William Ewart Gladstone

Juventus Mundi: The Gods and Men of the Heroic Age

William Ewart Gladstone

Juventus Mundi: The Gods and Men of the Heroic Age

ISBN/EAN: 9783742820686

Manufactured in Europe, USA, Canada, Australia, Japa

Cover: Foto ©Andreas Hilbeck / pixelio.de

Manufactured and distributed by brebook publishing software
(www.brebook.com)

William Ewart Gladstone

Juventus Mundi: The Gods and Men of the Heroic Age

PREFACE.

In this work, which is mainly the produce of the two Recesses of 1867 and 1868, I have endeavoured to embody the greater part of the results at which I arrived in the 'Studies on Homer and the Homeric Age,' 1858. Those results however are considerably modified in the Ethnological, and in the Mythological, portions of the inquiry. The chief source of modification in the former has been that a further prosecution of the subject with respect to the Phœnicians has brought out much more clearly and fully what I had only ventured to suspect or hint at, and gives them, if I am right, a highly influential function in forming the Greek nation. A fuller view of this element in its composition naturally acts in an important manner upon any estimate of Pelasgians and Hellenes respectively.

b

This Phœnician influence reaches far into the sphere of the mythology; and tends, as I think, greatly to clear the views we may reasonably take of that curious and interesting subject.

I have also greatly profited by the laborious and original treatise of Dr. Hahn, on Albanian Archaeology and Antiquities, as well as manners; which, although published at Jena in 1854, was scarcely, if at all, known in this country in 1858.

But, further, I have endeavoured to avoid a certain crudity of expression in some sections of the 'Olympos,' which led to misconceptions of my meaning with respect to the action of tradition (especially of sacred or Hebrew tradition) and invention respectively, in the genesis of the Greek mythological system.

In dealing with the Third portion of the 'Studies,' called Aoidos, I have contracted a great deal, but added and altered little.

The immediate purpose of the former work was to draw out of the text of Homer, by a minute investigation of particulars, the results that it appeared to me to justify. Many of them were more or less new, and the process of inquiry was therefore exhibited in great, perhaps in excessive or wearisome, detail. I have now felt warranted to give a larger space to deduction, and a smaller one to minute particulars of inquiry, in a work which aims at offering some practical assistance to Homeric study in our Schools and Universities, and even at conveying a partial knowledge of this subject to persons who are not habitual students. Of what appeared directly useful for this end, I have consciously omitted nothing.

I am anxious, then, to commend to inquirers, and to readers generally, conclusions from the Homeric Poems, which appear to me to be of great interest, with reference to the general history of human culture, and, in connection therewith, of the Providential government of the world. But I am much more anxious to encourage and facilitate the access of educated persons to the actual contents of the text. The amount and variety of these contents have not even yet been fully appreciated. The delight received from the Poems has possibly had some influence in disposing the generality of readers to rest satisfied with their enjoyment. The doubts cast upon their origin must have assisted in producing and fostering a vague instinctive indisposition to laborious examination. The very splendour of the poetry dazzles the eye as with whole sheets of light, and may often seem almost to give to analysis the character of vulgarity or impertinence.

My main object, then, in this, and in the former work, has been to encourage, or, if I may so say, to provoke, the close textual study of the Poet, as the condition of real progress in what is called the Homeric question, and as a substitute for that loose and second-hand method, not yet wholly out of vogue in this country, which seeks for information about Homer anywhere rather than in Homer himself.

In further prosecution of this purpose, I have begun, and carried forward at such intervals as I could make my own, another task. With patient toil, which applied to most authors would have been drudgery, I have tried to draw out, and to arrange in the most accessible form, resembling that of a Dictionary, what may be termed the body, or earthy and tangible part, of the contents of Homer. To a dissection of such a kind, the ethereal spirit cannot be submitted. This analysis will be separately published, so soon as other calls upon my time may permit. It must not be supposed that so homely a production aspires to exhibit Homer as a poet. Yet it exhibits

him as a chronicler and as an observer; it
helps to give an idea of his power by showing
some part at least of the copious materials
with which he executed his great synthesis, the
first, and also the best, composition of an Age,
the most perfect 'form and body of a time,' that
ever has been achieved by the hand of man.

Like Colonel Mure, I am convinced that the
one thing wanted in order to a full solution of
what is called the Homeric question is knowledge of the text. In an aggregate of 27,000
lines, as full of infinitely varied matter (to use
a familiar phrase) as an egg is full of meat,
this is not so commonplace an accomplishment
as might at first sight be supposed. I have
striven to attain it; yet, as I know, with very
partial success. And I do not hesitate to say,
with the productions of some recent writers
and critics on the Poet in my mind, that the
reading public ought to be very wary in accept-
ing unverified statements of what is or is not
in Homer. I eschew the invidious task of
illustrating this proposition from the pages of
others : possibly it might receive some illustration from my own.

I have felt great. embarrassment, in common
I suppose with many more, in consequence of

the unsettled and transitionary state of our
rules and practice with respect to Greek names,
and to the Latin forms of them.

Upon the whole, not without misgiving, but
not without consideration, I have acted upon
the belief that we cannot permanently fall
back into the system which we were content
until half a century ago to follow, and which
Mr. Mitford and Mr. Grote assailed in common; that we cannot well stand where we
are; and that we should, if possible, in this
as in all matters, try to make preparation for
the future, and make approaches at least towards a durable system.

First, then, I follow many high authorities
in adopting generally the names of the Greek
deities and mythological personages, instead of
the Latin ones.

Secondly, with respect to names which have
in no way become familiar to our ears or been
domesticated in the English tongue, instead of
the Latin forms and terminations, I adopt
commonly the Greek; and say Iasos, Acrisios,
Eurumachos, instead of Iasus, Acrisius, Eury-
machus: as also Achaioi, Hippemolgoi, Lotophagoi, Phaiakes, instead of Achaians, Hippe-
molgi, Lotophagi, Phæacians.

But I have usually followed the old custom in cases where Greek words have been, so to speak, translated, so that the English ear has become thoroughly accustomed to the rendering, whether it be effected by the Latin form, as Cyprus for Κύπρος, or by an English one, as Rhodes for Rhodos.

Yet a case like the first of these exhibits the practical mischief of a somewhat degenerate system; for the name Kupros would, more readily than Cyprus, have suggested the fact, that copper owes its name to that island, which first afforded to Europe and the Mediterranean a plentiful supply of so primitive and important a metal. In this matter of names I am less consistent than Mr. Grote; and less bold, for I have not the same title to expect obedience. I can only say that my practice is accommodated, as far as I am able, to a state of transition, and that I have no doubt it is open to criticism in detail, even from those who may accept the general rule.

Lastly, I have in many cases written a Greek word in Roman type. I know not whether it will or will not, at some time, be found practicable to serve the purposes of all languages by one and the same character. But the general knowledge of the relationship of tongues, and of particular languages, is increasing; and it may be both of interest and of use to the English reader, though unacquainted with Greek, to know the form and body of the words discussed in the text, when this advantage can be given without seriously distorting the words themselves.

HAWARDEN, NORTH WALES,
October, 1868.

CONTENTS.

CHAPTER I.

INTRODUCTION.

CHAPTER II.

THE THREE GREAT APPELLATIVES.

CHAPTER III.

THE PELASGOI.

CHAPTER IV.

HELLAS.

CHAPTER V.

THE PHŒNICIANS AND THE EGYPTIANS.

CHAPTER VI.

On the Title 'Anax Andrōn.'

CHAPTER VII.

THE OLYMPIAN SYSTEM.

CHAPTER VIII.

THE DIVINITIES OF OLYMPOS.

c

CHAPTER IX.

FURTHER SKETCH AND MORAL ASPECTS OF THE OLYMPIAN SYSTEM.

CHAPTER X.

ETHICS OF THE HEROIC AGE.

CHAPTER XI.

POLITY OF THE HEROIC AGE.

CHAPTER XII.

RESEMBLANCES AND DIFFERENCES BETWEEN THE GREEKS AND THE TROJANS.

CHAPTER XIII.

GEOGRAPHY OF HOMER.

CHAPTER XIV.

PLOTS, CHARACTERS, AND SIMILES.

CHAPTER XV.

MISCELLANEOUS.

CHAPTER I.

IF, as the general opinion holds, the Iliad and the Odyssey are the works of an individual poet (whom we term Homer), they are probably, as a connected whole, the oldest in the world; though a few of the Books of Scripture, and, in the opinion of some, a portion of the Vedas, may perhaps lay claim to a higher antiquity. They unquestionably contain a mass of information respecting man in a primitive or very early stage of society, which has not even yet been thoroughly digested, and such as is nowhere else to be found. They have also, through the intervention of the Greek and then of the Roman civilisation, for both of which they form the original literary base, entered far more largely than any other book, except the Holy Scriptures, into the formation of modern thought and life.

A main reason, which has prevented mankind from profiting to the full by these invaluable works, appears to have been this; that, except for the purposes of purely·poetical appreciation, they have been viewed

62   B

far too much through the medium of later traditions,
of the productions of the classic ages of Greece and
Rome, and especially of the great epic of Virgil; and
the multiform features of the picture which he draws
have thus been confounded with the representations
of much later, and in many respects very different
ages.

While the works of Homer have exercised an influence which has been greater than those of any
other poet, and which is rising apparently at the
present time, nothing is known of his person. His
blindness, but only in mature and late life, is allow-
ably conjectured from the fact that he has drawn a
careful and sympathising picture of the blind minstrel
Demodocos in Scheriè[1] (now Corfù), and has made
him more conspicuous than any other Bard mentioned
in the Poems. Absorbed in his subject, the Poet never
refers to himself: in half-a-dozen passages the personal
pronoun is used—'Tell me, O Muses[2],' and the like;
but it is a mere grammatical form, never specially
pointed to his own individuality. Of his character
we can only judge as far as different passages of the
Poems may enable us to trace his personal sympathies
in their tone and colour. The conjecture as to his
blindness is indeed in accordance with a passage
which Thucydides[3] quotes as his from the Hymn to
Apollo, and which mentions it: but the weight of
this evidence depends much more on the beauty and
pathos of the verses, than on the fact that the great
historian treats it as by Homer; since he does not
speak in the character of a witness, and the reference

---

[1] Od. viii. 64.   [2] Od. i. 1.   [3] iii. 104.

to Chios as the place of his residence is a circumstance
calculated to excite strong suspicion.

With respect to the date at which Homer lived,
nothing is known, except it be by recent and as yet
scarcely recognised discovery[1], from sources extrinsic
to the Poems. Herodotus places him at four hundred
years before himself, in the ninth century before Christ.
This would bring him nearly to the epoch of Lycurgus.
But the state of society and manners in Greece de-
picted by him is far anterior to all that is connected
with the name of that legislator; and betokens not
only priority, but long priority, to the historic period,
which is commonly said to begin with the Olympiad
of Corœbus, B. C. 776. The date of 1183 B. C. is
fixed by Eratosthenes for the fall of Troy: but it has
long been known to be no more than conjectural[2].
In my opinion, that event is quite as likely to have
been older, as to have been more recent. But there
are in reality no fully acknowledged measures of time
applicable to the decision of the question. Homer
alone seems to afford us, for his own age, any means
of estimating, however rudely, the lapse of years.
His only chronology is found in genealogies, given
by him in considerable numbers, and in singular correspondence with one another. But this knowledge,
if authentic, stands as an island separated from us by
a sea of unknown breadth. We have as yet no mode
of establishing a clear relation of time between it and
the historic era.

The Poems afford, however, partial means of estimating the date of Homer, relatively to the War of Troy.

---

[1] See Chap. V. on Phœnicia and Egypt.
[2] Clinton, Fasti Hellenici, i. 123.

He virtually states, that he was not an eye-witness
of the War [1]. Poseidon [2] prophesies that the grand-
children of Æneas shall reign in Troas; and it is
fairly argued that the Poet would not have ventured
on the prediction, if he had not lived to see its entire
or partial accomplishment. A grandson of Æneas
may well have reigned in Troas within fifty or even
forty years of the fall of the city; and a son within a
much shorter period. Arguments for a greater interval
have indeed been founded on the passages, in which the
Poet contrasts the might of the Troic heroes with the
lower standard of his own time. But a ready answer
is surely found in the fact that Nestor, in the First
Iliad [3], draws a somewhat similar contrast between
the heroes of his youth, and those of the Greek army
before Troy. Figure is, in truth, the main element
in all such comparisons. A third argument has been
founded on the passage, in which Here observes to
Zeus that he is free to destroy the cities she loves
the best—Argos, Sparta, and Mycenæ [4]. Hence, it is
thought, Homer must have lived after the Dorian
conquest. But (1) we do not find that any of these
cities were destroyed at that epoch; and (2) had
Homer lived in an age posterior to that great revolution, he must have betrayed his knowledge of it not
in one equivocal passage, but in many, and by a multitude of signs of later manners. (3) The Dorian conquest had the immediate effect of reducing Mycenæ to
obscurity, while it left Argos and Sparta at the head of
Greece; and it would be strange indeed that Homer,
if he had witnessed it, should join the three in a single

[1] Il. ii. 486.   [2] Il. xx. 307.
[3] Il. i. 260-272.   [4] Il. iv. 51.

category, and take no notice of the distinction. From
the manner in which the cities are mentioned, we may
indeed rather say, that the passage affords an argument to show that the Poet lived before that epoch,
and not after it. (4) It is urged also that Homer
mentions riding on horseback, and the trumpet, as in
use, but not as in use during the War. But in the
Tenth Iliad, Odysseus and Diomed ride the horses of
Rhesos; and the trumpet appears to be mentioned only
as used to summon a beleaguered place on the arrival
of the enemy[1]. On the other hand, Homer seems again
to glance at his own case in the words addressed by
Odysseus to Demodocos, respecting his Trojan lay:
'You have sung the Achaian woe right well, as if
you had yourself been a witness, or else had heard it
from one[2].' The idea seems here to be conveyed with
distinctness, that either actual experience or, at the
least, the evidence of those who had possessed it, was a
condition of true excellence in historic song. Again,
the elaborate plan by which, in the Twelfth Iliad, Homer
accounts for the disappearance of the defensive work
of the Greeks, seems to show that the interval since
the War must have been short, for if it had been long,
natural causes would have done more to account for it.

A cardinal argument for placing the date of the Poet
near that of his subject is, that he describes manners
from first to last with the easy, natural, and intimate
knowledge of a contemporary observer. He is in
truth in visible identity with the age, the altering but
not yet vanished age, of which he sings, while there is
a very broad interval of tone and feeling between him
and the very nearest of all that follow him. And even

---

[1] Il. xviii. 219, 220.   [2] Od. viii. 489–491.

the difference to be observed in the shade of style and
of manner between the Iliad and the Odyssey, is just
such as would be fairly due, in part to the difference of
the subjects, and in part to the shock of those alterations, which were evidently caused in Greece by the
absence of its kings and leaders, during a prolonged
period, at the War. I conjecture, without pretending to
do more, that Homer may well have been born before,
or during, the War; and that he probably was familiar,
during the years of his maturity, with those who had
fought in it. For treating Homer as an Asiatic Greek,
who lived after the migrations eastward, there is really
neither reason, nor trustworthy authority.

As to the place of Homer's birth and residence,
we are yet more in the dark than about his date.
The testimony of the Poems is both slight and equivocal; and no other testimony is authentic. In one
passage he says the Locrians dwell beyond, or it may
mean over against, Euboea[1], on the East of Greece;
in another, the Echinades and Doulichion[2] are beyond,
or over against, Elis, on the West of Greece. The
second passage seems to destroy any such inference as
Wood, in his ingenious Essay[3], drew from the first.
On the other hand, morning comes to Homer over
the sea[4]; an expression which seems to contemplate
a 'whereabout' on the West of the Ægean. The character given to Zephuros, the North-West wind, varies
according as it is a sea-wind, which it is in the description of the Elysian Fields; or a mountain-wind, when
it is described as charged with snow[5]: and no inference

---

[1] Il. ii. 535. [2] Il. ii. 626. [3] p. 8. (First Ed. in 1775.)
[4] Il. xxiii. 227. [5] Od. iv. 566-568; xix. 206.

can be drawn from it to show that Homer lived on
any particular coast. Every line of the Poems bears
testimony to the fact that Homer was not derivatively,
but immediately and intensely, Greek. Contented with
accumulated evidence of nationality in the highest
sense, we must leave the question of the precise birth-
place and dwelling of the Poet in the darkness in
which we find it.

It cannot be too strongly affirmed, that the song
of Homer is historic song. Indeed he has probably
told us more about the world and its inhabitants at
his own epoch, than any historian that ever lived.

But the primary and principal meaning of the assertion is, that he is historical as to manners, customs,
ideas, and institutions: whereas events and names are
the pegs on which they hang. It is with respect, not
to the dry bones of fact, but to all that gives them
life, beauty, and meaning, that he has supplied us with
a more complete picture of the Greek, or, as he would
probably say, Achaian, people of his time, than any
other author, it might almost be said than any number
of authors, have supplied with reference to any other
age and people.

There are however very strong presumptions that
Homer is also historical with respect to his chief
events and persons. For, 1. It is the chief business
of the Poet or Bard, as such, in early times to record
facts, while he records them in the forms of beauty
supplied by his art. 2. Especially of the Bard who
lives near the events of which he professes to sing.
3. It is plain that Homer so viewed the Poet's office,
from the nature of the lays which he introduces; from
his representing to us Achilles engaged in singing the

deeds of heroes [1]; and from his saying that the gods ordained the War of Troy that it might be sung to all posterity [2]; with other like sentiments. 4. The Poems were always viewed as historical by the Greeks. 5. If fictitious in their basis, they would have been far less likely to acquire and maintain such commanding interest. 6. The structure and tenour of the Poems throughout indicate the highest regard to national tastes and prepossessions: and these tastes were manifestly very strong as to all matters of tradition and hereditary fame. Of this we have an indication which may be taken by way of example, in the question usually put to a stranger, who are his parents? 7. The number, and the remarkable self-consistency of the Genealogies given in the Poems, appear almost of themselves to prove an historic design. 8. The Catalogue in the Second Iliad implies a purpose with reference to the nation, much the same as that indicated by the Genealogies with respect to particular persons or families. 9. The Aristeia of the greater chieftains respectively, in the intermediate Books of the Iliad, are thought to load the movement of the Poem; but they receive a natural and simple explanation from the tendency of a Poet at once itinerant and historical to distribute carefully the honours of the War between the different States and Heroes. 10. A considerable number of the minute particulars given, especially in the Iliad, are of a nature to derive their interest wholly from recording matter of fact; such for instance as the small stature of Tudeus, the *mare* driven by Menelaos, and many more. 11. Homer often introduces curious legends of genealogy and race, in a manner which is

[1] Il. ix. 186-189.   [2] Od. viii. 579.

palpably inopportune for the purposes of poetry, and
which is, on the other hand, fully accounted for by
the historic aim. These legends are not to be explained by the garrulity of Nestor; for, even if the
character of Nestor admitted of a garrulity wholly
apart from good sense, still these legends are not confined to him. Nor are they shared with him only by
Phœnix, who is likewise in years; they are spoken by
Æneas, Glaucos, and others, and this too even on the
field of battle: and, by means of them, Homer has supplied us with a great mass of curious knowledge, highly
interesting to his auditors, and eminently illustrative
of the first beginnings of the Greek nation, as yet in
embryo. His intermixture of supernatural agency with
human events must be judged on its own grounds; but
cannot by the laws of historical criticism be held of
itself to overthrow his general credit.

We must not however attempt to define with rigour
the limits, within which the Poems are to be considered ·
historical. The free intermixture of the supernatural
need not indeed constitute a serious difficulty. For the
theurgy of the Poems is, so to speak, self-subsistent. It
represents in the main a parallel and concurrent action,
rather than a mere ornament, or a simple portion of
one and the same narration with the War; and it lies
upon the human and visible tissue like a continuous
pattern of rich embroidery. But several points of the
story are presented to us in a dress apparently mythical;
for example, the distribution of the time into three
periods, each of ten years: and many of the names of
persons appear to have been invented, especially in
cases where they carry an etymological meaning calculated directly to serve the purpose of the Poem. Again,

if we suppose an historical existence for the persons indicated by the names, for example, of Achilles and Helen, it remains open to doubt, how large a proportion of the remarkable and characteristic features, with which they are invested, may be due to the imagination of the Poet. In the case of Achilles, whose qualities everywhere border on the superhuman, this question is especially relevant. Nor is the circumstance to be overlooked, that a goddess is assigned to him as a mother, and is stated to have sat commonly, or oftentimes, as queen in his father's palace [1].

It must also be fully admitted that, although the Troad may afford some physical indications favourable to the historic character of the Poems, yet the proof of that character chiefly, nay almost wholly, rests upon internal evidence [2]. But internal evidence, when carried to a certain point, is the very best we can desire in a case where we are obliged to travel back into the mist of ages, far beyond the limits of historical record.

Of all the features of the Homeric Poems, perhaps the most remarkable are the delineations of personal character which they contain. They are not only in a high degree varied and refined; but they are also marvellously comprehensive and profound. The proof of their extraordinary excellence as works of art is to be found in this, that from Homer's time to our own, with the single exception of the works of Shakespeare, they have never been equalled.

Homer is also admirable, when the specialties of his purpose are taken into view, in the arrangement of incidents: in keeping interest ever fresh: in his

---

[1] Il. i. 396.   [2] Mure, Literature of Greece, vol. I.

precise and copious observation of nature: in his
power of illustration, his use of epithets; in the freedom, simplicity, and power of his language; and in a
versification perfect in its application to all the diversified forms of human action, speech, and feeling.

It may probably have been the combined and intense effort of the Trojan War by which the Greeks
first felt themselves, and first became, a nation. At any
rate, from that epoch appears to date their community
of interest and life. Homer, then, was hardly less wonderful in the fortune of his opportunity, than in the
rarity of his gifts. In speaking of his theme, the two
Poems may be taken as virtually one. He supplied to
his country thenceforward, and for all periods, the bond
of an intellectual communion, and a common treasure
of ideas upon all the great subjects in which man is
concerned. He was not only the glory and delight,
but he was in a great degree the ποιητὴς, the maker,
of his nation.

I have spoken of the darkness which, as far as direct
testimony is concerned, envelopes the person of the
Poet. The same is the case with the Homeric Poems,
distinguished from every other work of the first rank
in these among other particulars: there is not one, of
which so little has been told us by contemporary or
early testimony; while there is not one which tells us
so much. Of their origin, their date, and their first
reception, we know nothing, except so far as we can
gather it. from themselves. The Cyclic Poems, which
aimed at completing the circle of events with which
they deal, never attained to an equal or competing
fame, and have long ago perished. Periods of darkness, the length of which we cannot determine, both

precede and follow the two great productions. At the
dawn of trustworthy tradition, we find them holding a
position of honour and authority among the Greeks, for
which, with respect to works professedly secular, history affords no parallel [1]. The Greeks had no sacred
books, properly so called: and it is probable that the
Poems of Homer filled in some particular respects the
place of Sacred Books [2] for that people.

By the Poems of Homer, I mean the Iliad and the
Odyssey. I can find no adequate reason for assigning
to him any other of the larger compositions of the early
Greek Bards. Of the other works more or less reputed
to be Homeric, not one can now be ascribed to him
with confidence, or has been shown ever to have been so
ascribed by the general and unhesitating opinion of the
Greeks. The Hymns contain very few passages of
such mark as even to allow the supposition that they
could have proceeded from him. Nor do they carry, so
to speak, his physiognomy. No writer of any period
has borne stronger and more characteristic notes of
style. We have seen that one beautiful passage is
quoted from the Hymn to Apollo, by Thucydides. He
describes that Hymn as a Hymn of Homer; and doubtless he represents a tradition of his day. There are
also one or two fragmentary verses ascribed to Homer:
one passage, in particular, is given by Aristotle [3], and
said to have been taken from a poem termed The
Margites. It may be observed that besides their
general inferiority, the Hymns in general, embody

---

[1] The case which comes nearest to this is perhaps that of the
Divina Commedia of Dante.
[2] Milman, Life of Horace, p. 1; Grote, Hist. of Greece, vol. i.
[3] Eth. Nicom. vi. 7

mythological traditions, evidently of a later stamp than those of the two great Epics.

The Iliad and Odyssey give a picture of the age to which they refer, alike copious and animated, comprehensive and minute. The Iliad represents that age in its vigour; the Odyssey paints it in the beginning of its decline, when Greece had been unsettled and disorganised by the prolonged absence of its chiefs at Troy. The Iliad gives us what it had been; the Odyssey indicates what it was about to be. The delineations embrace jointly all the materials that human life and society could then in their simplicity supply: when writing was either unknown or unavailable, when civil rights had not begun to take the form of law, and when visible Art, in its higher sense, was an exotic not yet naturalised in Greece. In a manner chiefly incidental, there is supplied to us a mass of information on history and legend, religion, polity, justice, domestic life and habits, ethnical and social relations, the conditions of warfare, navigation, industry, and of the useful arts, exceeding in amount what has ever at any other period been brought for us into one focus by a single mind; except possibly by the philosophical works of Aristotle, if we possessed them entire.

It has been doubted[1] at various times whether either Poem, and especially whether the Iliad, was the work of a single author; and also whether the two were due to the same hand. The Chorizontes, so called because they separate the authorship of the Iliad from that of the Odyssey, found themselves mainly,

[1] See the account of the controversy from its earliest phase among the Alexandrian Critics, in Mure, Hist. of Greek Lit. vol. I, ch. II. III. iv.

(*a*) On supposed discrepancies in the mythology of the two Poems respectively:
(*b*) On differences of manners and institutions:
(*c*) On differences in the language.

Those who destroy the unity of the Poems, and especially of the Iliad, altogether, contend,

(*a*) That the art of writing did not exist at the time of their composition, and that poems of such length could not have been orally transmitted. This was the famous argument of Wolf.

(*b*) That there are such discrepancies, anomalies, and defects of plan, in the Iliad, as to preclude the belief that it could be the work of a single mind.

With respect to the argument of Wolf, it is now commonly admitted that no such art of writing existed, as could be available for the transmission of the Poems: but his second proposition, that they could not be transmitted orally, is also very commonly denied. Quintilian says, 'Invenio apud Platonem obstare memoriæ usum literarum[1].' Even in the period when the exercise of the memory had become subject to this disadvantage, Niceratos, according to Xenophon[2], stated that he knew the Iliad and Odyssey by heart: and Athenæus[3] states, that Cassander, king of Macedon, could do nearly as much; he could repeat the chief part of the Poems. Even now, it would not be difficult to select youths, of strong memory, aided by poetic feeling, who, if they made it a profession, would be able to acquire by heart the whole of them: which however need not have been done by all those who recited them under a system apparently organised with a view to recitation in parts.

[1] xI. 2.   [2] Sympos. iiL 5.   [3] xiv. p. 620.

As respects the other heads of argument against the unity of the Poems generally, it may be sufficient for the present to reply as follows:—

(*a*) The plot of the Iliad (as will be shown) is admirably constructed for its purpose.

(*b*) Its internal discrepancies are both very few, and very insignificant.

(*c*) Some of the cases of alleged discrepancy are only such when the canons of modern prose are applied precipitately as the criteria of the oldest poetry.

As regards the arguments of the Chorizontes or separators of the authorship of the two Epics, let it be observed:—

(*a*) If the mythology of the Odyssey, in that region to which the voyage of Odysseus belongs, shall be shown to be Phœnician[1], the whole argument from discrepancy in that mythology will thereupon disappear.

(*b*) The differences in manners or institutions are not greater than may be explained by the action of a revolutionary crisis, like the crisis caused by the prolonged absence in Troas; and are really such as may be taken rather for an evidence of unity in authorship than the reverse.

(*c*) Some differences of language between the two Poems is required by the different character of the subjects: and the actual differences seem not to be thought by scholars in general to betoken their belonging to different ages.

(*d*) A careful comparison of style between the Odyssey and the Iliad, and of a number of particulars of turn and manner, will be found to supply a con-

[1] See *infra*, Chap. V. on the Phœnicians; and Chap. VII. on Mythology, sect. Poseidon.

siderable amount of very specific evidence for the unity
of authorship. No such resemblances could be shown
to the works of any other author, or to the Pseudo-
Homeric compositions.

(*e*) Those characters of the Iliad, which are also
found in the Odyssey, reappear in the later Poem
with a perfect preservation of identity, confirmed, not
impaired, by the altered shading which belongs to their
altered positions.

(*f*) The testimony of the Odyssey to facts, especially those connected with the War, is in no
case discordant with that of the Iliad. For if the
manhood of Neoptolemos[1] creates a certain amount
of difficulty, we should bear in mind that the
adjustment of time with reference to the Poem,
appears to be one of the points in which Homer
has allowed himself a certain licence, with a view
probably to poetical effect.

(*g*) But the overwhelming proof of the unity
of authorship, both for each Poem, and as between
the two, is really supplied by the innumerable particulars of manners, institutions, and ideas, which
pervade both the Iliad and the Odyssey with a marvellous consistency; and by the incommunicable
stamp of an extraordinary genius which they carry
throughout. If discrepancies exist, the difficulty they
present is not only small, but infinitesimal, compared
with the difficulty of that hypothesis which assumes
that Greece produced in early times a multitude of
Homers, and all of them with the very same stamp
of mind. Whether in short we consider these works
as poetry or as record, the marks of their unity are

[1] Od. xi. 506.

innumerable and ineffaceable. A part of their force is sensible to the ordinary reader; but it will be felt constantly and immensely to increase in proportion as the reader becomes the student, by virtue of a patient, constant, and thorough examination of the text.

Of the two Poems, it seems to me that, while both are wonderful, the Iliad is without doubt the greater. The plot of the Iliad, we shall find, is a marvellous combination of poetical skill with national spirit and practical prudence. The plot of the Odyssey, at first sight more organised and symmetrical, is in the first place of far easier construction, and in the second, is wound up in a manner which is feeble if not slovenly. The suspicions of the genuineness of the Twenty-fourth Book appear to me on the whole to be tolerably met by a general conformity of turn and handling, though with diminished force; and by many minute particulars of correspondence which, here as elsewhere, the text supplies. But they have perhaps been reasonably suggested by a perceptible inferiority of workmanship in this and, with some exceptions, in several Books preceding it. The vigour of the Iliad, on the other hand, continues quite unabated to the end. Again, in the Odyssey there is not a mere decline of vigour: the plan of the ending may be called degenerate and incomplete. The ends of some of the threads are dropped. If ever a peace was patched it is that which is announced in the closing passage. The intervention of Mentor, even though his exterior conceals a deity, is not what the dignity of the Sovereign or the grandeur of Odysseus would require. And the unexplained as well as unfulfilled prophecy[1] of

[1] Od. xi. 127; xxiii. 275.

the war, suggests that Homer had poetical intentions to which it was not permitted him to give effect.

Generally speaking, the Odyssey displays the same powers as the Iliad, but in less energetic manifestation. A faculty of debate, never surpassed if ever equalled in human history, is found in both; but though the flight of Odysseus in the Seventh Odyssey is, like that of the contention in the First Iliad, a lofty one, it cannot be compared with the wonderful speech of Achilles in the tent-scene of the Ninth. Again; no man but Homer could have reproduced in the Odyssey to the life the characters of the Iliad, or could have added the specific shading of their altered circumstances. But though Homer in each is stronger than any other of the Ancients, yet Homer of the Iliad is Homer at the height and maximum of his power in this transcendent quality; while in the Odyssey the great luminary seems to have just begun his descending course.

Next comes the question how far we may reckon on having substantially the same text as that of our author; not as to any minor detail, nor even so as to exclude occasional interpolations, but as to the style, diction, and language generally.

Mr. Paley [1] says (not that the Greek of the Iliad is greatly different from that of the Odyssey, but) that we find in the Poems two distinct and separate phases of the Greek tongue: first, the language of the earliest Trojan Epics, and secondly, the ordinary Ionic of the time of Herodotus, with a mixture of Attic idioms. The question is one evidently requiring minute examination; but it is beyond my competency to decide. I would observe, however,

[1] Athenæum, Aug. 10, 1867.

(*a*) That in an author who composed at a period of crisis, when all the elements of the Hellenic nation, that was to be, were settling down, we should look for, or at least should not be startled by, some mixture of older and younger forms.

(*b*) That considerable changes of the minor order might be made in the text of the Poems without seriously affecting the substance, if there was a great and constant anxiety to abide by the true sense of Homer.

(*c*) That if we find the internal evidence as to manners, institutions, and facts, singularly self-consistent, this goes far to show that alterations of the text have been generally confined within merely verbal and narrow limits.

(*d*) The antiquity of the present text is not overthrown by the fact that the later poets in many instances have followed other forms of legend in regard to the Troica: for they would necessarily consult the state of popular feeling from time to time; and tradition, which, as to religion, altered so greatly after the time of Homer, would, as to facts and persons, it is evident, vary materially according to the sympathies of blood and otherwise at different periods of Greek history. The displacement of the Achaians, and the rise of the Dorians and Ionians, must have occasioned great changes in this respect. It is also surprising, if such difference in the language really exists as is alleged by Mr. Paley, that it was not perceived by the Greeks of the classic period, who must surely be allowed to have known their own tongue.

There are passages of ancient writers, which tend to the disintegration of Homer. But they are late, and of small authority. Josephus [1] says it was reported, or thought, that from want of the aid afforded by the art of writing there were many discrepancies in the Poems. This was merely a current opinion, not of himself but of others, on the state of the text; an opinion which we can for ourselves see to have been erroneous. The Scholiast on Pindar [2] reports, and only reports, that Kunaithos and his school had made large interpolations. The Latin authors, such as Cicero or Paterculus, must be considered as giving their opinions, which cannot from the circumstances be of great critical weight, rather than as witnesses in the case.

The external evidence to a contrary effect, though fragmentary, is more considerable, and for the most part of much earlier date. Heraclides Ponticus [3], a pupil of Plato, declares that Lycurgus obtained the Homeric Poems from the descendants of Kreophulos, and was the first to bring them into Peloponnesos. Ælian [4] makes the slight but material addition, that he brought this poetry in a mass (ἀθρόαν). Plato states in the Republic [5] that Kreophulos was a companion of Homer; Strabo [6], that he was a Samian; Diogenes Laertius [7], that Hermodamas, the master of Pythagoras, was his descendant. Plutarch [8] states that some portions of Homer were known in Greece before Lycurgus brought the whole from Crete.

Herodotus [9] states that Cleisthenes, the tyrant of Sicyon, when he had been at war with Argos, put

[1] Contr. Ap. ii. 2.
[2] Nem. ii. 1.
[3] Fragm. περὶ πολιτειῶν.
[4] Var. Hist. xiii. 14.
[5] Rep. x. p. 600 B.
[6] xiv. p. 916.
[7] viii. 2.
[8] Lyc. p. 41.
[9] v. 67.

a stop to the competitions of the rhapsodists in
Sicyon, because the Homeric songs turned chiefly upon
the Argeians and Argos (ὅτι 'Αργεῖοί τε καὶ 'Αργος τὰ
πολλὰ πάντα ὑμνέαται). Also, that he sought to banish
from Sicyon the memory of Adrestos, as being an
Argive hero. Now the Iliad describes Greece not
seldom under the title of Argos, and the Greeks
frequently as Argeians; and it represents Adrestos
as the first king of Sicyon, while at the same time
it represents him as the father-in-law, or grandfather-
in-law, of Diomed the Argive chieftain.

From this passage it appears—

(a) That there were at Sicyon, six centuries before
Christ, State - recitations of the Homeric Poems,
attended with prizes.

(b) That they are not named as peculiar to Sicyon,
but rather as a customary institution, set aside in
that place at a certain epoch on special grounds.

(c) That the recitations depended chiefly on the
Homeric Poems; for they ceased when these were
prohibited.

Dieuchidas of Megara, an author placed by Heyne
after the time of Alexander the Great, is quoted by
Diogenes[1] as stating that Solon provided by law for
the recitation of the Homeric poems ἐξ ὑποβολῆς, one
reciter taking up another; and therefore that Solon did
more than Peisistratos to throw light upon the Poet.
And Lycurgus the orator, who was contemporary with
Demosthenes[2], tells the Athenian people that their
forefathers thought of him so highly as to provide by
law for the recitation of his songs, and his alone,
quinquennially at the Panathenaica; and such, he adds,

---

[1] Diog. Laert. i. 57.　　　　[2] In Leocritum, 104-8.

was then the valour of their ancestors, that the Spartans took Tyrtæus[1] from among them to be their general.

Hence it appears that—

(*a*) According to Lycurgus, Homer was recited at Athens in the time of Tyrtæus, nearly seven centuries before Christ.

(*b*) Just when Athens begins to rise, Solon appoints by public law competitive recitations of Homer, to be taken in turn by the reciters.

(*c*) And of Homer alone.

(*d*) It appears negatively that probably there were recitations at Athens before Solon, but without regular turns.

(*e*) If public authority thus established the recitation of the Poems, we may rest assured that care was taken, as far as possible, to preserve their text from corruption.

(*f*) The vanity or carelessness of a particular rhapsodist would tend to corrupt them; but the matches were free and competitive, and each reciter would be watched and checked by the vigilant jealousy of his rivals. This element of competition would in all likelihood have a highly conservative effect, before the art of writing had come into use. And it is plain, from Il. ii. 594-600, that the practice prevailed from before the time of Homer himself; as he tells us that Thamuris had challenged the Muses to compete with him, and was punished accordingly for his audacity. Hesiod witnesses to the matches, and says that in Aulis he himself won a tripod[2]. Thucydides also finds proof of them in the Hymn to Apollo[3].

---

[1] Smith's Dict., art. Tyrtæus.   [2] Opp. 654-657.
[3] Hymn Apoll. 146-150, 166-173.

(g) In a word, while there were at work what may
be called centrifugal forces, tending to impair and
vitiate the text of the Poems, there were also
centripetal forces tending to restore it; in the rivalry
of States as well as of Bards, in the intense love of
the song of Homer felt by every Greek, and in the
great value set by the whole people upon it as a record.

When we come down to the historic period, we
find in it full evidence of the standing anxiety both of
States and persons to preserve the text of Homer.
It appears probable that a common text was more or
less recognised, while many even of the Greek Colonies
had their public or State Recensions. Individuals of
eminence, or of literary taste, had their editions also.
The Venetian Scholiast constantly refers to these two
descriptions of copies, and while the references prove
that there were in this, as in every ancient document,
many variations of text, they also show that such
variations were confined within narrow limits, and
did not affect the body of the work. The State
editions were called αἱ πολιτικαὶ, αἱ ἐκ τῶν πόλεων,
αἱ ἀπὸ πόλεων: those prepared for individuals αἱ κατ'
ἄνδρα: and a third class, got up apparently for public
sale, and of very variable quality, were αἱ κοιναὶ, αἱ
δημοτικαὶ, αἱ δημώδεις.

Among the public or State Recensions, we hear of
those of Argos, Crete, Sinopè, Marseilles, Chios,
Cyprus; of the Aiolis or Aiolikè, a name which may
perhaps indicate the recognised text of what is called
Homer's Æolian Greek; the Recension of the Mou-
seion, or depository near the School at Alexandria;
and the Kuklikè, which is supposed to mean an edition
wherein Homer appeared with other poems of the Cycle.

It seems very probable, that the work of Peisistratos was in substance a critical recension of the text effected by a comparison of different versions, and a complete publication by authority of the several portions of the Poems in the order in which we now have them; in fact that it was an early and notable example of the reactive tendency to preserve the text by recurrence to a standard, and to check its variations, which I have mentioned as the natural counterpoise to disintegrating agencies.

We have no clear account of the proceedings of Peisistratos; but we know that when, at a later period, the Alexandrian School of Zenodotos, Aristophanes, and Aristarchos brought the best critical power of the time to bear upon the Poems, they found comparatively little to question. Nor have the suspicions they entertained of particular passages since received anything approaching to an unanimous approval.

As to more general reconstructions, it is allowed that the Odyssey does not admit of them; and such as have been proposed with regard to the Iliad have manifestly failed to obtain any sensible, much more any permanent, amount of assent.

But the strongest argument for the soundness of the text, as well as that for the unity of the Poems, hangs upon internal evidence. I do not hesitate to say that no work known to me presents, in any degree equal or approaching to these Poems, the proof, in kind among the strongest of all, which arises out of natural unstudied self-consistency in detail. The particulars in which the text confirms at one point what it conveys at another may be counted by many thousands: those where it appears to be inconsistent are but a few units to be reckoned by the primitive process of Proteus upon the fingers. Errors undoubtedly there must be. Still, if they were very serious, it is impossible but that a far greater number of them must have been tracked out, and their detection established to the general satisfaction of cultivated men. On one portion only of the Forty-eight Books, namely the close of the Odyssey, has there been thrown what may be termed grave or recognised doubt; and even here doubt is all that can be reasonably sustained. Indeed over and above correspondence of tangible particulars there is what I must call an unity of atmosphere in the Poems, such as I believe has never been achieved by forgery or imitation.

In this chapter I have not relied upon the tradition according to which Lycurgus, the great Spartan lawgiver, brought the Poems into use in Lacedæmon, because it is one belonging to the Roman rather than the Greek period. On the other hand I cannot attach great weight to the statement in the Hipparchos [1], which assigns to that Sovereign the original introduction of the Poems into Attica. It appears simply incredible that the Poems should have been unknown in Attica, when we learn from Herodotus that they had long before been recited in Sicyon.

On the whole, then, we are not in every case dogmatically to assert that each line of the Poems as they stand is the work of Homer; but while fairly weighing the evidence in the comparatively few cases where doubt sustained by argument has been raised, we may, as a general rule, proceed to handle the text with a reasonable confidence, that the ground is firm under

[1] Sect. iv.

our feet; a confidence, which experience in the work will, I think, be found progressively to confirm.

Thus far we have seen reason to suppose that the Iliad and the Odyssey are the work of a Poet who lived at a date that we are unable to define otherwise than by its nearness to the Trojan War; an event which, if we attempt to measure its distance from the historic era by manners and institutions, we must hold to be of a high antiquity.

At times it has been questioned, whether Homer or Hesiod was the older poet. We know of Hesiod that while the reputed authors of the Cyclic Poems belong to the historic era [1], he is pre-historic; and we must seek, therefore, in his works, as in those of Homer, for the means of estimating his probable 'whereabout' in the deep mist of ages. He gives us no sign that the instrument of writing had become available at his epoch for the preservation of poetry; and if his compositions, as being much shorter, taxed the memory more lightly, on the other hand we have no reason to believe that they were watched with the same jealous care to preserve, or to recover, the genuine text. But if the episode of the Five Ages be genuine, they are decisive of the question. For the composer of it had been witness to an iron age; and iron, as compared with copper, had in his time come to be the inferior, that is to say the cheaper, metal. The use of it therefore must have grown common, as, from remains still extant, it had evidently come to be common in Assyria at a period supposed to be about the eighth century before Christ. Homer lived at a period, as defined by economic laws, much earlier; at

[1] Mure, Lit. of Greece, ii. 282.

a time when the use of iron was but just commencing,
when the commodity was rare, and when its value was
very great. This argument appears to me so conclusive
as to the comparative dates, that I forbear to dwell
on other particulars, or upon the considerable difference
in the manners of the Hesiodic, as compared with the
Homeric, Poems.

We have also seen that in the state of primitive
society it was essential to the business of the Epic
Bard to commemorate, in poetic forms, actual events;
and that the works of Homer prove how he kept this
property of his art constantly in mind.

Viewing then his position in human history and his
profession, we find that he is an original and a solitary,
as he is also a most copious, witness to the condition
of mankind, and especially of the Greeks, at a period
to which we have no other direct literary access.
Traditions there are in abundance, reported by Apollodorus in mass, or scattered here and there through the
works of earlier writers; and these traditions may, in
any given case, contain matter relating to the age of
Homer, or to what preceded him, and may even in some
cases be true, or nearer the truth than his. But they
carry as a general rule no attestation; and their confused and promiscuous nature marks them as a miscel-
lany gradually accumulated in many ages and from many
lands. I submit then that we ought to make the
evidence of Homer in relation to his age and to what
had gone before, a separate study, and to assign to
it a primary authority. The testimony of later writers
should be handled in subordination to it, and in general
even tried by it as by a touchstone, on all the subjects
which it embraces. It will be seen, as we proceed

to deal with the contents of the Poems, that this is a proposition fruitful of important results as regards the religion, the polity, and the manners of early Greece.

In asking for the testimony of Homer a primary authority, I refer only to those cases where it stands in competition with other, and in truth inferior, literary evidence. The evidence of fact, whether in geography and topography, in language, or in archæology, stands upon its own ground, and Homer, like every other author, must yield, if a conflict arise, to its more cogent authority.

I will give a single example of the discrepancy between the Homeric, and the later, representations of the early Greek ethnology. According to a tradition founded in part upon Apollodoros[1], in part upon a fragment ascribed by Tzetzes to Hesiod[2], Deucalion was the son of Prometheus, and a certain Hellen was the son of Deucalion. Hellen had three sons, Aiolos, Doros, and Xouthos; and Xouthos again had two sons, Ion and Achaios.

It is impossible not to be struck with the convenient adaptation, speaking generally, of this tradition to the reputed descent and succession of the various Greek races, so as to give to each its share of fame and its order of seniority. All Greeks were Hellenes, so Hellen is made the father of them all. The oldest among these names in the Greek tradition is Aiolos; so an Aiolos is made the eldest son of Hellen. The great dominant race of the first historic ages of Greece was the Dorian; accordingly, Doros is the second son of Hellen. The Ionians, represented by Attica, came later to their repute and power; so they, and the Achaians

[1] Lib. vii. 2, 3.   [2] Fragm. xxviii. ap. Tzetz. ad Lyc. 284.

to whom they gave a refuge after the Dorian conquest,
appear as the children of the third and youngest son.
This tradition may be properly viewed as a pretty piece
of joinery. But Mure[1] has with justice observed that
the name Hellen bears witness against itself, being apparently derived from the territorial name Hellas, and
that in its turn from the Helloi. When we bring this
tradition,-thus discredited by internal evidence, to the
bar of Homer, we find him in discord with it on every
point. Of Hellen as a person he knows nothing: the
name would to all appearance have meant in his ear
most properly an inhabitant of Southern Thessaly.
Aiolos, if named by him at all, is named as a foreigner;
while only particular families, not a tribe descended
from him, are indicated as having borne or bearing rule
in parts of Greece. Doros is wholly unknown to him;
and the Dorians are a portion, apparently an obscure
portion at the time, of the inhabitants of Crete. Of
Xouthos we have no trace whatever; in fact this whole
family is, as such, utterly non-existent. There is no
Ion; and the Iaones who appear as settled in the Attica
of Homer, are without any tribal eponymist. Again,
there is no trace of an Achaios; but the name Achaioi
is the dominant name of the period, and the crown
of its celebrity.

Such, exhibited by an example, is the contrariety
between Homeric and post-Homeric tradition. We
shall see in due time what materials the text of Homer
can contribute towards the construction of the ethnology of Greece in the heroic age.

In the following pages I endeavour to give to the
testimony of Homer what I have described as its due

[1] Lit. of Greece, vol. i. p. 39 n.

place. They are based upon a wide collection of particulars from the text. And, as far as possible, I have supplied the reader with means of judging where it is Homer that speaks, and where it is an illustrative tradition, or an indication drawn from some other than a literary source; as also of distinguishing in all cases between evidence, and the inference or conjecture which I may have presumed to found upon it.

Upon the whole, I trust enough has been said to show that in the text of the Poet we may find solid materials to work upon for the handling of the Homeric question. With this encouragement, let us commence our inquiries.

CHAPTER II.

THE name of Greeks, as the modern equivalent of
the several appellatives by which Homer describes the
army engaged in the siege of Troy, is too firmly
established to be changed. But it is not a correct
name. The Greek equivalent of the word is Γραικοί.
The name Γραῖα[1] is found in the Iliad, but it is only
a local name of a settlement of Boiotoi or Bœotians.
The name applied to themselves by the Greek people
throughout the historic times, as at the present day,
was not Graikoi, but Hellenes. And even this name,
as Thucydides[2] observes, had not come into vogue in
the time of Homer. It was indeed, as we shall find,
creeping, so to speak, into use: but the standing appellations of the army in the Iliad are these three,
Danaoi, Argeioi, and Achaioi; and it is sufficiently
plain that the most proper national name for the
Greeks of the period was that of 'Αχαιοί, Achaians.
We call them Greeks conventionally: but with no
more accuracy than we should render the Galli of

---

[1] Il. il. 498. [2] L 3.

Cæsar by the word 'French.' We should bear in mind, then, that in strictness the Greeks of the Troica were Achaians.

We find in Homer traces, as of a religion, so of a race, or group of races, who inhabited the Greek peninsula before the Achaians, or any other tribe of the blood afterwards classed as Hellenic. These inhabitants passed in different places under a variety of designations; of which the most comprehensive and wide-spread[1] appears to have been Pelasgoi. They seem to have formed the base of the Greek army, and of the people subject to the sway of Achaian and other great families.

There is no trace in the poems of their having used a language different from that of their superiors in station, although the tradition of a difference in blood subsisted down to the historic time, and although the Pelasgian language, where the people using it had not been blended with the Hellenes, had then come to be accounted as a distinct, if not a foreign, tongue.

The relation between this older race and the Hellenic tribes leads to the conclusion that both were alike derived from the Aryan stem. And there is no reason to believe that there were any earlier occupants of the Greek, or of the Italian Peninsula[2], than the group of tribes that was called Pelasgian. Neither of these countries presents us with remains belonging to what is called the stone period of the human race, when implements and utensils were made of that material, and the use of metals was unknown. The first emigrants from the East may probably have worked their way by

---

[1] Thirlwall, Hist. of Greece, vol. l. chap. ii.
[2] Mommsen, Hist. of Rome, chap. i.

land to and along the comparatively level and easy
countries of Central Europe, and seem not to have
penetrated through the masses of mountain, which
inclose on their northern sides both Greece and Italy.
The boast of autochthonism, or birth from the soil, so
rife in the historic ages of Greece, was therefore not
irrational, if we consider it to betoken only the claim
to first occupancy. And it seems to have been principally in vogue among the people of Attica and
Arcadia, the former of which had long been impressed
with a markedly Pelasgian character, while the latter
retained that character even through the historic
period. The particulars which have been embraced
in this slight survey are partly suggested by, and are in
all cases accordant with, the Homeric testimony.

The Greeks of the Iliad are ordinarily called by
Homer

    1. Danaoi.
    2. Argeioi.
    3. Achaioi.

They are also called

    1. Panhellenes, Il. ii. 530.
    2. Panachaioi, Il. ii. 404; vii. 73, 159, 327;
       ix. 301; x. 1; xix. 193; xxiii. 236. Od. i.
       239; xiv. 369; xxiv. 32.

With respect to the three first, which may be called
the Great Appellatives of Homer, it is manifest that
the Poet frequently uses them as interchangeable and
synonymous. Yet, upon examination, important distinctions will be found to exist between them.

The various legends interspersed through the Poems,
carry back the Homeric tradition to a period several
generations earlier than the War of Troy: which War,

D

together with the attendant group of circumstances, I
shall commonly call the Troica. But we shall find that
Homer does not also carry backwards the use of these
appellatives indifferently through the pre-Troic period:
and thus we shall obtain pretty clear evidence of a
chronological succession among them.

This rule applies likewise to other Homeric names.
For example; when reference is made, in the narrative of the Iliad, to the soldiers belonging to the
country afterwards called Bœotia, he describes them as
Boiotoi. But where Agamemnon and Athenè introduce the legend[1] of Tudeus, which touches the people
of the same district at a prior epoch, they are called
not Boiotoi but Kadmeioi and Kadmeiones. Moreover, in this same legend appear the people of Argos,
and the people of Mycenæ. They are both called
Achaioi, a name never given to the Kadmeioi.

In the legend of the birth of Eurustheus[2], the scene
is laid in Ἄργος Ἀχαιϊκόν. This name we shall find
still attached perhaps to the Peloponnesos, and certainly to the Eastern Peloponnesos, in the time of
Homer. Its inhabitants, who are described as we
have seen, in the time of Tudeus, that is to say one
generation before the War, as Achaioi, are called, in
the time of Eurustheus, and therefore before the period
of the Pelopids, not Achaioi but Argeioi[3]. It seems
impossible to treat these very marked usages as accidental.

About the same period Proitos, whom the post-
Homeric tradition represents as a brother of Eurustheus, expelled Bellerophon from Ephurè[4]. The text,

[1] Il. iv. 385, 391; v. 800-7.   [2] Il. xix. 95 seqq.
[3] Il. xix. 122, 124.   [4] Il. vi. 158.

true to itself, describes the people over whom Proitos ruled, not as Danaoi or Achaioi, but as Argeioi. In the same manner the Poet here describes as Ephurè what in the Catalogue he calls Corinth[1].

Homer then appears to point to Argeioi as the more ancient, and Achaioi as the more recent, name. But, moreover, he uses the two designations with marked respect to place as well as time.

In the Eleventh Iliad[2], Nestor details to Patroclos the legend of the war between the Pulians, and the Epeians who inhabited Elis. He calls the Pulians dis tinctively Achaians, where he is speaking of them as the conquering party. He seems to withhold that name from the conquered : and he gives it to the Pulians at a period which must have been within the life and reign of Eurustheus, that is to say, the period when the name of Argeians was attached to those who inhabited the ruling quarter of Greece, or the Eastern Peloponnesos.

But the word Argeioi, used freely by Homer as a national designation, has also a marked local sense in the poems. It is a standing epithet, in the singular, of Helen, and this too in the mouth of Greeks, and of deities, whose use of it gives it a force quite different from that which it might have had among the Trojans. The purely national name would in such a case have been void of distinctive meaning ; but now we naturally interpret the epithet as referring to the part of Greece with which Helen was especially connected. According to the post-Homeric tradition, confirmed by the Iliad, which makes Lacedæmon the country of Castor and Poludeukes[3], Tundareos, her father, was

[1] Il. ii. 570.   [2] Il. xi. 670-761.   [3] Il. iii. 244.

king of Sparta. Till the Pelopid House acquired it, and thus the Achaian sway began, this would be an Argeian kingdom; and thus Helen, though the wife of Menelaos, represents by her descent an Argeian title to it, so that the epithet thus acquires a full significance.

Thus far I have cited some examples to illustrate the practice of Homer. Let us now consider the leading particulars connected with the use of the three Great Appellatives.

The name Danaoi is used in the Iliad 147 times: in the Odyssey thirteen. Once it is combined with Argeioi, in Od. viii. 578, and appears to serve as an epithet. It is never used in the feminine. It is never used in the singular; and never locally. It seems never to signify the people inhabiting the Greek peninsula and islands, nor their ancestors in prior history: but invariably and only the Greeks of the army. It has therefore all the appearance of being an heroic and poetical rather than an historical appellation, and thus it is well adapted to describe men engaged in a military expedition surrounded with the most romantic associations.

Accordingly, the epithets applied to Δαναοί are exclusively of a military character. They are

1. ἥρωες, Il. ii. 110, 256; xv. 733 (heroes).
2. θεράποντες Ἄρηος, Il. vii. 382; xix. 78 (comrades of Arès).
3. φιλοπτόλεμοι, Il. xx. 351 (war-loving).
4. αἰχμηταί, Il. xii. 419 (spearmen).
5. ἀσπισταί, Il. xiii. 680 (shielded, heavy-armed).
6. ἴφθιμοι, Il. xi. 290 (stalwart).
7. ταχύπωλοι, Il. viii. 161 (of swift steeds).

It being then plain that Danaoi was not the proper contemporary name of the Greeks, it is also plain that it could not have been applied to the Greeks as an army before Troy, unless it had had some root lying deep in the history or legends of Greece.

National or tribal names in Homer usually come

1. From an eponymist or founder of a state, directly as Dardanoi or Troes, or Kadmeioi; or indirectly, when they proceed from the name of a country, which name has been acquired from an eponymist. Such is Ithakesioi from Ithakè, Ithakè itself being derived from Ithakos, who is mentioned in Od. xvii. 207.

2. In like manner a name may come mediately from a race instead of an individual. Thus it seems that Hellas is derived from Helloi, and is in its turn the source of the great national name Hellen.

3. From the physical character of the country inhabited, as Threkes (Thracians), from θρῇξ, describing a rough highland country[1]: or Aigialeis, from Αἰγιαλός, the district of coast to the south of the Gulf of Corinth.

4. In the single case of the Athenians, we find the name of a population derived from that of a deity.

Besides the Homeric names which can be traced to one or other of these sources, there are names of which the connection with any of them is not established, or even where it is improbable.

The text of Homer affords very slender aid for tracing the name Danaoi up to its source. But we must combine the fact of its application, limited as it is, to the nation, with the negative evidence afforded by this fact, that Homer nowhere uses the name as a domestic

[1] Cf. Od. ix. 27.

name, either for his own, or for the immediately preceding generations. This seems to throw back the
origin of the name to a period comparatively remote.

And when we reach such a period, we find at least
a clue. In Il. xiv. 319 we hear of the amour of Zeus
with a beautiful Danaè, of the royal house of Acrisios,
from which union sprang Perseus and his line. The
presumption then arises, that this Danaè, being the
daughter and mother of princes, was of the lineage of a
Danaos, that this Danaos was himself a real or reputed
prince of celebrity, and that he gave his name to the
people with whom, and among whom, he effected a
settlement in Greece.

This may be the proper place to observe that, on the
subject of the foreign origin of Greek races or houses,
Homer is what is termed an unwilling witness. Intensely national in feeling, he represents the first form
of that peculiar sentiment which, in the historic period,
divided mankind into Greeks and Barbarians; much
as the Hebrew race, upon grounds of a more definite
character, made their division of the world into Jew
and Gentile. There can be little doubt that Homer
could, if he would, have told us much respecting immi-
grations and settlements in Greece, which now remains
the subject of comparatively dark conjecture. But it
may be broadly laid down that he systematically eschews
tracing either a family or a tribe to an origin abroad.
It seems to be his intention that we should assume all
Greek families and races, and further all Greek manners and institutions, to have sprung out of the soil.
The sources of silver and copper and some other commodities, and moreover of works of art, he is willing, or

even careful, to point out. But not so as to man and
his highest operations. Though he tells us sometimes
of foreign persons and events, he never, I think, consciously supplies, but seems habitually to keep back, the
link between them and his own beloved Greek nation.

All this seems to be conformable to the course of
natural feeling. Arrivals from abroad, in the earliest
periods of the life of a nation, usually indicate either
the conquest, or at least the superiority, in one form or
another, of foreigners over natives, of what is strange
to the soil over what is associated with it. In this
there is some violation of that feeling of simple reverence for the past, which is so conspicuous among the
Greeks of Homer, and which is jarred by the memory
of all disturbances of its even tenour. It can hardly be
that, in any country, such narratives should be popular
at or near the time of the events. Even the process by
which Hellenes mastered Pelasgians, or by which Pelopids put themselves in the place of Perseids, is nowhere
disclosed to us by Homer: whose purpose it was to unite
more closely the elements of the nation, and not to
record that they had once been separate.

When Homer tells us of descendants of a Tantalos,
or an Aiolos, and of a people called Kadmeiones, but
gives us no clue to the extraction, or to the habitation,
of any of these personages themselves, we may conclude,
without much risk of error, that none of them were
native Greeks, and that their names mark the point of
transition from a foreign to a Greek domicile for their
respective families. He never even names the connection of Kadmeiones with Kadmos, or of Pelopidai with
Pelops: both these great personages are only named by
him incidentally, in remote portions of the Poems; and

as to Aiolos, the ancestor of the Aiolids, it has not yet
been generally recognized that the Poet names him at all.

Without, then, calling in the aid of extraneous traditions, it appears highly probable that the Danaoi bore
the same relation to a Danaos, as the Kadmeioi obviously bear to a real or imaginary Kadmos.

It is also probable, that Danaè stands in the generation next to Danaos. For Danaè herself stands, as we
shall see, in the sixth generation before the Troica;
and the knowledge and traditions of Homer nowhere go
back beyond the seventh generation. But as Danaè is
the daughter of Acrisios, not of Danaos, it is probable
that Acrisios was a younger brother of Danaos; and
that the genealogy stands as follows :

1. Danaos = Acrisios.
   2. Danae.
    3. Perseus.
    4. Sthenelos.
    5. Eurustheus. Contemporary with Heracles and Pelops.
         6. Atreus = Thuestes.
         7. Agamemnon = Aigisthos.

It will here be perceived that the text of Homer is
altogether at variance with those later legends, which
throw back the first Greek dynasties into a very remote
comparative antiquity. There is, I apprehend, an intrinsic improbability in such legends as affect to trace
prolonged lines of sovereigns through ages of darkness
and barbarism, not possessed of the ordinary means of
record ; but there is also this strong presumption in
favour of the Homeric text, that his genealogies, gathered indiscriminately as they are from different parts
of the Poems, are in singular, if not absolutely un-
varying, accordance with each other.

According to the post-Homeric tradition, Danaos

was an Egyptian, and was brother of Aiguptos. He migrated into Greece, and became king of Argos. Proitos was his great-grandson; and as, according to the legend of the Sixth Iliad[1], Proitos stands at two or two and a-half generations before the war, there is here an apparent agreement with Homer; but as Acrisios also is made the brother of Proitos, a much greater antiquity is in effect claimed for the immigration of Danaos. So far, however, as respects his personality, the seat of his kingdom, and his being of foreign origin, the later tradition sustains the presumptions arising from the text of Homer.

The early disappearance of the name from the roll of tradition would be easily accounted for by that change of the dynasty in the male line which takes place at the time of Danaè.

From what country Danaos came, we shall hereafter have occasion to consider. For the present we may take him to have been one of the personages who arrived in Greece as a stranger, and who there founded such a dynasty, among the primitive or Pelasgian population, as became naturalised. This foundation seems to have taken place at the very commencement of what we may call the traditionary, as opposed to the merely mythical, period, about two hundred years before the Trojan War.

Even this is considerably older than the date of any family which we can connect with the Achaian name, or with the Hellenic stock. It seems, however, quite possible that Perseus and his race may on the father's side have descended from an Hellenic ancestry, and that the fable of Zeus and Danaè may be no more

[1] Il. vi. 158.

than a veil employed to cover the transition, and to dignify the origin of the incoming family.

Hesiod[1] terms Perseus both Danaïdes, and son of Danaè, and states that Danaos relieved Argos from drought. Æschylus in the Supplices[2] represents the whole Greek Peninsula as having been originally subject to one and the same sway under Pelasgos. Euripides[3] says that Danaos changed the name of the Peloponnesians from Pelasgiotai to Danaoi. These reports are in no way at variance with the Homeric text.

Upon the whole, then, the probable conclusions are :

1. That the Danaan name was dynastic.

2. That the dynasty was pre-Hellenic.

3. That it stands next in chronological succession to the Pelasgic time ; and

4. That it makes its appearance at about two centuries, more or less, before the War of Troy.

We have next to deal with the name Argeioi. And first as to the facts connected with its use in the Poems.

It is found 177 times in the Iliad, and seventeen times in the Odyssey. I speak of the plural form. The singular is also used eleven times in the Iliad, and seventeen times in the Odyssey.

Of the seventeen passages in the Odyssey, not one refers to the Greeks as a nation, or as contemporary with the action of the Poem. In two of them, Od. iii. 309 and xv. 240, the word signifies the inhabitants of Argolis or the North-Eastern Peloponnesos. In the other fifteen, it is always applied to the Greek army before Troy.

---

[1] Fragm. 58, and Scut. Herc. 216, 229.   [2] v. 263.
[3] Ar. Fr. li. 7.

In the Iliad, we have certain cases of the local use. Proitos[1], who was nearly contemporary with Eurustheus, ruled over Argeians. From the text it would seem as if he were a neighbour to Sisuphos, of Ephurè or Corinth: and if so, his subjects may have been Argives of Argolis, taken largely; of the Eastern, or Eastern and Northern, Peloponnesos. Such is evidently the meaning of Argeioi in the legend of the birth of Eurustheus[2]. On the other hand, the name of Proitos was attached to one of the Gates of Thebes. It was plainly therefore a Phœnician name. It is far from clear that he reigned in Thebes; but, if he did so, then the name Argeioi is applicable to the inhabitants of Bœotia. This slender probability is the only presumption afforded us of the use of the name Argeioi beyond the limits of the Perseid or Pelopid dominions in Peloponnesos, except as a designation for the army before Troy. Again, in the chariot race of the Twenty-third Iliad, Diomed is described as Ætolian by birth, but as ruling among Argeioi[3].

These, it seems plain, must be the Argives of Argos, who formed his contingent. Still, upon this local name there had supervened, since the accession of the Pelopid dynasty, as we shall find from the legend of Tudeus, the paramount and wider name of Achaioi[4].

The name of Argeioi, then, appears to stand partially in the same category with Danaoi, as a name rather poetic and archaic, than actually current; and as one of which the common application to the Greeks in general, at any period, is uncertain; but which had, several generations before, been the proper designation

[1] Il. vi. 159.　　　[2] Il. xix. 122.
[3] Il. xxiii. 470.　　[4] Il. iv. 384; v. 803.

at least of the inhabitants of the ruling portion of the peninsula.

This name is, on the other hand, so far unlike the Danaan name, that we find it in the singular number and the feminine gender. But it is only thus applied to two persons; Helen, and the goddess Herè. It is plain, as we have seen, that, for the former, it means not Greek Helen, but Argive Helen. It is but twice given to Herè: both times where she is acting with Athenè in the fifth Iliad[1]; in the first passage Zeus cites them as helpers of Menelaos, in the second, as having restrained and baffled Arès on the field. The meaning of Argeiè, when applied to a goddess, according to analogy, must be, 'worshipped in Argos,' as Aphroditè is called Kuthereia, and Apollo Smintheus. The local worship of Herè continued, as is well known, to characterize Argos throughout the historic period. It was to this local point in particular that her tenacious attachment was constantly directed. It survived dynastic changes; watched over Eurustheus; reappeared in hatred of Heracles; and protected Agamemnon. Three cities, we know, she loved beyond all others[2]: Mycenæ, Argos, and Sparta; and her attachment to the Greeks in the War possibly may have its root in this more special and local affection; or may, on the other hand, be due to the representative character of that district as the political centre of the whole of Greece.

If in one point of view, as has been suggested, the use of the Argeian name by Homer was poetic and archaic, on the other hand, we may compare this employment of the designation of the ruling part to signify the whole with the cases of more extended empires. All the races,

[1] Il. v. 8, 908.   [2] Il. iv. 51.

that served under Xerxes and Darius in their expeditions against Greece, were regarded as Persians. The Roman name was applicable to the people of Campania or Calabria, as forming parts of the Roman dominion; while in any domestic or Italian matter their local name would naturally revive. So it may be that while all the Greeks of Homer are Argeians on the field of Troas, a portion of them may also be Argeians in the local sense afterwards given to Argives; with regard, like Kadmeians, Ætolians, Arcadians, or Locrians, to their own local habitation.

We have thus traced back this, the second of the Great Appellatives for the Greek army, to a more ancient and also more limited use for the inhabitants of the ruling part of Greece; but we have still to ask, how came it originally to be so applied in either way, and what is the root and meaning of the name?

Plainly its root is that of the word Argos; and plainly also, as we shall find, the application of the territorial name Argos is wider than that of its derivative.

There are several forms of geographical expression under which Homer appears to signify the entire territory inhabited by Greek races, or subject to Greek sway.

(*a*) The only word which manifestly, without addition of any kind, suffices with the Poet for this purpose is Achaiis. It is used either substantively, or adjectively with γαῖα or αῖα, in eight passages. It will suffice to quote one in which Nestor describes the gathering of the army, a process that manifestly included the whole dominion:

λαὸν ἀγείροντες κατ' Ἀχαιΐδα πουλυβότειραν[1].

[1] Il. xi. 770. 'Collecting an army through fertile Achaiis.' Cf. Il. l. 254; vii. 124.

In a line twice used, indeed, it is combined with Argos:

Ἄργος ἐς ἱππόβοτον καὶ Ἀχαιίδα καλλιγύναικα ¹.

But there is no reason why in this line the word should not follow what we have seen to be the ruling sense, Argos meaning the more famous part, and Achaiis meaning the whole.

(*b*) A second and compound form of expression, evidently conveying, as a compound, the same sense, is found in the combination of Argos with Hellas:

ἀνδρὸς, τοῦ κλέος εὐρὺ καθ᾽ Ἑλλάδα καὶ μέσον Ἄργος ².

The meaning of the line plainly is, a reputation reaching over all Greece. It is not conceivable that Penelopè, who uses the phrase more than once, could mean to assign to her husband's fame a limit narrower than the Greek nationality. But we shall find that the name Hellas evidently has a special affinity with the north of Greece. Presumably, then, this line may mean,

'Through Northern and through Southern Greece.'

(*c*) But we find also a third form of expression, in which the word Argos, with the affix πᾶν, appears to cover the whole, at least, of continental Greece, and thus to be equivalent, or nearly so, to Achaiis, and also to Hellas combined with Argos:

πολλῇσιν νήσοισι καὶ Ἄργεϊ παντὶ ἀνάσσειν ³.

For this line, joining Argos with the islands, describes the range of the whole empire, or (to use a modern phrase) suzerainty, of Agamemnon.

---

¹ 'Horse-feeding Argos and Achalis with beautiful women.'
² Od. i. 344. 'Whose fame extends through Hellas and mid-Argos.'
³ Il. ii. 108. 'To rule over many islands and all Argos.'

(*d*) Next it appears that we have the word Argos, with particular ethnical or tribal affixes, used distributively for each of the chief parts of Greece.

In the Catalogue, after Homer has enumerated all the contingents drawn from the Islands, as well as from Southern and Middle Greece, he opens a new division with the line:

Νῦν αὖ τοὺς ὅσσοι τὸ Πελασγικὸν "Αργος ἔναιον[1].

And he then proceeds to reckon nine contingents, all of which were drawn from Greece north of Mount Othrûs, or, in other words, from Thessaly.

It appears, then, that by Pelasgic Argos Homer meant Thessaly.

(*e*) Next we have an Achaiic Argos mentioned in five passages.

In the first[2] (of which the words are repeated in the second), Agamemnon is speaking of the return to Greece. While the phrase therefore might carry the sense of that country at large, it may also very properly mean the seat of the Pelopid power, or the Eastern Peloponnesos.

In the third, Herè goes to Achaiic Argos[3] to hasten the birth of Eurustheus. The meaning appears to be that she went to the kingdom of Sthenelos his father, which again will mean the Eastern Peloponnesos.

In the fourth, Telemachos asks where was Menelaos whilst Aigisthos was engaged in the work of treachery and murder. ' Was he away from Achaiic Argos, and travelling abroad[4]?' Here, while Sparta only might (as far

---

[1] Il. ii. 681.   'But now (recount) those, as many as inhabited Pelasgian Argos.'

[2] Il. ix. 141, 283.   [3] Il. xix. 115.   [4] Od. iii. 249.

as the meaning goes) be signified, the sense of ' Eastern Peloponnesos,' or the ' Pelopid dominion,' is perfectly suitable, and appears to be the true sense of the phrase.

(*f*) Further we find an Iason Argos. Eurumachos, the suitor, pays a compliment to the beauty of Penelope by saying, ' You would have more suitors than you now have,' i. e. than these islands yield you :

εἰ πάντες σε ἴδοιεν ἀν' Ἴασον "Αργος Ἀχαιοί[1].

He evidently goes beyond the dominions of Odysseus. But then he probably speaks only of the territory lying nearest to them, and in habitual intercourse with them. Now this was Western Peloponnesos: as we know from the limited range of Greek navigation; from the direct testimony of the Poems, which tell us of the journey of Odysseus to Ephurè[2], and of the debt which Odysseus went to Messenè[3] to recover; and (not to mention other circumstances) from the apprehension of the Suitors that Telemachos would at once repair to Elis, or to Pulos[1], for aid. In the same manner the relations of Crete were with Eastern Peloponnesos; and therefore Helen at Troy easily recognizes Idomeneus, because, as she says, she has often seen him in Sparta[6]. So far, then, Iasian Argos would seem to consist of Western Peloponnesos, including therein the dominions of Elis, Pulos, and perhaps parts at least of Messenè.

We have other means of connecting the name of Iasos with Western Peloponnesos. For Amphion, the king of the Minueïan Orchomenos, was the son of Iasos. He was also the father of Chloris, whom

---

[1] ' If all the Achaians of Iasian Argos could see you.'
[2] Od. i. 260.
[3] Od. xxi. 15.
[4] Od. xxiv. 431.
[6] Il. iii. 232.

Neleus married, and who became queen of Pulos. Now
there was a river Minueïos[1] between Pulos and Elis;
and not only is there an Orchomenos included in the
places which supplied the Arcadian contingent[2], but
also Agamemnon asks of Odysseus, in Hades, whether
his son Orestes is at Orchomenos, or at Pulos, or at
Sparta[3]; as if it were some considerable seat of power
where a prince might find refuge. Thus Amphion, the
son of Iasos, is placed in close connection both with
Bœotia and with Western Peloponnesos.

Further, Homer acquaints us that he and his brother
Zethos first founded and fortified Thebes; for, says the
Poet, not even they could hold it unfortified[4]. As his
daughter married Neleus, this fortification must have
been effected from four to five generations before the
Troica. But he founded no dynasty in Thebes. On
the contrary, we find from Homer that Œdipus ruled
there, apparently in succession to his father, two generations before the War[5]. And, according to tradition,
he was the descendant of Kadmos, who had colonised
Thebes from Phœnicia. It seems very possible that
Amphion, like so many others[6], was expelled from the
fat soil of Bœotia; that he passed into Western Peloponnesos; and that he carried thither both the names
of Orchemenos and Minueïos, which we find undeniably
existing in that region, and the name Iasos, which thus
receives a probable and natural application.

Iasian Argos then is the Western Peloponnesos.

And thus moreover we find Argos, with adjuncts,
running over the three most famous portions of Greece.
It is the common term in three distinct territorial

[1] Il. xi. 722.   [2] Il. ii. 605.   [3] Od. xi. 459.
[4] Od. xi. 264.   [5] Od. xi. 273–276.   [6] Thuc. I. 2.

E

names, as if it meant 'a settlement,' and as if they respectively signified

1. Thessaly, the settlement named from the Pelasgoi.
2. Eastern Peloponnesos, the settlement named from the Achaioi.
3. Western Peloponnesos, the settlement named from Iasos.

. (g) Further, it is incontestable that Argos sometimes means the city known in history by that name, or rather that city with its immediately contiguous territory: for example, in the Catalogue[1], where it is mentioned with Tiruns and other places, as making up the contingent of Diomed; and where it is named with Mycenæ and Sparta as being together the favourite cities of Herè (πόλης). The word polis does not indeed invariably include a district; for in certain cases we find it used for the town, in opposition to agros, the country[2]. But this seems to be the only case where the word is applied to Argos. We have a similar use, when, as Telemachos is quitting Sparta, he is joined by Theoclumenos, 'a fugitive from Argos[3].'

On the other hand, the signification, though still local, must be enlarged where Agamemnon says that Briseis shall pass her life at his palace 'in Argos[4],' since the city of Argos was under the sway of Diomed, and the residence of Agamemnon was at Mycenæ. The same will hold good of the passage in which Ephurè, afterwards Corinth, is described as situate in a nook of horse-feeding Argos, μυχῷ Ἀργεος Ἱπποβότοιο[5].

The epithet 'horse-feeding' has the effect of showing that the country designated is a plain country. Thus

[1] Il. ii. 559.   [2] Il. xxiii. 832, 835; Od. xvii. 182.
[3] Od. xv. 223.   [4] Il. i. 30.   [5] Il. vi. 152.

the island of Ithaca is described as a goat-feeding[1] spot, and more beautiful than a horse-feeding district. Of course the phrase is to be understood by comparison.

(*b*) Lastly, there are one or two passages in which the name Argos may be held to stand alone for Greece at large: as when Nestor declares it shameful for the army to return to Argos ("Αργοσδε ἰέναι[2]) before the mind of Zeus is known. And Poludamas, speaking of the possible destruction of the Greek army in Troas, thus describes that contingency:

νωνύμνους ἀπολίσθαι ἀπ' Ἄργεος ἐνθάδ' Ἀχαιούς[3].

Paris, too, says he brought home property from Argos. This may mean from Sparta as part of the Pelopid dominion; or it may mean from Greece at large. But perhaps we cannot be sure that in these passages Argos stands for more than a description of the whole by its capital part.

Argos, then, with Homer has these four uses:

1. It may be held to mean, alone or with πᾶν, Greece at large; but, if so, it is rarely thus used.

2. It may mean the Pelopid dominions, or, taken roughly, the Eastern Peloponnesos.

3. It may mean the city of Argos, with the immediately surrounding district attached to it. In this sense it accepts the epithet πολυδίψιον: and the epithets ἱππόβοτον, πολύπυρον, and οὖθαρ ἀρούρης, appear to apply to it both in this and in the last-named sense.

4. When joined with distinctive epithets of an historical, not a physical, character, it seems to be applicable to most portions of Greek territory, as if a

---

[1] Od. iv. 606.   [2] Il. ii. 348.
[3] Il. xii. 70.   'That the Achaians perish inglorious away from Argos.'

radical signification, such as settlement, or colony in the original sense of the word, still adhered to it.

When we proceed to examine the etymology of the word, we find that, as it is but once combined with polis, so the epithets attaching to it (as above), all of them indicate a tract of country; like 'land' among the Scotch, as in the expression ' landward parishes.' And again, on comparing it with agros, the proper term for describing a rural tract, this latter appears to be the very same word with the middle consonants transposed. So far, then, the meaning may be that of a tract of land suited for, or brought under, cultivation.

The Homeric names of countries and places, as far as we can trace them, appear to be derived—

1. From an individual founder: as Ithakè from Ithakos, Dardaniè from Dardanos[1].

2. From a race in occupation or in ascendancy: as Achaïis from Achaoi, Cretè or Cretai, from Cretes[2].

3. From a race in occupation, which race has itself derived its name from features or circumstances of the country: as Threkè from Threkes, Thracians; the race in turn taking a name related to the rough character of a highland country, and probably proceeding from the same root with τρῆχυς. So again, Aigialeia from the Aigialeis, these being named from Aigialos, the strip of coast afterwards called Achaia.

4. From these local features or physical incidents directly, like Aigialos: or like Euboiè, which apparently signifies the adaptation of that fertile island to tillage ; an adaptation which afterwards made it the granary of Athens.

---

[1] Od. xvii. 207; Il. xx. 216.   [2] Od. xiv. 199.

It is plain, negatively, that the word Argos has no connection with any of the three first-named sources. The suggestion already made would attach it to the fourth. It would then apply to Argos of the Eastern Peloponnesos, as the Argos κατ' ἐξοχήν.

The word argos is used adjectively by Homer for dogs, Il. i. 50; for oxen, Il. xxiii. 30; and for a goose, Od. xv. 161. And we have these compounds into which it enters:

1. ἀργῆς (κεραυνός).
2. ἀργικέραυνος.
3. ἀργεστῆς (Νότος).
4. ἀργενναὶ ὄιες, ὀθόναι.
5. ἀργινόεις (Κάμειρος).
6. ἀργιόδοντες (ὕες).
7. ἀργιπόδες (κύνες).
8. Ποδάργης, a horse of Achilles.

The sense of whiteness or brightness may apply to every one of these uses, both primitive and derivative: but whiteness or brightness could only be applicable to such districts of country as might be chalky or sandy; and this sense therefore will in no way assist us towards an explanation of the territorial name Argos with its very wide application.

If Argos have a connection with ἔργον, then it at once admits the sense of an extent of land tilled or suitable for tillage, a sense nearly akin, though not similar in etymology, to that of the word 'lowlands.' For ergon in Homer, while it is applicable to industrial operations generally, is primarily and specially applied to agriculture[1].

We can, then, conceive how, out of many districts, all fitly described as lowlands, in one, from being merely a description, it would become a proper name; and how, at the next stage in the process, it would

[1] Od. vi. 259.

give a designation to its inhabitants. In accordance
with this supposition, we have more than one Argos
in Homer: and in the historic period we have Argos
of Orestis in Macedonia, Argos of Amphilochia in
Western Greece, and Argos near Larissa in Thessaly.
But only one Argos is inhabited by Argeioi. Just as
there are Highlands of Saxony no less than of Scotland,
but only the Scotch mountaineers acquired the name of
Highlanders, as a standing and ordinary name.

In referring Argos to a common root and significance
with ἔργον, we are not bound to hold that it attains its
initial vowel by junction with the particle α in its in-
tensive, or in any other, sense. For we have the word
ergon, and also its derivatives, in this form, handed
down from very ancient Greek. Among the four tribes
of Attica, which subsisted until the time of Cleisthenes,
one was that of the husbandmen, called Argades. And
in the Elian Inscription, supposed to date about the
fortieth Olympiad, or more than six hundred years before Christ, we have the word ergon, in the form argon
with the digamma, as follows—

αἴτε ϝεϝος αἴτε ϝαργον[1].

Another probable example of the exchange of these
vowels is in aroō, to plough, compared with era,
the earth. In the Latin tongue we find both forms
preserved, in aro, to plough, and sero, to sow, respectively.

We need not here inquire what is the common root
of ἔργον and of Argos. But, if labour be the idea conveyed, this may perhaps suggest a meaning for the

----

[1] Museum Criticum, i. 536; and Marsh, Horæ Pelasgicæ,
p. 70.

Homeric adjective argos and for all its compounds. The groundwork of that meaning may be conveyed by the word 'strenuous.' Sometimes this takes the form of keenness, and then follows the idea of swiftness: sometimes it takes the form of a persevering patience, and then slowness is not less appropriately suggested. The labour of a dog is swift, that of an ox is patient: hence we have laborious oxen, moving slow; laborious dogs, moving fast. The sense of whiteness legitimately attaches to the effect of rapid motion on the eye. This explanation will perhaps be found to suit all the diversified phrases which have been cited above.

And (reverting to the fountain-head), we perceive that the notion of strenuous labour will adapt itself to other uses of Argos. We may consider the name of the ship Argo as meaning possibly 'swift,' but preferably 'stout,' able to do battle with the waves, as we now say a good or a gallant ship. Again, this sense suits, far more fully than the mere idea of speed, the noble dog Argos of the Odyssey; for whom mere whiteness would be a vapid description. Once more, we have in the 'Αργειφόντης of Homer a glimpse of the tradition of Argos the spy, to whom we naturally ascribe a strenuous vigilance. The epithet ἀργαλέος, 'hard or difficult to cope with,' follows in the train: while the later word ἀργοῦντες[1], 'idle,' takes up the idea of slowness at the point where it passes into inertness.

When we turn from Argos to its derivative Argeioi, we find subsidiary evidence to the effect that the word properly meant a husbandman, a rustic. In Suidas[2] we have the proverb 'Αργείους ὁρᾶς, 'You see Argeioi,' with the explanation παροιμία ἐπὶ τῶν ἀτενῶς καὶ κατα-

<hr />

[1] Soph. Fr. 288.   [2] Suid. in voce.

πληκτικῶς ὁρώντων [1]. Now we know nothing of the
Argives as inhabitants of Argolis, which would lead
to the belief that they stared hard, or conveyed
alarm by their looks. But if the word Argeioi
meant husbandmen, then, as the population, instead
of living dispersedly in hamlets (κωμηδόν) gathered
into towns, the rural part of the community would
gradually become also the ruder part, and from this
point the transition is easy to the sense of a wild
and savage aspect.

The Latin word agrestis stands to ager as Argeios,
according to the foregoing argument, stands to Argos.
The agrestis, or countryman, was opposed to the ur-
banus, or townsman. The latter, with its Greek correlative ἀστεῖος, came by degrees to mean a person of
polished manners; but agrestis, following the movement I have supposed in the case of Argeios, came to
mean coarse, wild, barbarous. Thus Ovid says of the
River Acheloos, when mutilated by the loss of his horn
in the combat with Heracles,

       ' Vultus Achelous agrestes
   Et lacerum cornu mediis caput abdidit undis[2].'

And Cicero, after describing the battles of the Spartan
youth, carried on with nails and teeth as well as fists
and feet, asks, ' Quæ barbaries Indica vastior atque
agrestior [3]?'

Again, Suidas gives us the expression 'Αργεῖοι [4], which
he says is used for sheer villains, because the Argeioi
are held up in plays as noted thieves; for which he
refers to a lost play of Aristophanes. According to the

---

[1] 'A proverb concerning people who stare hard and whose
looks cause alarm.'   [2] Ov. Met. ix. 96.
[3] Cic. Tusc. Disp. v. 27.   [4] In voc. 'Αργεῖοι φῶρες.

view I have given, the word may well mean robbers, since theft in the early stages of society always frequents solitary places.

Again, Æschines[1] charges Demosthenes with gross offences, which had brought upon him disparaging nicknames. One of these was Argas; which Suidas and Hesychius explain as the name of a snake, signifying sharp and crafty. But Æschines says he was called Argas, each of his guardians having suits against him to recover money. So that the meaning would be 'crafty in getting hold of the money of others,' *homo trium literarum*, a sharper.

Once more. Hesychius on the name Argeioi says, ἐκ τῶν Εἱλώτων οἱ πιστευόμενοι οὕτως ἐλέγοντο, ἢ λαμπροί, 'those Helots distinguished for fidelity are so called.' Why was it that select and confidential Helots thus received the name of Argeioi ? That name may have retained its local force, as applicable to the whole Pelopid dominion, long after Homer : and it may also, apart from its use as a proper name, have borne the meaning of a free or ordinary agricultural settler. The Helot was a serf by the fortune of war; but he was a serf whose forefathers had, according to this view, been Argeioi. If then a Helot made himself conspicuous, and acquired the confidence of his lord by fidelity and smartness, it would seem a very natural reward to efface from him the brand of his captivity, and give him the old name of the free countryman of that part of Greece. In this case Argeios might mean a libertus, without a defined *formula* of emancipation.

It is worth remark that the cognate word agrios appears to have gone through the same process as

[1] De Falsâ Legat. p. 41, l. 14.

agrestis and Argeios. For there was an Ætolian
prince Agrios[1], a grand-uncle of Diomed, two generations before the War of Troy. In the contemporary
language of the Poet, Agrios had come to mean savage
and cruel, and is so applied to Poluphemos[2]. The intermediate meaning probably was that of a dweller in
a wild and unsettled place. The word is never used to
describe the passion, or the cruelty, of Achilles.

It should also be noted that Argeioi, where applied
to the Greeks at large, never means the chiefs,
but always the mass; whereas the word Achaios has,
as we shall see, in many places a decided leaning
towards the aristocracy. Epithets are scarcely ever
given by Homer to the Argeian name. Only in four
passages do they appear. In Il. iv. 242 they are ἰόμωροι
and ἐλεγχέες, 'dishonoured:' in Il. xiv. 479 ἰόμωροι[3], and
ἀπειλάων ἀκόρητοι. These are in each case, not descriptive epithets attaching to or indicating general character,
but reproaches growing out of the occasion. In Il. xxi.
429 they are θωρηκτοί, clad in breastplates, which,
from the context, seems to do no more than state
a fact: the phrase is equivalent to 'the Greeks in
arms.' In Il. xix. 269, the Argeioi are called φιλοπτόλεμοι, lovers of battle; and this appears to be the
sole passage in which an epithet of description, properly so called, is attached to the word. But the
Danaan name, though more rarely used, has epithets
in twenty-two passages; and the Achaian name in

---

[1] Il. xiv. 117.   [2] Od. ix. 215, 494.

[3] I render ἰόμωροι, not archers, a sense neither suited to the
passage nor to the general armament of the Greeks, who were
not as a rule archers; but braggarts, loud talkers, in close harmony with the sister-phrase ἀπειλάων ἀκόρητοι = insatiate of boasts.

nearly 130. This circumstance tends to show, that the Argeian name properly belongs to the commonalty or masses, rather than to the chiefs.

We have assumed above, in accordance with the general Greek tradition, that the Pelasgoi were the first agricultural settlers of the peninsula; but that their name, and any other cognate names, were suppressed or thrown into the shade by the dynastic name, which a Danaos probably gave to his people. That name, again, naturally disappearing with the accession of another line to his throne and dominions, the name Argeioi, taken either from the occupation of the people (like Argades), or from the settlement they had made, would take its place with great propriety, in lieu of reverting to the Pelasgic name, which would silently pass out of use, as that of a race conquered and therefore comparatively depressed.

The third and most weighty of the Great Appellatives is Achaioi.

The evidence of the Poems will I think suffice to show—

1. That this is the most familiar designation of the Greeks of Homer.

2. That the manner of its use indicates, among the Greeks of Homer, the political predominance of an Achaian race over other races ranged by its side in the War, and composing along with it the nation which owned Agamemnon for its head.

3. That, besides its national use, the name of the Achaioi has a local use in many parts of Greece.

4. That the manner of this local use points out with sufficient clearness, that the rise of the Achaian name was contemporary with that of the family of Pelops.

The first proposition may be at once settled by the rude, but not inconclusive, test of numbers. While the Danaan name is used about 160 times, of which thirteen are in the Odyssey; and the Argeian 205 times, of which twenty-eight are in the Odyssey; the Achaian name is used about 597 times in the Iliad, and 117 in the Odyssey, making 714 in all. This frequency of use in the two poems of itself goes far to determine that the Achaian designation was the most modern of the three.

It is also worth observing, that in the opening of the Iliad the word Achaioi is used five times, before Danaoi or Argeioi are introduced at all.

We have seen that the Danaan name is never used in the singular; and that the Argeian name is so used only in its local sense. But the Achaian name, and that only, is used in the singular to designate an individual as belonging to the nation; with the reserve, however, of a separate shade of meaning, sometimes [1] tending to attach it to a class. So the Poet uses Δάρδανος ἀνήρ [2] for a Trojan or a Dardanian.

Again, Homer has worked this name into the female forms Achaiides, Achaiiades, Achaiai, to signify the women of Greece; but has made no such use of the Danaan or Argeian [3] names.

Also the phrase υἷες 'Αχαιῶν, sons of the Achaians, has no correlation with the Danaan or Argeian names, and further helps to show the predominant familiarity of this designation. What the patronymic was to the individual, this form of speech was to the nation—an appeal to a standard of honour, an incentive under the form of an embellishment.

---

[1] Il. iii. 167, 226.   [2] Il. ii. 701.   [3] *Supra*, pp. 36, 44.

Epithets are given to the name Achaioi in 130 places, besides eight or ten more in which they are used either for the women, or for the word in its territorial sense. And the familiar use of the word Achaiis for the country is a proof of the prevalence, ascendancy, and familiarity of the name, which was thus applied on its own merits, so to speak, and not, like Argos, because it was the proper designation of the most eminent part of the country.

When we look to the character of these epithets, we find them such as point to the Achaians in the character of a dominant race or aristocracy.

In one or two cases we have epithets of reproach, such as were addressed to the army at critical moments: ἀνάλκιδες, Il. xv. 326; ἀπειλητῆρες, Il. vii. 96, and in the same passage 'Αχαιΐδες. In a few others we have them as simple descriptions of circumstances of the moment[1]. But the pointed epithets, descriptive of character, are as follows:—

1. δῖοι, worthy or noble: Il. v. 451; Od. iii. 161, *et alibi*.

2. ἑλικῶπες, from the rapid motion of the eye giving brightness: Il. iii. 389, *et alibi*.

3. ἐϋκνήμιδες, stoutly-greaved: Il. iii. 304; Od. iii. 149, and in thirty-two other places.

4. ἥρωες, heroes: Il. xii. 165, *et alibi*.

5. καρηκομόωντες, with flowing or abundant hair: Il. ii. 11; Od. i. 90, and in twenty-seven other places.

6. μεγάθυμοι, high-spirited: Il. i. 123, 135; Od. xxiv. 57.

7. μένεα πνείοντες, ardent: Il. iii. 8.

8. χαλκοκνήμιδες, with greaves of χαλκὸς or copper: Il. vii. 41.

[1] Il. xii. 29; xiii. 15; xv. 44.

9. χαλκοχίτωνες, with armour for tunics: Il. i. 371; Od. i. 286, and in twenty-two other places.

10. ὑπερκύδαντες, exulting: Il. iv. 66, 71.

11. ἀρηίφιλοι, lovers of war: Il. vi. 73; xvi. 303; xvii. 319.

12. φιλοπτόλεμοι, lovers of battle: Il. xvii. 224.

These epithets are very marked in character; they describe courage, personal beauty, well-made and well-finished arms, or excellence generally.

The epithets given to Danaoi are exclusively those of a soldiery: those of Achaioi are more extended, and seem to extend to nobility of race.

The epithet dios is, in my opinion, wrongly translated 'divine;' and much confusion arises from the attempt to apply that sense to the various uses of the word. But if we understand it to mean a limited or special excellence, excellence in its own kind, we have no difficulty in understanding how Eumaios [1] and Clytemnestra [2] can both receive it, the one for his trusty character, the other, the sister of Helen, for her beauty. There is, however, one other sense which might be given to it, that of high-born, well-descended, which perhaps would not be less adapted to all the cases of its use.

In the plural, Homer applies it to Achaians and Pelasgians only. This rare use supplies a presumption of some peculiar meaning; and it may be thought that the Achaians are δῖοι because both of their blood and of their power and predominance, the Pelasgians because of their antiquity.

It is Thersites, who in the Second Iliad attempts to stir up the soldiery by calling them Achaiides, or she-Greeks. It is to be noted, that in his short speech,

[1] Od. xiv. 48, and in ten other places.   [2] Od. iii. 266.

of which an inflated presumption is the principal
mark, the Achaian name is used five times within
nine lines, and neither of the other names is used
at all. In two of these cases, the speaker pointedly
calls himself an Achaian. Probably the upstart and
braggart uses this name only because it was the most
distinguished or aristocratic name, as an ill-bred person
always takes peculiar care to call himself a gentleman.

There are, however, numerous single passages, in
which the simple term Achaioi appears from the
context to have a special, sometimes perhaps even
an exclusive reference to the chiefs and leaders, or
to the officers and higher class, of the army. And
if this be so, then we must consider the national use of
the name as derivative like that of Argeioi, the whole
being named from the prime part; but with this difference, that in the case of Achaioi it is the prime
blood of the country, in that of Argeioi the prime
seat of power.

The injured priest, Chruses, solicits all the Achaioi,
and most of all the two Atridai. All the Achaians
assent, except Agamemnon [1]. There is no sign that
he solicited the army. In truth, this could only be
done in an Assembly; and there was no Assembly. It
follows, that the Achaioi here mean the chiefs. But
when Chruses invokes the vengeance of the god upon
the army at large, the phrase alters to Danaoi [2].

The actual division of booty is, from the nature
of the case, a matter that must have rested principally
or wholly in the hands of the chiefs. When this
matter is referred to, Agamemnon says, Do not let me,
alone of the Argeians, that is, of all the Greeks, go

[1] Il. i. 15, 22, 26-32.   [2] Il. i. 42.

without a prize[1]; and Nestor uses the same word, when he stimulates the army at large by the hope of booty[2]. But Achilles replies to Agamemnon that the Achaians have no means of compensating him[3] there and then, since they hold no common stock in reserve. The phrase is the same in subsequent passages[4]. So far then the Achaian name seems to fall especially to the chiefs.

The same leaning may be observed, when reference is made to other governing duties. Achilles, in his adjuration by the staff or sceptre, the symbol of governing power, describes it as borne by the sons of the Achaians, obviously the kings, chiefs, or persons in authority.

When Priam on the wall of Troy inquires from Helen the names of two prominent commanders, he both times asks, who is that Achaian[5]? and in the second case, the king describes him as out-topping the Argeians by his head and his broad shoulders. Here the Achaian seems to mean the prince or noble; the Argeians, the soldiery at large. Indeed, the words are hardly susceptible of any other construction; and they seem almost to warrant of themselves the conclusion that the Achaian name is properly that of a dominant race, grown, generally speaking, into a class, and possibly including others of that class, although not of Achaian descent.

In the historic ages of Greece, the Achaian name acquired a local force, similar to that of the Argive name, in exclusive, or almost exclusive, connection with one particular district. We cannot say that it

---

[1] Il. l. 118.   [2] Il. il. 350–356.   [3] Il. i. 123.
[4] Il. i. 135, 262, 392; ii. 227. In Il. li. 256 the giving is by the ἥρως Δαναοί. The passage has the obelos; but it is not out of harmony with my argument.   [5] Il. iii. 167, 226.

has in this sense, if strictly taken, a local use in Homer. Yet we find the Achaians in many parts of Greece mentioned in such a way, as to distinguish them from other inhabitants of the country, either in the same or in neighbouring tracts.

1. We have already seen that the name Achaioi had come into use among the people of Mycenæ and of Argos a generation before the War; and that it is used of them in contradistinction to the Kadmeioi of Bœotia[1]. At earlier epochs they are called Argeioi; but we are not to suppose that this name had fallen into local desuetude, even though the other might be more in vogue. We shall see that the Myrmidons of Achilles afford us an example of a race, or body, who bore more names than one.

2. It has also been shown that, in the legend of the Eleventh Iliad about the Epeian War, the Pulian party are called Achaians at the period of the youth of Nestor; and this in apparent contradistinction to their opponents, who therefore were not Achaian at all at that time, or not Achaian in the same eminent sense.

3. The troops of Achilles, always called Myrmidons among the other divisions of the army in the field, inhabited, as we find from the Catalogue, Hellas and Phthie[2], and bore, evidently with some distinctive force, the name of Hellenes, and likewise that of Achaioi[3]. In the Ninth Iliad, Achilles describes the women of the same tract of country as Achaiides[4]. On the origin of the name 'Myrmidon,' which this

[1] Il. iv. 384; v. 803; vi. 223.   [2] Il. ii. 683.
[3] Il. ii. 624.   [4] Il. ix. 395.

division of the army had wholly to itself, Homer throws no light. Hellenes they were, as inhabitants of Hellas [1] in the special sense of the word. And as the Achaian name in Homer is not territorial, we must suppose them to have borne it in virtue of their blood, the Myrmidons being probably a subdivision of the great Achaian family.

4. Of the five races [2] who inhabited Crete at the time of the Troica, four were named Eteocretes, Pelasgoi, Kudones, and Dorieis: the fifth, which is named first, perhaps by reason of political predominance, was Achaian. The appearance in this passage of the Dorian name together with the Achaian, subdivides, more pointedly than any other passage in the Poems, the Hellenic family.

5. Again, a portion of the force of Diomed is described as composed of those 'who held Ægina and Mases, Achaian youths [3].' The site of Mases appears to be unknown. But tradition, according to Pausanias, gave the name of Pelops to the small islands off the coast of Troizen [4]. Such a tradition corresponds remarkably with the indirect testimony of the verse I have quoted, if there be a relation, as I suppose, between the rise of the family of Pelops and the predominance of the Achaians.

6. On turning to the dominions of Odysseus, we find that three names are used to describe their inhabitants: Kephallenes, Ithakesioi, and Achaioi.

The first is used four times in the Odyssey [5], and is the distinctive. name in the Iliad of the military

---

[1] See *infra*, Chap. IV.   [2] Od. xix. 175-177.   [3] Il. II. 562.
[4] Paus. II. 34. 4, p. 191.   [5] Od. xxi. 210; xxiv. 354, 377, 428.

contingent led by Odysseus. We shall find that it
appears to indicate the predominance of the Hellenic
element [1].

The Suitors [2] are ordinarily called 'Αχαιοί, never
'Αργεῖοι or Δαναοί. They constituted the aristocracy
of the islands. It appears that either they were an
Achaian race, or else they were called Achaian because
they were an aristocracy.

The sway of Odysseus appears to have depended
upon his personal qualities. Like his father Laertes [3],
he was both a conqueror and an economist. Accordingly, his long absence is fatal to his power; though
Menelaos, after an absence almost as long [4], resumed
his throne without impediment. When Odysseus
re-appears, his final proceedings against the Suitors
are attended with precautions, evidently dictated by
his fear of the people. And in the Assembly of the
last Book, whilst more than one half take up arms
against him [5], the rest simply remain neutral: he has
no positive aid to rely on, except that of his father,
his son, and a mere handful of immediate dependants.
During his absence the Suitors are ruining him, but
are not said to oppress the people. All this looks as
if his family was perhaps of foreign or extraneous origin,
and in any case had recently attained to power.

Autolucos, the maternal grandfather of Odysseus,
resided at Parnesos in Phokis [6]: Penelopè has no
trace of connection with Southern Greece: her sister
Iphthimè was married to Eumelos, heir-apparent of

---

[1] Infra, Chap. IV.
[2] Od. ii. 51; xvi. 122.
[3] Od. xxiv. 205-207, 377.
[4] Od. iv. 82.
[5] Od. xxiv. 463.
[6] Od. xix. 394.

Pherai in Thessaly[1]. Of Arkeisios, the father of
Laertes, with whom the genealogy begins, we have
no trace in Ithaca. But we do hear of an eponymist
or founder, Ithacos[2], who, with Neritos the eponymist
of the chief mountain of the island, and Poluctor,
constructed the fountain, from which the city was
supplied with water. A descendant of this Poluctor,
probably his son, by name Peisandros[3], appears, with
the title of anax, among the leading Suitors. He
may not impossibly have represented a family, displaced by Laertes from the sovereignty of this island
dominion. I say by Laertes, because if Arkeisios
had founded the sovereignty in Ithaca, it appears
probable that Odysseus would have taken his patronymic from that personage, and not from his father.

But, apart from the question to what root the
family of Odysseus is to be referred, it seems plain
that either the Suitors, being the aristocracy, were
Achaian in blood; or, because they were the aristocracy, they fell under the designation of Achaians.

When the mass of the people are gathered in
Assembly, they are invariably addressed, not as
Achaioi, but as Ithakesioi[4]. And when, instead
of the inhabitants of the island, the subjects throughout the dominion are spoken of, they are called
Kephallenes, the name always given to the military
division in the Iliad[5].

When the Suitor Eurumachos expresses a misgiving
lest, in lieu of Penelopè, it should prove he would
have done more wisely in courting some other dame,

[1] Od. iv. 798.   [2] Od. xvii. 203,-207.   [3] Od. xviii. 299.
[4] Od. ii. 25, 161, 229; xxiv. 453, 531.   [5] Od. xxiv. 354.

he says there are many (other) Achaiides [1] in Ithaca,
and in the other territories. This must surely refer
to women of noble birth.

It is true that, in the Second Odyssey, Telemachos
summons 'the Achaians' to the Assembly [2]. But we
find in Scherie that principal persons only seem to
have been summoned man by man [3], though all classes
usually attended. Again, in the Ithacan Assembly
of the Twenty-fourth Book, Eupeithes complains
of the harm Odysseus has done the Achaians [4]. The
Suitors, whom he has slain, were (he says) far and
away, the ἄριστοι, the aristocracy, of the Kephallenes.
This is exactly conformable to the view I have taken.
When Eupeithes ceases, we are told that pity seized
all the Achaians [5]. This seems to mean the party
of the Suitors, those allied with them by blood or
interest, or near them in station. For, shortly after,
the Assembly divides, part taking arms against
Odysseus, and part, by the advice of Halitherses,
remaining neutral.

We have also to consider the word Panachaioi.
It is used eleven times in Homer. We cannot take
it for a mere synonym of Achaioi. Seven times
out of the eleven, it appears in the expression ἀριστῆες
Παναχαιῶν. In conformity with the sense of the word
πᾶν, we may assign to the compound a cumulative
and collective force: so that Panachaioi would mean
the entire body of the Achaians, or all classes of the
Greeks. In the other passages [6] where the word
occurs, this sense is very suitable, and especially in

---

[1] Od. xxi. 251.   [2] Od. ii. 7.   [3] Od. viii. 11.
[4] Od. xxiv. 426.   [5] Od. xxiv. 438.
[6] Il. ix. 300; Od. i. 239; xiv. 369; xxiv. 32.

the passage of the Iliad where Odysseus, interceding with Achilles, says, 'If you do not care for Agamemnon, yet pity the Panachaioi,' or the Greeks at large [1].

I have now collected the particulars connected with the use of the three Great Appellatives in Homer, and presented them to the reader sufficiently, as I hope, for certain purposes. These purposes are, first to establish in their due order the succession of the periods at which they had respectively obtained some root in the country: next to show that the most proper national name of the Greeks at the time of Homer, the name most nearly approaching to what we mean by a national name, was that of the Achaioi: thirdly, to exhibit, as the specific shades of meaning attaching to the three Appellatives respectively, (1) for Danaoi, the soldiery, the people in warfare; (2) for Argeioi, the masses, the people engaged in tillage; (3) for Achaioi, the chiefs or aristocracy, the people regarded through the governing class.

This class, and the race that formed it, appear to me to be entitled to a more separate and concentrated attention than it has as yet received in the investigation of Greek history. It forms a distinct type of Hellenic character, the earliest in time, and certainly not the least remarkable in grandeur or in completeness. The Greek of Homer is neither the man of Athens nor the man of Sparta: he is neither cast in the Dorian nor in the Ionian pattern: he is the Achaian Greek. Simple, and yet shrewd; passionate, and yet self-contained; brave in battle, and gentle in converse; keenly living in the present, yet with a 'large discourse' over the future and the past; as he is in

[1] Il. ix. 300.

body ' full-limbed and tall,' so is he in mind towering and full-formed. His portrait could never have been drawn but from the life: and, disregarding what I conceive to have been the figments of the first *renaissance* after the wild and rude Dorian revolution, I set down Homer himself as the Achaian painter of his own kith and kin.

It will however be requisite to inquire,

1. What light can be thrown on the origin of the Achaian name through the growth of the power that brought it into vogue.

2. How it was superseded; and what place the three Appellatives respectively occupy in the later tradition and literature.

But this will best be done after we have examined and illustrated, as far as may be, the Homeric use of other national and tribal names, especially four of them, which, though of much rarer occurrence, are of an importance scarcely second to the names already discussed. These are—

1. Pelasgoi.
2. Hellenes.
3. Phoinikes.
4. Aiolidai.

We may then sketch in outline the relative position of the families or races respectively embraced by these Appellatives, and consider what they severally contributed to the formation of the great Greek nationality.

CHAPTER III.

RESPECTING the Pelasgoi, we have some direct and some indirect testimony from Homer. And we have also certain supplements to this Homeric information—

(1) In the later Greek and classical tradition;

(2) In the results of modern ethnological and archæological research.

The direct testimony of Homer establishes—

The wide extension of the Pelasgoi.

The country afterwards called Thessaly bears in the Iliad the name of Pelasgic Argos[1]. It furnished to the Greek army nine contingents, and 280 ships, or about one fourth of the entire fleet. And this seems to be the only name which it bears as a whole. The line, in which this name is given, is evidently prefatory to the great Thessalian division of the Catalogue[2]. Pelasgic Argos appears to be included with other countries in the wider name of Hellas; a name which probably may also have had an especial application to the part

[1] Il. ii. 681.   [2] Studies on Homer, vol. I. pp. 100–105.

of Thessaly ruled by Peleus, and inhabited by the Myrmidons.

It further appears, from the Odyssey, that the Pelasgoi were one of the five nations of Crete [1].

And we learn from the Trojan Catalogue in the Second Iliad, that the Pelasgoi of Larissa served in the War among the allies of Troy [2].

The facts thus exhibited, though few and simple, indicate the wide extension of the Pelasgoi, who thus appear on both sides, in a war which draws the armies engaged in it from so considerable an extent of country.

But further; Zeus, the Zeus of Dodona, the Zeus served by Hellic interpreters of his will, is, in the most solemn invocation of the Iliad, addressed as Pelasgic Zeus [3] by Achilles, the greatest representative of the Hellenic mind and life.

This was at a period of complete and well established Hellenic predominance. The name Pelasgicos is, then, evidently an archaic name of Zeus; and it is not easy to see how he could have received it, unless the inhabitants of the country from Dodona, at least as far as the kingdom of Peleus, had been known as Pelasgoi. The concurrent evidence of this passage with that of the line in which all Thessaly is called Pelasgic Argos, appears to demonstrate that Thessaly had formerly been known as a country of Pelasgoi, and that these Pelasgoi were worshippers of Zeus.

Accordingly, of the nine Thessalian contingents, seven are described by the places they inhabit, without any national or tribal name. It is probable that in

---

[1] Od. xix. 177.   [2] Il. ii. 840.   [3] Il. xvi. 233.

these districts the Pelasgian name had not yet been
superseded by any other designation for the purposes
of familiar use. The only territorial name used in this
part of the Catalogue, besides Pelasgic Argos, is in the
case of the eminently Hellenic dominions of Peleus.

When Homer names the Pelasgoi of the Trojan
Catalogue, he describes them as those Pelasgoi who
inhabited the deep-loamed Larissa[1]. He therefore distinguishes them from other Pelasgoi. But he cannot
possibly mean, in composing for a Greek audience,
to distinguish them from the only other Pelasgoi
mentioned by him, those of Crete, who are not named
in the Catalogue or in the Iliad at all. It is likely,
then, that he refers to other Pelasgoi of the Trojan
army; of which the two contingents immediately preceding this one are described without any national or
tribal designation.

Again, the Poet does not simply say, 'Hippothoos
led Pelasgians,' but, 'he led tribes (φῦλα) of Pelasgians,'
thus pointing again to a variety of tribes comprised
under that name. This has been observed by Strabo[2].

If in general the Achaians were paramount, and the
Pelasgoi were subordinate members of one and the
same community, it is not difficult to see why Homer
should nowhere apply the Pelasgian name to any
portion of the Greek army; and again, why the same
scruples should not bind him as to a portion of the
Trojan force.

He has pursued an exactly similar course with
respect to the Thracians. He mentions them in the
Trojan Catalogue, and again in the Trojan army[3].

[1] Il. ii. 841.   [2] xiii, 3, p. 620.   [3] Il. ii. 844; x. 434.

They have no recognised place among the Greeks,
and yet Thamuris, evidently a Greek, is described
as Thracian [1]. And the word Threx seems to mean
Highlander, in opposition to Pelasgos as Lowlander.
Probably Thracians existed diffusively, like Pelasgians,
among the Greeks; but were absorbed in designations
more prominent and splendid.

We have yet a third example. The Kaukones appear
in the Tenth Iliad as part of the Trojan force [2]. They
are nowhere found in the Greek host, or in the Greek
Catalogue. But in the Odyssey, where there was no
reason for keeping the name in the background, as
the same national distinctions did not require to be
kept in view, Homer mentions the Kaukones apparently as a people dwelling on the west side of Greece,
for the Pseudo-Mentor [3] is going among them from Ithaca
to claim payment of a debt. They were probably, then,
near neighbours. He distinguishes them as high-
spirited, μεγάθυμοι: which reminds us of the reverence
he has shown for the ancient possessors of the country
by calling the Pelasgians dioi.

Again, Homer, in the three passages where he names
Pelasgians, names them each time with a laudatory
epithet; a circumstance deserving some notice, when
we observe to how small a proportion of his national
or tribal names epithets are attached.

Once he calls them ἐγχεσίμωροι [4], addicted to the
spear. He elsewhere uses this epithet but thrice;
once for the Arcadians [5], whom, in the only other
place where they are named, he describes as skilled
in fight; once for two royal warriors individually [6];

[1] Il. ii. 594-600. [2] Il. x. 429; xx. 329. [3] Od. lii. 366.
[4] Il. vii. 134. [5] Il. ii. 611. [6] Il. ii. 692.

and once for the Myrmidons[1]. This epithet then is
of high rank as describing valour.

On the other two occasions he calls the Pelasgians
dioi[2]. This epithet implies, sometimes perhaps a narrow, but always a special and peculiar excellence. And
it is one which Homer allows to no race except only
the Pelasgians and Achaians[3]. There is no difficulty
in explaining the latter use of it. The former is also
appropriate, if we suppose the Pelasgoi to be the
ancient and primary base of the Greek nation.

The leaders of the Pelasgoi before Troy are
themselves the sons of Pelasgos, who was the son of
Teutamos.

Only then in five places altogether does Homer
give us traces of this name or its derivatives. But
this affords no presumption adverse to the hypothesis
that the Pelasgians were the base of the Greek nation;
because it is his uniform practice to throw into the
background whatever tends to connect the Hellenic
race with foreign origin or blood; and the currency
of the Pelasgian name beyond the limits of Greece,
and among its foes, evidently had this tendency in a
marked degree.

The Larissè[4] mentioned in the Trojan Catalogue
appears once more[5]; and on both occasions it has
an epithet denoting fertility. The tendency of this
epithet is to show that the Pelasgoi were an agricultural and settled people. Of this we shall find
other signs.

When we come to the historic age, we find many

---

[1] Od. lil. 188.   [2] Il. x. 429; Od. xix. 177.
[3] Il. v. 451, *et alibi.*   [4] Il. ll. 841.   [5] Il. xvll. 301.

Larissès[1]; and the mere name is commonly believed
to indicate a seat of the Pelasgians. But in Homer
we have only one Larissè. A possible explanation is,
that Larissè was properly the name of a fort or place of
refuge, somewhat like the bell-towers of Ireland and
other countries, to which the people of the district be-
took themselves for refuge on an emergency, from their
dwellings in the surrounding country. Around these
forts, as happened in our own country about the feudal
castles, towns would gather by a gradual process.
And so the application of the word Larissè to the
town conjointly with the district[2], of which we seem
to have this single example in Homer, might by degrees
become common. That which was an Argos, or settlement for tillage, in the original or Pelasgian stage,
might, after wars had taught the necessity of defence,
become in some cases a Larissè; while in others the
old name might continue: or the one name might be
applied to the part for habitation, the other to the part
for defence. This hypothesis is supported by the fact
that the citadel of the historic Argos, which stood
upon an eminence, was called Larissè[3].

Such are the direct notices of the Pelasgoi in
Homer. They are scanty in amount. But there are
three other heads of Homeric evidence relating to
them.

1. The signs of alliance between the Pelasgoi and
the inhabitants of particular parts of the country :

2. The signs of a difference of race, pervading the

---

[1] Cramer's Greece, vol. iii. p. 244.
[2] Comp. εὐρύχορος Θήβη, and the passage Od. xi. 260–265.
[3] Strabo viii. 6, p. 370.

population, and more or less running parallel with
differences of rank:

3. The signs of an occupation of the country prior
to that by the Hellenic tribes:

Independently of another head of inquiry, to be dealt
with at a later stage, namely the relation of the Trojan
to the Greek race:

And, again, independently of evidence supplied by
the later tradition.

1. The Arcades[1] of Homer show signs of connection
with the Pelasgoi.

In the Catalogue the Arcades are described as ἀγχιμα-
χηταί, or heavy-armed [2]; and we are also told that they
had no care for maritime pursuits. In both respects,
their relation to the people of Troas is remarkable.
Homer nowhere else uses the epithet except for the
Dardanians, whose position in Troas resembled that of
the Arcadians in Peloponnesos. And the Trojans were
so destitute of vessels, that the shipwright who built
for Paris is mentioned as on that account a notable
character[3]. Nor do we hear of a Trojan ship in any
case but his. Heavy-armed troops are furnished by
a settled peasantry, light-armed by a population of
less settled habits. The absence of maritime pursuits
tends to imply a pacific character, in an age when
enterprise by sea was so intimately connected with
kidnapping and rapine. Arcadia was not a poor
country. In historic times it was, next to Laconia,

---

[1] Niebuhr, Hist. of Rome, vol. i. p. 29, sets down as Pelasgian
the Arcadians, the Argives, probably all the original inhabitants
of Peloponnesos, the Ionians, and the people of Attica and
Thessaly.

[2] Il. ii. 604, 614.   [3] Il. v. 54-64.

the most populous province of Peloponnesos [1]. In the
Troica it supplied sixty ships with large crews [2]. All
this is accordant with Pelasgian associations.

Again, the Arcadians were commanded by Agapenor [3]
the son of Ankaios. But Ankaios was of Ætolia.
Ships supplied by Agamemnon [4], and a chief not indigenous, tend to mark the Arcadians as politically subordinate, therefore as Pelasgian.

At the funeral games of Amarunkeus there were
present Epeians, Pulians, and Ætolians [5]; that is to
say, all the neighbouring tribes except the Arcadians.
Now the Homeric indications respecting the origin of
games, in a marked manner tend to connect them, as
we shall find, with sources other than Pelasgic [6].

In the Seventh Iliad, Nestor relates that in his youth
the Pulians and Arcadians fought, near the river Iardanos. The former seem to have been victorious;
which accords with the military inferiority of Pelasgoi
to an Hellenic force. Clearly, when Nestor killed
their king Ereuthalion [7], it was by the aid of Pallas;
and Pallas, we shall find, is always a Hellenising deity
against Pelasgians. The Pulians, as we have seen, are
Achaian in a special degree.

In marked accordance with this indirect testimony,
the later tradition places Lucaon son of Pelasgos in
Arcadia; represents the people as autochthonous; and
makes the district compete with Argolis for having
given them their first seat in Peloponnesos.

We have here, too, some aid from philology. The

---

[1] Xen. Hell. vii. 1. 23. Cramer, lii. 299.   [2] Il. il. 610.
[3] Il. ii. 609; xxiil. 630–635.   [4] Il. ii. 612.
[5] Il. xxiil. 630–635.   [6] See *infra*, Ch. V.   [7] Il. vii. 154.

Arcadians called themselves Προσέληνοι, which is commonly rendered 'anterior to the moon.' Now it is difficult to see why the moon, which continually waxes, wanes, and disappears, should be selected as the type of stability and longevity among natural objects. But if we refer the origin of the word to πρὸ and Σελλοὶ or Σέλληνες, then it becomes the appropriate form in which the Arcadian, or Pelasgian, people assert their priority in the Peloponnesos to the Hellic or Sellic races.

Until very late in the historic period, the Arcadians remained an undistinguished people. But they were the Swiss of Greece ; and they supplied a hardy soldiery to any state in want of mercenary assistance, without reference to attachments of race as between Dorian and Ionian. With the Lacedæmonians they invaded Attica : with the Thebans they invaded Lacedæmon [1] : in the great siege of Syracuse, one contingent fought by the side of the invaders, the other along with the besieged [2].

2. The Ionians (Iaones) are but once mentioned in Homer. They are one of five divisions appointed, in the Thirteenth Iliad [3], to meet the attack of Hector, when that attack is destined to prevail. The others are the Locrians, Phthians, Epeians, and Boiotians. The same spirit of nationality, which prevents Homer from allowing any eminent Greek chieftain to be slain or wounded in fair conflict with the Trojans, apparently leads him in this place to select, (perhaps with the exception of the Epeians [4],) some of the less distin-

[1] Xen. Hell. vii. 1. 23.   [2] Thuc. vii. 57.   [3] v. 635.
[4] They have laudatory epithets in Il. xi. 732 and xiii. 636. They were, however, worsted by the men of Pulos.

guished portions of the army to resist the Trojans, on
an occasion when the resistance is to be ineffectual.
The Myrmidons are of necessity absent: but he might
have placed in the post of danger those troops whom
he pointedly commends, the troops of Agamemnon, or
the Abantes[1]. Our finding the Ionians among undistinguished contingents tends to fix upon them a like
character.

Further, they are called ἑλκεχίτωνές[2], men with long
flowing tunics. As Homer has nowhere else used the
epithet, he gives us no direct aid in illustrating it.
But it clearly has more or less of disparaging effect,
since such an habiliment is ill-suited for military purposes. And it is in direct contrast with the epithet
ἀμιτροχίτωνες of the valiant Lukioi or Lycians, whose
short and spare tunic required no cincture to confine it.

These Ionians were, as it would seem, the ruling
class of the Athenians, the 'Αθηναίων προλελεγμένοι[3];
or, it may be, their picked men. The praise awarded
to Menestheus in the Catalogue, even if the passage be
genuine, is only that of being good, to use a modern
phrase, at putting his men into line[4]. The Athenian
soldiers, indeed, are declared in Il. iv. 328 to be valiant,
μήστωρες ἀϋτῆς; but the character of the commander is
less than negative. Though of kingly parentage, he
nowhere appears among the governing spirits of the
army, nor is he called one of the kings, although his
father Peteos had enjoyed the title[5]; and on the only
occasion when we find him amid the clash of arms,
namely, when the brave Lycians are threatening the

---

[1] Il. ii. 577, 542.   [2] Il. xiii. 685.   [3] Il. xiii. 689.
[4] Il. ii. 554.   [5] Il. iv. 338.

part of the rampart committed to his charge, he shudders, and looks about him for aid[1]. The inferiority extends to the other Athenian chiefs, Pheidas, Stichios, Bias, and Iasos[2]; of whom all are undistinguished, and two, Stichios and Iasos, are 'food for powder,' slain by Hector and Æneas respectively. Here then there seems to have been bravery without qualities for command; and all this tends to exhibit the Athenians as in a marked degree Pelasgian at this epoch, stout but passive, without any of the ardour or the κῖκυς[3] of the Hellenic character.

Something will hereafter be added to this evidence from an examination of the etymology of names in Homer.

The close relation between Athenè and Athens, however, is a sign that seems to tell in the opposite direction. But upon examining into it, we perceive that it is a local and not a personal relation. Ever active in the protection or guidance of Achilles, Agamemnon, Diomed, Odysseus, Athenè says and does nothing whatever in the War for any Athenian. Yet Athens has the epithet 'sacred[4],' the unfailing mark in Homer of special relation to some deity; and, as far as Athenè has any favourite place of earthly residence or resort, it appears to be Athens, to which, seemingly as matter of course, she repairs from Scheriè[5], in the Odyssey. There is something remarkable, and not easy to explain, in this combination of strong local connection with a total absence of personal care and patronage.

It is to be borne in mind that Athenè appears to

---

[1] Il. xII. 331.   [2] Il. xiii. 691; xviiI. 329, 332.
[3] Od. 2L. 392.   [4] Od. xi. 332.   [5] Od. vii. 30.

have been a deity of universal worship[1]. She was regularly adored by the Trojans[2], whom she laboured to ruin.

On both the occasions when Athens is placed in direct connection with the goddess, the name of Erechtheus is introduced: in the Catalogue he is stated to have been nursed by Athenè, and he was the child of Aroura[3]. She (probably Athenè) set him in Athens, in her (or his) rich or well-endowed temple (ἐῷ ἐνὶ πίονι νηῷ).

It is impossible wholly to shake off the apprehension of forgery in dealing with this passage, which falls short in the grammatical clearness usually so notable in Homer. On the other hand, the objections which have been taken to it seem insufficient to condemn it; to condemn at any rate the part of it I have cited, which remarkably corresponds with Od. v. 81 : there she enters the well-built house (πυκινὸν δόμον) of Erechtheus.

Erechtheus appears in the Catalogue to be described as an autochthon; and therefore probably as Pelasgian. The wealthy temple may perhaps mean a temple with a τέμενος or glebe for a priest, which we shall find to be a sign, not of Hellenic, but of Pelasgian nationality. On the whole, we cannot ignore the existence of Pelasgian signs, while we cannot find in the text of Homer any full explanation of the fact that Athenè is the eponymist of Athens.

The type of Athenè, however, is far too high to allow us to view her as a deity merely national. She is not circumscribed by any limits either of blood or place. This does not exclude specialties of attachment; but

---

[1] *Infra*, Ch. VIII.   [2] Il. vi. 300.   [3] Il. ii. 547-549.

her special attachment to the Greeks is one apparently having reference to great qualities of mind and character. The Pelasgianism of the Trojans does not, before the great quarrel, cut them off from her. She singularly loved Phereclos, who built the ships of Paris[1]; and she aided the Trojans in erecting the rampart which sheltered Heracles from the pursuing monster[2].

There is, however, very powerful evidence outside the text of Homer to show the strongly Pelasgian character of Attica in early times. Her subsequent greatness was evidently connected with a remarkable mixture of blood, arising from her having been, during long periods, a place of refuge for fugitives, and for the worsted party expelled from other portions of Greece.

Thucydides[3] states that, from early times, Attica was inhabited by one and the same race, because the poverty of the soil offered no temptations to an invader. Hence it is, without doubt, that we find the Athenians of history ever claiming the character of autochthons. But this is in effect to call them Pelasgians.

Herodotus[4] declares the Athenians to have been Ionian, and the Ionians to be Pelasgian. Having been Pelasgians, he says, the Attican people became Hellenic, apparently by the reception of immigrants, and by a gradual amalgamation. Evidently, according to this historian, the change did not take place by an arrival of Ionians, for he declares that which Homer only suggests, that the Ionians were Pelasgian.

Some conflict, however, there was, apparently, be-

---

[1] Il. v. 59.   [2] Il. xx. 146.   [3] i. 2.   [4] i. 56.

tween the urban and the rural population. The Pelasgians complained, said Hecatæus[1], that the Athenians
drove them from the soil, which they had improved in
such a degree as to excite envy. The Athenians alleged
that their children, when they went forth to draw
water, were insulted by the Pelasgians. The Dorian
Tau, Herodotus[2] adds, was the Ionian Sigma.

Thucydides[3] says the Athenians were the first among
the Greeks to lay aside the custom of bearing arms,
and to cultivate ease and luxury. We may naturally
connect this fact with the undisturbed condition and
pacific habits of the people : and perhaps it is partially
indicated by the word ἑλκεχίτωνες, 'tunic-trailers,'
already cited.

The Hesiodic tradition of Hellen and his sons does
not mention Ion. It is remarkable that Euripides does
not represent Ion as Hellenic, but as the adopted son
of Xouthos, the real son of Creusa, an Erechtheid ; in
entire conformity with what, as I conceive, the text of
Homer suggests.

Peisistratos and his family claimed a Neleid, that is,
a non-Pelasgian descent ; recognising as it were the
difference of the ruling blood.

According to Herodotus[4], there remained in the
Athens of history a portion of the wall called Pelasgic ;
and the primitive Athenians were called Pelasgoi Cra-
naoi, and were reputed to be autochthonous.

Eleusis, in Attica, was the chief seat of the worship
of Demeter—a deity, as we shall find, of eminently
Pelasgian character and associations.

Strabo declares that ancient Attica was Ias, with an

[1] As quoted in Herod. vi. 137, 138.   [2] i. 139.
[3] i. 6.   [4] i. 56; iii. 44; v. 64.

Ionian people, who supplied Asia Minor with the colonists of the Ionian migration[1].

The careful researches of Dr. Hahn in Albania have accumulated much evidence of the Pelasgian character of the population. It includes remarkable coincidences with the institutions of Attica: for example, the fourfold division of the tribes[2].

To us the origin of the Ionian name remains in great obscurity. It is probably related to the Pelasgian stock. It certainly appears not to be Hellenic.

3. In the Thessaly of the Greek Catalogue, not only does the paucity of tribal names leave us to suppose that the population of the districts generally had not yet distinctly emerged from what may be called Pelasgianism, and not only is this supposition confirmed by the name of Pelasgic Argos, but there are other confirmatory signs.

One of them is the worship of the River Spercheios[3]; which, though offered by Achilles for a special purpose, was also practised by Peleus, and is probably due to a strong local tradition of a Pelasgian character. His τέμενος, or glebe, also connects him with the Pelasgians[4].

Another sign is the τέμενος or sacred glebe of Demeter at Purasos[5]. Possibly the name may be related to πυρός, wheat. Apart from this, the associations of Demeter in Homer are never Hellenic[6]. The appearance of a τέμενος in this case is also a Pelasgian sign.

---

[1] Bk. viii. p. 333.
[2] Hahn, 'Albanesische Studien,' Abschn. li. pp. 43-46, and note 19, p. 130.
[3] Il. xxiii. 144.   [4] See *infra*, Ch. VII.; also p. 106.
[5] Il. ii. 696.   [6] See *infra*, Ch. VIII.

The historical growth of the Graian[1] (Greek) name
out of the Greek settlements in Italy connects it with
communities highly Pelasgian. In Homer we find that
name only in Boiotia, a land of rich cultivation, like the
Italian colonies. But Aristotle[2] places the Graicoi in
the ancient Hellas, a portion of Thessaly, about Dodona
and the Acheloos, which, he says, was inhabited by
them and by the Selloi. Thus the Graian name serves
further to associate Thessaly with the Pelasgoi.

4. The name Iasos has an early and important place
in the Homeric tradition.

(*a*) The phrase 'Iason Argos,' which means Western
Peloponnesos[3], appears to indicate a dynasty, or dominion, of an Iasos in that country.

(*b*) Demeter (in Crete, according to Hesiod) gives
way to her passion for Iasion[4], a son or descendant of
Iasos, in a tilled field.

(*c*) Demetor Iasides, a son, or rather a descendant, of
Iasos, is represented by the pseud-Odysseus as reigning
in Cyprus[5] at the period of his return to Ithaca, and
as being in xenial relations with Egypt, the people of
which, he says, made a present of him to Demetor.
This clearly shows that there had been an Iasid dominion in Cyprus.

(*d*) Amphion and Zethos, who first founded and walled
in the city of Thebes, were Iasids[6]: Amphion at one
time (ποτε) reigned in Minyan Orchomenos.

(*e*) Iasos[7], son of Sphelos and grandson of Boukolos,

---

[1] The name Graicos, according to K. O. Müller, came back into
use with the Alexandrian poets, through the old common tongue
of Macedonia. Müller's Orchomenos, p. 119.
[2] Meteorol. l. 14.   [3] See above, Ch. II. p. 48.   [4] Od. v. 125.
[5] Od. xvii. 442.   [6] Od. xi. 262, 283.   [7] Il. xv. 337.

was one of the Athenian commanders, and fell by the
hand of Æneas; this too without any commemora-
tion: from both which circumstances we perceive that
he was in no great esteem, and was most probably not
of Hellenic, but of Pelasgian blood.

The attachment of Demeter to Crete was plainly
connected with the Pelasgian period. The secondary
place given to Iasos in the war, and the etymology
of the names of his ancestry, seem to establish his Pelasgian extraction. If Amphion and Zethos were, as
it appears probable, displaced from Bœotia by Kadmos
and the Phœnicians, they were probably of a Pelasgian
family: and indeed it would be very difficult to give
evidence of any Hellenic race or family at their epoch,
which is between four and five generations before the
Troica. Lastly, Cyprus, distant as it was from
Greece, was evidently in some position of qualified
subordination to its ruling house; because, when the
expedition to Troy was meditated, Kinures[1], its ruler,
sent a beautiful gift to Agamemnon, probably more as
an apology for non-appearance, than as a disinterested
token of good-will.

All the several indications then converge upon this
point, that the name of Iasos appears to bear no Hellenic character. It has certain points of contact at
least with some of the races that dwelt in Egypt; and
likewise with Phœnicia through the city of Thebes,
and through the indubitable presence of a Phœnician
influence in Cyprus. Anterior to, and apparently reaching beyond the Hellenic name, its most marked associations appear to be Pelasgian.

[1] Il. xi. 19-23.

5. There are abundant marks of a Pelasgian character in the population of Crete.

We know that the ruling family in Crete was Phœnician; but the wealth of the hundred-citied island[1] was just what might be expected to arise from the early combination of Phœnician enterprise with Pelasgian industry.

There were many races in Crete, and there was a mixture of tongue[2]. This appears to indicate the presence of the Phœnician element in considerable force with its Semitic form of speech, as we have no reason to suppose, among the races actually named, any radical difference of language. In this passage the speaker is addressing Penelope, and it is in accordance with the uniform usage of the Poems, that he should mention only races which had been domesticated in Greece.

Those races are, 1. Achaioi, 2. Eteocretes, 3. Kudones, 4. Dorieis, 5. Pelasgoi. Of these, the first and fourth may at once be classed as Hellenic. With respect to the Eteocretes, we may most naturally suppose them to have been part of the Pelasgian family, whose date of arrival was more remote, in relation to whom all the other races had thus been strangers, and to whom therefore is given a name that is the equivalent of autochthons. The Kudones appear to be of similar origin. They lived on a Cretan river Iardanos[3]. This was the name of the river in Peloponnesos, on the banks of which the Pulians fought the Arcadians. The battle[4], as being one between Achaians and Pelasgians, was probably on Arcadian ground; and

---

[1] Il. ii. 649. In Od. xix. 174, ninety.   [2] Od. xix. 175.
[3] Od. iii. 292.   [4] Il. vii. 134; xi. 735, 752 (?).

the name of *rapid* Keladon, given to the stream, also shows that it was on the high land.

This Pelasgian population, with its less warlike, possibly also less energetic, habits, appears to have sunk at a later period into servitude. According to Ephorus, as quoted by Athenæus[1], there were in Crete festivals of the slave population, during which freemen were not permitted to come within the town walls, while the slaves were supreme, and were competent to flog the free. These festivals were held in Kudonia, the city of the Kudones.

Fifthly, the name of Pelasgoi speaks for itself.

6. The Leleges have a place on the Trojan side, apparently more important than that of the Kaukones. They appear, with the Kaukones and Pelasgoi[2], as part of the force which was encamped upon the plain during the period when the Greeks were shut up within their entrenchment. Priam had for one of his wives Laothee, daughter of their king Altes[3]. He calls them lovers of battle. Æneas says[4] that Pallas ' incited Achilles to make havock of Trojans and Leleges.' Homer can hardly mean, under the name of Leleges, to speak of the whole body of allies, which included both Pelasgians and his favourite Lycians. The name may be one covering some of the allied contingents; or it may signify the fourth and fifth divisions of the Trojan army, which appear in the Catalogue[5] without any national or tribal designation, immediately before the Pelasgoi and the rest of the allies.

We have abundant instances in *Homer* of double names attaching to the same population. The people

[1] vi. p. 263. [2] Il. x. 429. [3] Il. xxi. 25.
[4] Il. xx. 96. [5] Il. ii. 828, 839.

of Elis are Eleioi and Epeioi. The Dolopians are
included under the Phthians; perhaps under Achaians
and Hellenes[1]. Five races in particular are named as
inhabiting Crete; but all, possibly with others, are
included in the Cretes[2] of the Second Iliad. The
Ionian name, with that of the Kaukones, and of Leleges, not to speak of the Temnikes, Aones, Huantes,
Telebooi, of whom we do not hear in Homer, are most
probably subdivisions of the great Pelasgian category.
On the whole, it seems safest to adopt the conclusion
of Bishop Thirlwall, that in all likelihood 'the name
Pelasgians was a general one, like that of Saxons,
Franks, or Alemanni; but that each of the Pelasgian tribes had also one peculiar to itself[3].' The evidence directly deducible from Homer tends to this
conclusion; and it is powerfully sustained, as we shall
see, by more copious indirect testimony.

The work of Dr. Hahn affords ample evidence of
their occupation of Epiros, which was also recognised
by the tradition of the ancients[4].

The belief that the Pelasgoi were the original inhabitants of Greece, appears to be held undoubtingly by
the modern Greeks, if we may trust the recent work
of Petrides[5] upon the ancient history of his country.

We are in no way obliged to suppose that tribes
of so wide a diffusion came into Greece by a single
route. The prevailing opinion[6] of the ancient writers
was that their first seat was in the Peloponnesos.

---

[1] Il. ii. 683; ix. 484; κτλ. 186.   [2] Od. xix. 175; Il. ii. 645.
[3] History of Greece, vol. i. ch. ii.
[4] Strabo, bk. v. p. 221. Leake's Travels in Northern Greece,
vol. iv. p. 174.
[5] Chap. I. pp. 2, 3 (Corfu, 1830).   [6] Cramer's Greece, L 17.

Homer gives abundant signs of them in Thessaly, but
also in Crete and in Cyprus. It seems probable that
they may have arrived both by the landward route of
the Thracian coast, and by the stepping-stones, so to
speak, which the southern islands afforded them.

If there has been presented reasonable ground for the
conclusion that the Pelasgians formed the base of the
Greek nation, it is interesting to observe, by the light
of history, how the most durable vitality of a people
resides in the mass, while the energies of mere class,
or of any branch socially separate from the trunk, are
liable to exhaustion if they are not refreshed by popular
contact; as water taken from the sea grows foul, while
the sea itself is ever fresh. The astute Aiolid, the
high-souled and fiery Achaian, the Dorian with his iron
will and unconquerable tenacity—each for a time enjoys
ascendancy and disappears; and the districts which successively attain to military pre-eminence in the later
historic ages, are Bœotia, Macedonia, Arcadia, Epiros,
none of which had been the early depositories of powerful Hellenic influences. Lastly, Achaia emerged into a
late celebrity. It is probable that we ought to consider
this name, not so much in connection with the old and
famous Achaian race, as with the party worsted in the
great Dorian conquest: and if this be so, we shall be safe
in concluding that, in all likelihood, the province had
retained throughout a dominant Pelasgian character.

The etymology of the Pelasgian name has been long
and variously discussed without any conclusive issue.
Some draw it from Peleg of the tenth chapter of Genesis, a name said to mean 'partition,' that is, of the
earth: this opinion is questioned by Marsh[1], and re-

[1] Horæ Pelasg. c. i. sub fin.

jected by Clinton[1]. Again, it has been derived from pelargoi, the Greek name for storks. This, according to some, because the Pelasgians were wanderers, and the stork is migratory. But the periodical movement of the stork seems to have no great correspondence with an irregularly roving habit in a people. Aristophanes[2] appears undoubtedly to make the name of storks a vehicle for a jest on the Pelasgian origin of the Athenians. Another plea seems to me more plausible. The stork is a social bird: in the East it settles on the roofs of houses; it freely follows the ploughman along his furrow; and its habits thus, in both points, supply links of association with the first appearance of a people of husbandmen. The stork was one of the sacred birds of the Egyptians.

Some have derived the name from pelagos, a word used in Greek for the sea. And this, either because the Pelasgians came by sea, or because they came from beyond sea. It seems doubtful, however, whether ' sea' was the proper or only the second meaning of pelagos. We have the phrases, ἅλος ἐν πελάγεσσι (Homer), πόντιον πέλαγος (Pindar), ἅλς πελαγία (Æschylus), πέλαγος θαλάσσης (Apollonius), all of which seem to show that pelagos, like aequor, may mean ' a plain,' and may thus come to mean the expanse or level of the sea. Strabo tells us of a people called Pelagones in Macedonia, and in Homer we find the names Pelagon and Pelegon. Hesychius renders the word πέλαγος as meaning greatness or depth, or the breadth of the sea. If the name of Pelasgoi be related to the word pelagos, it may be either because they were great and numerous, or because they were settlers upon plains. So Thrēx,

[1] Fasti Hellenici, i. 97.　　　　[2] Aves, 1354.

its counterpart, akin to τρηχύς, meant the inhabitant of a rough or rocky place, a mountaineer[1].

Of the signs of a difference of race among the Greek population more or less in correspondence with a difference of ranks, some have been exhibited in the examination of the Achaian name, which appears properly to have designated an aristocracy formed from a conquering or dominant race, and placed amid a population of distinct and less aspiring blood.

Yet the difference must not be overstated. By common consent we are dealing with different branches from the Aryan stem: and the distinction of Hellic and Pelasgic finds a correlative classification in the Italian races, where the Oscans hold the place of the Helloi. It is represented indeed in our country by the distinction among Normans, Scandinavians, Saxons (or the group of tribes collectively so called with no great propriety), and Celts; though it may be more or less doubtful at which point of division we should draw the line among these several races.

I shall endeavour to show that the Trojan War may in some sense be considesed as the conflict of Hellic with Pelasgic elements. But it is remarkable, 1. that Homer nowhere represents the Trojans as speaking a tongue different from that of the Greeks; 2. that the Trojan soldiery are nowhere represented as generally inferior to the Greek force; it is the superiority of the chiefs which determines the fate of battle throughout the Poems.

[1] K. O. Müller (Orchomenos, p. 119), assuming Pelasgos to be identical with Pelargos, derives the word from πλω, 'to be,' 'to be wont to be,' and so 'to frequent' or 'inhabit,' together with Ἀργος.

With respect indeed to tongue, Homer tells us that
the Trojan public called the son of Hector by the name
of Astuanax, which is of Greek etymology; and we
have in Troas[1] examples of that double nomenclature
which is commonly interpreted as referring to the
epochs of two different nationalities, the second of
them corresponding, for all we know, with the contemporary Greek tongue, though we are made aware
that a variety of languages were spoken among the
allies of Troy[2]. A long list of names, common to
Greek and Trojan personages, may be drawn out from
the Poems.

But while we greatly lack positive information in the
case of Troas, we possess it in the case of Italy. Care
indeed must be taken to exclude from any comparison
those words which were transported bodily out of the
Greek into the Latin tongue after literary communion
had begun, and according to the practice which Horace[3]
has described and recommended.

Niebuhr[4] laid down these propositions, which appear
to be reasonable.

1. That the words truly common to the Greek and
Latin languages are Pelasgian:

2. That they chiefly relate to tillage and to peaceful
life:

3. That, accordingly, the Pelasgians were given to
peace and to husbandry:

4. Conversely, that the words in which the two
tongues differ are due to another race, and indicate its
pursuits.

[1] Il. ii. 813; xx. 74.   [2] Il. iv. 438; x. 420.
[3] De Arte Poet. 53.
[4] Hare and Thirlwall's Transl. vol. i. p. 65.

Speaking generally, those words of the Latin and Greek which most closely correspond, are

1. First elements of the structure of a language, such as pronouns, prepositions, numerals.

2. Words relating to the commonest objects of perception, and the primary wants of life, and forms of labour.

Under the second head the following lists are presented, by way not of exhaustion, but of example.

I. OBJECTS OF INANIMATE NATURE.

ἀήρ	aer	νέφος	nebula
αἰθήρ	æther	(νίξ) νεφός	nix
ἅλς, θάλασσα	salum	νύξ	nox
ἄντρον	antrum	πεύκη	pix
ἀστήρ	astrum	πόλος	polus
αὔρα	aura	πόντος	pontus
Διός (Ζεύς)	dies	ῥῖγος	frigus
δρόσος	ros	σελήνη	luna
ἔαρ	ver	σκόπελος	scopulus
ἐνιαυτός, ἦνις	annus	σπίος, σπήλαιον	spelunca
ἔρα	terra	ὕδωρ	sudor
ἕσπερος	vesper	ὑετός	{ fluvius / pluvius }
ἥλιος	sol		
κοῖλον	cœlum	ὕλη	sylva
λᾶας	lapis	φῦκος	fucus
λάκκος / λάχυς }	lacus	φύλλον	folium
		χαμαί	humus
λεύσσω / λύκη in λυκάβας }	lux	χειμών	hyems
		ὥρη	hora
μήν	mensis		

II. TREES, PLANTS.

ἴον	viola	φηγός	fagus
ῥόδον	rosa		

III. OF ANIMATED NATURE.

ἀλώπηξ	. . . .	vulpes	κύων, κυνός . . .	canis
ἀμνός	. . . .	agnus	λέων	leo
βοῦς	. . . .	bos	λύκος	lupus
ἔγχελυς	. . . .	anguilla	ὅῖς	ovis
θήρ	. . . . .	fera	οὖθαρ	uber
ἵππος	. . . .	equus	πῶλος	pullus
ἰχθύς	. . . .	piscis	ταῦρος	taurus
κάπρος	. . . .	aper	ὗς	sus
κριός	. . . .	aries	ὠκύπτερος	accipiter

IV. OBJECTS CONNECTED WITH FOOD.

ἄμπελος	. . . .	pampinus	μέλι	mel
γάλα, γάλακτος γλάγος	}	lac, lactis	μῆλον	malum
			οἶνος	vinum
δαίς	. . . .	dapes	σῖτος	cibus
ἐλαία	. . . .	olea	σῦκον	ficus
ἔλαιον	. . . .	oleum	τρύγη	fruges
κάλαμος	. . . .	calamus	ἀ-τρύγετος . . .	triticum
κοινή	. . . .	cœna	ᾠόν	ovum
κρέας	. . . .	caro		

V. RELATED TO OUTDOOR LABOUR.

ἀγρός	. . . . .	ager	ζεῦγος ζυγόν }	jugum
ἄροτρον	. . . .	aratrum		
ἄρουρα	. . . . .	arvum	κῆπος, σηκός . . .	sepes
			ὄρχατος	hortus

VI. NAVIGATION.

ἄγκυρα	. . . . .	ancora	λιμήν	limen
ἐρετμόν	. . . .	remus	ναῦς	navis
κυβερνήτης	. . .	gubernator	πούς	pes

H

VII. DWELLINGS.

αἰθάλη	favilla	θύραι	fores
αὐλή	aula	κληίς	clavis
δόμος	domus	λίχος	lectus
ἶδος	sedes	οἶκος	vicus
θάλαμος	thalamus		

VIII. CLOTHING.

ἐσθής	vestis	χλαῖνα	læna

IX. THE HUMAN BODY.

γόνυ	genu	μηρός	femur
δείκνυμι	digitus	μυελός	medulla
ἕλκος	ulcus	ὀδούς	dens
ἔντερον	venter	ὀστέον	os (ossis)
ἧπαρ	jecur	παλάμη	palma
καρδίη } κέαρ }	cor	-πέζα (comp.) } πούς }	pes, pedis
κεφαλή	caput	ὠλένη	ulna
κόμη	coma	ὦμος	armus
λάξ	calx	ὤψ	os (oris)
λάπτω	labrum		

X. THE FAMILY.

γένος	gens, genus	φρήτηρ } φρήτρη }	frater
ἑκυρός	socer		
μήτηρ	mater	χήρη } χηρωστής }	heres
πατήρ	pater		
υἱός	filius		

XI. SOCIETY.

ἐλεύθερος	liber	τέκτων (στέγω)	{ tectum, tego
παλλακίς	pellex		
ῥέζω (ῥέξω)	rex	φώρ	fur

XII. GENERAL IDEAS.

αἰών	. . . .	ævum	λήθη ⎱	. . . letum
πλγος	. . . .	algor	Λήτω ⎰	
ἄνεμος	. . . .	animus	μένος	. . . . mens
αὐδή	. . . .	audio	μόρος	. . . . mors
βίος	. . . .	vita	μορφή	. . . . forma
βίοτος	. . . .	victus	νεύω	. . . . numen
γεύω, γεύσω	. .	gustus	νόος	. . . . nosco
δόσις	. . . .	dos	ὀδμή	. . . . odor
δῶρον	. . . .	donum	ὀδύνη	. . . . odium
εἴδω	. . . .	video	ὄνομα	. . . . nomen
θεός	. . . .	deus	ῥώμη	. . . . Roma, robur
θιγγάνω	. . .	tango	ὕπνος	. . . . somnus
θυμός	. . . .	fumus	φάτις, φατόν	. . fatum
ἴς	. . . .	vis	φήμη	. . . . fama
κνίσση	. . .	nidor	φυγή, φύζα	. . fuga

XIII. ADJECTIVES OF COMMON USE.

ἄγκος	. . . .	uncus	μέγας	. . . . magnus
ἄλλος	. . . .	alius	μείων	. . . . minor
βραδύς, βαρδύς	.	tardus	νέος	. . . . novus
βραχύς	. . .	brevis	ὅλος	. . . . solus
γενναῖος	. . .	gnavus	ὀρθός	. . . . ordo
γραῦς	. . . .	gravis	παῦρος	. . . ⎰ parvus
γυρός	. . . .	curvus		⎱ paucus
δεξιός	. . .	dexter	παχύς	. . . . pinguis
ἐρυθρός	. . .	ruber, rufus	πικρός	. . . . acris
ἡδύς	. . . .	suavis	πλατύς	. . . . latus
κυρτός	. . . .	curvus	πλέος	. . . . plenus
λεῖος	. . . .	lævis	πυρρός	. . . . furvus
λιπτός ⎱	. . ⎰ lentus		τέρην	. . . . tener
λιγύς ⎰	. . ⎱ levis		ὕπτιος	. . . . supinus
μάσσων	. . .	major	χάος	. . . . cavus

For such a people as we have supposed the Pelasgians

H 2

to be, here is no inconsiderable equipment of words. But there are exceptions.

1. In regard to religion, the stock is scanty. We have deus related to θεός, numen to νεύω, rex to ῥέζω, in virtue probably of the sacrificial office of a primitive king: and we may add, as correlatives, λοιβή to libo, and ἀράομαι, ἀρητήρ to ara, orare, orator. But this is little: and there is a great lack of correspondence in the principal words, such as, on the Greek side, ἱερός, ἅγιος, θύω, βωμός, νηός, ἄγαλμα, τέμενος, εὔχομαι, and on the other, sacer, sanctus, pius, templum, preces, vates, macto, mola. In one case, or in both, there must have been a great displacement of the Pelasgic vocabulary. And as the Roman religion was far more Pelasgian than the Greek, it is probable that this displacement, if it occurred in one only of the two peninsulas, occurred in Greece.

2. The words relating to war are almost without exception irreducible to agreement.

αἰχμή	cuspis	κλισίαι . . . castra
	mucro	κνημίς . . . . ocrea
	acies	κολεός . . . . vagina
Ἄρης	Mars	κύκλος . . . rota
ἅρμα, δίφρος .	currus	κυνέη . . . . galea
	rheda	μάχη, ὑσμίνη . . pugna
ἀσπίς, σάκος .	scutum		proelium
	clypeus	ὀϊστός, ἰός . . sagitta
βέλος	telum	πόλεμος . . . bellum
βιός, τόξον . .	arcus	ῥυμός . . . . temo
δόρυ, ἔγχος . .	hasta	σάλπιγξ . . . tuba
θώρηξ . . .	lorica		classicum
κλισίη[1] . . .	tabernaculum	φάσγανον, ξίφος ensis.

[1] Cæsar, De Bell. Civil. b. iii. c. 96.

Here the most striking correspondence is that of
Arès with Mars, both used to signify war itself, as well
as to mean the god of war. But Arès, though he is not
easy to trace, appears to be a deity whose origin would
assign him exclusively neither to the Pelasgian nor to
the Hellenic family[1]. The relationship of βέλος to
telum appears clear enough. Except a rather faint
similarity of πόλεμος to bellum, and of θώρηξ to lorica,
there is no apparent connection between any other
words in the list.

It is also worth observing that, while the Greeks derive the important ethical words βέλτερος, better, from
βέλος, and ἄριστος, best, from ἄρης, the Latins are content with optimus, obtained from a common root with
opes, wealth; possibly, however, as we, not much to
our honour, say that one man is *worth* more than
another.

With respect to the terms belonging to navigation,
it is remarkable how they bear upon rowing, its rudest
form, and do not include the names for mast, yard, or sail.

Again, the use of metals is slight in the earliest stage
of society.   Even with the Greeks of Homer only one,
χαλκός, or copper, was at all common; and we may
observe a great want of correspondence between the
Greek and the Roman names for these invaluable commodities.

1. χρυσός	. . .	aurum	4. σίδηρος	. . . .	ferrum
2. ἄργυρος	. . .	argentum	5. κασσίτερος	. . .	stannum
3. χαλκός	. . .	æs	6. μόλιβος, μόλυβδος	.	plumbus.

The Greek δοῦλος, again, is in marked contrast with

---

[1] See *infra*, Chap. VIII.

the Latin ser v us. We might on the whole plausibly suppose that slavery was not a Pelasgian institution at the
time when the Greek and Italian branches of the race
parted company. War and maritime adventure were the
chief feeders of that institution; and the Pelasgians,
as we see, were not of themselves addicted to either,
however good the materials they afforded for a soldiery.

Nearly all those Greek words which are in close
affinity with the Latin are found in Homer.

It seems then, in sum, that the Pelasgian tongue
supplied both peninsulas with most of the words relating
to the primary experience, and to the elementary wants
and productions, of life; but not with those of a more
arduous range, such as war, art, policy, and song. And
the religious vocabulary of the Greeks was probably
supplied from Hellenic sources.

There is also a very traceable distinction in the
names of persons throughout the Iliad. I am far from
contending, that we are to suppose them to be in general
authentic. But the elements, out of which Homer has
constructed them, will indicate a marked difference
of character and pursuits. Homer gives his Phaiakes
names generally connected with nautical habits, in accordance with his picture of the people. It is probable
that he proceeds on a similar principle in other cases.
The evidence which names, analysed according to this
hypothesis, will supply, tends to show the strength of
the Pelasgian element—1. among the Trojans; 2. in
the inferior class of Greeks; 3. particularly in certain
portions of Greece; while 4. the Lycian names, though
on the Trojan side, appear to fall into an opposite
class.

The test of a Pelasgian leaning in the names I

suppose to be their connection with rural, pacific, or
industrious habits, and the like. The opposite class
express ideas belonging to glory, policy, mental powers,
martial vigour and operations.

We must not apply the rule too closely to slaves:
such as Eumaios, Eurucleia, Eurumedousa, Alkippè; for
high-born slaves were frequently obtained by policy
and by the chances of war[1].

It is also to be observed that the names etymologically related to the horse are almost exclusively on the
Trojan side. Such are Hippasos, Hippothoos, Hippo-
lochos (Lycian), Hippodamas, Hippodamos, Hippocoon,
Hippomachos, Hippotion, Melanippos, Euippos, Eche-
polos. Hippodamos, too, will be remembered as one of
the stock or staple epithets of Hector. On the other
side I have only noticed Hipponoos[2]. In Homer, the
horse-feeding country is the plain country[3]. And
Thessaly had already begun to obtain the pre-emi
nence in its breed of horses, which distinguished it in
the historic period; for the two best teams 'by far[4],'
in the Greek army, were Thessalian. This may perhaps be the link of association between the horse and
our Pelasgian lowlanders.

Again, the names connected with gates are generally
of the Trojan party. There are Pulaios, Pulon, Pu-
lartes, and Pulaimenes. Of the Greeks we have Eurupulos. But all these appear to be the names of leaders
or prominent personages.

Among Attic names we find Pheidas, Stichios, Sphelos, Boucolos. These names belong to prominent personages. But an etymology relating to such ideas as

[1] Od. xv. 413.
[3] Od. iii. 263.
[2] Il. xi. 303.
[4] Il. ii. 763, 770.

parsimony and tillage is such as we do not find among the Hellenic races in a corresponding rank.

Among Trojans slain, without much note of distinction, we find Amphiteros, Echios, Puris, Polumelos, Argeas (compare Argeioi), Dresos, Opheltios, Boucolion, Melanthios (compare Melanthios and Melantho of the Odyssey, both servants). Many of the names accompanying these are of doubtful etymology: comparatively few relate to high qualities or pursuits.

In the Eleventh Iliad, Hector slays in a mass nine persons[1], who are called ἡγεμόνες, or leaders, as opposed to the πληθύς or common soldiery. But as none of these are anywhere else even mentioned, and as Homer never allows Greeks really distinguished to fall wholesale by the Trojan sword or spear, we cannot render this as meaning more than that they were officers. Accordingly we find a mixture of names; Aisumnos, Autonoos, Agelaos, are of the Hellenic class: Dolops, Opites, Opheltios, Oros, and perhaps Hipponoos, of the Pelasgic. Dolops, however, is the son of Clutos, a name belonging to another order.

When we turn to the Lycians, whose affinities are plainly not Pelasgian[2], we find that Odysseus slays in succession Koiranos, Alastor, Chromios, Alcandros, Halios, Noemon, Prutanis. These names are all probably of the Hellenic class; for Halios means maritime, and we find no presumably Pelasgian names which point to maritime pursuits (Astualos[3] is simply local); while Chromios seems to mean bright-coloured (χρῶμα), i. e. beautiful. All the others are clearly of a patrician cast.

We find in the Iliad ten legitimate sons of Antenor,

---

[1] Il. xi. 304.   [2] Il. v. 677.   [3] Il. vi. 29.

and one bastard. Eight of the ten have names palpably
of the Hellenic order: Agenor, Acamas, Archilochos,
Demoleon, Echeclos, Iphidamas, Laodamas, Laodocos.
Nor can the other two, Coon and Helicaon, be referred
to the Pelasgian class. The bastard is Pedaios, Il. v.
70: he was brought up on the same footing as the rest.

It will be remembered that Homer expressly declares
the Myrmidons to be Hellenic and Achaian. Now
we have named among them Patroclos, Menoitios,
Menesthios, Eudoros, Peisandros, Maimalos (μαιμάω),
Alkimedon, Laerkes, Automedon. Every one of these
names is of what I have described as the Hellenic
character.

Upon the whole, and without any allegation of a
rigid uniformity, indeed with a confessed inability to
assign an etymology for many of the Homeric names,
still it may be held that, where we have already on
other grounds found reason to presume Pelasgian blood,
there the names are frequently related to peace, industry, wealth, and are not of a soaring character:
whereas in cases of high station generally, and of clear
Hellenic blood, they refer to valour, fame, command,
mental power, and the like.

The chief of all the Homeric signs that Greece had
been occupied, before the Achaian period, by a non-
Hellenic race, is to be found in the sphere of religion.
I will not anticipate what there will be an opportunity
of unfolding in detail hereafter[1]. It may suffice for the
present to observe, that while the genius of the Olympian system of Homer is intensely human or anthropomorphic, we can trace, especially outside of that system,

---

[1] *Infra,* Chap. VII.

but partially as adopted into it, the remains of a religion of a different order, based, principally at the least, upon the worship of Nature-Powers, that is to say, of the powers discerned in material and sensible nature.

I now turn to glance at some of the extra-Homeric evidence of the wide extension of the Pelasgoi at an early period[1].

Besides associating Dodona both with Hellic and Pelasgic races, Hesiod may be interpreted as personifying Pelasgos: a testimony legendary in itself, but betokening the importance of the race[2].

Asios, a very ancient poet, as quoted by Pausanias, represents Pelasgos to have been the child of Earth, born upon the mountains that he might be the father of men[3]. Æschylus, in the Supplices[4], makes him the son of the earth-born Palaichthon; from him the Pelasgians take their name: his dominion reaches from the Strumon northwards to the Peloponnesos. In the reign of this Pelasgos, Danaos comes to Greece. Of Pelasgos, Argos in the historic period professed to show the tomb. Arcadia held the tradition that he taught the use of dwellings and clothes, and to eat chestnuts instead of roots, grass, and leaves[5]. Thessaly had its separate tradition of him.

According to Herodotus, Greece was anciently called Pelasgia: the Peloponnesian women under Danaos were Pelasgiotides: the Arcadians and people of Aigialeia (afterwards Achaia) were Pelasgian: the case of Attica has already been mentioned: recollections of the Pelasgian worship were preserved in his day at

---

[1] See Bishop Marsh, Horæ Pelasgicæ, Cambridge, 1815.
[2] Hes. Fragm. ii. 2.   [3] Paus. viii. 1. 2.   [4] v. 247.
[5] Paus. viii. 2. 2.

Dodona: the Pelasgian race subsisted in Samothrace and Lemnos, and in Plakiè and Skulakè, settlements on the Hellespònt[1]. He writes[2] that they use a foreign tongue; and at this we need not wonder, when they and the Pelasgians of the Greek peninsula had moved for so many generations on separate and diverging lines.

Thucydides places the spot, or building, called Pelasgicon, under the Acropolis at Athens; and states that the Pelasgian race was the race principally diffused over Greece in early times. He also calls the Pelasgians of his own day barbaroi; the name then applied by Greeks to everything not Greek. He adds that they were of the same family, the Tursenoi, who anciently occupied Athens[3].

Theocritus, early in the third century before Christ, describes the Pelasgians as the principal race in Greece before the Troïca; and Apollonius, two generations later, calls Thessaly their country. The Scholiast on this passage quotes Sophocles in the Inachos as declaring that Pelasgoi and Argeioi were the same: which, for those within the limits of Greece, is very nearly the conclusion suggested by the text of Homer as a whole[4].

Strabo states that the Pelasgoi were the earliest lords of Greece; that the oracle of Dodona was a Pelasgian foundation; that Thessaly was called Pelasgic Argos; that, according to Ephorus, Pelasgia was a name of the Peloponnesos; and he gives us the fragment of

---

[1] Herod. I. 146; ii. 52, 56, 171; vii. 94.
[2] Herod. I. 57.   [3] Thucyd. i. 3; v. 109.
[4] Theocr. Idyll. xv. 136-140; Apoll. Argonaut. i. 580; and Schol. Paris.

Euripides, which reports that Danaos changed the name of its inhabitants from Pelasgiotai to Danaoi[1].

Dionysius looks upon Peloponnesos as the first seat of the race, and affirms that it was Hellenic: meaning, probably, that it entered into the composition of the Hellenic body[2].

Niebuhr[3] shows the wide range of Pelasgian occupancy in Italy: Cramer, in Greece and Asia Minor[4].

---

[1] Strabo, vii. p. 327; v. p. 221.   [2] Dion. Halic. i. 17.
[3] Hist. chap. iii.   [4] Geogr. of Ancient Greece, vol. i. p. 15.

CHAPTER IV.

HELLAS.

THE name which the Greeks have given their country for a period approaching three thousand years, and which foreign countries have incorrectly rendered by the term Greece, is Hellas. It has a secondary place in Homer; and yet there are indications of its coming greatness. With Hellas as a territorial name, we meet not unfrequently in Homer; but we likewise have the derivatives of that word,—

1. Hellenes, Il. ii. 684.
2. Panhellenes, Il. ii. 530.
3. Kephallenes, Il. ii. 631 *et alibi.*

And we have also the primitive tribal name from which it is itself derived, Helloi, or Selloi, Il. xvi. 234.

We first make acquaintance with the Hellas of Homer in the Catalogue. He takes unusual pains to fix in his picture, as it were with fast colours, the contingent of Achilles. In four lines he represents them,—

1. As occupying a part of Pelasgic Argos or Thessaly.

2. As occupying Alos, Alope, Trechin, with Phthiè and Hellas. The three places named are probably the chief or only towns [1].

3. As bearing the designations (1) of Myrmidons, (2) of Hellenes, (3) of Achaioi.

In Homer, great part of Greece is wholly without territorial names; and, when such names appear, we must not at once assume that they are employed with the same precision as in later times, when they came to signify districts of fixed and known delimitation.

Hellas is named ten times in the Poems; four times together with Argos, in the set phrase καθ' Ἑλλάδα καὶ μέσον Ἄργος [2], 'throughout Hellas and mid-Argos:' four times obviously in the same sense as in Il. ii. 633; and three of the four times in immediate connection with Phthiè, and with reference to territory under the dominion of Peleus [3].

But, in Il. ix. 447, Phœnix says that he left Hellas to enter the dominions of Peleus, and in Il. v. 478, that he left Hellas, and entered Phthiè. Yet the Catalogue, and three other passages, show us, that a part at least of the dominions of Peleus was called Hellas; and the Myrmidons were also called Hellenes, and are indeed the only people to whom that designation is expressly given.

Now, when Phœnix thus took refuge, he was flying from his father Amuntor, who dwelt in Eleon [4]; and this Eleon, as we find from the Catalogue, was in the land of the Boiotoi [5]. Consequently the name Hellas,

---

[1] See the Catalogue, Il. ii. 603 seqq., 615 seqq.
[2] Od. i. 344; iv. 724, 816; xv. 80.
[3] Il. il. 683; ix. 395; xvi. 595: Od. xi. 494.
[4] Il. x. 367.   [5] Il. ii. 500.

besides designating at least a part of the kingdom of Peleus, embraced the country as far as to include Bœotia.

Accordingly, it must have included the country of the Locroi, afterwards called Locris. So that, when Homer says the Oilean Ajax excelled, in the art of casting the spear, 'the Panhellenes,' that is, all the Hellenes, 'and the Achaians,' it is pretty plain that the name Hellenes in his view embraced the Locroi.

We find, then, that the two passages, where Hellas is named by Phœnix in contradistinction to Phthiè, are in general harmony (according to the results of our previous inquiry [1]) with those where it is mentioned with Argos; and that, in both, it is, without any rigid definition of boundary, a general name for the parts of Greece north of the Peloponnesos.

And the four passages, in which the name Hellas is applied to territory under the sway of Peleus, do not compel us to give a second sense to the term; for they do not imply that Peleus ruled all Hellas, but only that his dominions extended beyond the territory specially called Phthiè, and included part of what had Hellas for its ruling appellation.

Phthiè itself is remarkable as the only territorial name, denoting a district of country without reference to a town, which we find in the Greece of Homer north of the Isthmus of Corinth. We may regard it as carved out of Hellas, and so distinguished from it when mentioned alone; yet included in it when Northern Greece is named as a whole. The phrase 'Pelasgic Argos' is hardly an exception, since that

[1] *Supra*, Ch. II.

appears rather to be a description given by the Poet
of the great Pelasgian Lowlands, than a recognized
and current title. So 'the plain of York' is a descriptive phrase, not an established territorial name.

It is plain that Phthiè was the principal part of the
dominions of Peleus, since it is used for the whole
of them[1], like England for the United Kingdom. It
was a rich and fertile country.

Yet its inhabitants are never called Phthioi. This
name is given to two other Thessalian contingents, the
second under Podarkes, and the fourth under Medon[2].
And here we have a remarkable indication of the
distinction between the Hellenic and the Pelasgian
races. We cannot doubt that the kingdom of Peleus
had been inhabited by Phthioi, since they had given
it the name Phthiè. We have no reason to suppose
these Phthians were displaced by the Myrmidons, since
we find Phthians and Myrmidons side by side in the
same army. But the more distinguished title effaces
the more obscure; and while the Phthian name continues to attach to the population of other less Hellen-
ized parts of Thessaly, in Phthiè itself the people have
in lieu of it the three designations of Myrmidon,
Hellene, and Achaian; Achaian, as a great and leading branch of the illustrious Achaian family; Hellene,
as inhabiting a country included under the overriding
name of Hellas; and Myrmidon, probably as a subsept
of the Achaians.

It is plain, that Homer has made use of special
means to mark the Hellenic and Achaian character
of the kingdom of Peleus, and to exclude it in a marked

---

[1] Il. i. 155, 169; ix. 363; xix. 299.
[2] Il. xiii. 685, 693; cf. Il. ii. 704, 727.

manner from the category of Pelasgian influences.
This observation, however, opens up another subject,
to which we may revert.

The word Panhellenes, though only once used, in the
description of the Oilean Ajax, is of great importance.
'In spear-casting he excelled the Panhellenes and
Achaians[1].' These two names cannot refer to the
inhabitants of different territories. Even if they did,
the former would include the inhabitants of all Hellas,
that is, of all Northern and Middle Greece. But we
know (1) that there were Achaians there ; (2) that
these Achaians were also, in the case of the Myrmidons, called Hellenes. Homer may seem, then, to
designate, though not as by absolute and well-under-
stood synonyms, but rather with a certain vagueness,
substantially the same persons, namely all the Greeks ;
but to give them both their territorial name, and their
blood-name.

Though Thucydides[2] is right in saying Homer does
not call the Greeks Hellenes, yet it thus appears not
improbable that, once at least, he calls them Panhellenes. Yet the verse ought hardly to attract suspicion on account of the word, since independently of
it we have sufficient proof that the territorial name of
Hellas might be applied without impropriety to
describe the range at least of Northern and Middle
Greece. Nor do I broadly deny that this may be the
meaning of the word Panhellenes. If such be the true
construction, then the use of Panhellenes and Achaians
to signify all Greeks, may be compared with the use
of 'Hellas and the breadth of Argos' in the Odyssey
to describe all Greece. It is also just possible that, as

---

[1] Il. il. 530.   [2] i. 3.

the Achaian name has a leaning to the dominant class or aristocracy, the Hellenic name may in this passage have a similar leaning, and may, like the other, be used to denote the community, as the part supposed more excellent often is used to denote the whole.

There is another designation in Homer which seems probably, if not certainly, to be a derivative from the same stock — the name Kephallenes, a name still engraved on the island of Cefalonia. This word is used in the Iliad to describe the subjects of Odysseus. It however appears but twice. It might be expected to recur frequently in the Odyssey. But it is employed only five times, and never for the inhabitants of Ithaka, taken alone, who are always called either Ithakesioi, or Achaioi. In Od. xx. 210 it refers specially to those who inhabited the continental pasture lands of Odysseus. In Od. xxiv. 355, 377, 428 it seems to be capable of no meaning except the subjects of Laertes and those of Odysseus generally, as in the Iliad. Generally, I mean, as opposed to any narrower territorial limitation; for I do not exclude the belief that the name of Kephallenes may imply the better blood of the community. It may moreover be conjectured that this was a word, like Hellenes, creeping into use, but not as yet fully established.

It appears to be formed from the word Hellenes, with the prefix κεφ-, meaning 'head,' which appears in κεφάλη, in the Sanscrit kapâla, the Latin caput, and the German kopf[1], not to mention other words.

Let us now ascend to the word from which Hellas itself is derived; since it obviously means, according to a regular Greek formation, the country which had

[1] Donaldson, New Cratylus, p. 291.

been occupied by, and which had come to be named
from, the Helloi. These Helloi appear to be the
Selloi of Il. xvi. 234. They seem also to be a people
of the rudest habits, dwellers in the mountains; having
prophets or interpreters, it is said, not priests, of Zeus,
and being especially devoted to him in that capacity.
We have other vestiges of this race in Homer; in
the name of a river Selleeis, which we find in or near
Troas [1], as well as (probably) at more than one point in
Greece; and especially in the name Hellespontos,
which in Homer means not the narrow strait merely,
but the whole sea between Troas and Thessaly at the
least, or the northern Ægean [2].

Independently of the grammatical connection between Helloi, Hellas, and Hellene, there can be little
doubt that in his solemn invocation, Achilles, himself
described as a Hellene, means to invoke Zeus by the
tie of race. This, then, is signified in the recital
concerning the Selloi, or Helloi, the *sigma* and the
aspirate here representing one another as in many
other cases; for example, hex, hepta, hudor, hus,
and sex, septem, sudor, sus. The one form reappears
in Selleeis, and in the Proselenoi [3] of Arcadia; the
other in Hellespont, and in the Hellopia of Hesiod.

The Scholiast on the Birds of Aristophanes [4] informs
us that braggarts were called Selloi; and that the word
σελλίζειν meant to vapour or brag. He derives this
sense of the word from Sellos, the father of one
Æschines, satirised by the dramatist. Now it seems
very little probable that the name of the obscure father
of an obscure man should thus have given by metaphor

[1] Il. ii. 839.   [2] Il. ix. 360.
[3] See *supra*, Chap. II. p. 80.   [4] v. 824.

a word to the Greek tongue; and again, that the explanation should have been handed down from the time of Aristophanes to that of the Scholiast. Such words as 'hectoring' and 'rhodomontading' presuppose a great celebrity in the personage on whose name they are based, as without this they would not be intelligible. But if we refer this phrase to the ancient Selloi, the explanation is easy. In Greece, and especially in Attica, to be autochthonous or indigenous, and consequently to be of a very ancient race, was notoriously matter not only of credit but of vainglory, and thus to play the Sellos would be a natural and effective way of describing the manners of a vainglorious person.

The great Greek chieftains of the war are supplied as follows: Achilles, from a district of which the whole military class is expressly described as Hellene and Achaian; Idomeneus, from Phœnician ancestry; Odysseus also, from a region in which the upper class is Achaian; Agamemnon, Menelaos, Diomed, Nestor, from districts in which Pelasgianism is wholly submerged. The greater Ajax is the near kinsman of Achilles, and we must therefore suppose the Telamonian race to be strongly marked with Hellenism.

It may reasonably be asked, how it happens that if Southern Greece, meaning the Peloponnesos with the adjoining islands, thus abounds in Hellenic elements, we should be entirely without traces of the name of Hellas in that portion of the country.

We find indeed its kindred there; the name Selleeis for a river, and Kephallenes for a people. But these are not very prominent. The proper answer seems to be that, as the name Hellas took a natural precedence over names of Pelasgian associations, so the Achaians were probably the flower and the ruling order of Hellenes. Consequently, their name, where they were largely spread, might tend to suppress that of Hellas; or to prevent its formation, by filling already the place it would occupy with the territorial name Achaiis. This Achaian name is here found prevailing in the dominions of Agamemnon, of Diomed, of Nestor, of Odysseus: the same must be presumed of those of Menelaos. And at least much the larger part of the Peloponnesos seems to be included in the Achaic Argos, besides that the word Achaiis unquestionably includes the whole country from north to south.

There may however be an inference drawn from the local concatenation of names. Beginning at or near Troas, and moving towards the west, we have Selleeis, Hellespont, Helloi, Hellenes, and (from Hesiod) Hellopia. Probably we have here an indication that the route of the Hellic tribes into Greece was by the Hellespont and the northern extremity of the country. They were not, like the Pelasgians, an essentially lowland people, as we perceive from the brief description in the Invocation of Achilles. The name Trechin, as one of the settlements in the kingdom of Peleus, allied as it is with Threx, or Thracian, affords a similar indication. Again, Thamuris, the Bard who attended the solemn public competitions of song, and challenged the Muses, and whom I suppose, like those competitions themselves, to be Hellenic, was a Thracian. There is therefore less difficulty in assigning this route unequivocally to the Hellic than to the Pelasgian race.

CHAPTER V.

Direct Notices.

1. Minos, who is stated by Thucydides[1] to have been the first known founder of a maritime empire, appears in Homer as the greatest and most important of his archaic personages. The achievements of Heracles are personal, indeed corporal; but the name of Minos, whether mythical or not, is a symbol of political power, of the administration of justice, in a word, of civilisation. He is the only person, indeed, lying so far back in time as three generations before the War, about whom Homer has supplied us with any details of real and historic interest.

Minos had Zeus for his father, and the daughter of a distinguished Phœnician[2] (such appears to be the most probable interpretation, but in substance there is little doubt about the meaning) for his mother. At nine years old he received revelations from Zeus[3], and reigned over all Crete, at that early age, in the great

---

[1] i. 4.   [2] Il. xiv. 321.   [3] Il. xiii. 450–453; Od. xix. 178.

city of Knossos[1], named first among the Cretan cities
in the Catalogue. He was the father of Deucalion,
and the grandfather of Idomeneus[2], who, at the period
of the War, was passing from middle life into old age[3],
and had begun to feel its effects in failure of the
organs of sense. After death, the Cretan sovereign
exercised the office of a ruler in the realm of Aïdoneus,
and administered justice among the dead[4], as a king
does among his subjects upon earth. His brother Rhadamanthûs[5], hardly less distinguished, has the custody
of the Elysian Plain. Him the Phaiakes conveyed (by
water from Scheriè[6]) to Euboea, on his way to Pano-
peus of the Phokes, for the purpose, apparently, of his
passing judgment upon Tituos, son of Gaia, who had
offered violence to Leto, as she was on her way (probably from Delos) to Putho or Delphi[7]. The presumption arising upon these passages is, that Rhadamanthûs
was acting for his brother Minos, and that the authority
of that sovereign prevailed not only in Scheriè but in
Phokis; in other words, that he bore sway over a considerable dominion, both maritime and continental, in
Greece.

This connection with Scheriè confirms his Phœnician character: and the signs of an authority extending
to the mainland of Greece, and to the islands on its
western coast, appear to be plain. It may be as a relic
of this dominion, that we find in Ithaca a harbour of
Phorcûs[8], who is a maritime god of the Phœnicians.
General tradition reports that Minos laid a tribute

---

[1] Il. li. 646.　　[2] Il. xix. 180.　　[3] Il. xxiii. 469, 476.

[4] Od. xi. 569.　　[5] Od. iv. 564.

[6] See the Outer Geography, *infra*, Ch. XIV.

[7] Od. vil. 321-324; xi. 576-581.　　[8] Od. xiii. 96.

upon Attica[1]. Of this we have no direct evidence
from Homer; but the fact that Theseus went to Crete
to seek Ariadne the daughter of Minos to wife[2], indicates a political relation between them, and in this
way partially sustains the tradition.

Minos is in the last-named passage called oloo-
phrōn[3]. This is a word confined by Homer to the
circle of Phœnician personages. The epithet seems to
imply in some form a formidable if not injurious craft.
It may apply to the character of the Phœnicians as
astute and tricky merchants, who acted at times as
kidnappers and pirates: but as it is applied to great
personages[4], Atlas, Aietes, and Minos, it may probably
refer to what is politically formidable; and, if so, it
may well be a trace of a former supremacy in Greece,
standing in connection with the Phœnician name.

It may even be doubted whether Homer does not
mean to describe the Phœnician tongue as still spoken
in Crete; for he says[5] that in that island there is a
mixture of languages. This with him is a significant
and rare expression. It is difficult to suppose that he
would have used it merely because the island contained
Pelasgian as well as Hellenic races. For he speaks
of the mixed tongue of the Trojan army, not in connection with the people of Troas, who probably spoke
the same or nearly the same language with the Greeks,
but with the allies[6], of whom he distinctively calls the
Carians barbarophonoi[7]. He applies the phrase

---

[1] See the Dialogue Minos, ascribed to Plato, 16, 17.

[2] Od. xi. 322.

[3] Oloos is applied to an adverse divinity. See Il. iii. 365;
xxii. 15.   [4] Od. i. 52; x. 137.

[5] Od. xix. 175.   [6] Il. ii. 203, 204.   [7] Ib. 867.

allothrooi [1] to the people of Temese in Cyprus, who were probably Phœnician. If the Phœnicians gave Crete its name, then the Eteocretes of this passage of the Odyssey may be a Phœnician race, amidst the other four, which are apparently Hellenic and Pelasgian. This conjecture is in some degree supported by the fact that the Poet calls them megaletores, or haughty; an epithet suited to a race in possession of political ascendancy, much in accordance with the oloophrôn already cited, and yet more closely with another of his Phœnician epithets, agauos [2].

It is possible that the Deucalion whom the later tradition connects with Thessaly, may have been the son of Minos; and that his appearance there ought to be taken as another indication that the power of Minos reached to that region. Thucydides [3] states that this personage appointed his children to be hegemones or rulers; which implies a dominion distributed in provinces, and also Asiatic in some of its features.

If this be so, then, on finding Minos installed as a ruler in the Underworld, we reasonably conclude that he is not so placed by the arbitrary choice of the Poet, but that he governs below the same persons, of the same countries, which he had governed upon earth. In short, that his office there is a testimony to the existence of a bygone Phœnician dominion, exercised in Greece from Crete as a centre. The great wealth of Crete is eminently in harmony with this hypothesis.

Bishop Thirlwall [4] has explained the position of Minos, as it is defined by general tradition. Again, the existence of an empire connected with his name

---

[1] Od. l. 183.   [2] Od. xiii. 272.
[3] i. 4.   [4] Hist. of Greece, L 5.

best explains the partial introduction of Cretan institutions into Laconia. I have elsewhere [1] ventured on
the conjecture that the mnoia, or public slavery, of
Crete was an institution of Minos, and is named
after him.

Herodotus repeats, that Minos expelled his brother
Sarpedon from Crete; and that Sarpedon colonised
Lycia, which, even in the time of the historian, was
governed by laws partly Cretan. If the royal house
of Lycia was thus connected with that of Crete, and
with the man who made the first recorded effort to
bind Greece together in civil order, it gives a satisfactory explanation to the remarkable partiality which
the poet always shows in the Iliad for the Lukioi or
Lycians, far above all the other portions of the Trojan
force.

Again, Homer places Daidalos in Crete; and says
that he wrought there for Ariadne, in metal, a dance,
which formed the model of that wrought by Hephaistos
on the shield of Achilles [2]. He could not more distinctly have connected the Crete of Minos with the
Phoenicians than by placing there the great traditional
producer of works in metallic art, from whose name
was taken the verb δαιδάλλειν, to embellish.

Next to Minos we may consider the case of Kadmos
in connection with the Phoenician name and race.
Homer gives us conclusive evidence of the migration
of such a person into Greece, by calling the inhabitants
of Thebes, one generation before the Troïca, by the
names of Kadmeioi and Kadmeiones. His proper
name is only mentioned in the Odyssey as the father

---

[1] Studies on Homer, vol. i. p. 179.
[2] Il. xviii. 592.

of Leukotheè [1], once a mortal, now deified in the Sea-region, who appears to Odysseus after the wreck of his raft on the way from Ogugiè, and provides him with a girdle for his preservation from the angry flood. There could hardly be a more distinct intimation of the Phœnician extraction of Ino than her deification, not in Greece, but in the Sea-sphere, and her appearing to Odysseus before he had regained the threshold of the Greek world.

We learn from general tradition that the Thebes of Kadmos had seven gates, which were in correspondence with the sevenfold planetary worship of the East. And Homer[2] calls the Thebes of the Kadmeioi seven-gated. But Kadmos was not the first founder of the city: its first founders were Amphion and Zethos[3]: and Homer, when he mentions the foundation by them, does not call it seven-gated, but champaign, from the character of the country, conformably to the description given by Thucydides.

In the Underworld of the Odyssey we find a great proportion of persons having Phœnician associations. Again, the name Phoinix had, at the epoch of the War, been variously naturalised in Greece. Besides being a Greek proper name, it also meant a Phœnician, a palm-tree, and a purple dye[4].

The most important works of art named in the poems are obtained from the Phœnicians. Not only was this the case with works in metal, but it was from Sidonia that Paris brought the beautifully wrought tissues which were so prized by the royal family of Troy[5]. And all navigation, except that of the coasts

[1] Od. v. 333.　　　　[2] Il. iv. 406.　　　[3] Od. xi. 263.
[4] Od. xiv. 288; v. 163; Il. iv. 141.　　　[5] Il. vi. 289.

and the Ægean, appears to be, at the Homeric period, practically in the hands of the same people. The Taphians, who carry iron to Temesè[1] in Cyprus, and mean to bring back copper, appear clearly to be a Phœnician colony. Odysseus, feigning that he had escaped from Crete to Ithaca[2], speaks, as if it had been a matter of course, about the ship's company who brought him, as Phœnicians. In his second fiction[3], and here again as if it were a matter of course, it is a Phœnician rogue who inveigled him in Egypt, carried him to Phœnicia, and then intended to take him to Libya and sell him for a slave. When Odysseus represents himself in another of his fictions as a practised navigator, he is a Cretan, but he is one of the highest station, and represents himself as having been the colleague of Idomeneus in the Trojan command; therefore, probably, as like him of a Phœnician family[4]. Eumaios, telling of his own home in the distant Suriè[5], describes how the Phœnicians came thither for trade or kidnapping, and how a Phœnician woman was a domestic in his father's house[6]. Alone among the races of the epoch, the Phoinikes, with their imagined counterparts, the Phaiakes, are called nausiclutoi[7], 'ship-famous.'

The immense fame acquired, and the mythical character assumed, by the single great Achaian voyage of the traditionary fore-time, that of the ship Argo to the Euxine, combine with all the other negative evidence of the Poems to prove to us how completely the Greeks of the Homeric age were de-

---

[1] Od. i. 184.   [2] Od. xiii. 272.   [3] Od. xviii. 290-300.
[4] Od. xiv. 230, 237.   [5] Od. xv. 415.   [6] Ib. 417.
[7] Od. xv. 414; vii. 39; xvi. 227.

pendent on the Phœnicians for their ordinary intercourse with the outer world; and the outer world
here means everything beyond the Greek Peninsula,
with the islands coasting it to the south of the Corin-
thian Gulf, and with the islands and coasts of the
Ægean.

Besides the name Phoinix, we have in the poems
the names of Marathon, Turo (Tyre), and Danae[1],
which are all apparently represented in Phœnician
names still traceable on that coast.

The direct notices of Egypt in the Poems are much
narrower than those of Phœnicia; and the name
Aiguptios[2], borne by an Ithacan noble, is perhaps
the sole positive trace which we find of an Egyptian
influence within the limits of Greece.

Egyptian Thebes was known as a city of vast
wealth, with twenty thousand persons possessed of
chariots, and with an hundred gates[3].

In the Odyssey we learn that Menelaos, driven
by the winds, visited the Aiguptioi[4]. In the palace
of Menelaos[5], one of the attendants of Helen carried
her silver basket[6], given her by Alkandrè, wife of
Polubos, who dwelt in Egyptian Thebes. Helen had
likewise the drug of marvellous effects, which may
have been opium. This drug had been presented to her
by the Egyptian Poludamna, wife of Thon[7]. It grew
in Egypt, which abounds in drugs, and where all the
inhabitants are unrivalled physicians, being of the
race of Paieon[8].

---

[1] See Renan's Phenicie. [2] Od. ii. 15.
[3] Il. ix. 381-384; Od. iv. 127. [4] Od. iii. 300.
[5] Od. iv. 87. [6] Od. iv. 125.
[7] Od. iv. 227-232. [8] See Paieon, infra, Ch. VIII.

In this region Menelaos was detained by the gods
for neglecting to offer the proper sacrifices, at Pharos [1],
a day's sail from the mainland. There he had his
interview with Eidotheè, and his conflict with Proteus,
the servant of Poseidon [2]. By Proteus, after his
victory, he was directed to return to the mouth of
the river Nile, which, as well as the country, was
called Aiguptos. At that point he was to make his
offerings, which he did. And there he erected a
funeral mound in honour of Agamemnon, 'for his
eternal fame [3].' This passage seems to show either
that Agamemnon was already known in Egypt, or
that the memorial would make him famous because
it was in so famous a country. In either sense, particularly in the latter, the recital savours of some tradition which exhibited Egypt as a great centre of power.

In the fiction where Odysseus pretends to be a
Cretan, and the bastard son of Kastor, he relates
that he sailed to Egypt with a crew, who in spite of
him began to lay waste the exceeding fine fields (peri-
calleas agrous) of the Egyptians [4], and to assail the
inhabitants. Next morning the Egyptians gather in
great numbers and drive off the marauders, killing
many, and reducing the rest to slavery. As being
their chief, he besought the king's mercy. He was
treated with exceeding kindness both by the king,
and, after the first excitement, by the people. In
this passage [5] Homer calls Egypt 'the well-watered.'

In another fiction Odysseus relates that he went
with free-wandering pirates, probably meaning Phœnicians, to Egypt, and the very same circumstances

[1] Od. iv. 351 seqq.   [2] Od. v. 386.   [3] Ib. 584.
[4] Od. xiv. 249-287.   [5] Ib. 257.

are repeated; but this time, instead of his applying
to the king and obtaining mercy, he reports that they
made him over to Demetor, the lord of Cyprus [1].

We have no such thing as a voluntary voyage to
Egypt by a pure Greek, or as any voyage to Greece by
an Egyptian. The sea which separates them is so wide,
that the very birds can traverse it but once a year [2].

And yet, though Homer knew little of Egypt, he had
informants who told him of what lay beyond it.
Most strange it is to find that his account of the
Pugmaioi or Pigmies [3], so long regarded as pure fable,
has been found, according to recent travellers, to be
founded in fact.

Such are the direct Homeric notices of these two
countries. But eight Books of the Odyssey (v-xii)
describe the adventures of the hero on his way home.
From the time when he leaves the Kikones, whose
country is his very first halting-place, and passes Cape
Malea, the scene of these adventures is in an outer
world, evidently foreign to Greek experience. They
are made up from materials just such as the tales of
daring seamen would supply, with the double resource of
strange fact and of embellishment at will: and, in all
probability, also with a tendency to give to places and
persons an aspect not too inviting to the Greeks, who
might have seemed capable of becoming, as indeed they
did become, their competitors in a lucrative pursuit.

Among the reasons for supposing the materials of

---

[1] Od. xvii. 424-444.   [2] Od. iii. 318-322.

[3] Il. iii. 6. See in the Revue des Deux Mondes for Oct. 1855,
Review of the work of the German missionary Dr. Krapf,
pp. 886, 904. These Pigmies are 'hauts d'un mètre à un mètre
trente centimètres.'

this part of the Odyssey to be Phœnician, come first
these two, that Greek experience could not have supplied them, and that the Phœnicians could.

Thirdly, we are brought into contact, while the scene
is laid in this region, with an altered mythology.
Most of the Olympian deities retire, for the time,
from the stage. On the other hand, the prerogatives
of Poseidon are enhanced; and we even find him
apparently presiding at an Olympian meeting[1]. A
new deity, faintly glanced at in the Iliad as having
Trojan sympathies, comes forward in full personality
and with distinct attributes. Poseidon's sway seems
to lie towards the west and north: it is as we move
eastward that we encounter Helios, the Sun. He
appears as a recognised member of the Court of
Immortals: he has descendants, and satellites, and
an island on earth especially consecrated to him. Here
too we trace the strongest marks of the sacredness
of the ox, an idea wholly alien to the Hellenic mythology. And, in these Books of the Poem, both sea and
land are peopled with new and strange half-human
races, and with a fresh series or cycle of personages
properly mythological, who stand in no relations to the
most familiar of the Greek deities, but only to Poseidon
and Helios. Nay a change even of diet confronts us;
and, as we get clear away from the Hellenic world,
the ox ceases to be used as food, his place being taken
by sheep and swine. In short the evidence is full and
thick, to the effect that we have passed into a new
and foreign world.

When such evidence has reached the point of suffi-
ciency for a legitimate induction, it gives us authority

[1] Od. viii. 321, 344.

to pronounce Phœnician, from the company in which
we find it, even what may not of itself and directly
bear the stamp: and further, when reflected on the
Hellenic world, it enables us to discern and identify
many notes of Phœnician influence, which, but for
this clue, we should have been unable to detect.

And the consequence is, that we find the debt of
Greece to Phœnicia to be very large: so large as to
be inexplicable, until we bear in mind that, if the
Phœnicians were the only foreigners at that time in
ordinary contact with Greece, it is highly probable
that all, which the Greeks knew or received through
the arrival of Phœnician vessels, would with them
commonly bear the Phœnician name. It may indeed
well have happened that the name Phœnician should,
for the Greek people of that day, become the synonym
or representative of ' foreign;' so that whatever came
from Syria, Assyria, or Egypt, would sound as Phœnician to the Homeric ear, much as in later times
every foreigner in the Levant was a Frank, and as
in Abyssinia (we are told) a foreigner is, at this our
own epoch, termed an Egyptian.

Phœnicia, so understood, comes to mean for Homer,
when taken in its widest sense, the East: and the
conclusion to which I am led, as the probable result
of an inquiry much too large to be here set out in detail, is no less than this: that, under cover of the Phœnician name, we can trace the channels, through which
the old parental East poured into the fertile soil of the
Greek mind the seeds of civilisation in very many (to
speak moderately) of its most conspicuous provinces [1].

[1] The argument is partly stated in the Quarterly Review for
January 1868, art. ' Phœnicia and Greece.'

K

To begin with Greek commerce and navigation. Both these pursuits were in Phœnician hands at the epoch of the Poems. Ever since the time of Minos, without doubt, the Greeks had been their apt pupils: but, even at the epoch of the Troïca, they were far behind their masters. From what Homer says of the Arcades[1], I conclude that the Pelasgian tribes were not apt to acquire nautical habits.

It is on general tradition that we must in a great degree rely for showing that Greece owed to Phœnicia, by the immigration of Kadmos, the gift of letters: and these were probably at first rudimentary symbolical signs, rather than a regular alphabet. For, had an alphabet been conveyed to Greece several generations before the War, we must surely have perceived more of its results. But the general tradition, thus understood, receives both direct and indirect support from the text of Homer. Proitos, ruling over, or, as it might well be rendered, mightier than, the Argeioi[2], sends by Bellerophon a fatal message, couched in signs which were intelligible, not to the bearer, but to the receiver. Now one of the seven gates of Thebes bore the name of Proitos[3]. He is spoken of as one who had come in and acquired a sovereignty in Greece by strength or talent[4]. On the one side, he is in relations with the family of Sisuphos, which we shall find reason to suppose Phœnician; on the other side, with the royal house of Lycia, as to which we have already found similar presumptions[5]. And these facts date from a period of two generations before the War. Yet, in the

[1] Il. ll. 614.   [2] Il. vi. 157.   [3] Paus. ix. 8. 4; Æsch. Sept. 360; Eurip. Phœn. 1109.   [4] Il. vi. 159.   [5] Il. vi. 157, 168.

ordinary dealings of the Greeks, we find nothing like
written memorial or record. It appears, then, as if
an art of writing, but one of rude and ill-developed
contrivance, remained in Greece as an occult art, the
privileged possession of a few Phœnician families.

The Pelasgians have been sometimes supposed to
have brought the art of building with hewn stone into
Greece. And yet the rival name, commonly given to
the ancient remains of this class, is Cyclopian. But
what is Cyclopian is, as we see from the Odyssey, immediately related to Poseidon and to the cycle of Phœnician tradition. Now I think we may lay down this
rule: that wherever Homer mentions solid building,
or the use of hewn or polished stone, we find it always
in some relation to the Phœnicians. Tirûns is 'the
well-walled [1].' But Apollodorus, Strabo, and Pausanias [2]
report (in no conflict with Homer) that it belonged
to Proitos, and was built for him by the Cyclops. The
wall of Troy [3], which so long defied the Greeks, was
built by Poseidon [4] the Phœnician god: that is to say,
by Phœnician artisans. The same supposition will
apply to another Trojan edifice, the palace of Priam [5].
Again, there were polished stones in the mansion of
Kirkè [6]; a Phœnician goddess. There was a court
before the cave of the Cyclops [7] built with hewn stone;
and the Agorè or market-place of Scheriè [8] was constructed in like manner; both scenes belonging to the
Outer or Phœnician world.

[1] Il. ll. 559.
[2] Apollodorus, B. ll. c. 2; Strabo, viii. p. 372; Paus. ii. 16. 4;
Pind. Fragm. 642.
[3] Il. xxi. 516.   [4] Il. xxi. 446.   [5] Il. vi. 242, 243.
[6] Od. x. 211.   [7] Od. ix. 185.   [8] Od. vi. 267.

That the Phaiakes, the people of Scheriè, now Corfù, were Phœnicians, has been argued by Col. Mure[1] from their name and their pursuits. There are abundance of confirmatory arguments; such as the worship of Poseidon as their chief god; the descent of their royal house from him[2]: the return of Athenè from Scheriè to Athens by Marathon[3], a place which was out of her way, but which appears, from a comparison of the word with the Marathus of Phœnicia[4], to have been a Phœnician settlement. Now we observe, that these Phaiakes prided themselves especially on their skill in games: in boxing, wrestling, leaping, running[5]: and Odysseus gained immense honour by his successful cast of the quoit[6]. The games in Scheriè are the only games regularly described in Homer, besides those of the Twenty-third Iliad. They do not include the horse or the chariot race, nor is the horse mentioned anywhere in Scheriè. But they appear to give us a clear indication that the use of these competitive matches in feats of bodily strength was derived from the Phœnicians. And if so, then, taken in connection with the absence of the horse from Scheriè, they suggest a natural explanation of what I for one have found a most difficult subject, namely, the close connection between the horse and the god Poseidon, by the following hypothesis. That the institution of games, being Phœnician, was under the god Poseidon. That the legend of the Centaurs, and the immense preponderance of interest attaching to the chariot-race in Il. xxiii., warrant us in the

[1] History of Greek Literature, i. 510.   [2] Od. vi. 266.
[3] Od. vii. 56.   [4] Renan, Phénicie, pp. 20, 97.
[5] Od. viii. 100-103, 158-164.   [6] Od. viii. 235, seqq.

belief that the Hellenic tribes, much given to horse-manship, introduced the horse into the institution of the Games. And lastly, that the horse, by his introduction into the Games, which (from Il. xi.) we know to have taken place at least two generations before the Troïca, came under the special care and patronage of Poseidon.

With respect to fine art, it seems impossible to resist the clear and ample evidence of the Homeric text, to the effect, first, that works well deserving that name in all essentials existed in the time of Homer [1]; and secondly, that they are exhibited to us as proceeding from a Phœnician source.

Lastly, there is reason from Homer to suppose, that not perhaps the vital spark of poetry, but yet the use and art of music came to Greece from those whom he calls Phœnicians. In the first place, it is only in the palace of Alkinoos that Homer has presented us with the Bard actually at work; not only as one regularly installed in the household, but with his successive lays given at length. In the palace of Odysseus, the Poet only mentions, and that but once [2], the subject of the lay: in the palaces of Menelaos and Nestor, which afforded ad-mirable opportunities, we do not hear of the Bard at all. Again, when we enter the mythologic circle of the Phœ-nicians, we have all the beings of the highest order, whom it contains, engaged in music: the Sirens, who may be called goddesses of the chant; Calypso and Kirkè, who have no special connection with the art, but both of whom are found singing in their respective abodes [3].

If these reasonings be well founded, it may be asked

---

[1] See 'Hephaistos' and 'Art,' *infra*, Chap. VIII. sect. ix.; and Chap. XIV. sect. ii.

[2] Od. i. 327.   [3] Od. v. 61; x. 221.

what contributions were made by Pelasgians and
Hellenes to that marvellous aggregate which we know
as the Greek nation. The answer, I presume, would
be this. That the Pelasgian races brought into Greece
the pursuits of agriculture, and the habits of a settled
life. That the practice, or discipline (it was more than
a sport), of hunting, which had so powerful a hold on
the mind of Homer, and that a high political genius,
together with an extraordinary excellence in war, were
rather due to the masculine habits, both mental and
bodily, of the Hellenic tribes. But that the main
question is not the actual possession of this or that
accomplishment, of this or that institution; it is the
possession of the quality, in soul or body, which is
adapted first to receive the gift as into a genial bed,
and then so to develope its latent capabilities as to carry
them onwards, and upwards, to its perfection. Among
all the gifts of the great nations of modern Europe, how
many are there which we can affirm to be, in each case,
absolutely original [1]?

But then follows the just demand of a sound criticism,
that for such gifts as it may seem that the East may
have conveyed to Greece at the time when its energies
were beginning to expand, we ought to be able to
point out an adequate personal medium, through which
the communication was effected. It would be much
to lay all this honour upon Minos, whose empire, whatever it was, had passed away, and the more enduring
fruits of whose political achievements do not seem, for
the time, to have reached beyond the bounds of Crete;
or upon Kadmos, whose influence, whatever it had been,

---

[1] It seems to be admitted that the very bagpipe of the Highlander is a comparatively modern introduction.

certainly had not made the Thebes of the Troic period
an 'eye of Greece' or a recognised centre of its
civilisation, as it ought to have done had he supplied
the channel through which were so largely transmitted
by his mother-country the gifts of civilisation: not
to mention, that with respect to each of these personages it is questioned whether they were real, or only
mythical. Minos, indeed, stands near the period of
the War. But Kadmos is more remote; and I learn
from distinguished authority that his name signifies
simply one coming from the East. Either way, it may
justly be urged that a channel should be indicated for
those most fruitful communications, which I suppose to
have taken place. To this reasonable demand I propose to suggest a reply.

But here our path must be a little circuitous. In my
Studies on Homer I have endeavoured to point out,
that we have no warrant from the Poems for speaking
of an Æolic dialect of the Greek tongue, or of supposed
Æolians as the prevailing race of Greeks at the Troic
or the Homeric period. Nor is Homer merely silent
on the subject; for while he tells us nothing of the
existence of the Æolians as a tribe, he tells us of
Aiolid houses, and gives us to understand that from
this stock proceeded a considerable proportion of the
reigning families of Greece during and before his time.
From him we hear of Sisuphos reigning in Corinth,
descended from Aiolos: of the Neleids in Pulos, of
Pelias, of Aison, Pheres, Amuthaon, all similarly descended: of Augeias reigning in fertile Elis, to whom
tradition gives a similar extraction. The question
arises, were these Aiolids Phœnician?

If they were, we have to add to them, first, Kadmos

and Minos, already reckoned; then the great house of
the Actoridai, which is described as being descended
from Poseidon; then Proitos, who made himself King
of the Argeioi; and, lastly, there is every reason to
suppose that Danaos was a Phœnician. That in the
later tradition he stands for an Egyptian is not to be
wondered at, when we consider how the two countries
melted into one another, in the view of the early
Greeks, like a concave line of bays upon a coast trend-
ing towards a distant horizon; and while Phœnician
vessels were the channel of communication, Phœnicia
itself was, before the time of the Troïca, deeply charged
with Egyptian elements. M. Rénan has found a district in the neighbourhood of Tripoli called Danniè[1], or
Dyanniyeh. So in the old Irish histories we find that
the third recorded invasion of the island was effected
by the Tuath-de-Danaans, who are stated to have
been a Greek people[2]. No doubt they are set down
as Greek, because of the connection established in
Homer between Greece and the Danaan name. But
we see at once, so far as the Irish tradition is concerned, how much more appropriate it becomes, if the
name Danaan be of Phœnician extraction. Again:
Pausanias tells us[3] that there stood at the reputed land-
ing-place of Danaos, on the Argive coast, a temple
of Poseidon Genesios, an association which at once
assigns to that personage a Phœnician origin.

I return, then, to the question of the Aiolids. And,
first, as to Troas. We have found signs that in Ilios,
Troy of the plain, the Phœnicians themselves, or the

[1] Phénicle, p. 123.
[2] The Irish before the Conquest, by M. C. Ferguson, p. 7.
[3] Ii. 16. 4.

Phœnician worship of Poseidon, had been cast out; and
this ejection is probably represented in the poetic or
traditionary fiction, that the god Poseidon had become
bitterly hostile to the city of Priam. Not so in Dardania; for Poseidon specially protects Æneas, the heir
to that sovereignty, and rescues him, at the critical
moment, from the attack of Achilles[1]. This at once
betokens a relation between Poseidon and the Dardanian branch of the royal house of Troas.

Here history comes in to our aid. Pausanias[2] and
others assure us that, in the historic period, there were
Æolians at a place called Assos in Troas, and that an
Æolian race held what was reputed to have been Troy.
And the general connection of Æolians with the worship of Poseidon may, I believe, be taken as an uncon-
tested fact.

Everything combines to raise the presumption thus
obtained, about the Phœnicianism of the Aiolids, to
the rank of a rational conclusion. Take, for example,
the fact that Homer never mentions Aiolos himself in
conjunction with his Aiolids. Considering their illustrious position, this reticence demands observation;
especially as in almost every case Homer names the
person who stands at the head of one of his genealogies.
If Aiolos were a Greek, either born or naturalised, it
seems wholly inexplicable. But if Aiolos were an immigrant who never lost his foreign character, or if he
were the famous foreign sire or ancestor of men who
acquired sovereignties in Greece; or, thirdly, if he were
only a mythical formation, representing the foreign
paternity of a group of distinguished men who had cast
their lot in that country, then nothing can be more in

[1] Il. xx. 318-340.   [2] vi. 4. 5.

keeping with the general method of the Poet than that, just as he cuts the thread which connects the Pelopids with Tantalos (and, in the preternatural order, the thread which connects Demeter with Persephonè), so he should cut the thread which connects the Aiolids with Aiolos.

Again, observe the link supplied by horse-breeding, and by the introduction of the horse into the Games. Two generations before the Troïca, Augeias, a reputed Aiolid, holds Games in Elis[1], probably at what was afterwards Olympia: and at these Games there were chariot-races: and it is in direct connection with Games that all which relates to horses is placed under the sanction of Poseidon[2], whom tradition so long connected with the Olympian contests[3]. Eumelos, an Aiolid, has the finest mortal horses of the army[4]. The Trojans, who had Æolian relations, are famous for their horses. Sisuphos, an Aiolid, reigns in Corinth[5]: and this is one of the districts where Poseidon strives against another deity for the sovereign worship[6], and obtains it as far as the low ground is concerned[7].

If then Aiolos was foreign, and was connected with Poseidon, he could hardly be other than Phœnician. We turn then to those books of the Odyssey which we have found to have been constructed out of Phœnician materials. And here we meet him, exactly such as we might have anticipated, in consonance with the foregoing *data*. If Aiolids, settled in Greece, had

---

[1] Il. xl. 699-702.   [3] Il. xxiii. 581-585.
[2] Pindar, in the Olympic Odes.   [4] Il. ii. 763.
[5] Il. vi. 152.   [6] Pind. Ol. xiii. 4.
[7] For a large collection of particulars about Poseidon, see Gerhard, Ursprung, &c. des Poseidon, in the Berlin Transactions; and Preller, Gr. Mythologie, vol. i. p. 452.

brought the use of the horse into the Games, nothing
could be more natural than that Homer should mythically connect Aiolos with the horse: accordingly, even
in this foreign region, and upon this sea-girt isle,
Aiolos is the son of Hippotas[1], a name of Greek etymology. If the Aiolids were sea-borne to Greece, so
Aiolos dwells in a sea-island, and is the guardian of
the winds. If they were a large variety of houses from
one ancestor, either real or supposed, so we find him
supplied with six prolific pairs of children: brothers
and sisters, coupled together in a way which was alien
to Greek manners, but which we may, reasoning from
analogy, suppose to have been much more agreeable to
Phœnician customs and ideas. If the actual or ideal
person represented in Greece by the name of Aiolos
was popularly taken to be connected with the ruling
houses of Greece, and with Troy, then it is quite
natural that he should feel an interest in the Trojan
War. Accordingly, the Aiolos of the Odyssey inquires
minutely of Odysseus about both Troy and the Greeks[2]:
which, be it observed, neither Kirkè nor Calypso does,
nor does any other of the foreign personages encountered by Odysseus in his tour.

I suppose, then, that the Aiolos of the Tenth Odyssey
is the ancestor, real or reputed, of the Aiolid houses
of Greece named in Homer; and I remark with some
confidence, that if he is not this, he is a personage
wholly unaccountable and unintelligible.

This somewhat lengthened though inadequate statement will, I hope, appear to be justified, when it is
remembered that the historical question, which under
the legendary veil invites investigation, is one of

[1] Od. x. 1-4.   [2] Od. x. 14-16.

extreme interest: it is the question of the amount, the nature, and the channels of the earliest powerful Semitic influence upon an Aryan or Japhetic people.

And this leads me to my concluding point in the present argument. It may naturally be asked, is there anything in the name Aiolos, which is a Greek name and perhaps a mythical one, to account for its being applied by Homer to Phœnician or Semitic families? This question has been considered by Dr. Hahn[1], who offers his solution of it. He observes that, among many nations, warriors have been tattooed, to make them look terrible: and that a tattooed man might very well be called Aiolos, or ' variegated.' He thinks, therefore, that the name Aiolos, which ran, as we see, wholly in the ruling class, meant a warrior.

Without denying the ingenuity of this hypothesis, I offer another: for I feel that Dr. Hahn's interpretation is scarcely applicable to the Greeks of Homer. Among them we hear nothing whatever of tattooing; nor is the name Aiolos, with its derivatives, particularly attached to warriors; nor have we reason to suppose that the Phœnicians were in any manner superior to Hellenes in war, however they may have acted as teachers, or as forerunners, in arts and knowledge.

I lean to another explanation of the name, which appears to me very simple and sufficient. I find it in a fact stated incidentally by Professor Rawlinson[2]. He tells us that, among the Persians, dresses were not often patterned, but depended generally for their effect on make and uniform colour only. And he adds, ' In all these respects we observe a remarkable contrast

[1] Hahn, Alb. Stud. p. 247.
[2] Ancient Monarchies, vol. iv. p. 326.

between the Aryan and the Semitic races, extreme simplicity characterising the one, while the most elaborate ornamentation was affected by the other.'

If this were so, then nothing could be more natural than that when a few prominent and conspicuous persons from a Semitic country came to settle in Greece, and especially when they held there a position and attitude of superiority, they should bring with them the customs and dress of their country, and that to them, in respect of the style of their habiliments, the name of Aiolos, meaning patterned or variegated, should attach.

Let our line of thought now enter upon a somewhat wider field.

If an empire, connected with the Phœnician name, had already weighed upon Greece within the memory of man; if Phœnicians, very probably officers of that empire, had penetrated the country at a number of points, and had usually been able, wherever they appeared, to obtain the ruling power; we can have no cause to wonder that Homer should have regarded them as a great power in the past, even if to the Greeks of his day they were chiefly known as merchants or as freebooters. Hence we can be at no loss to comprehend how it is that his epithets for them, oloophrones, olophoïa eidotes, agauoi, go much beyond what was necessary to describe the astute man of business, or even the daring kidnapper.

The detection, if it be a real one, of these powerful Semitic influences, both in the Greece of Homer, and as they had operated before his time, opens a new perspective into the ancient history of the world. The knowledge of this history has recently much advanced, through research of many kinds in various quarters, and especially through the interpretation of the Egyptian hieroglyphics. Before this region of knowledge was unbarred to us, the poems of Homer were justly regarded, even by those who appreciated the evidences for their unity of authorship, as might have been some isle of Delos floating on the sea of time, without possessing root or anchor visible to human eye, and without affording us any *data* whereby we might measure the distance of the extraordinary phenomenon from the continuous and solid ground, the true ἤπειρος, or continent, of history. But now the case is altered. Men of learning think themselves to have obtained means of computation, whereby they can follow the annals of Egypt, and, in a degree, of the countries related to it, upwards, for thousands of years before the Advent, along the stream of time. So far as I understand the matter, modern Egyptology adopts in general the chronological computations of the priest Manetho, as sufficiently corroborated by the deciphered records of the country. For myself, I do not understand by what certain criterion Manetho could distinguish, at the period when he wrote, between the contemporaneous and the successive dynasties of the far olden time. It seems that he attempted it, and in some cases refrained accordingly from heaping together in series all the years of all the recorded reigns. He may not have been very far wrong: but how can we know that he was right? To me the constant changes[1] of the chief seat of government, which are allowed to have taken place, suggest the suspicion that there may be more of contemporary and less of successive power than is sup-

[1] Le Normant, Histoire Ancienne de l'Orient, Paris, 1868, vol. I. p. 187.

posed, and that the gross figures of the chronology may be exaggerated. But I take them as very rough approximations to the truth, which doubtless lies, not beyond, but within them. And, so viewing them, it appears to me that the period perhaps has arrived when the Poems of Homer may, for the first time, be regarded as becoming gradually susceptible of chronological handling, and when attempts may not be hopeless to give them their approximate if not exact place in relation to the main chain of events, which marks for those ancient times the central movement of the history of man.

And this with reference firstly to Phœnicia; secondly and principally to Egypt; which, as I have shown, the Greeks of that early day could hardly have the means of distinguishing from Phœnicia with regularity or precision.

It is plain, from both the Poems, that, at the epoch of the Troïca, Sidon was in its vigour. The Sidonians are mentioned apart from Phoinikè, in the list of the countries which Menelaos visited [1]. Here, as we find, were produced the noblest works of metallic art [2]; here the richly embroidered robes [3]. From the king of Sidon (who has the poetical name of Phaidimos) Menelaos receives a noble gift [4]. And some of Homer's Phœnician personages are also called Sidonian.

Now the period of the Sidonian supremacy closed, as we are told, with the rasing of that city by the Philistines in the year 1209 B.C. [5] Then began the supremacy of Tyre; a city of which we have no indication throughout the poems, unless we may be thought

---

[1] Od. iv. 84.   [2] Od. iv. 618.   [3] Il. vi. 290.
[4] Od. iv. 617; xv. 117.   [5] Le Normant, vol. ii. p. 286.

to find one in the name of Turo[1], the grandmother of
Nestor. From many signs it appears that Turo must
have been Phœnician. But Homer tells nothing,
knows nothing, of a Tyrian. It seems pretty clear,
then, that the epoch of the War, and probably of the
Poems, must have been antecedent to the fall of Sidon,
reputed to have taken place in 1209 B.C. I do not here
attempt to enter into the complicated questions with
reference to the succession, juxtaposition, and intermixture of races in Phœnicia, where all the three great
families of Noachian man seem to come in turn upon
the stage; but I simply treat their influence as a Semitic influence, on the evidence of their Semitic tongue,
and in conformity I believe with the general judgment
of persons entitled to authority.

Now with respect to Egypt. Ample proof is afforded
by the verse of Homer that the Greeks of the Troic
period had for their proper national name the name of
Achaians. We also see very clearly that it had come
into vogue but one or two generations before the
Troïca. We know that it lost its hold as a national
name at, if not before, the conquest of the Heracleidai,
two or three generations later.

At the end of the nineteenth Egyptian Dynasty[2],
and with the reputed date of the fourteenth century
before Christ, under Merephtah, successor of Rhamses II or Sesostris, it appears from the inscriptions that
the people of Libya and of the North, who had formerly
succumbed to the Egyptian power, effected an invasion
of that country in return. In this invasion participated,
among others, Achaians of the Peloponnesos, and La-
konians. · They made great havock in the country;

---

[1] Od. xi. 235.   [2] Le Normant, ii. 286.

but a great battle was fought, in which they were entirely defeated, and their enterprise was broken up.

It seems in a high degree probable, that this invasion occurred during the period which I have described as defining the prevalence of the Achaian name, and the duration of the supremacy of that noble race of Greeks.

It is much more likely that the effort was made before the War of Troy, than after it; for the condition of Greece was then less impaired by exhaustion and by internal revolutions. We have no means of saying whether, so far as Greece was concerned, it was a national, or only a local effort. It is probable that Crete may have been its base: that island was nearest to Egypt; it had a strong Phœnician element, and probably a considerable marine; and in one of the fictions of the pseud-Odysseus, when representing himself as a Cretan of high rank, he declares that he undertook a voyage to Egypt [1], an effort in navigation of which we hear in no other quarter.

We need feel no surprise at the silence of Homer with respect to this daring enterprise. The Poet, frequent and even copious in his allusions to the minor legends of his country, seems almost jealous of the greater ones. The ship Argo is mentioned but once in the Poems [2]; the allusions to the war of Thebes are slight. But if little careful to mix with his own great theme the records of what he might deem rival histories, in a case like this invasion, another and more powerful order of motives would come into play. He sang for the glory of Greece; and as on this occasion, sharing the disastrous fate of their Libyan allies, his country-

---

[1] Od. xiv. 246.   [2] Od. xii. 70.

men were utterly worsted by the foreigner, it was no fit subject for his minstrelsy. Yet it is very remarkable that in the fictitious narrative just made, the expedition takes the form of an invasion. Great havock at first takes place [1]. But the Egyptians are roused; a battle is fought; the invaders are slain or taken; a pretty exact counterpart, although in miniature, of the history of the actual invasion, as it appears in the Egyptian records.

Under Thouthmes III [2], of what is termed the eighteenth dynasty, and at a date taken to be about 1600 B.C., the military power of Egypt reached its zenith. The Empire extended east and northwards over Mesopotamia, Syria, Phœnicia, and even into Armenia. This military dominion was, so constructed as to recognise the local governments, under the suzerainty of the Pharaohs. Among the supports of its power was a fleet [3], which established its supremacy in the Mediterranean waters. There can be little doubt that this fleet was, both in its men and material, Phœnician. An inscription at Karnak [4] shows that it conquered Crete, the islands of the Archipelago, and portions of the coast, at least of Greece and Asia Minor. It penetrated into the Black Sea; and it acted on the populations of the Libyan coast. Centuries appear to have passed away before this empire, probably not too stringent in its action, crumbled into fragments. But it subsisted amid much vicissitude. In 1462 B.C. the nineteenth dynasty is reckoned to commence. It seems doubtful whether the maritime supremacy, which there was no native marine able to

[1] Od. xiv. 263.
[2] Le Normant, II. 239.
[3] Le Normant, II. 246.
[4] Ib. p. 247.

maintain, had not already dwindled to nothing. The second monarch of this dynasty, Seti I, was a great warrior; but he made no effort to retrieve the dominion of the sea.

Here I may venture conjecturally on the following observations. The Egyptian history of the maritime conquests of Thouthmes III, if we are allowed the almost inevitable assumption that the nautical instrument for creating the supremacy was Phœnician[1], reads like an account in other words of what Thucydides has slightly but firmly sketched from general tradition, and what we are enabled to gather with a considerable amount of proof from Homer, respecting the empire of Minos in Crete, over the Archipelago, and on the continent of Greece.

But the empire by sea soon vanished; while the empire by land, extending it appears into Asia Minor, continued, though in varying phases, to subsist. There is at least one indication gathered from Homer and the general tradition jointly, which would lead to the conclusion that the War of Troy took place after the fall of the first, but before the disappearance of the second, portion of the Egyptian power. The Poems are altogether opposed to any idea that a maritime Egyptian Empire still existed. Crete, apparently its old head-quarter, was not at the Troïc period the centre of prevailing power that it had been before. But Memnon was among the allies of Troy[2]; and all tradition reports that Memnon was Egyptian. It may perhaps be worth noting, that the Memnon of Homer

[1] In much later times we find Phœnicia performing much the same office for the Persian king. Herod. ii. 19; vii. 44.

[2] Od. xi. 522.

is gifted with the highest personal beauty, and that
this honour would not have been awarded by the
Poet, who above all things admired the lighter hair
and complexion, to the swarthy, nay tawny, natives
of the Egypt of our geography. Is it not also highly
improbable that Priam, whose list of allies in the
Catalogue stops at Lycia and Caria, should have been
able to draw an auxiliary force from so great a distance? But if the political Egypt, the Egyptian supremacy or empire of that day, reached as far as Armenia
or Asia Minor, the difficulty disappears at once; from
such a region Memnon might have come, and the
account of Homer, together with the later tradition,
becomes natural and intelligible.

In the year 1311 B.C., which is considered as a date
astronomically ascertained [1], Rhamses III, the last
great military monarch of Egypt, came to the throne.
Mesopotamia, however, was under Egyptian rule as
late as 1150 B.C.

The time may be at hand, when, from further investigations, it will be possible to define with greater
precision those periods of the Egyptian chronology
to which the Homeric Poems, and their subject, thus
appear to be related.

In the meantime it may reasonably be pointed out [2]
that the discoveries already made tend to show that
those inquirers have not been wrong, who have assigned
the greatest measure of antiquity, and of historical
character, to the works of Homer.

---

[1] Le Normant, p. 200.   [2] Ib. p. 302.

CHAPTER VI.

THERE is a substantial distinction between titles, and epithets descriptive of station or office. Titles are in effect that class of descriptions which have been gradually accepted by society and established in common usage for the purpose of indicating a certain rank or function, just as a given weight and form of the precious metals is appointed by law or custom to indicate a certain value. In both cases the symbol, becoming familiar to the minds of all, is accepted in common use without examination.

By titles, and also by epithets, I understand, for the present purpose, either adjectives or substantives, as the case may be.

Epithets, or descriptive phrases, may by degrees grow into titles: and it is probable that all titles, properly so called (I do not now speak of those denoting relationship), may begin in descriptive phrases.

One sign of a title is, that it can either be combined with the name of the person to whom it belongs, or substituted for it.

In Homer, the substantives hegemones, aristees,

and the adjectives skēptouchoi (of kings), theioi (of bards), are epithets or descriptive phrases. Again, with respect to individuals, echephron (for Penelope), pepnumenos (for Telemachos), polumetis (for Odysseus), are descriptive phrases. But Basileus, Basileia, for king and queen, are titles. Anax sometimes means ruler or lord, somewhat vaguely, as a title; sometimes noble, as a class; sometimes lord, as a master or proprietor, for example, of slaves or animals. It differs from Basileus in these particulars: first, that it is more rarely used as a title; secondly, that, while both indicate a superiority, the idea conveyed by anax leans to ownership and absolute command, while the Basileus is a ruler not an owner, a ruler of freemen organised under the social bond, and limited by civil right which he is himself bound to observe.

As a designation of dignity, Basileus is the higher, as well as the more definite. The word nearest to it is koiranos; but this has hardly, in Homer, settled down into a title. The ruling office is also more vaguely indicated by the expressions κρείων, and ποιμὴν λαῶν, shepherd of the people. Basileus is well rendered by 'king:' anax by 'lord,' a word at once wider, more absolute, and less elevated in the sense it conveys.

But we find in Homer the remarkable phrase anax andrŏn, lord of men; and this is used, not descriptively, but, beyond all question, as a title. Now, as the word anax has no reference to reciprocal rights and duties, it is very remarkable that we should find it thus used with regard to relations towards men, and evidently freemen, in a title enjoyed by certain individuals. The physiognomy of the phrase, so to speak, is not that of

Hellenic society; for Hellenic society was already founded in *rights*. It suggests therefore a history of its own, and a character either foreign, or archaic, or both.

The facts relating to the use of this phrase are as follows :—

It is applied to Agamemnon forty-four times in the Iliad, and twice in the Odyssey.

It is also applied to

Æneas, Il. v. 311.	Augeias, Il. xi. 700, 739.
Euphetes, Il. xv. 532.	Eumelos, Il. xxiii. 288.
Anchises, Il. v. 268.	

Thus then anax andrōn is a stock or staple phrase for Agamemnon. Yet it is applied to five other persons, all of them sovereigns; but none of them at all approaching Agamemnon in point either of personal eminence, or of power. It is not therefore on account of his personal eminence or of his power that the title is bestowed on Agamemnon.

But again. While it is given thus frequently to Agamemnon, it is given but once to four of the other five, and but twice to Augeias. One of these personages, Euphetes, is named but once in the Poems[1], and then he is named with the title. Augeias (except once in a patronymic) is only mentioned twice[2], in the legend of the Eleventh Iliad; and twice with the title. Eumelos has the title once, out of five passages in which he is named. Anchises once only, out of thirteen. But Æneas is very frequently named in the Poem, and yet never with the title except once. He appears to hold it as heir-apparent to his father's throne; and his

---

[1] Il. xv. 532.   [2] Il. xi. 700, 738.

possession of it marks its hereditary character under such circumstances.

It is to be noticed, that all the six names to which Homer annexes the title are virtually of the same metrical value in the place of the verse where it is almost invariably so annexed. The same observation applies to the word Atreides joined with it in Il. i. 8. At first sight, then, it might appear that metrical convenience had prompted the use of the phrase. But then,

1. Two of the six names, in their simpler forms, Aineas and Augeas, are modified into Aineias and Augeias in order to fall in with the title.

2. It cannot be metrical convenience which gives it so very frequently to Agamemnon, and so rarely to the others.

3. There are at least from thirty to forty names of equivalent metrical value in the Poems, including many princes, heroes, and notable persons, which never receive the title. Among these are, of the living, Patroclos, Sarpedon, Antenor, Diomedes, Agapenor, Menelaos, Aigisthos; and of the dead, Amphion, Heracles, Eurustheus, Adrestos, Rhadamanthos, Meleagros.

Homer never inflects the title, giving it always in the nominative. He never severs the phrase by tmesis, except once only, through inserting the copulative particle τε. Once, in Il. i. 7, it lies between the second and fourth foot of the verse; in every other case it is found between the third and fifth. Some of these particulars may be held, according to the laws of Homeric use, to add dignity to the title. In illustration of this proposition, I will observe that, conversely, in the few instances where the Poet introduces himself into the verse, he never once uses the nominative. Again, Enosicthon is used for Poseidon forty times; thirty-nine of them in the nominative. Diogenes is found in the nominative and vocative only. The masculine kudistos is used sixteen times, all in the vocative. Eurucreion twelve times, only in the nominative.

The phrase anax andrōn entirely disappears from use after Homer.

Let us now look to particulars connected with the application of the phrase to each of the six names severally, in order to discover the thread, if there be one, on which in common all are hung.

I. AGAMEMNON.

The sovereign of all the Greeks is nowhere described by personal epithets of pointed characteristic force. Eight times he is called by the epithet dios, which indicates some specialty of excellence, and which was fairly due to his prominence whether among rulers or among warriors. Generally he is marked either by the patronymic, which is simply historical, or by what may be called official epithets, creion, eurucreion, poimēn laōn. But the staple or stock phrase is anax andrōn.

I have already given a reason why this cannot be on account of his great power and sway. Again, the passages which most forcibly describe these are the lines about the Sceptre in Il. ii. 100–108, and that which gives him his place in the Catalogue, Il. ii. 576–580. In these he is not called anax andrōn, but creion. In two other passages of the Poem he is personally glorified: as to his appearance in Il. ii. 477–483, and as to his arming in Il. xi. 15–46. In neither of these is he

anax andrōn. Neither corporal distinctions, then, nor
official position thus far appear to supply a basis for
the phrase. Yet the very emphatic use of it after the
proper name in the prefatory passage of the Poem,
which contains so much, as well as its frequent reitera-
tion, prove its general dignity and importance. Again,
therefore, it seems likely that we are to look somewhere
in the past for the secret of its meaning.

Unfortunately, in the case of this great family of the
Pelopidai, the past at a certain point, and that too one
soon reached, becomes obscure.

All that Homer desires or intends us to know of the
extraction of Agamemnon is contained in the famous
and very significant passage of the Sceptre, Il. ii. 101–
108. Here we are informed that

1. Hephaistos fashioned it.

2. He gave it to Zeus.

3. Zeus gave it over to Hermes Diactoros, the Agent,
or Go-between; or Ambassador.

4. Hermes gave it to Pelops 'the driver of horses.'

5. Pelops gave it to Atreus, shepherd of the people
(δῶκε).

6. Atreus dying left it (ἔλιπε); it remained or passed
over to Thuestes, rich in flocks.

7. From Thuestes in like manner it was left to
Agamemnon (λεῖπε).

8. It conveyed suzerainty (at the least) over all Greece
and its numerous islands.

The first question is, what are we to say to the theotechny or preternatural machinery here introduced?
If we are to give it an ethnological meaning, the names
of Hephaistos and of Hermes give it a colour foreign,
and such as I have called Phœnician. Little stress

could be placed upon this, if it were an isolated phenomenon. But the sphere of the art of Hephaistos, and
of the general activity of Hermes, lies so completely
beyond the limits of Greece, that I cannot but attach
weight to their names as indicating that, before Pelops,
the family had been foreign, and probably Asiatic. The
passage also demonstrates that the starting-point of the
house is one at which it had attained to princely rank.

Next, the epithet given to Pelops tends to support
the tradition, which places him in relations with the
Olympian Games, and with the god Poseidon.

Further; Atreus first appears in the Pelopid time as
'shepherd of the (or a) people.' There is something in
this phrase which seems to point him out as the first head,
in the Pelopid line, of a settled and consolidated Greek
sovereignty. The same inference may be drawn from
the fact that his name supplies the standing patronymic;
as Neleus supplies it to Nestor. There is also some
more direct evidence. Heracles may be reckoned as
living one generation and a half before the War; since
he has in it both a son and grandsons; and Eurustheus,
who was his contemporary, reigned in Achaic Argos,
which afterwards became the seat of the Pelopid power.
There seems to be only room, therefore, in the natural
course, for one generation of sovereigns in Achaic Argos
after Eurustheus and before Agamemnon.

To this generation probably belong both Atreus and
Thuestes, the father of Aigisthos. In the change of
phrase from δῶκε, 'gave,' to ἔλιπε and λεῖπε, Homer may
seem to glance at a departure from the common line of
direct succession, and a return to it. Thuestes, then,
not being in that line (or, if we were to suppose him in
it, being in it only as the brother of Agamemnon), we

have but two generations of ancestry, and but one of established sovereignty, given for the house of Agamemnon; Pelops having probably founded the power of the house, but not placed it in its fixed seat, or obtained for it the full measure of acknowledgment and positive authority.

We see plainly, from this circumstantial account of the derivation of the Sceptre, that the Pelopids did not simply subvert, or succeed to, a prior dynasty; but that they held a new dominion, legitimated, in poetic phrase, by the gift of Zeus. And we know, from the comparison of dates and particulars already made, that this was the great Achaian dynasty, having the old Argeian dominion for its centre, but reaching much beyond its bounds, with an undefined though acknowledged supremacy over Greece and its whole coronet of islands.

The joint and simultaneous rise of the Achaian race, and of the house of Pelops, is well and clearly founded in the facts of the text: which, however, carries us but little farther. Tradition asserts that Pelops was the son of Tantalos, and Tantalos the king of a race of Phruges. Homer introduces him to us in the Underworld, together with a variety of personages, all of whom have relations, in one form or other, with Greece. Placing him among such persons, he still conforms to his rule by not naming him in the passage of the Sceptre; since he never, on any occasion, deduces a Greek dynasty from a confessedly foreign ancestor.

The nature of his punishment, pointing to some form of greed as his offence, is also well assorted with the tradition which represents him as the last holder of his inherited power, and his son as an immigrant in a foreign land.

We have no means of determining, from the Poems, whether Tantalos was reputed to be of divine descent; but it is far from improbable, since most of those among whom he appears in the Odyssey were so descended.

Post-Homeric tradition makes Niobe the daughter of Tantalos. The tradition of Niobe herself is recited by Achilles [1], and from this we may infer, first, her dignity and fame; next, her having relations with Greece. The theotechny, too, of the tradition exhibits her as one of the great of the earth; and the term laous [2], applied to those who were vicariously punished for her offence, evidently means her subjects. Very possibly, the epithet ἠύκομος, commending the beauty of her hair, may indicate that the Poet regarded her as a Greek, either born or naturalised.

Homer places the mourning Niobe on Mount Sipulos, near the Acheloos; and Pausanias found the reputed tomb of Pelops on the summit of the hill. The Phruges of Tantalos are reputed to have been a Thracian people [3]. Their name [4] appears even in Attica; and a harbour in Elis was called after Tantalos [5].

Pelops is commonly said to have gained the hand of Hippodameia, and the throne of Elis, by success in the chariot-race. Local traces of him remained. He was worshipped in a sanctuary hard by the temple of Zeus Olympios [6]; and revered there among heroes, says Pausanias, as Zeus was among gods. He is the reputed founder or restorer of the Games who raised them to their historic celebrity. Another tradition brings him

---

[1] Il. xxiv. 602.
[2] Il. xxiv. 611.
[3] Strabo, xii. p. 579; xiv. p. 680.
[4] Thuc. ii. 22.
[6] Paus. V. xiii. 1-4.
[6] Paus. V. xiii. 5.

from Olenos into Elis; no improbable indication of his
route from the north. Nine islands off the coast of
Methana were called the islands of Pelops in the time
of Pausanias[1]; and we have already noticed in that
quarter traces of the Achaian name.

That the Achaians were Hellenes, and that they
rise to pre-eminence with the Pelopids, are circumstances which lead us to look for further traces of the
connection. Now Strabo[2] seems to attach a great
value to a tradition which he repeats, that the Achaians
of Phthiotis came with Pelops into the Peloponnesos, occupied Laconia, and gave it the name of Achaic Argos;
and subsequently, when the Achaians were driven out
of Laconia, they drove out an Ionian race from Aigialos,
and gave their name to that region. This account
of the journey of the race, and of Pelops, is in accordance with the traces we have found in Homer and elsewhere of the passage of the family of Pelops towards
the south, and with the emergence of the dynasty of
Atreus. It is also in marked accordance with the emphatic application of the Achaian name to the inhabitants of Phthiè, and with the prominence that the Poet
gives to that district in the War, through its Myrmidon
soldiery and its illustrious chief, who are thus placed in
near relations with Agamemnon and his adherents.
Although we have found in many places vestiges of the
local use of the Achaian name, this is one of only two
where it is expressly and directly assigned to the inhabitants of a district as such. The other is in Crete;
and there no such great importance attaches to the
statement, which exhibits them in conjunction with
Dorians and other races.

[1] Il. 34.   [2] Bk. viii. 5, p. 365.

History at this point comes in to our aid. Down to the late era of Polybius, the connection of the Achaian name with Phthiè still subsisted. There were always Achaians of Phthiotis; and in the year 205 B.C. Quintius, the Roman general, recognised the Achaians, upon inquiry, as a Thessalian race[1].

And the close relation of this race to the Pelopids is in no respect more clear than in this, that as they rose, so they fell, with that particular dynasty. In the post-Homeric literature, all of which follows the Dorian conquest, the Achaian name has ceased to be a current designation for the Greeks.

We are not entitled, however, to carry the connection backwards in time beyond Pelops. We may reckon with confidence that, if Tantalos had been recognised as a Greek, he would have been named by Homer in the line of the ancestry of Agamemnon.

Yet not even the Heracleid victors in the struggle could afford to let slip the repute and credit of the Achaian sovereignty. So although Tisamenos, their representative in blood, had been expelled, and had betaken himself with his followers to Aigialos, his tomb in aftertimes was shown at Sparta; and hard by it the feast of Pheiditia was kept: with an explanatory tradition that their fathers, admonished by an oracle, had fetched the remains of the last Pelopid sovereign from their home at Helikè, in Achaia. On the other hand, the Achaians had now set up a legendary ancestor, Achaios by name, whose image they professed to exhibit; and along with it they cherished a tradition, that the family of Tisamenos had continued to reign among them down to the time of Ogugos, in the third

[1] Polyb. xviii. 30-37.

century before Christ, when their league was formed
upon the basis of democratic institutions. In neither
quarter do we see any such honour paid to the yet older
dynasty of Danaos or of Perseus. All this seems to enhance the dignity of this Achaian sovereignty, to which
the title of anax andrön was attached, as if it were
possessed of some peculiar attribute which it had not
received, and which it did not transmit.

We have now examined the proper import of the
phrase, and its use in the case of Agamemnon. We
have found that its groundwork does not lie either in
his personal qualities or in his position as general-in-
chief or as king. It appears to point backwards to a
state of things anterior to the constitution of Achaian
society; which, as we find it in Homer, though imma-
ture in its forms of administration, was profoundly
penetrated with a political spirit, and had completely
possessed itself of the substance of civil right, though
not in the form of law. It suggests, then, a chieftaincy
or hereditary superiority, older than the settlement of
the family in its present form of power, and, whether
founded in blood or otherwise, having reference to an
origin in time and place beyond the limit of Greek
history, even in that wide sense of the phrase in which
we apply it to the chronicles of Homer.

Let us now see what further lights can be supplied
from the cases of the five personages who share this
title with Agamemnon.

II. ANCHISES, and III. ÆNEAS.

If the strong sense of nationality in Homer has led
him everywhere to keep back from his hearers what he
may have known or heard of a foreign origin for any
Greek race or family, it seems plain that least of all

would he be disposed to lift the veil in the case of a
people whom the Greeks had conquered, and whose
great chieftains especially he exhibits throughout in
marked though skilfully softened and disguised inferiority.

As the Helloi are first introduced to us in the
mountains above Thessaly, so the Dardanians appear
in the recesses of Ida, above the Ilian plain. Dardanos
is expressly declared to be the son of Zeus; as Agamemnon may probably have been his reputed descendant. On the one side we have Zeus, with the Helloi
for his prophets: on the other, Zeus of Ida, Zeus
Idaios. The term anax andrôn applied to a father
and his son, both living, shows the derivative and more
than hereditary character of the title, and supports the
hypothesis that it springs from some remote fountain-
head. But why is it that, given both to Anchises and
Æneas, it is not given to Priam or to any of his family?
Here there is opened to us a curious field of inquiry.

Certain facts are on the face of the Poems.

Priam[1] had, before the war, been a potentate, excelling all in that vicinity. Besides the Allies, and
besides his own troops under the command of Hector,
who are described in terms somewhat like those applied
to the troops of Agamemnon in the Greek army, the
Dardanians appear as a separate contingent; and there
are three other military contingents[2], one certainly, but
perhaps all, included under the name of Tröes, forming
the third, fourth, and fifth divisions of the army. The
King of Troy, then, probably held a position less
powerful indeed, yet resembling that of Agamemnon

[1] Il. xxv. 543-546.   [2] Il. II. 224-239.

M

in having, besides his immediate subjects, various
princes under his suzerainty.

There was at Troy an Union or Chamber of δημογέροντες[1], which occupied the same relative place as the
βουλή or Council among the Greeks. It was composed
of royal and princely persons; yet Anchises appears
neither in this body, nor anywhere upon the scene of
the poem. It is not directly stated that he was alive;
yet it seems to be assumed[2]. If he lived, his absence
from the Council is remarkable, as his dominions were
engaged in the war, and Æneas, before he came to
Troy, had only been rescued by Poseidon from the
hands of Achilles[3]. This prince is never spoken of as
in possession of his inheritance.

The sovereignty held by Anchises was the older of
the two; for Dardania was built by Dardanos[4], Troy
apparently by his grandson Tros, or his great-grandson
Ilos. Priam was the great-grandson of Tros through
Ilos and Laomedon, Anchises through Assaracos and
Capūs. We cannot judge with certainty from this
genealogy, the longest and most detailed in the Poems,
whether the branch of Ilos or that of Assaracos was the
younger. But the presumption arising out of his removal from the original seat into the plain seems to be
against Ilos. It is true he is named before Assaracos:
but in Il. vi. 76 we have Æneas named before Hector
by Helenos; and here likewise he gives precedence to
his own birth. Again, Æneas takes no part in the
councils of Hector; and his personal qualities are very
faintly marked. Yet, like Hector, he is honoured as a

---

[1] Il. iii. 146-148.
[2] Il. xx. 240.
[3] Il. xx. 90-93; 128-131.
[4] Il. xx. 215-240.

god[1]; and the special protection given him by Poseidon marks him as a most important personage. His name is combined with that of Hector[2] in a way which almost implies a parity of military command. Moreover, there is jealousy between him and the house of King Priam. He hangs on the outskirt of the battle[3], and cherishes resentment, because he does not receive due honour from the monarch. Yet the character of Priam was genial and kindly. Again, Æneas is taunted by Achilles[4] with entertaining the hope of succeeding to the throne of Troy. In answer to this taunt, he utters no contradiction of it, but simply gives his genealogy. This seems very like an assertion of his title, which, if it existed, could only rest on seniority.

Æneas does not thwart Hector in counsel like Poludamas: so that there could be no umbrage taken on that ground.

Zeus had presented Tros with certain horses, in compensation for the loss of Ganymede. These horses remained with Laomedon in the plain. But Anchises[5] brought his mares to them surreptitiously, and got possession of the breed. And it is here that this prince is called anax andrōn, as though to say, in virtue of his being the lineal representative of the elder branch, he thus asserted his claim to the use of a gift which had been presented to Tros the common ancestor.

I have said, that the import of this title seems to carry it back to a period anterior to the political organisation of society which we find in Greece. Are we then to suppose, that it also came into the family of

---

[1] Il. xi. 53; cf. v. 467.   [2] Il. vi. 75-77.   [3] Il. x. 459.
[4] Il. xx. 179-183.   [5] Il. v. 268.

Dardanos before his settlement on Mount Ida? I reply
that first there is not the same cogency of reason for
supposing it: for the relation of the Asiatic king to his
people was far more accordant than that of the Greek
to the idea implied in anax andrōn. But neither
need it be rejected on the ground that Dardanos is the
son of Zeus. For, in these remote ascriptions of Divine
origin[1] to royal houses, possibly little more in substance
is intended than is less pointedly conveyed in the peculiar and exclusive ascription to Kings of the epithets
Diogenes, Zeus-born, and Diotrephes, Zeus-nurtured.
Certainly they are to be distinguished from cases of
nearer mythological parentage; and they can hardly
mean more than something of special dignity as among
kingly houses, or else a simple attribute of the class.
But in truth the case of Dardanos and his family will,
if I mistake not, be found to fall in with the general
course of the argument.

The use of this title is a remarkable sign of affinity
between the Trojans and the Greeks: but here is not
the place most convenient for examining into the
general signs of that affinity.

We have seen that, in the case of Anchises, the title
anax andrōn is employed as if to justify him in an
act of aggression in virtue of this dignity. Again, in
the case of Æneas, we are told at a great crisis, 'and
now would have perished utterly the anax andrōn
Æneas, had not Aphrodite perceived his plight[2].' As if
to say, 'great though he was, it would have been all
over with him.' There will be occasion to notice in
other cases, how pointedly this phrase is used in con-

[1] Il. xx. 215.   [2] Il. v. 311.

nection with some striking act or crisis, and by no
means as an otiose or merely ornamental epithet.

IV. Auoeias.

The Elian contingent is sent to the War under four
separate leaders; of whom one is Poluxeinos, son of
Agasthenes. He is termed a prince or lord, and (by
patronymic) descendant of Augeias[1].

In the Nestorian legend of the Eleventh Iliad, we
are told that Neleus[2] sent to Elis a four-horsed chariot
to contend in the Games; but Augeias, who is here
termed anax andrōn, laid hands on the horses, and
detained them. Hence the invasion from Pulos, effected by Achaians, under the guidance of Athenè.
Agamedè, the daughter of Augeias, was profoundly
versed in drugs[3]. And she was married to Molios,
a descendant of Poseidon through Actor; who resided at court, and was slain by Nestor in the Pulian
raid[4].

We may justly suppose that Augeias ruled over Elis,
because the noble Actorid family were attached to his
court as the court of a superior. Whereas at the time
of the Troïca, when the unity of the Elian State
appears to have been broken up, the Actorids of the
time command distinct military divisions, upon a
footing of equality with the descendant of Augeias.
It is probable that Elis, like Bœotia, had already undergone revolutions; and for the same cause, namely,
its fertility.

Other circumstances enhance the presumption of the

[1] Il. ii. 615–624.
[2] Il. xi. 670 seqq.
[3] Il. v. 741.
[4] Il. v. 738, 740, 741.

great position and high descent of Augeias; especially,
his presiding over the Games. To these Games, as we
see, the neighbouring States, some half-century before
the war, already sent their chariots to compete. To
these it seems probable that Thamuris[1] was on his way,
when he met with the calamity which deprived him of
the gift of song; for we find he had reached the
Alpheos, at a distance from his own country, and
from the court of Eurutos, to which he apparently
belonged.

With respect to the descent of Augeias, Homer is
silent, and we must look for the aid of general tradition. He was reputed to be the son of Salmoneus,
and thus a descendant of Aiolos. In this manner he
comes within the circle of the Phœnician traditions.
And though Aiolos is of divine descent, like Bellerophon[2], the text of the Odyssey supports this tradition[3]
(1) by giving him the epithet of amumōn, which
appears to be used by Homer not as an epithet of character, but most commonly as one indicating a divine
descent, of the same class as that of the Dardanids;
(2) Because the name of his daughter Turo points to
Tyre; (3) Because she is called εὐπατέρεια[4], an epithet
only used in two other places[5], and both times with
respect to Helen, who is treated as the daughter of
Zeus, Διὸς ἐκγεγαυῖα[6].

Tradition also places in Elis one of the ancient
towns called Ephurè. The text of Homer, without
directly confirming the tradition, is more than pro-

---

[1] Il. ll. 594–600.   [2] Il. vi. 191.   [3] Od. xl. 235 seqq.
[4] 'daughter of a noble sire.'   [5] Il. vi. 292; Od. xxii. 227.
[6] Il. lii. 199, 418, *et alibi.* Cf. Od. iv. 569.

bably in accordance with it. For Odysseus visited Ephurè to obtain poison for arrows[1]. And it was feared that Telemachos might pay a like visit[2]. Now it is certain (1) that this must have been an Ephurè on the west coast of Greece; therefore probably in Peloponnesos, for intercourse does not appear to pass northwards beyond the gulf of Corinth; (2) that it could not be the Ephurè of Sisuphos, since this to all appearance had now become Corinth, and is so named in the Catalogue[3]. Furthermore, in both cases Ephurè was a place where the use of drugs was studied; and in this use the daughter of Augeias, as we have seen, was skilled. We may, then, reasonably assume that Augeias dwelt at Ephurè, though at the period of the Troïca the place was not significant enough to be named in connection with the force from Elis; but few towns or settlements of which, however, are recited in the Catalogue.

In the case of Augeias, as of Anchises and Æneas, we may observe the very emphatic use of the phrase. The anax andrón detained the mares: i.e. he kept the mares, as if presuming upon his dignity of anax andrón.

V. EUPHETES.

Euphetes is named but once by Homer. Meges, a Greek chieftain, is saved from the spear-stroke of Dolops by the stoutness of his many-layered breastplate[4], brought by his father Phuleus from Ephurè, hard

---

[1] Od. l. 257.
[2] IL ii. 570.
[3] Od. ii. 326.
[4] IL xv. 530.

by the River Selleeis, where it was given him by his
host the anax andrōn Euphetes.

Euphetes, then, is manifestly the king of Ephurè:
and is at once brought within the circle of those traditions to which the name belongs.

The question, over which Ephurè Euphetes reigned,
is at first sight less important than the relation established by the name itself. Strabo[1] reckons, besides
Corinth, an Ephurè in Elis, one in Thesprotia, one in
Thessaly, and five others, which had fallen to the condition of mere villages. In Homer, we hear (1) of the
Ephurè of Corinth, (2) indirectly of that of Elis, (3) of
the Ephurè from which Heracles carried off Astuocheia,
the mother of Tlepolemos, after a destructive raid.
This would appear to have been in Thessaly; since
Tlepolemos comes from Rhodes, and we have other
examples of connection between Thessaly and the
southern islands in the persons of the descendants of
Heracles[2]; but none between those islands and the
west of Peloponnesos.

According to Strabo[3], Euphetes was the son of
Augeias. If so, nothing can better accord with the
Homeric text, which makes Meges[4] the commander of
a contingent from the coast over against Elis; which
places him in battle at the head of the Epeian troops[5];
and which states that Phuleus, his parent, had emi-
grated on account of a feud with his own father[6].
Phuleus is not condemned on account of this feud, but
on the contrary is commended as dear to Zeus. It
was in every way fit, then, that he should con-

---

[1] p. 332.   [2] Il. ii. 676–680.   [3] p. 459.
[4] Il. ii. 625.   [5] Il. xiii. 692.   [6] Il. ii. 629.

tinue to be united by the ties of guestship with the
lord of Elis. And as to the use of the title anax
andrōn, the case of Euphetes may thus in all probability fall under that of Augeias. It appears indeed
possible, though I will not now venture to dwell upon
it, that the name Ephurè may of itself be a sign of
Phœnician relations.

VI. EUMELOS.

Eumelos commands before Troy the forces of his
father Admetos. The seat of his throne seems to have
been at Pherai, a name not improbably akin to Ephurè[1].
And here we find it holding the same relation to the
anax andrōn Eumelos, as Ephurè holds to two other
bearers of the same title, namely Augeias and Euphetes.
Further, we have seen that the name Ephurè is also connected with the Aiolid line in the person of Sisuphos.
Now we find from Homer that Alcestis the mother of
Eumelos was the daughter of Pelias, and that Pelias
was the spurious child of Poseidon, by Turo afterwards
the wife of Cretheus the Aiolid: while in the male
line, which would govern the descent, the family was
descended from Pheres[2], and Pheres was one of the
legitimate sons of Cretheus. Eumelos therefore is an
Aiolid, and as such is sprung from Zeus.

He is mentioned six times in oblique cases, either
of his own name or of his patronymic Pheretiades,
and five times in the nominative; but only once as
anax andrōn[3]. This again is on the only occasion that called for the use of an emphatic phrase,

---

[1] Il. ii. 711–715; Od. iv. 798.   [2] Il. ii. 763.   [3] Il. xxiii. 288.

since his only conspicuous action in the Poems is that, being possessed of the finest horses[1], and excelling in their management, he springs up much more rapidly than any other chieftain, to accept the challenge of the chariot-race in the Twenty-third Iliad[2].

The Homeric evidence then, gathered from various parts of the Poems, and slightly aided by the filling in of blanks from tradition, may be summed up as follows:—

1. The employment of this phrase seems not to be accidental or to be meant for mere ornament; but to rest upon a common character attaching to those who bear it.

2. It is borne only by ruling princes, or their heirs.

3. But though a title of peculiar dignity, it does not indicate a present superiority of power or prerogative to other contemporary rulers.

4. In the cases of the Dardan princes, and of Eumelos, the text shows expressly that it accompanies descent from Zeus, at a remote date, and without the name of a mother.

5. In the cases of Euphetes and Augeias, tradition states, and the text indirectly but strongly supports, a similar descent.

6. In the case of the Pelopids, all direct indications fail us; but even here, Pelops, or his reputed father Tantalos, would appear to be a personage standing relatively to Greek history in much the same position as Aiolos, that is, as the foreign head and founder of

---

[1] Il. ii. 763.　　　　[2] Il. xxiii. 289.

a ruling race; a character, which also apparently attaches to Dardanos in Troas.

7. In each and all of these cases, the ancestor appears upon the scene of Greek tradition as already a prince; and always at a period antecedent to the formation of anything like polity in Greece.

8. It is in this attitude that we are justified in believing Homer presents to us those archaic characters in Greece, whose prior history and descent were foreign, so that if distinctly unfolded they would have broken his uniform rule by representing leading elements of Greek society and nationality as derived from foreign sources.

9. The nature of the phrase anax andrón, meaning nearly, as it does, 'master of men,' seems to bear a foreign rather than a Hellenic colour, and is probably drawn from a state of civil society, which may be called either more patriarchal, or more Asiatic, than that of the Hellenes: a state where power was more absolute, and right less distinctly recognised, than they were respectively in the Greece of Homer. It is a title which, whatever be its lingering glories, has not in it any savour of liberty.

10. The name is nowhere found in connection with Pelasgian associations; but it attaches strongly to what had been all along the ruling element in Greek society from its first recorded formation, whether in connection with the Achaian or with the Phœnician name; namely, a primitive chiefship or superiority, linked to something which, as to time and place, lay beyond the Greek horizon proper.

11. Under these conditions, it is not difficult to see that the title of anax andrón could not apply (for

example) to Achilles or Odysseus, whose families were
not the representatives of these ancient sovereignties:
or to Nestor, whose descent from Poseidon was veiled
by spurious birth, and who was connected with Aiolos
only in the female line: or to Sarpedon, who is directly
affiliated to Zeus: neither do any of them, nor does
Diomed or Ajax, stand in any relation to the characteristic name of Ephurè, or of the Selleeis.

12. Nor is it difficult to understand why this title
of sovereignty and honour, alone among those employed by Homer, passes away with him.

We cannot say whether it was accompanied with
any prerogatives of a substantive character, as it evidently was with a peculiar form of dignity. Those
characters and families, who had not risen by effort
and degree, of whom no human memory bore record
that they had at any period been less than the leaders
and the lords of men, and whose names were associated
with the earliest guidance lent to Greece in her first
struggles for civilisation, might well remain as bright
luminaries adorning the past of the race, until either
a great lapse of time, or, more probably, a breaking up
of the social and political system they had taken a lead
in creating, should bring about their extinction. And
it is change of this kind, on the brink of which Homer
leaves us, as he disappears from us in the distance. In
soft music, he sings out the heroic age of heroes: and
after him, as Hesiod tells us, a ruder and a darker
age is sung in with a wilder music. The traditions,
and the families, of the older time are submerged
by the flood of Dorian conquest. The noble and
refined Achaian succumbs to the half-savage Heraclid. The Hellenic world is resolved into a chaos,

which devours its ancient ideas and institutions:
though the spirit of life still breathes over the form-
less mass, and gradually moulds it into a new and
more organised and splendid, if not a more pure and
healthful civilisation.

CHAPTER VII.

HOMER was the maker not only of Poems; but also, in a degree never equalled by any other poet,

      1. Of a language;
      2. Of a nation;
      3. Of a religion.

The common tradition of Greece recognised the poets, as having had a large share in the formation of the religion of the country. These poets were in particular Homer and Hesiod, as represented by the works ascribed to them. But the difference is immense between the work performed by the author of the Iliad and Odyssey, and the author of the Theogony respectively. The latter, at a date very early without doubt, though sensibly later than that of Homer, placed upon record, and arranged, the mythological legends of the portion of country, supposed to have been Bœotia, within which he lived; and the late position, given in the poem to the gods of the Olympian dynasty, is in accordance with all the indications of the Homeric productions. But the mythology of Homer, instead of being a chronicle or a catalogue, is a supreme work of art, that lives, breathes, and moves, like the metallic statues of his own Hephaistos. And it is precisely the contrast between this wonderful performance and the Theogony of Hesiod, which enables us to conceive in some degree the immense power with which the imagination of Homer operated in shaping the characters of the Olympian gods, in adjusting their relations to one another, and in fixing the conditions of their government of the world, and of their intercourse with the children of men. On these great matters, a poem like that of Hesiod could have no other influence, than a register of births and deaths could have upon the social and political fortunes of a community.

In the supernatural world of Homer, we find deities not only of different ranks and attributes, but marked with very great varieties of moral character and tone ; bearing marks of connection with different places, countries, races of men, and celestial dynasties, or theogonies, with very different degrees of respect paid to them; and these again varying with races of men and local situations.

At the same time, these beings have a head, a central place of habitation, a system and polity among themselves ; to which, however, the various members of the supernatural order are very variously related.

In a word, we appear to see a great mass of heterogeneous materials having reference to the unseen world, which, as they were probably settling down in the world of fact, from their recent contact, into more stable and normal relations, so, in the world of poetry, they receive from the hand of the master an unity fitting them to constitute that intellectual and ideal

whole, which we know as the Hellenic religion. In
this process of construction, the actual belief, traditions, and tendencies of the people could not but be
the chief determining force. But the potent mind and
imagination of the Poet, in all likelihood, exercised
an influence in modifying the stages and fixing the
consummation of the process, which, if secondary and
subsidiary only with reference to the powers before
mentioned, may still be justly supposed to have been
far greater than any ever wielded by any other Greek,
whether legislator, poet, or philosopher.

There is nothing contrary to reason in the supposition that the condition of religion in Greece, at the
epoch of Homer's existence, may have offered remarkable opportunities for the formative influence even of
an individual mind.

In a nation of one blood, which claims to be autochthonous or indigenous, because, since first the migration of the primitive tribe was arrested, it has never
changed its seat, we may look for a religion based upon
the predominance of some single idea, and invested
with great uniformity of colour.

But where, as in Greece, the nation itself is compounded out of a variety of factors, the religion will
naturally assume a variegated aspect.

Each race or family of immigrants arrives *cum Pe-
natibus et magnis Dis;* brings with it its own conceptions and names of deity. These they set down
for themselves upon ground already occupied by the
religion of the former inhabitants, and by their traditional conceptions. These conceptions will be in
many cases representatives of the same original ideas;
and though diversely modified, after the separation of

the races, according to the genius and associations of each branch, they will often claim the same attributes, and the respective worships will tend to compete and even clash together.

Of this clashing we find the mark in Homer, when two deities have the same function. Thus Athenè is even more supreme over war than Arès. A Paieon has to do with healing as well as Apollo. Poseidon is god of the sea; but beneath him, yet in independence of him, is Nereus, inhabiting the depths; and the sea is affected by the agency of Zeus, or Herè, or Athenè [1], or Apollo, with respect to breeze, and storm, and shipwreck, as well as by his own agency.

The same kind of competition is represented in Homer by the deposition, and relegation to a distance, of the older gods of the Nature-system, and by the legends of the youth, or infancy, of Hephaistos and Dionusos.

Also this conflict of religions, growing out of the relations and conflicts of races, is powerfully exhibited in Homer by the division of Olympos into two factions during the Trojan War, and by the bold and effective, if to us incongruous, conception of the Theomachy, or Battle of the gods.

In the later tradition, this clashing comes to be represented by the legends of contests between two deities for a given territory. Poseidon contends with Helios (the Sun) for Corinth; and with Athenè for Athens. A variety of other cases may be cited.

Had the Poet worked up his mythological scheme out of Greek materials alone, we may be sure that the relations of subordination among the gods would have

[1] Od. v. 108, 109.

been at least as well defined, as those subsisting among the leaders of the army, or perhaps even the members of a well-ordered family. Whereas now we find first that Okeanos, as the head of an older though superseded dynasty, stands aloof, and is exempt from attendance at the Olympian court [1]; and that the position of Zeus among its members reminds us of the position of the kings of France before Louis XI among their great feudatories. Poseidon, even singly, is not without pretensions to an equality of force: Athenè, without proceeding to physical resistance, does not hesitate to oppose in debate, as well as in veiled action, the councils of her father: and a combination of these two with Herè had once proved too much for his solitary strength.

When the various worships thus met in competition on the same soil, the result could not but be, either that the objects of them were amalgamated; or that some of them were expelled; or that by division of functions, that is a compromise, their differences were adjusted.

Of amalgamation we observe an example in the first deity of the Homeric poems. The Zeus of Dodona, and of the Pelasgians, becomes also the Zeus of the Hellic tribes.

Of permanent expulsion we have examples in the Okeanos, and also in the Kronos, of Homer, with their followings respectively.

Of the resistance to a new worship, and of its temporary exile, we have an instance in the driving of Dionusos into the sea by Lukourgos.

But the great principle of the Homeric mythology

[1] Il. xx. 7.

is, adjustment by distribution of offices. And the anthropomorphic idea greatly favoured the application of this principle; since it gave to the Poet all the varied functions and orders of humane society, both domestic and political, as a framework after which to arrange his Olympian personages.

And thus it is that Homer, from living in the midst of an intermixture and fusion of bloods continually proceeding in Greece, acquired a vast command of materials, and by his skilful use of them exercised an immense influence in the construction of the Greek religion.

It became with him, what it probably had never been before, and what it was not in the works of any later writer, a most gorgeous and imposing, and even in a certain sense a highly self-consistent, whole : containing in itself, without doubt, many weak and many tarnished elements, but yet serving in an important degree the purpose of a religion to control the passions and acts of men.

The Olympian system of Homer is eminently what Horace describes as

> ' Speciosa locis, morataque rectè
> Fabula.'

It is wrought out with pains and care, full of character and individuality, marvellous alike in the grandeur and the weaknesses of its personages—a work, in the very highest sense that is applicable to any human production, of true and vast creative power.

Even without the attestation of Plato, we might have been able to judge that it was in all likelihood a main instrument in establishing the dominant features of the Hellenic religion, such as we know them from

the historic ages. Partly it reduced to unity the competing elements of the true Hellenic tradition, of the
old Pelasgian Nature-worship, and of the Phœnician,
Syrian, and Egyptian mythologies: partly it cast them
into the shade of local, as opposed to national, devotion.
In the poems of Hesiod, it appears to us as the latest
form of Greek religion; but, more artfully compacted
than the rest, it acquired and retained a real supremacy
among them, although the diversity of aspect never was
effaced.

Yet its character continually altered; and altered
for the worse. It has features which are sublime, and
features which are debased. But the sublime features
of the Olympian characters became, with the lapse of
generations, less and less observable. The debased ones
grew more and more prominent. And the profoundly
interesting specialties of the several deities, indicating their respective origins, at length became apparently imperceptible even to the Greeks themselves.
No one can closely and carefully examine the system
of Homer without a deep interest: no one can find
much ground for such an interest in the theological
part of the religion of the historic period. Only its
ethical ideas, and the highly poetic ideas connected
with destiny, retain any attractive power; and from
the mythology these ideas are, in the later stages of the
Olympian system, almost wholly dissociated.

The wonder indeed is, not that the Olympian
religion should have failed to resist the corrosion
of change, but that it should have been able in any
manner to retain its identity. Devoid as it was of
all authority, and even of the allegation of authority,
for its origin, and not only unsustained, but belied,

by the witness of surrounding nations, it probably had
little else of unity than such as it derived from the
great Bard of the nation, and from its imaginative
splendour; while it had none of the guarantees, real
even if partial, which are afforded either by Books
known and recognised as sacred, or by a compact and
permanent hierarchy, dating, or professing to date,
from the beginning of the system. If the Homeric
poems stood in the place of the former, yet we can
perceive for them no avenue to the mind and heart
of man, except that of the poet, and the delight he
gives ;

ἦ καὶ θέσπιν ἀοιδὸν ὅ κεν τέρπῃσιν ἀείδων[1].

And as respects the latter, neither was the priest, as
such, a significant personage in Greece at any period,
nor had the priest of any one place or deity, so far as
we know, any organic connection with the priest of
any other ; so that if there were priests, yet there was
not a priesthood. Its strength lay, then, in its beauty;
a beauty which, surviving the death of the subject in
which it resided, had power to ravish the mind of
Goethe, one among the greatest of modern poets ; and
probably we could not name in all human experience
a more signal instance of the vast power of the imagination, than is to be found in the long life, and the
extended influences, of the Greek religion.

It found a way to the mind of man through his
sympathies and propensities. Homer reflected upon
his Olympos the ideas, passions and appetites known
to us all, with such a force, that they became with
him the paramount power in the construction of the
Greek religion. This humanitarian element gradually

[1] Od. xvii. 385.

subdued to itself all that it found in Greece of traditions already recognised, whether primitive or modern,
whether Hellenic, Pelasgian, or foreign.   The governing idea of the character of deity in Homer is a nature
essentially human, with the addition of unmeasured
power.   It is at once obvious, then, that the elements
of a profound corruption abound in his Olympian
Court, although they affect very variously the personages
who fill it.   And the principle upon which it is constructed makes but too copious a provision for further
deterioration.

Such accordingly was the actual working of that
Hellenic Theo-mythology, of which we must regard
Homer as the great founder.   With the progress of
time it became more and more debased, and the distinctions originally perceptible among its elements
being worn away, it likewise fell into such a state of
complexity as approached to chaos.

But, while the popular creed thus degenerated, the
intelligence and the speculative mind of the Greeks
became more and more estranged from it.   With the
lapse of time we must learn to regard it, not as in
Homer, under a single aspect, but under three: as a
religion of philosophers, a religion of legislators, and a
religion of the people.   By the philosophers, the abstract idea of deity was greatly purified and reformed;
but the sense of personality connected with it became
feebler and more remote.   In Aristotle, the most profound and powerful mind of Greece in the classical
ages, as well as perhaps among the purest which the
country produced, it is reduced, as a practical principle,
to zero.   Still, the lofty sentiments, thus elaborated
in the abstract, again acquired much of the warmth of

life in the writings of some at least of the dramatic
poets; and may thus have exercised influence in a wider
sphere than that supplied to the few by the thoughtful
studies of the Schools.

Meantime the mythology, with its constant development and deterioration, continued to be accepted by
the people; while with a view, as must be supposed,
to public order, all its institutions had the steady countenance of the ruling authorities.

It may then be believed that there resided among
men, six, eight, or ten centuries after Homer, a much
purer intellectual conception of deity than can be
collected from his poems; while, as a first necessity of
wealth and civilisation, a defined but narrow morality
of property, so to call it, arose; both in a form more
determinate than any known to the Poet, and also sustained by the machinery of law and public policy.

But, notwithstanding all this, a great real declension
in other, and perhaps yet graver, respects had taken
place. For the mass of the population, the abuses and
corruptions of the older creed 'did not pass, but grew.'
Not perhaps against society, which had learned to take.
care of itself, but against the unseen Ruler of the
world, and against the sanctity of human nature, sins
and loathsome abominations had come in, and were
flourishing in a rank and foul luxuriance, which seem to
have been unknown to the Greece of Homer. For the
religion of his day had not ceased to be a power.
Variously and imperfectly, but truly, men were commanded and restrained by it. It presented a system of
rewards and punishments, intelligible to its votaries,
and operative, as it appears, to no small extent upon
human conduct. And whatever may have been, as it is

represented, the personal practice of the Homeric
deities, their system of government was addressed in
the main to good ends. It exhibited, generally speaking, though in an imperfect, yet in a real manner,
superior power, armed and active on behalf of truth,
justice, and humanity. This could not but be an
engine of great good. That it was so, we may learn
from a tone of general character, which certainly did
not afterwards improve, and from the absence of the
horrors already named, which afterwards abounded
even in the more refined regions and in the educated
classes of society.

It may seem strange that the two processes of a
speculative ascent and a practical decline, a mental
discipline of the few and a general dissoluteness of
life, should be simultaneous. But so it was, even to
the day of the last dying throes of paganism. Never
was the heathen creed, on its intellectual side, in
a condition so sublimated, as when it perished under
the blows of the Christian apologists and the influence
of the Church. But also, never had its practical power,
as a religious system elevating or constraining action,
fallen so low, as in the days when its votaries were
habitually content to deify even monsters in human
shape, if they wore the imperial purple.

To say, then, *simpliciter*, either that the Greek religion as it grew old improved, or that it degenerated,
would be to use equivocal and misleading language.
By its side, and never in any degree taking its place in
the minds of the many, there grew up a speculation,
which was hardly a belief, but which put aside a mass
of fables, and in many points approximated to the
truth, concerning the nature of God. But as a living

creed it worsened; and as an instrument for the government of conduct, it more and more lost its power.

The reproaches of Plato against Homer, for the unworthy treatment of the gods, can have little influence on our minds in the light of such knowledge as we now possess. It would appear, from the Cratylus for example, that Plato had little knowledge of the origin of the Hellenic mythology; and the personages, who filled the chief places in it, had in his day assumed a sameness of colour and position, which they had not in the time of Homer. In order to comprehend the method of the Poet, we must bear in mind (1) that many deities, afterwards completely naturalised, were in his day only making the first steps of their way into Greece; (2) that deity is with him a most elastic idea, susceptible of infinite diversities, in point both of virtue and of power; (3) that he has a vivid conception of intercommunion between the two natures, divine and human, which was probably lost in the time of Plato.

If Arès and Aphroditè are exhibited by Homer in lights which are even ridiculous, we have to observe that nothing can be more profound, more entire, than the reverence of his mortals for Apollo and Athenè, nay often for Poseidon and Herè. This difference is not casual; it is in the whole manner of treatment: and what we seem to learn from it is, that, among the Hellenes of his time, Arès and Aphroditè had as yet no regular recognition, no established worship. There is not a single indication of either in the Poems; though it appears from them that these deities were worshipped in Thrace and in Cyprus respectively.

Apart from this, Homer's system of thought included

a number of beings, whom he calls divine, but in whom the divine attributes are minimised. The Gigantes, who rushed to their own ruin; the Kuklopes, who exhibit a perfectly brutalised humanity; the Phaiakes, who in all manly qualities are represented as much below the Greek level; all these were kinsfolk of the gods.

A slight circumstance shows us how, in Homer, the divine idea could be reduced to the smallest dimensions of power. When the comrades of Odysseus ate the oxen of the Sun, Lampetiè, his daughter by Neaira, expressly called a goddess[1], carried the news of the deed to her father. Obviously, then, she had not herself sufficient power to prevent or punish this offence, committed by a mere handful of exhausted mariners. Neither could the Sun, who is called all-beholding, see the act from his pathway in the heavens, without her intervention as a messenger.

The principal materials of religion which Homer found ready to his hand were, so far as appears, supplied by

1. The Pelasgian or other archaic races, which had had possession of the Peninsula prior to the Hellenes.

2. The Hellic families and tribes.

3. The Phœnician immigration.

4. An Egyptian and oriental influence which we trace (*a*) in obscure traditions, and (*b*) in the actual remains of a worship clearly proceeding from this origin, which endured down to the time of Pausanias. This was probably brought to Greece through the Phœnician vehicle.

[1] Od. xii. 131-133.

The Zeus of Homer is equally Pelasgian and Hellenic.

The Apollo, the Athenè, and the Herè appear to belong especially to Hellenic traditions. But the two first carry marks, which can hardly be mistaken, of an affinity, probably dating from a very early period, to the Hebrew traditions, recorded in the sacred Scriptures.

The Poseidon of Homer is manifestly Phœnician. This deity waives as it were his supremacy on coming into Greece, in deference to the paramount force of the religion of the major number, and to the ruling influences. Yet the character and worship of Poseidon may occasionally in Greece, as well as elsewhere, have been preserved under the name of Zeus.

These five are the five great deities of the Poems. But it may be convenient to consider first the mode which Homer has devised for dealing with the elder gods.

It is in a far-distant perspective that he places the Elemental or Nature powers; which are thus removed from inconvenient contact with the actual governors of the world, and yet are subjected to no indignity.

At the head of these is Okeanos; whom Homer regards as the source (not the father, that title being reserved for Zeus) of all the gods. He is not invested with anthropomorphic attributes, a circumstance which indicates the distinctness of the race which had worshipped him. But Homer, paying a marked respect to his dignity, does not summon him to the great Olympian Assembly of the Twentieth Book[1], where, if he had appeared, he must have been second to Zeus. It is

[1] Il. xx. 7.

possible even that the relations of this deity to mankind were pre-Pelasgic; as Zeus appears to have been in the Pelasgian system, and Okeanos could hardly have been there except as its head.

In no case is the Homeric treatment more artful, than in that of the sea- or water-god Nereus. He is completely invested with the anthropomorphic character; for he is blessed with an abundant progeny of daughters. But his place was wanted for Poseidon: he is therefore confined to the sea-deep; and he is in no manner or degree an object of worship in the Poems.

While the Olympian system generally is to be regarded as alien to elemental worship, and as founded on a different basis, it is important to trace nevertheless such vestiges of the elder religion as are to be found among the Greeks of Homer.

1. In the Pact of the Third Iliad, the original terms were[1] that the Greeks should offer a lamb to Zeus; the Trojans two, the one black, the other white, to Gaia and Helios, the Earth and the Sun. This appears to draw the line pretty clearly between some leading ideas of the worship of the two countries; which nevertheless had, as is plain, many points of contact.

When we come to the actual Invocation, Agamemnon officiates on behalf of both parties[2]. Accordingly he first invokes Zeus (but as ruling from Ida); then the all-seeing, all-hearing Helios; and then he inserts, before Gaia, the Rivers; and he adds the deities (without naming them) who dwell beneath, and who punish perjurers in the Future State, or Underworld.

[1] Il. iii. 103.   [2] Il. iii. 276-280.

2. In the Nineteenth Iliad we have an oath and Invocation purely Greek[1]; and on comparing it with the former we find

a. That Zeus is invoked without any mention of Ida.

b. The Earth is next named.

c. The Sun is invoked without any special words of personification.

d. The Erinues, strictly ethical personages, are named as the deities below, unnamed in the previous Invocation.

e. The Rivers do not appear.

3. We also have, in the Ninth Iliad, another imprecatory Invocation; that of Althaia, mother of Meleagros. She addresses herself to (*a*) the Earth, (*b*) Aïdoneus, and (*c*) Persephone: and her prayer is heard, and evidently granted as well as heard, by the air-stalking Erinūs. The offence here was not perjury, but the slaying of her brother by her son.

We thus perceive, from the first Invocation, either that the Earth and Sun stood to the Trojans as Zeus did to the Greeks, or that, when all were to be addressed, the Earth and Sun fell to the Trojans from some greater affinity to their creed. But when we come to an Invocation affecting the Greeks alone, in the Nineteenth Book, the Sun is less prominently named, and the purely ethical element is introduced in the Erinues, avengers of perjury in the nether world.

In the mixed Invocation the Erinues are not named, but are evidently the personages glanced at as avengers beneath the earth and after death.

[1] Il. xix. 258–260.

We also find it clearly established by these passages, that the Nature-gods in general were treated by Homer as subterranean: though this did not absolutely and invariably exclude them from the Olympian family. And the office generally assigned to them is not' a share in the ordinary government of the world, but is the infliction of punishment, both for perjury and also for other offences, in a future state.

Hence it is that Achilles, a lock of whose hair had been promised by his father Peleus to be dedicated to the River Spercheios on his return home, deposits such a lock, at the time when he knows he shall not return home at all, in the hands of the dead Patroclos; that his spirit may carry it to the River-god, in the Underworld[1]. Here we have the clearest evidence that the Underworld, into which Patroclos was about to find entrance, was the ordinary residence of the River-gods.

Nor is this the only case of River-worship in the Poems. The Pulians in the Epeian even sacrificed a bull to Alpheios[2], when they reached his banks; and Odysseus likewise invokes the unnamed River of Scherie, at whose mouth he touches the shore[3]. These two, it will be observed, were plainly acts of worship with reference to some immediate result, and implied the exercise by the Rivers respectively of some present prerogatives. On the other hand we may notice their strictly local character, as well as that of the act done by Achilles.

To the great Olympian Assembly of the Twentieth Book, which is to prepare the way for a decisive issue

---

[1] Il. xxiii. 144-151.   [2] Il. xi. 728.   [3] Od. v. 445.

to the war, Themis summons the Rivers (except old Okeanos) and the Nymphs who frequent or inhabit the groves and fountains. These latter, both here and elsewhere, are evidently conceived under the conditions of the human form. A like process had been begun with the Rivers; because Poseidon[1] accomplishes his purpose with Turo in the form of the River Enipeus. Others, too, of the Rivers have human sons. Nay, they even sate on the burnished chairs of the Olympian Hall[2].

Nor let it be thought strange, that while the worship (except for imprecation) of the greater deities of the old Pelasgian system had been superseded, that of smaller ones had thus survived. For the Dii majores of that system, by reason of their very greatness, had no one exclusive residence. But the River-worship was strictly local; and it is the nature of this local worship, in whatever age, and in connection with whatever creed, to take a deep hold, and live a tenacious life. Of this there can be no stronger proof than the great number of temples recorded in Pausanias as having been erected in honour of deities, whose existence is hardly traceable in the public and national religion of historic Greece. Just so it was that the heathen system, when it was slowly and reluctantly yielding its ground to Christianity, lingered long in the villages and remoter districts, and thus gave us, as if by caprice, the singular name of Paganism for the religion, which had blazed with such extraordinary splendour in the Forum of Rome, and on the Acropolis of Athens.

[1] Od. xl. 241.   [2] Il. xx. 11.

There is another form of relation between the older and the younger scheme. While the anthropomorphic spirit of the Olympian religion repels the counter-system of elemental worship, it nevertheless appropriates its materials, and even exhibits occasionally traces of its form. Thus, while the air- or sky-god becomes Zeus, the rainbow becomes Iris: and, as the rainbow in nature belongs strictly and exclusively to the sky-region, so Iris remains in the closest adherence to Zeus. She is his messenger, not the messenger of the gods in general; and even when he sits on Ida, she is in attendance on him, and available for a mission [1]. And as we may suppose that Ida was the habitual resort of Zeus when the armies were on the field, we can thus understand, not only why it is Iris who informs the Trojans about the Greek array [2], but how she is at hand to prompt Helen's going to the Wall [3], and to take Aphroditè out of the turmoil, and drive her, in the chariot of Arès, to Olympos [4].

In like manner, Herè appears to be constructed out of the old traditions which treated the Earth as a divine power: Demeter from a like source: and Hephaistos from an elemental god of fire.

If the local cultus thus survived in fact long after the central system had been eclipsed and superseded by one founded on ideas of greater vigour and elevation, then Homer, who of course had to exercise his plastic powers as a poet upon traditions which he found ready to hand, could not wholly extinguish the representation of these minor nature-powers in his Olympian system. And the ultimate form of recon-

[1] Il. viii. 399.   [2] Il. ii. 786.
[3] Il. iii. 121.   [4] Il. v. 353-369.

ciliation for the two systems was not in the ejection of the minor powers, but in the establishment of their assumption of human form, and with it the presidency over the object in which they at first inhered, as the condition of enlistment, so to speak, in the popular religion. Such was the basis of compromise, so to call it, which secured to Rivers, Fountains, Hills, and Woods, in each case their proper place in the Olympian system.

To obtain a right view of its nature, the Homeric mythology must be carefully severed, not only from the bygone schemes of Nature-worship, but likewise from (1) the Roman mythology, and (2) the mythology of classical Greece; from this classical system even as we have it in the poets, and much more as we draw it from the later writers.

We then find that the Homeric formation consists of a Polity, framed on the human model, with a king, an aristocracy, and even a people or multitude; and that its seat is on Olympos. The king is Zeus. The aristocracy consists of a number not precisely defined. Somewhere about eight or ten deities take actual part in the debates of Olympos. The ordinary meetings are strictly analagous to those of the βουλή or council of the Greek army. But, like that council, the Olympian court has its silent members: and as Hephaistos prepared for it twenty chairs[1] or thrones, we must suppose this to have been the approximate number of those who were entitled to attend. This is the body, of which the feastings are so gorgeously described; and in it are, probably, included all the deities, who had obtained more than a narrowly local recognition in the Greece of Homer.

[1] Il. xviii. 373.

O

But sometimes the gods meet in (ἀγορὴ) their Assembly [1]. Homer appears to use this phrase on occasions when a great resolution is about to be taken.
The Assembly of the Fourth Book defeats the Pact of
the Third, and brings the Greeks into the field against
the Trojans during the isolation of Achilles. That of the
Eighth is designed to insure the absence of their potent
patrons from the field of battle. Greatest of all, the
Assembly of the Twentieth Book is brought together
by a wider summons, including Nymphs and Rivers.
This Assembly removes the embargo, and by permitting
the battle of the gods, forecasts the corresponding victory of the stronger party upon earth.

In the members of the Olympian Court itself we discern every kind of heterogeneity. There seems to be
scarcely a single definite feature that they possess in
common: only we may assert that every one of them
has a preternatural superiority to man in some one or
more particulars, while a few approximate to divine
perfections.

They seem, indeed, in no case to be liable to total and
final extinction [2]. Yet Ares, having fled from Diomed,
declares, not only that he might have remained sense-
less under the blows of the warrior, but might have
suffered (δηρὸν) indefinitely long, left among the slain.
And the gods may be deposed from Olympos, as Zeus
says he would have deposed Ares, if born from any
other divine sire than himself.

In the Fifteenth Iliad, Poseidon appears to be threatened with Tartaros, as the consequence of the formidable conflict between Zeus and himself, which had
seemed so imminent. The gods beneath, says Zeus,

[1] Il. iv. 1; viii. 2; xx. 4.   [2] Il. v. 901.

who form the Court of Kronos, would have become right well acquainted with the battle. As those gods are wholly cut off from Olympian action, this could only have been, as it seems, if Zeus had placed Poseidon where he had already placed Kronos [1]. Even Herè and Athenè may suffer wounds, from which ten whole years will not suffice for their recovery [2]. And if they had persisted in the second descent, then, smitten by the thunderbolt, they would not have been again admitted to Olympos [3].

The same notion of right which binds men together, prevails among the gods, but may be set at nought by them [4]. The happiness of Olympian Immortals is liable to be impaired and disturbed by quarrels on account of their partialities to men this way or that, as the happiness of men would be disturbed [5]. The community of gods is no less emphatically humanised, than are the individuals. The relations of its members to one another are, however, but partially defined, and are subject to contingency.

Hardly any two deities are of the same dignity; and even when they discharge the same function, they do it under different conditions. Thus Athenè and Arès are the deities of war [6]. Arès fights with his own hand against a mortal: his opponent Athenè does not deign to enter into conflict herself; she incites [7] the mind, drives [8] the chariot, but only against a god, and impels or diverts the weapon [9].

While however Athenè thus behaves in relation to Arès, we have no similar example in the action of the

[1] Il. xv. 221-228.　　[2] Il. viii. 404.　　[3] Il. viii. 455.
[4] Il. v. 761.　　[5] Il. l. 573-576; v. 383, 384, and 873, 874.
[6] Il. v. 430.　　[7] Il. v. 500.　　[8] Il. v. 840.　　[9] Il. v. 290, 856.

Poems, of matters carried to extremity in the upper rank of the Olympian Court. On the contrary, the highest deities of Homer are bound together by a law of mutual respect, even when they take opposite sides of a question or a quarrel, and they show the utmost anxiety to avoid carrying their differences to issue. After all, is it not a folly, they commonly say, to diminish our own happiness on account of beings so inferior to ourselves?

See the language of Zeus to Athenè, Il. viii. 39;
Of Zeus about Poseidon, Il. xv. 226-228;
Of Apollo to Poseidon, Il. xxi. 462-467;
Of Herè about Zeus, Il. viii. 427-431;
Of Athenè about Poseidon, Od. xiii. 341-343;
And, although Hermes is a god of lower stamp, of Hermes to Leto, Il. xxi. 498.

Again, with a great delicacy, Homer never allows any of the higher deities to be named to mortals as being in conflict one with another. Thus when Diomed ascribes to Apollo the escape of Hector, and makes an appeal for himself to divine aid [1], he does not, as on other occasions (e. g. Il. x. 284), name Athenè as his protectress, but says,

' If perchance I too may have a god for my ally.'

So Poseidon, in the form of Calchas, urging on the two Aiantes, and referring to Hector as claiming to be the son of Zeus, and as perhaps having his aid [2], suggests that ' some one of the gods' might help one of them to make an effectual resistance. In reply, the Oilean Ajax observes that the pretended Calchas is some one of the gods of Olympos [3]. Thus no deity is placed by name in opposition to Zeus.

[1] Il. xi. 362-366.   [2] Il. xiii. 54-58.   [3] Il. xiii. 68.

And thus it is contrived, that Poseidon shall retire
from the field (Il. xv. 218) before Apollo arrives there
to renovate Hector (239).

In the Seventeenth Book, when Athenè[1] appears, that
she may give effect to the altered policy of Zeus,
Apollo does not absolutely retire, but the agency of
the two is so directed as to avoid collision. For when
Athenè has incited Menelaos, and Apollo then kindles
Hector, the two warriors do not meet in fight. Once
more, when Achilles (Il. xx. 450) recognises the fact
that Apollo has carried off Hector, he expresses a hope
that τὶς θεῶν may aid him too. In a word, the greater
gods of Homer never are brought into conflict, nor
do they exhibit their differences within the human
sphere.

In Book xx, Herè consults Poseidon and Athenè
(v. 115) as to the mode of counteracting the agency
of Apollo, who is accompanying Æneas against
Achilles. ' Let us,' she says, ' force him back: and
then some one of us can go to attend Achilles' (119–
121). Poseidon, in his reply, is unwilling to bring
gods into conflict, ' unless Ares or Apollo should begin,
or should hinder Achilles' (132–143) in his work of
havoc.

And when, finally, Zeus exhibits the golden scales
in the air, that which holds the fate of Hector sinks
to Hades, and thereupon Apollo quits him. It is then
only that Athenè, who was at hand and ready (see
v. 187), joins and accompanies Achilles[2].

But this mutual respect is only one among many
notes of difference, which separate the orders of deity
in the Olympian Court.

---

[1] Il. xvii. 544.   [2] Il. xxii. 208-214.

The Olympian personages of Homer may be divided into several classes, in several respects.

Firstly. We may consider them as background and foreground personages. The background personages are little heard of, and scarcely affect the machinery of government for the Homeric world. Such are Demeter, Themis, Leto, Dionè, Hebè; such are the Muses, and the Charites or Graces; independently of the Nature-powers, who are summoned to Olympos on great and special occasions, but who take no active part in superintending human affairs at large.

Secondly. The foreground personages may be divided into those of higher and of lower power.

Of higher power we have only Zeus, Herè, Poseidon, Athenè, and Apollo.

Thirdly. The Olympian deities may again be divided into two classes, of the higher and the lower ἦθος, or moral tone, respectively. The three first divinities are of the lower, and the two last of the higher, in regard to all those matters which pertain to the morality and to the infirmity, or ἀσρασία, of man.

Zeus, in his Olympian personality, stands with the class to which Herè and Poseidon belong; while, as the traditional representative of providence and the Theistic idea, he ranks more justly with Athenè and Apollo.

Of the class lower both in power, and in moral tone, we have Hephaistos, Arès, Hermes, Aphroditè.

All, except the highest gods, in Homer may be said generally to be subject to the following limitations and liabilities:—

1. They do not know what events take place among men, except by the common senses of sound or sight,

and when favourably placed; for example, when near at hand, or when sound is loud.

2. They do not know what is in the mind, and must ask to be informed.

3. They shriek or cry aloud from emotion.

4. When they move, it is (*a*) by gradual progression; (*b*) with means of conveyance.

5. They are liable to be hurt and wounded.

6. Human warriors can contend against them.

7. Their worship is peculiar to some races or places.

8. They are even liable to disparagement in communications held by the higher gods with men.

9. They have little or no command over outward nature and the elements.

10. They do not habitually repair to Olympos[1].

11. Their partialities and propensities are without system, policy, or governing mind.

12. They neither have divine foreknowledge, nor, in many cases, have they prudence or forethought equal to the human.

13. They are not able immediately to influence the human mind.

The only deities who may be called absolutely free from all these limitations are Zeus, Athenè, and Apollo.

Even Herè is subject to some of them: Poseidon to more.

Not even those deities, who are omnipresent upon earth, and take cognisance of all human affairs, are precisely informed as to what takes place in the supernal region; for when Herè sent Iris to Achilles, in

---

[1] Where, however, Hephaistos lived (Il. xviii. 143–147); but perhaps for special reasons.

the Eighteenth Iliad[1], to urge him to appear before the
contending armies, it was done without the knowledge
either of Zeus or of any other deity.

Certain special features, as we have seen, and shall
further see, are traceable, most of all in the Athenè
and Apollo of the Homeric Poems, but also in Zeus,
and (more forcibly) in Leto and in Iris, as well as in
one or two other Olympian personages: and these features, in the case of the two first-named deities particularly, impart to the pictures of them an extraordinary
elevation and force, such as to distinguish them broadly
from the delineations of other gods, in whom these particular features are wanting. The features themselves
are in the most marked correspondence with the Hebraic
traditions, as conveyed in the books of Holy Scripture,
and also as handed down in the auxiliary sacred learning
of the Jews. But while it seems impossible to deny the
correspondence without doing violence to facts, on the
other hand we are not able to point out historically the
channel of communication through which these traditions were conveyed into Greece, and became operative
in the formation of the Olympian scheme.

At first sight we should be tempted to suppose that
the Phœnician navigators offered the natural and probable explanation of any such phenomena. Because,
on the one hand, we know, from the historic books of
Scripture, that the Phœnicians were at an early date
in habits of intercourse with the Jews; while, on the
other hand, they not only were in like habits with the
Achaian Greeks of Homer, but also, as far as we can
discern, no other nation had a sensible amount of

[1] vv. 183-186.

intercourse with Greece, or if there were such, it passed under the Phœnician name.

And again, there is one of the legends of Homer with reference to which the presumption arises with a peculiar force.

Apart from any disposition to premature deduction or imaginative interpretation, it seems obvious to observe upon the striking similarity between the legend of Bellerophon, solicited by the wife of Proitos, and that of Joseph, by the wife of Potiphar.

And the great abundance of tales forming the outer circle of the Odyssey, which (it is hardly too much to say) can only have had a Phœnician origin, and which touch almost every point of the compass except that to the eastward of Phœnicia itself, suggests the likelihood that this enterprising people would not be destitute of reports from that quarter also.

The name of Proitos[1], appearing on one of the seven gates of Thebes, which mark its Phœnician re-foundation, supplies a positive link between the legend of Bellerophon and the source to which I am ascribing it.

A second such link is supplied by the written characters, in which Proitos communicated with the King of Lycia respecting Bellerophon. The art of writing, according to the later tradition, was brought by Phœnicians into Greece; and the name of Proitos distinctly connects the text of Homer with that belief.

Our finding the family of Bellerophon in close relations with Proitos tends, of itself, to induce a belief in their ethnical connection. This presumption comes into clearer light when we observe that Bellerophon was an Aiolid.

[1] Paus. p. 727.

It must also be admitted that, in supposing any other channels than the Phœnician for the conveyance of these traditions, we should force them up to a very early point of time, namely, that of the separation of the Semitic, and the Japhetic or Aryan, branches of the human family.

It is however admitted that the Olympian scheme has for its distinctive character, or *differentia*, the intense action of the anthropomorphic principle ; which pervades and moulds the whole, repelling, and as it were repudiating, on the one hand all abstract speculations about the Deity, on the other the worship of Nature-Powers and of the animal creation. It is also clear, that some of the Hebraic traditions were eminently calculated to develop the anthropomorphic principle. The promise or expectation of a Redeemer, or Deliverer, of man, who should be at once human and divine, laid a basis for the entire system, by annexing the glory of divine attributes to the corporeal form of man. And the seed thus supplied was vivified, so to speak, by the familiar belief in the intercourse of God with the patriarchs, which so readily adapts itself to, if indeed it does not require, the use of a form approaching at least to the human type.

Every race had its own religious traditions. Each modified, or kept, or lost them, in obedience to its ruling tendencies. It does not seem strange that the tribe or tribes, whatever they were, which brought into Greek life and religion what proved to be their central principle, should have clung with a great tenacity to, and preserved far more faithfully than other races of a less fine composition, those traditions which were so well adapted to the effective development of their peculiar genius.

Among the Hebrews, besides what has been enshrined in the Sacred Scriptures, there was a stream
of tradition [1] otherwise delivered and relating to the
Messiah, which, though it nowhere impugns or even
varies, yet vividly illustrates the written record. I
subjoin some particulars.

1. The Messiah was to be divine.

2. He was conceived of as 'the Glory of God' in the
feminine gender.

3. The relation of His two natures was set forth
in the figure of mother and daughter.

4. He was to be the Logos, the Word or Wisdom
of God.

5. He was the Lord of Hosts—an idea which would
naturally take form in some martial development.

6. He was especially The Light.

7. He was to be the Mediator, through whom the
counsels of God take effect upon man.

8. He was to perform miracles.

9. He was to conquer the Evil One, and to libe-
rate the dead from the grave and from the power of
hell.

10. And, generally, the divine qualities were all
to be reflected in the Messiah (conceived as masculine)
or Shechinah (as feminine) [2].

We may probably regard the use of the feminine
gender in these traditions as having been either (1) the
most convenient mode of impersonating an abstract
idea of the Wisdom of God, or (2) as suggested by

---

[1] Studies, vol. ii. pp. 48–51.

[2] Ib. vol. ii. pp. 51–53. Taken principally from Schüttgen's
Horae Hebraicae.

the arrangements of the Egyptian, or other Eastern religions.

This is not the place to discuss at large the origin of the numerous religions which have existed outside the pale of the Divine revelation. It was a favourite opinion with the Christian apologists, Eusebius and others, that the pagan deities represented deified men [1]. Others consider them to signify the powers of external nature personified. For others they are, in many cases, impersonations of human passions and propensities, reflected back from the mind of man. A fourth mode of interpretation would treat them as copies, distorted and depraved, of a primitive system of religion given by God to man. The Apostle St. Paul speaks of them as devils [2]; by which he may perhaps intend to convey that, under the names and in connection with the worship of those deities, the worst influences of the Evil One were at work. This would rather be a subjective than an objective description; and would rather convey an account of the practical working of a corrupted religion, than an explanation of its origin or its early course. As between the other four, it seems probable that they all, in various degrees and manners, entered into the composition of the later paganism, and also of the Homeric or Olympian system. That system, however, was profoundly adverse to mere Nature-worship; while the care of departments or provinces of external nature were assigned to its leading personages. Such worship of natural objects or elemental powers, as prevailed in connection with it, was in general local or secondary. And the deifi-

---

[1] See the Propaldeia or Præparatio Evangelica of Eusebius, *passim.*   [2] 1 Cor. x. 20.

cation of heroes in the age of Homer was rare and
merely titular. We do not find that any cult or
system of devotion was attached to it.

The preternatural machinery of the Homeric Poems,
besides its other qualities, is singularly complex and
comprehensive. Its complexity is doubtless due to the
fact, that Homer had to represent and to harmonise
the several varieties of religion, which had found its
way into the country in company with immigrating
races, families, or persons. Its comprehensiveness is
owing to that anthropomorphic principle on which it is
framed, and which borrowed from earth, and carried up
to Olympos, the state, the family, and the individual,
as they exist among men.

The bold invention by which the gods take sides
in the War of Troy, and decide the controversy by
main force in heaven, before it can finally be brought to
issue on the plain between the Achaian and Trojan
armies, is not a flight of the imagination only. The
partisanship of the respective deities, this way and
that, is evidently dictated by sympathies of race.
Neither the blood, nor yet the religion, of the two
countries were wholly separate; but differences of
leaning and of colour between them may readily be
discerned upon a close examination. And again,
the mode in which general rules are occasionally
varied in the Poems, irresistibly suggests that there
is a reason both for the rule and for the exceptions;
as, for example, in the care of Poseidon for Æneas
the Trojan, and in his persecution of Odysseus the
Greek. We may also discern the marks of subdivided
attachments. The care of Athenè is exercised chiefly
on behalf first of Odysseus, next to him of Achilles,

and next to him of Diomed. The care of Herè is
for the Pelopid family, and apparently for the Greeks
as the people whom they lead. Irrespectively, then,
of the manifold interest attaching to the Homeric
mythology, both as a religion and as poetry, it is
in truth a main key to the ethnography of the Poems,
and even might on this account be taken as a point of
departure in an investigation, which it influences from
first to last.

The personages of the Homeric Theotechny, under
which name I include the whole of the supernatural
beings, of whatever rank, introduced into the Poems,
are so diversified in character, intellect, and power,
that while they cannot be described under any one
common form, it is difficult to divide them into classes
with anything like precision. Into the following categories, however, we may distribute them with a
tolerable approach to accuracy.

1. The Olympian deities; recognised and actual
governors, but with immensely different titles and
prerogatives, either of the inner and Greek world, or
of the outer world known more faintly and indirectly
to the Greeks.

2. The greater Nature-Powers, with Okeanos at their
head, who had apparently been supreme in the prior or
Pelasgian Theogony.

3. The lesser Nature-Powers, who continued to hold
their ground, at least in local influence.

4. Minor deities of foreign tradition, neither naturalised nor acknowledged in Greece, as not being of
sufficient significance to claim admission to Olympos.

5. Rebellious powers.

6. Ministers of Doom and Justice, real or reputed;

less than divinities in rank, but more closely associated with the moral order.

7. Impersonated ideas connected with the objects of human desire and aversion, hope and fear.

8. Translated, or deified, heroes.

9. Races intermediate between gods and men.

Again. Many elements of the Hebrew traditions recorded in the Holy Scriptures, or otherwise preserved among the Jews down to later times, appear in the Olympian Court of Homer. But they are not found in all the personages that compose the assemblage; nor even in all those deities whom, from various kinds of evidence in the Poems, we perceive to have been fully recognised as objects of the national worship. Further, in the characters where the features corresponding with Hebrew traditions mainly appear, there is a peculiar elevation of tone, and a remarkable degree of reverence is maintained towards them, so as to separate them, not indeed by an uniform, but commonly by a perceptible and even a broad line, from the remainder of the gods.

Besides the idea of a Deity which in some sense is three in one, the traditions traceable in Homer, which appear to be drawn from the same source as those of Holy Scripture, are chiefly these :—(1) A Deliverer, conceived under the double form, first of the 'seed of the woman'—a being at once Divine and human, secondly of the Logos, the Word or Wisdom of God. (2) Next, the woman whose seed this Redeemer was to be. (3) Next, the rainbow considered as a means, or a sign, of communication between God and man. And finally the tradition of an Evil Being, together with his ministers, working

under the double form described by Moloch in his
speech, of 'open war,' and of 'wiles;' as a rebel,
and as a tempter. This last tradition is indeed
shivered into fragments, such as the giants precipitated
into Tartaros, and as Atè roaming on the earth; with
perhaps a portion of the idea lodged in Kronos, whose
common and only description in Homer is 'Kronos
of the crooked thought' (ἀγκυλομήτης). The other four
traditions appear to be represented in the persons
of Apollo, Athenè, Leto, and Iris. Of course it by
no means follows that they have no other origin than
in these traditions, or that, as they stand in Homer,
they represent such traditions and nothing else. Iris,
for example, must evidently be considered as an impersonation of a Nature-Power. What seems to me
undeniable is that, in the Poems of Homer, the traditions I have named are at the least copiously and
richly embroidered upon the tissue, supplied by other
accounts of the mythological persons I have named;
and that they give to those persons a distinctiveness
of character and form, which upon a close and detailed
view of the Olympian system, as it is unfolded in the
Poems of Homer, cannot well be mistaken by a pains-
taking and unprejudiced observer. If, in the progress
of time, and with the mutations which that system
gradually underwent, the marks of correspondence with
the Hebrew records became more faint, the fact even
raises some presumption that, were we enabled to
go yet further back, we should obtain yet fuller and
clearer evidence of their identity of origin in certain
respects.

Even the highest conception of deity in Homer does
not exclude the element of fraud. I will give an

example. There can be no question that the prize of
the loftiest, most free, and most constant and unvary-
ing intelligence in the whole catalogue of Olympian
deities must be given to Athenè; who, alone among
them, is never ignorant of what it concerns her to
know, never exposed to disrespect, never outwitted by
an opponent, never disappointed of an end. But, in
the great crisis of Hector and Achilles, when the intrinsic superiority of the Greek hero makes him independent of any even more honourable aid, she descends
to the mean and shameful artifice of assuming the form
of his brother Deiphobos, whom he especially loved and
trusted, to induce him to turn and meet his adversary[1].
This arrangement is the more remarkable, because it
is somewhat difficult to discern the motive for such an
intervention, or to see why Achilles could not, with
his extraordinary swiftness of foot, have overtaken
Hector apart from any assistance whatever. Perhaps
it was an artifice of the Poet to uplift the character of
Hector, of course in order to glorify yet further the
Greek hero, who was to overcome him.

Those pure and lofty traditions, then, which we are
justly wont to refer to a primitive revelation as their
fountain-head, had already begun to be impaired. And
it is only what we ought to expect, if we find that with
the lapse of time they suffered further deterioration,
and if the persons representing them gradually sunk
nearer and nearer to the level of those other Olympian
deities who had already in the time of Homer lost, or
who perhaps never had possessed, any notes of the sublime conceptions which the Holy Scriptures, and in some
degree the auxiliary traditions of the Hebrews, have

[1] Il. xxii. 214-247.

P

handed down to us in the greatest purity, and which
the peculiar genius that became dominant in the Greek
religion had, for a time at least, been able to preserve,
if not from all injurious contact, yet from anything like
absolute immersion in the mire. The Athenè and
Apollo of the Olympian system may be compared with
the Child in the noble Ode of Wordsworth; about
whom, in his infancy, Heaven is lying, who as boy and
youth

> Yet by the vision splendid
> Is on his way attended;

but who in process of time parts from it altogether:

> At length the man perceives it die away,
> And fade into the light of common day[1].

It is no part of the object of this work to institute
a detailed comparison between the earliest and the
later stages of the morality and religion of the heathen
world; but I shall now state summarily the results
which such a comparison would, I think, reasonably
suggest, so far as religion is concerned.

Religion and race have ever run much together. We
find in Homer the clear tokens of a composite people,
and of a composite belief. With the lapse of time the
edges and angles of ethnical differences are worn down.
The nation and the creed settle down upon an acknowledged platform; and the distinctive features, though
they do not wholly vanish, take a form which it is difficult to trace back to their first origin. All formations,
especially if complex, must be examined in their beginnings. The religion of classical and historic Greece
is already an old religion. The Poems of Homer enable

---

[1] Wordsworth's Ode on the Recollections of Childhood.

us to investigate its first inception. We can trace the very finger of the artist on the clay he moulded for his countrymen's behoof. But as the nation was compacted and consolidated, the component parts of the religion also settled down, and their specific differences, like colours running, lost all definite outline.

This loss of distinctive notes in the Greek mythology was a deteriorating and not an improving process. The gods of later times were not relieved from the stains which attach to them in Homer. Some legends, which with him appear in a beautiful and noble shape, became utterly abominable and base. While the level of the higher characters of his Theogony was reduced till it nearly reached that of the lower, the level of the lower was in no way raised. In the processes of change, nothing was given, all was taken away.

But the grand distinction between the Homeric and the later systems was this: that the earlier scheme was a real, though it was a corrupt, religion. It acted upon life. It menaced the excesses of power. It prescribed the duties of reverence to age and authority, of hospitality to the stranger, and of mercy to the poor. It had one and the same standing with reference to all classes. It did not assign to deity that most ungodlike quality, respect of persons. But in after times, apart from its deeper moral stains, it became wholly severed from the cultured mind; and subsisted mainly as the jest of philosophers and men of the world, the tool of priests and rulers, the bugbear of the vulgar.

Again, it may be noticed that the religion of Homer, subject to varying closeness of relation between different places and particular deities, is, though not an uniform, yet an universal religion.

The Poet evidently supposed that in some manner
the Olympian gods governed not the Greeks only, but
all mankind. This perhaps is the reason why he has
admitted into the Olympian family personages like
Arès, Aphroditè, and the Sun, whom we cannot affirm
to have been worshipped at the time in Greece; the
evidence being, indeed, adverse to any such supposition.
This element of truth in his conceptions of Deity is
clearly exhibited by the banquets provided for his gods
among the Aithiopes; by the scene of the Iliad, in
which Zeus turns his eyes over the country of the Hippemolgoi and the Abioi[1]; and especially by this, that,
in the wide range of the Voyage of Odysseus, though
he comes within the special jurisdiction first of Poseidon, and next of Helios, still there is always a power
of supreme control lodged in the Olympian Assembly;
a power, by means of which his release from the island
of Calypso is finally obtained.

It seems as if his primitive spirit had been unable
to embrace the conception, which in later times came
into vogue, of different and unconnected deities ruling
different portions of mankind; and as if both his own
and the prevailing religious sense required that, although
the name and worship of many among them had originally come from, or even still belonged to, a foreign
shore, yet they should, as far as their importance required him to take notice of them, be bound together
into a supreme and organised unity. But, notwithstanding, within the bosom of this unity the character and
associations of his own race, which, without doubt, he
placed at the head of all mankind, were to be predomi-

[1] Il. xiii. 3-6.

nant. In this combination of ideas we find the basis, and the warrant, of his Olympian system.

The collective action of the Olympian deities in the government of men is less infirm, more venerable, more divine, than their individual action. When they move together, the mere idiosyncracies, in which they abound, appear to be in a great degree lost and absorbed. The co-operation of the three great Hellenising deities in the War against Troy is, indeed, the efficient cause of the divine decision in favour of the Greeks. And this again is mythically referred to a vindictive sentiment on the part of each of the men; yet the decision is a righteous decision. And, speaking generally, while the individual members of the Olympian Court are swayed by hate, lust, and greed, they have not any objects which they can pursue in common for the gratification of these appetites or passions; and thus is neutralised the personal bias which so frequently draws them off the line of moral obligation, and more free scope is given, in all their common action, to the exercise of the true governing office.

It is somewhat singular that we have not, in the true Olympian religion, any clear instance of a married deity, except Zeus. Hephaistos is married to Aphroditè only in the Phœnician, or rather perhaps Syrian, mythology of the Eighth Odyssey. In the Iliad he is but wooing Charis[1]. That Amphitritè is the wife of Poseidon is a purely gratuitous assumption, and is in every way improbable, since Amphitritè has no clear or definite impersonation. Helios and Persè had children; but they are wholly within the Eastern mythology. The names of Aïdes and Persephonè are commonly

---

[1] Il. xviii. 382.

combined in such a way as would be consistent with, and as may even suggest, their being married. But this would scarcely harmonise with his general arrangements, if Demeter was the mother of Persephonè, and if Aïdoneus[1] was an earthy Zeus. And Homer has carefully avoided using any words which would directly place them in this relation. Okeanos and Tethūs, Kronos and Rhea, lie outside the Olympian scheme.

If this observation be correct, the fact is probably to be accounted for in this way: Homer had no idea of a normal marriage without issue. Where there were none, it was a heaven-sent calamity. He could not, then, have divinities distributed in barren pairs. But to have provided them with families would have placed him in difficulties, such as may sometimes be felt by royalty on earth, with respect to the means of providing for a numerous offspring. It would have been difficult to weave them into the stock of traditions which supplied his raw material. Moreover, as between brothers and sisters, the Greek horror of incest perhaps would ill have allowed the general use of the idea of a matrimonial connection; though Herè was the sister as well as the wife of Zeus, and though this double relation was not at all foreign to such Eastern traditions[2] as he had received through the Phœnicians. Thus he was shut up on all sides to arranging his Olympos, as to its younger generation, in the form of the single though manifold family of Zeus.

Again. Within the theological system of Homer, and as a kind of kernel to it, there lies a system which may be called one of deontology, or that which ought to be, and to be done. 'Will' is the supreme element

---

[1] See *infra*, Aïdoneus.   [2] Od. x. 5–9.

in the mythological action; or, at the least, it is in
practice co-ordinate with 'ought,' and it seems to be
in conduct the livelier principle of the two. But
the idea conveyed in 'ought' has a separate sphere,
and ministers of its own, to which even Olympian
personages pay regard. Its laws are expressed sometimes in terms relating to destiny: most purely of all
in ὅπις and in νέμεσις; which may truly be said to
reflect the moral sense of the gods, and which are
never used by Homer to express a mere mental emotion of mankind. They may convey more or less the
sense of an emotion, but it is an emotion always
springing from and regulated by a regard to the essential laws of right, to the themistes of heaven. A third
form, in which the dictates of the moral law are expressed and enforced, is in the action of its mute but
ever active ministers, the Erinues.

These topics will be opened in their due order. I
pass to another head.

Homer informs us in the Eighteenth Iliad that
Hephaistos was found by Thetis busy in finishing a
set of twenty seats[1], for the members of the Olympian Court to use in their assemblies. I have observed
that, with some allowance for the vagueness common
with the Poet in the use of figures, we may take this
incident as indicating pretty closely what he meant to
be understood as the number of the Dî majores, or
personages qualified to attend at the Council (boulè) of
the gods.

As to nearly the whole of them, there is no difficulty
in drawing out the roll :—

[1] Il. xviii. 372-377.

I. The children of Kronos:—

    1. Zeus
•   2. Poseidon
    3. Aïdoneus   } 4
    4. Herè

II. The secondary wives of Zeus:—

    1. Leto
    2. Demeter   } 3
    3. Dionè

III. The children of Zeus:—

    1. Athenè
    2. Apollo
    3. Hephaistos
    4. Hermes
    5. Artemis   } 8
    6. Arès
    7. Persephonè
    8. Aphroditè

IV. Personages not classified, but performing
    Olympian offices:—

    1. Themis, the Summoner
    2. Iris, the Envoy   } 3
    3. Hebè, the Cupbearer

                                18

Besides these eighteen we have

1. Helios, the Sun, taking part in Olympian proceedings[1].

2. Paieon, who appears to be ordinarily present there as Healer[2].

Both these personages came to be absorbed in Apollo: but in Homer they are distinct from him: and, so far as the poet may have had a distinct intention as to number, these two have perhaps the best claim to the Nineteenth and Twentieth places.

3. Another claim, making the Twenty-first, is that of Dionusos; whose position, however, in Homer is faintly marked and somewhat equivocal[3].

On the whole we ought perhaps to reject two other names.

1. Eris, or Enuo, the sister and the paramour of Arès[4]. She grows up, and this as it seems habitually, from small to huge dimensions. She remains to witness the battle of the Eleventh Iliad, while the other deities withdraw to their Olympian palaces respectively[5]. She is sent down to the camp at the beginning of the same Book, and shouts from the ship of Odysseus. She is named, too, together with Pallas[6], in contrast with the effeminate Aphroditè. Yet, on the whole, she is probably no more than a vivid poetical impersonation. In conformity with this supposition, while Arès carries a spear as he leads the Trojans to the fight, she conducts, instead, another form yet more shadowy than her own, that of Kudoimos, or Tumult.

2. Histiè, who is Vesta, and one of the Dî majores,

---

[1] Od. vîli. 270, 302, and xii. 374-376.
[2] Il. v. 401, 899.
[3] *Infra,* ch. viii. sect. Dionusos.
[4] Il. iv. 441.
[5] Il. xi. 3, 4, 73.
[6] Il. v. 333, 592.

in the Roman mythology, and who is also fully personified in the post-Homeric poetry of the Greeks, can scarcely be considered as a person in the view of Homer. There are indeed invocations to her name[1], which signifies ' the hearth,' in the Odyssey; but in three cases out of the five it is combined with that of the table for guests.

[1] Od. xiv. 159; xvii. 160; xix. 304; xx. 230.

CHAPTER VIII.

The Divinities of Olympos.

Section I. *Zeus.*

Zeus presents to us a character more heterogeneous and less consistent than that of any other Homeric deity.

He claims a strength superior to the united strength of all the gods[1]; yet he admits that he would have some difficulty[2] in putting down Poseidon singlehanded; and he was actually delivered by a giant[3] from fetters into which he had been, or was about to be, thrown by a combination of that god with Athenè and Herè.

In many points he inherits the traditions, and is formed upon the conception, of the One and Supreme God. Yet he was one of three brothers, who had parents preceding them: the three were born to equal honour[4]: lot alone decided their several domains. Seniority gives Zeus the first place: yet the filial tie had not prevented him from imprisoning his own father in perpetuity. He is alike the depository of high moral ideas, and of intense, as well as of debased, human

[1] Il. iv. 17-27.
[2] Il. xv. 228.
[3] Il. i. 399-406.
[4] Il. xv. 209.

attributes. He bears many different characters; and no one of them is altogether consistent with the rest.

There are five different capacities in which, in order to embrace the entire picture drawn by the Poet, he must be regarded. Four of them are Olympian: one appertains to an earlier theogonic scheme.

1. Zeus is the meeting-point of the Pelasgic with the Olympian or Hellenic system of religion.

2. He is the depository of the principal remnants of monotheistic and providential ideas.

3. He is the sovereign lord of meteorological phenomena.

4. He is the head of the Olympian Court.

5. He is the most marked receptacle of all such earthly, sensual, and appetitive elements as, at the time of Homer, anthropophuism had obtruded into the sphere of deity.

On the epithets and verbal ascriptions of Zeus, we may observe,

1. That they much exceed in number and variety those of any other deity.

2. That with few and special exceptions they are applied to him exclusively.

3. That they divide themselves into classes according as they belong to him,

a. In respect of national or special worship, as Dodonaios, Idaios, Pelasgicos, Olumpios.

b. In respect of his chief place in the Hellenic theogony, as air-god: such as ἀστεροπητής, νεφεληγερέτης, κελαινεφής, τερπικέραυνος, ἐρίγδουπος, εὐρύοπης.

c. In respect of his character as the Providence and Governor of mankind, and the defender of social and

moral laws: such as θεῶν ὕπατος καὶ ἄριστος, πατὴρ ἀν-
δρῶν τε θεῶν τε, μητιέτης, ξείνιος, ἱκετήσιος: highest and
best of gods, father of gods and men, the Zeus of
counsel, the Zeus of the guest, the Zeus of the suppliant.

Let us now proceed to this fivefold observation of
the Homeric Zeus.

1. *The Pelasgian Zeus.*

At times, the Zeus of Homer appears to border upon
the mere Nature-Power: as in the epithet Διιπετής,
'falling from Zeus,' applied to rivers: in Ἔνδιος,
meaning 'at noontide,' and recalling the 'sub dio, sub
Jove,' of the Latins. Also the expressions, Διὸς ὄμβρος,
αὐγαί, νιφάδες, ὦραι, the rain, rays, snow-flakes, hours
or seasons of Zeus, may all be compared with analogous expressions applied to Demeter and to Hephaistos.
We may consider all these as being, in their various
shades, relics of the Pelasgian worship of Nature-
Powers.

We may in fact either consider the Pelasgian Zeus,
and the Zeus of the anthropomorphic system, as one
or as two. It is probable that two separate clusters
of tradition may have belonged to the same name, and
that in time they coalesced together, in obedience to
the law of public feeling, combined with their respective internal aptitudes. And this condition may have
been the solution no less of a great ethnical than a
great mythological question.

According to the legend of Thetis, in the First
Iliad, there was a time when Herè, Poseidon, and
Athenè combined to put him in bonds. He was saved
from this peril by Thetis, who fetched Briareus, or

Aigaion of the Hundred Hands, to his aid. This giant was stronger than his father Poseidon, and on his arrival the plan was abandoned. Of the three deities named, Herè and Athenè are eminently Hellenic, and Poseidon appears to be Phœnician. The meaning of the legend therefore probably is, that the supremacy of the old, and perhaps purely elemental, Zeus of the Pelasgians was endangered by the arrival of the Phœnician and Hellenic immigrants with their respective religious associations: but that an accommodation was afterwards effected, and a Zeus acknowledged, who sufficiently took into himself the Pelasgian element.

The Zeus of Homer is the Pelasgic Zeus, and the Zeus of Dodona; and he is also worshipped by the Helloi[1]. These Helloi appear to represent the Hellenic race in its pre-Hellenic form; and the Pelasgian name, with that of Dodona, places the throne of Zeus within the shadows of the pre-Hellenic period. It is true that, in the Theogony of Homer, this deity has ancestors and antecessors: and he alone, of the family of gods proper to the Pelasgians, is carried over at once into the Hellenic and Olympian system. This may have been both because, as the god of air and light, he answered best among them to that more abstracted and less materialised conception of Deity which the Hellenic mind required; and because there clustered around him whatever traditions of a supreme and single Being the world of human thought had either fashioned or retained. In any case it is plain that the Poet, having got rid of all claims of priority by relegating the Nature-Powers to the Underworld, or to the sea-floor, or to the extremities of the earth, is thus enabled to

[1] Il. xvi. 233-235.

leave his Zeus firmly grounded in authority as the
senior god of the Olympian system. And this claim
of seniority is the true basis of his supremacy. To
this it is, and by no means to mere excess of force,
that Poseidon defers in the Fifteenth Iliad, as to a
claim profoundly rooted in that moral order, which
even gods acknowledge and respect.

It is at the stage where the Past, having been before
only cloud and mist, becomes for Homer that shaped
tradition which occupied, relatively to his time, the
place of History, that Zeus offers to the mind of the
Greek hearer the earliest definite point upon which
understanding and memory can fix, so that he can be
chosen as, for practical purposes, the origin to which
all things are to be traced up and referred.

It seems likely that this priority of Zeus may lie at
the root of his preference for Troy: a state and people
in which we discern the predominance of a mere Pelasgian character, and where the royal family mounts to a
greater antiquity than that of any properly Hellenic or
Achaian race.

2. *The Divine Zeus.*

To Zeus as Providence belong both a number of
separate ascriptions, and a general position, which
underlies the whole action of the Iliad. The grandeur
of his figure and attributes transcends every other composition. He is identified, in perhaps an hundred
places of the Poems, with the word theos, in its more
abstracted signification as Providence, or the moral
governor of the world. He is the ταμίης πολέμοιο, the
arbiter of war: and he exhibits in the sky, on great

occasions, the scales in which are weighed contending
fates. He is the source of governing authority, and he
shows his displeasure when it is abused[1]. He is the
distributor in general of good and evil among mortals;
for it is on his floor that the two caskets[2] stand, from
which are dispensed the mixed and the unmixed lots of
men. He has the care of the guest, the suppliant, and
the poor; and thus his name becomes the guarantee for
three relations, which were and are fundamental to the
condition of mankind, considered with reference to
social existence. Indeed in this character he is himself a source of Destiny, as we find from the remarkable phrase Διὸς αἶσα, the fate of, or proceeding from,
Zeus.

Zeus approximates to, and perhaps possesses, an ubiquitous or universal supremacy. Hellie and Pelasgian,
Idaian and Olympian, he leads the band of the Immortals to feast during an eleven days' absence on the sacrifices offered by the Aithiopes or Ethiopians, who
occupied the whole southern line of the world of
Homer[3]: and he likewise, in an interval of his cares
respecting Troy, casts his eyes in the far north not
only over Thracians and Mycians, but over Hippemolgoi and Abioi[4]. His name is likewise acknowledged in the border land of Scheriè, and in the outer
sphere where Poseidon rules: for, say the brother Cyclops to the brutal Poluphemos, 'Disease comes from
the mighty Zeus, and cannot be escaped: pray however to thy father the lord Poseidon[5].' From this
passage we perceive that Zeus was not for Homer a
mere name for Poseidon in his own kingdom, as

[1] Il. xvi. 387.   [2] Il. xxiv. 527.   [3] Od. i. 23.
[4] Il. xiii. 1–6.   [5] Od. ix. 411.

Aidoneus is called 'the Zeus beneath[1].' The meaning
more nearly approaches to a recognition of the Providential character of Zeus, as contradistinguished from
his Olympian capacity. In this larger conception his
individual existence at times appears almost wholly to
merge.

Zeus, however, although no positive limits are affixed
to his capacities of perception and knowledge, does not
as a matter of course perceive all that is going on among
mortals. By an expedient of some *naïveté*, he turns
his eyes away from Troy towards Thrace and the
righteous nations of the North, when Poseidon is about
to come into the field. This god, assuming a disguise,
remains there long without being observed, although
the sleep of Zeus has not yet come[2].

And again, to save the body of Patroclos, Herè sends
Iris on a mission to Achilles, which is concealed from
Zeus as well as from the other gods[3] (κρύβδα Διὸς ἄλλων
τε θεῶν).

After the Theomachy also, he inquires of Artemis
who it was that had maltreated her. Yet he had seen,
and had exulted in seeing, the gods as they engaged in
conflict[4].

Besides these physical limitations, Zeus is subject to
deceit. He is entrapped by Herè through the medium
of his passion[5], and is lulled into a sleep, in order that
during his inaction his decree may be disobeyed. In
like manner[6] that goddess had completely outwitted
him at the time of the birth of Heracles, by obtaining
a promise on behalf of a descendant of his who was to

---

[1] Il. ix. 457.   [3] Il. xiii. 1-16, 352-356.   [5] Il. xviii. 165-169.
[2] Il. xxi. 389, 509.   [4] Il. xiv. 352.   [6] Il. xix. 97 seqq.

be born on that day, and by then accelerating the birth of Eurustheus in Argos, and stopping that of Heracles in Thebes.

On certain occasions, we find Zeus acting as supreme and single-handed, neither against nor with the Olympian assembly. The grandest of these is at the close of the Odyssey[1]. Athenè, stimulated by her sympathising keenness, appears to have winked at the natural, but vengeful, disposition of Odysseus towards his ungrateful and rebellious subjects. Zeus, who had previously counselled moderation, launches his thunderbolt; and it falls at the foot of Athenè, who thereupon gives the required caution to the exasperated sovereign. Peace immediately follows[2].

He has also this marked and paramount distinction, that he never descends to earth to execute his own purposes, but in general sends other deities as his organs, to give effect to his will, or else operates himself from afar, by signs, or by positive exertions of the power which he possesses as god of air.

Zeus, however, is not absolutely omnipresent; for his journey, and his consequent absence from Olympos, are described[3]. But, unlike the case of Poseidon, we have no detail, no succession in his movement. Again, unlike Poseidon, he hears prayer irrespective of the particular place or point from which it is offered.

---

[1] Od. xxiv. 481, 525-541, 546.   [2] Od. xxiv. 546.
[3] Il. i. 420-425.

3, 4. *The Olympian Zeus, and the Lord of Air.*

The chief agency of Zeus in the Poems is as head of the Olympian family and Court.

In this character he is the governor of the air and all its phenomena; the eldest of the trine brotherhood, and the owner of the Aigis, which is the symbol of sovereign power, like the crown, or sword of state, in an European kingdom. To him the gods rise up at their meetings. Though he swears, as other deities do, in confirmation of his word, we have no details as to the form: but we know that the highest mode of conveying his will and word is by the nod peculiar to himself[1].

Besides those offices in relation to the air, which are more capable of an elemental interpretation, he commands the clouds, the tempests, the winds, the thunder and lightning, the years; he impels the falling star, or launches the thunderbolt[2]. All signs in air belong to him, as does especially the rainbow, which he planted in the clouds[3]. Iris, accordingly, is his personal messenger in the Olympian Court. And when any of the attributes belonging to the region of air are employed by other deities, it is in virtue of a special relation to him. These partners of his power appear to be, exclusively of the rest, Herè as his wife; with Athenè and Apollo, in virtue of moral and traditional relations with the Supreme Deity, belonging to them respectively.

The arrangement of the trine brotherhood seems to

---

[1] Il. l. 524-530. Compare Hebrews vi. 13.
[2] Od. xii. 415-417; xxiv. 559.　　　　　[3] Il. xi. 27.

bear peculiar marks of a traditional origin. For, besides the division of power between three, the mode is
remarkable. The Greek ideas and practice were
founded, more or less, on primogeniture. Yet it is by
lot that Zeus receives the air, Poseidon the sea, Aïdoneus the Underworld. This method of division is
evidently meant to save the principle of equality,
which the Poet thus curiously interweaves with the
superiority of Zeus.

For, as the head of the Olympian Court, it is clear
that Zeus is stronger than any single god. It is in
doubt whether he is, as he boasts, stronger than the
whole. We see that at a former period three were
able to coerce him. Perhaps we are to understand this
legend as referring to a period of crisis: the conditions
of human life may enter into the problem, and his
sovereignty may be meant to be understood as one
which when once vindicated, became resistless, and was
thoroughly consolidated by time. His superiority, however, must in the last resort, like that of other governors, be maintained by main force[1], when persuasion or
verbal command has failed. Nor could it be exercised over the great Poseidon without a struggle[2].
Herè and Athenè, however, single or combined, he
threatens freely; and the first of these he had once
punished with severity[3].

Of omnipotence, properly so called, Homer does not
seem to have embraced the idea. To this height, indeed,
even the philosophy of the ancients never ascended.
But none of the epithets of Zeus go so far as to
express it, even in forms which might be supposed
figurative.

[1] Il. xv. 164–167.   [2] Il. xv. 228.   [3] Il. xv. 18.

The headship of Zeus, however, is established not only in superior force but, as has been shown, by special marks of respect, and by symbols of sovereignty: it may be added, by the general deference of the gods. Other tokens are observable. There is no patronymic among the gods, except that of Zeus himself. And further, in the Olympian system proper, there is no god born of any divine sire other than Zeus; nor any god born of a goddess, except he be the father; nor any god born of a human mother.

Again, he is undisguisedly the arbiter among the gods. Herè appeals to him on the conduct of Arès, and he permits his Queen to let loose Athenè on the Trojans[1]. Arès, when wounded, carries his complaint to Zeus[2]; and Artemis also sits on his knee and makes known to him her woes[3]. This office, as a kind of judgeship in appeal, is a great stay to the power of Zeus.

This headship of Zeus in the Olympian polity is not merely ornamental; it entails the weight of government. The careful reader of the Iliad will be struck by the resemblance between his position among the gods, and that of Agamemnon in the circle of his chieftains. As heralds upon earth are his messengers, so it is at his command that a messenger goes to summon the Olympian assemblies: he commonly[4], though not universally[5], introduces the subject of discussion, and, so to speak, manages the debate. He also feels the burden of government over man, when the divine Assemblies are not in session. After the gorgeous scene of the banquet in the First Iliad, the other gods

---

[1] Il. v. 765.   [2] Il. v. 782.   [3] Il. xxl. 705.
[4] Il. iv. 7; viii. 41; Od. l. 32.   [5] Il. xx. 13.

slept, but Zeus slept not; he had in his hands the
charge of the Executive, and he summoned Dream to
do his bidding[1].

The idea, to which we give the name of responsibility, is represented in Zeus, and in him only. Other
gods appear in the movement of the Iliad with an
intermittent agency. But it is Zeus who is charged
with the general conduct of affairs, with seeing that
the government of the world is carried on. There is
no better example of this, than in the Olympian Assembly at the opening of the Odyssey. Odysseus is at
the time detained by Calypso in the Island of Ogugiè.
The care of Athenè does not reach to him, because he
is in the Outer world, under the government, apparently, of Poseidon, his great enemy. Meanwhile, his
substance is wasted, and his wife tormented, by the
dissolute Suitors. All this exhibits a sad rent in the
established terrestrial order. Consequently the gods
in general are affected with compassion[2]. But it is
the business of Zeus to introduce the subject to them,
for their opinion and decree.

At the same time we must observe the skill with
which he manages the Assembly. He avoids placing
himself in conflict with Poseidon by any hasty assumption of the initiative; and only gives his sanction to
the plan of the Return, when Athenè has complained
of the detention, and thrown the responsibility of this
evil upon Zeus[3]. We may observe a like refinement
in the Assembly of the Fourth Iliad. The real object
of Zeus in that Assembly is to draw the Greeks into
the field, which can only be done by bringing about
a breach of the Pact of the Third Book. And this

---

[1] Il. ii. 1-7.   [2] Od. i. 28.   [3] Od. i. 62, 76.

must be done by the Trojans, since the Achaians were keepers of their oaths. But his mode of action is to propose that the accommodation just effected shall be made permanent, and that Troy shall continue to subsist. For he knows very well, that this will put the Hellenising deities upon proposing a scheme for the renewal of the war, and thus that they will save him from giving offence to those of the Trojan party.

It is not only in the individual characters and the family order, but also in the general form of the polity of Olympos, that we may trace the anthropomorphic spirit of the Homeric religion. That polity is more aristocratic than monarchical. It does not exclude the idea of coercion, even as applied to Zeus himself; for he was put in chains by the united action of Herè, Athenè, and Poseidon[1]. Upon the whole, notwithstanding the mutterings of Poseidon in the Fifteenth Iliad, the superiority of Zeus to any single deity is sufficiently established. But although he boasts, that he is able to overcome in mere force the whole Assembly[2], it is incontestable that the will which ultimately prevails is that of the body, and not of the individual who is its head. His effort[3] to obtain a more favourable solution entirely fails. Homer indeed has balanced the question with his usual adroitness; for, as far as the comparatively narrow plot of the Iliad is concerned, Zeus effects his purpose of glorifying Achilles, by the temporary success of the Trojans whom he loved. But it is the Battle of the gods, and the decisive superiority of the Hellenising deities, which foreshadows, and makes way for, the victory of Achilles over Hector. And, as regards the general issue of the War, it is

[1] Il. i. 399-401.   [2] Il. viii. 18-27.   [3] Il. iv. 14-19.

evident that the preference of Zeus lies with the Trojans and not with the Greeks. It is then the prevailing
sense of the Olympian Court, already represented to us
in the Theomachy under the form of physical force,
which determines the doom of Troy, and determines it
in conformity with justice, but clearly against the bias,
if not the outspoken will, of Zeus.

5. *Zeus the type of anthropomorphism.*

The framework of the Olympian system is in itself
the most imposing form of development ever given to
the principle of anthropomorphism; that principle which,
to define it briefly, casts the divine life into human
forms. This is effected by Homer with reference to
all the main relations of life; the State, the family,
and the individual. The State is represented by the
Olympian polity as a whole. The relations of the
deities among themselves are all thrown into the form
of the family. Perhaps it was the sheer necessity of
the case, perhaps the fact that the stream of tradition
came from the East, which carried with it the consequence that, while the Greek family was thoroughly
normal, the family of the Greek gods was based upon
polygamy[1], and upon polygamy attended with what
would among men be deemed a licence yet more relaxed. In truth, it is the domestic organization of
Troy, rather than of Greece, which supplies the earthly
original from which the family in Olympos is a copy;
although this is a feature accidental in reference to the
main design.

[1] Il. xxi. 499.

For, in Olympos, we have Zeus with Herè as his
principal wife; with Leto, Dionè, and perhaps Demeter, as the secondary or subordinate wives. In the
rear of these, came all the persons who were the subjects of his adulterous intrigues on earth. Herè alone
is the Queen, who by reflection attracts, and who
exercises, though with a contracted power, the air-
governing prerogatives of her husband. The other
goddesses I have named are personages, differing in
dignity, but agreeing in this, that they are mute and
blind in reference to the governing office.

While the Olympian Court, and Zeus as its head,
present to our view the weight of political care, and
are commonly seen working for good the individual
character of Zeus is of a far lower order than his public
capacity would lead us to expect. Into this there
enters almost as much of Falstaff, as of Lear into the
character of Priam. The basis of it is radically Epi-
curean. A profound attachment to ease and self-en-
joyment is its first governing principle. Except for
his pleasures, and indeed with a view to indulging in
them, he never disturbs the established order; and he
resents in a high degree the fiery restlessness, as well as
the jealousy[1], of Herè. The sacrificing man is the pious
man: but the love of Zeus for such men appears to be
closely associated with the animal enjoyment of the
libation and the reek[2]. To avoid trouble, he acquiesces
in the death of Sarpedon, whom he singularly loves: he
dreads to give offence to the goddess of Night[3]; and he
hesitates to grant the request of Thetis, notwithstanding the debt of gratitude he owes her. And generally

[1] Il. l. 562.   [2] Il. iv. 48, 49; xxiv. 69, 70.   [3] Il. xiv. 261.

he hates those gods who trouble him, and in proportion
as they trouble him; especially his son Arès[1].

He is not, indeed, devoid of affections; for he is
moved by pity, now for Agamemnon or a Greek chieftain, now for Priam[2]; and he is wrung with genuine
grief, as a father, for Sarpedon, over whom he even
weeps tears of blood[3]. But he delights to sit on Gargaros, and there to behold the bloody spectacle of the war;
he keenly longs to see the ships on fire; he anticipates a
lively pleasure from witnessing the very gods in conflict
with one another[4]. Not only does he rejoice in the
feast, but he glows with sexual passion, and he is subject to the power of Sleep, although that deity can only
subdue him by working hard, and moreover somewhat
at his peril, so that Herè is obliged to bribe him with a
high reward, promised under the sanction of an oath[5].

In a word, Zeus is the masterpiece of the Homeric
mythology, if we consider it with reference to that
humanising or anthropomorphic element, which gave to
the religion of Greece its specific national character.

Section II. *Herè.*

The Herè of Homer is a deity of all others the most
exclusively and intensely national.

Being such, she is modelled strictly according to that
anthropomorphic instinct which governed throughout
the formation of the Olympian system. She is proud,
passionate, sensual, jealous, vindictive; but all these in

---

[1] Il. v. 890.   [2] Il. xxiv. 174.
[3] Il. xvi. 459.   [4] Il. viii. 47-52; xv. 600; xx. 23.
[5] Il. xiv. 233, 236, 252, 268, 359.

strict subordination to the great end, which she pursues with unremitting perseverance, the glorification of the Greeks. She has no personal or moral preferences, like the regard of Athenè for Odysseus, founded upon qualities of character. Zeus is obliged to conceal from her the concession which he has made to Thetis on behalf of her son, the greatest of Greek warriors, but to the detriment of the host at large[1]. She loves Achilles and Agamemnon with an equal love[2]; that is, she loves them, not personally, but for their cause.

Herè is a deity much superior to Poseidon, as exhibiting higher intelligence, with more capacity of far-reaching design, and of the adaptation of means to an end; matters these, in which we have no manifestation of Poseidon's faculties, except in his purely obstinate persecution of Odysseus, for having used with energy the resources of self-defence against a monster[3]. Still there is a total absence of moral elements from the character as it is presented to us. Angered at the lameness of her child Hephaistos, she desires to conceal his birth[4]. Zeus charges her with being ready to eat Priam and his children raw[5]. She borrows the kestos of Aphroditè, and entices Zeus in a scene where sensuality is freely used, though as the instrument of a deeply laid and artful scheme[6]. The motive assigned for her hostility to Troy, is the insult she had suffered by the adverse judgment of Paris[7].

In the Odyssey, she may be said for practical purposes entirely to disappear. She is mentioned but seven times in the whole poem: thrice, quite incidentally, in

---

[1] Il. l. 545-550.　　[2] Il. l. 196.　　[3] Od. i. 20.
[4] Il. xviii. 495.　　[5] Il. iv. 34-36.　　[6] Il. xiv. 190.
[7] Il. xxiv. 27.

a formula where Zeus is called the loud-thundering
husband of Herè, and is himself the true subject of the
passage; once as the mother of Hebè; and thrice in
legend or narrative extraneous to the subject of the
poem. Nor is this unnatural. For, in the domestic
part of it, there is no question of the Greek nationality:
while amidst the Phœnician and Eastern associations
of the Outer Geography, a conception so strictly Hellenic could have no part to play.

Though the power of Herè is immense, yet she is
not surrounded with that reverence which the Poet
always maintains towards Athenè and Apollo. She is
not exempted from the touch of defeat and dishonour.
She was subjected to ignominious punishment by Zeus,
who suspended her with her hands in chains, and with
anvils hanging from her feet[1]. And, in the course of
her long feud with Heracles, that hero wounded her
with a three-pronged arrow in the right breast, and
caused her to suffer intolerable pain [2].

She alone among the deities is called Argeian Herè,
as Helen is called Argeian Helen. In both instances,
the epithet appears to be founded on the special
relation between the person to whom it is applied,
and the head-quarter of Greek power, especially as
that power was associated with the Argeian name,
and therefore probably with the period of the Perseids.
This connection subsisted in Argolis throughout the
historic period. In the Iliad, Herè is said to regard
the Greeks as her children [3]. She collected the armament against Troy [4]. She carried Agamemnon safely

---

[1] Il. xv. 18-21.   [2] Il. v. 392.
[3] Il. xviii. 358.   [4] Il. iv. 24-29.

back to Greece[1]. She conducted Jason and the Argo
through the terrible rocks[2], the Planctai, afterwards
Sumplegades. She hates Heracles, apparently because
he is in antagonism to the Perseid dynasty[3]. It can
hardly be from conjugal jealousy, since Jupiter recounts
his conquests in addressing her on mount Ida. In a
word, the vigour and activity of her partisanship
are such, as to make the more dignified conduct of
Athenè seem almost tame by comparison.

Her rank in Olympos is among the highest: she
must be supposed to sit by Zeus on one side, as we
are told Athenè did on the other[4]. The gods rise
from their seats to her as well as to Zeus, when
she comes among them[5]. At times, she acts immediately on the thoughts of man; as when she prompts
Achilles to call the Assembly of the First Book, in
order to stay the plague[6]; or impels Agamemnon
to stay the victorious course of Hector[7]. At other
times, Athenè is content to be her agent; as when,
in the debate with Agamemnon, she stays the wrath
of Achilles[8]. But by way of counterpoise, when the
two goddesses are about to descend together from
heaven, it is Herè who harnesses the chariot, and
plays in it the inferior part of driver, while Athenè
bears the Aigis[9]. The promise of her aid against
Poseidon greatly relieves the mind of Zeus[10].

She assumes, like the other higher deities, the
human form[11]; and exhibits an extraordinary power

---

[1] Od. iv. 513.   [1] Od. xii. 72.   [3] Il. xix. 130-133.
[4] Il. xxiv. 100.   [6] Il. xv. 85.   [5] Il. i. 55.
[7] Il. viii. 218.   [6] Il. i. 194-196: cf. ii. 156; v. 711; viii. 331.
[9] Il. v. 745-748.   [10] Il. xv. 49-52.   [11] Il. v. 784-792.

over nature, as if entitled, in virtue of her wifehood, to exercise in a manner the attributes of Zeus. Iris is her messenger as well as his [1]. Not only does she order the Winds [2], but she sends the sun [3], in spite of his reluctance, to his setting. When, indignant at the boast of Hector, she rocks upon her throne [4], Olympos shakes beneath her, as it did under the nod of Zeus. She endows the horses of Achilles with a voice [5]. And, conjointly with Athenè, she thunders in honour of the crowning of Agamemnon [6].

We learn from a speech of Phœnix, that, together with Athenè, she can confer valour. The daughters of Pandareus she endows both with beauty and with sense, while Athenè and Aphroditè provide them with industrial skill and bodily food respectively, and Artemis bestows upon them stature [7].

Herè takes part, with Athenè and Poseidon, in the great rebellion against Zeus, which all but effected his deposition. She had also been personally favoured with a special protection, at the time when Zeus himself deposed his father Kronos, and thrust him into the Underworld.

Of these two myths, the latter seems to suggest its own interpretation. Its scene is fixed in the midst of the great Theogonic crisis, at the point of the transition from the Pelasgian to the Hellenic or Olympian system. That was a moment of danger to her; but we read of no such danger to Poseidon. From this we may naturally infer that Poseidon had no concern

---

[1] Il. xviii. 168.

[2] This seems the natural construction of Od. iv. 513, and xii. 69-72.   [3] Il. xviii. 239.   [4] Il. viii. 193.

[5] Il. xix. 407.   [6] Il. xi. 45.   [7] Od. xx. 68-72.

at all with the Pelasgian system, and was an importation from a source altogether distinct. Herè, however, had a counterpart below, with which she might readily have been confounded. In that superseded system we find a Γαῖα, or Earth, who, with other Nature-Powers, inhabits, and is invoked in, the Underworld. Rescued from that danger, and set high in Olympos, she stands in marked opposition, as an Hellenic goddess, to the older and coarser conception of the same idea, with which she is in direct competition. This will account for the attitude she holds in the Poems. For here she is not only Hellenic, but she is nothing else; and the principle and groundwork of her Hellenism seem to be an intense untiring hatred of what is Pelasgian by race and association, just as if she were the preferred rival of an old Pelasgian deity; as if she had the very root of her being in a strong recoil from the superseded Nature-Power, into which she might relapse, if Hellenism were ever swallowed up by a victorious return of the Pelasgian worship. Born of the Hellenic reaction, its life and hers were bound up together.

Hence too, in all likelihood, we are to account for her place in the legend of the War in heaven. Zeus, like Janus, has two faces. When he deposes Kronos, he shows us his Hellenic, or Hellic, face. But this rebellion is a rebellion of deities, all of them having the most marked Hellenic sympathies, which evidently run against him in this legend, as the head of the old Pelasgian order.

The functional attribute, specially entrusted to Herè in her Olympian character, appears to be only that of regulating birth, through the medium of the Eilithuiai. This appears to be an ascription derived from

the original character of the all-producing Earth. And
the anthropomorphic spirit of the Olympian religion
is well illustrated by the fact that Homer cuts her off
from all other production, both animal and vegetable,
but leaves to her only the bringing of man to birth.
Human birth bears to Herè the same relation, as birth
generally to Gaia.

Though the Eilithuiai are mentioned as under the
control of Herè, they were objects of worship; for the
pseud-Odysseus mentions the case of Eilithuiè at
Amnisos in Crete [1].

On the whole, then, it seems likely that Herè, with
a name representing 'Epa, or the earth, is treated
by Homer with a transformation suited to the anthropomorphic and personifying spirit of the Olympian
religion; divorced, as to her personality, from Gaia,
much as Poseidon is held apart from Nereus, and
standing towards Gaia as soul to body: the body taking
its place with the old elemental deities of the Pelasgians in the Underworld, the soul rising to higher
offices.   Herè, thus detached from gross matter, carries
off with her, as to man alone, the great prerogative
of earth, that she is the all-feeding and all-bearing;
the τραφερὴ, the πολύφορβος, the φερέσβιος.   Accordingly, Herè becomes, or remains rather than becomes,
the great mother.   She is the wife of Zeus, father of
gods and men, and she holds among his wives and
concubines the queenly prerogative, like Hecuba in
Troy; the mother in heaven of some of his children,
as Hebè, Arès, and Hephaistos; and, with the Eili-
thuai for her ministers, the goddess of all motherhood
on earth [2].

[1] Od. xix. 188.   [2] Il. xix. 119.

This last, indeed, is her only specialty. Those other and high prerogatives, which invest her with command over Nature, and with the power of direct action on the mind, probably accrue to her as the consort of Zeus, and are therefore not her original gifts, but the reflection of his glory.

We have, perhaps, in the Theomachy, at least one vestige of the prerogative of Herè as a Nature-Power. It is she who excites Hephaistos against the river Xanthos[1]; and again, the River, parched by fire, makes his appeal to her to relieve him from suffering, with an engagement which he takes to aid Troy no more, not even in its last necessity. Herè accedes to his prayer, and checks the action of Hephaistos, who thereupon desists[2]. It seems as if the ground for choosing Herè to interpose on this occasion lay in the relation between rivers and the Earth along which they trace their course. This is the only act of a definite nature, with a sensible result performed by Herè within the limits of Troas, a fact which is again in accordance with the construction I have given it, and the apparent bias of the Troic religion towards Nature-worship.

Section III   *Poseidon.*

The most striking feature of the Homeric Poseidon, or rather Poseidaon, is vast force combined with a total absence of the higher elements of deity, whether intellectual or moral. A persistent vindictiveness, indeed, we trace as the groundwork of his entire action in

[1] Il. xxi. 328-330.   [2] Ib. 367-381.

both the Poems: he hates the Trojans, for the offence of Laomedon; he hates Odysseus, because, in the strictest self-defence, he had blinded Poluphemos. By no worthy word or act is he marked in any part either of Iliad or Odyssey, unless it be by some natural affection for his descendants, whether they be the youthful warriors of the house of Actor [1], or the savage, cruel, atheistic Cyclop.

One of the three sons of Kronos and Rhea, he comes next to Zeus in order of birth [2]. He claims an equality [3] of rank; and avers, that the distribution of sovereignties among the three brothers was made only by lot. More than indirectly, he asserts equality, as well as independence. When admonished by Iris that he is junior to Zeus, he acknowledges that there is force in the plea, and he withdraws from the plain of battle as he had been bid; but he reserves a right of resentment, in case Zeus shall not fulfil the decree against Troy. Zeus on his part is delighted at the news; and observes, that it would have cost much labour to coerce him [4]. Again, it is plain that, in the conspiracies against Zeus, he was the acting partner. For it is the superiority of his son to him, that frustrates the design of the whole party [5]; and when Herè attempts to revive the scheme, he pleads in reply, not their collective inferiority, but his own singly [6], as if he thought that it was, in point of mere force, well-nigh all they would have to rely on.

Apollo is restrained, in the Theomachy, by a sentiment of respect, from coming to blows with Poseidon,

---

[1] Il. xi. 749–751.   [2] Il. iv. 174–217.   [3] Ib. 186–209.
[4] Il. iv. 220–235.   [5] Il. l. 404.   [6] Il. viii. 211.

as his paternal uncle [1]. And a sentiment precisely
similar prevents Athenè in the Odyssey from comfort-
ing Odysseus by her visible presence, even at her own
sanctuary in Scheriè [2].

Though god of the sea, he is not, so to speak, the
Sea-god, or the Water-god. He has in him nothing of an
elemental deity. He is not placed in as near a relation
to water as Zeus is to air, by the epithet Διιπέτης, and
the phrase Διὸς ὄμβρος [3]. These very phrases show us
that he was not, in Homer's view, the god of moisture,
or even of water, generally. The attempts to derive
his name from a common root with πόσις, 'drink,' or
ποταμὸς, 'a river,' would therefore be insufficient or
inappropriate, even if they were not, as they are, somewhat equivocal. It is remarkable that, while Poseidon
supplied a sea-deluge as his contribution towards effacing
the Greek trench, it was Apollo who turned upon it
the mouths of all the rivers that descend from Ida [4];
which, when Poseidon had accomplished his labour,
he in turn sent back again to their proper channels.

Nereus, the true Sea-god of Homer, gave to the
element of water that name of nero, in the popular
speech of the Greeks, which it still retains [5]. He ever
dwells in the depths of the sea, as if he belonged to
them, and as if they supplied his atmosphere. But
Poseidon has a palace there near Aigai, where his
chariot was kept, where the Poet seems to imply that
he resided [6]. Yet not exclusively; for he appears at

---

[1] Il. xxi. 468.   [2] Od. vi. 329; xiii. 341.
[3] Διιπέτης = fallen from Zeus. Διὸς ὄμβρος = Zeus-rain.
[4] Il. xii. 13–35.
[5] Comp. the adj. neros, wet, in the late Greek of Phrynichus
the grammarian, A.D. 180.   [6] Il. xiii. 15; xv. 219.

the Olympian Court, on the plain of Troy, on the hill-tops of Samothrace[1], or on the Solyman[2] mountains; and he singly visits the Ethiopians, to partake of the sacrifices they offered him[3]. This reference to his being worshipped in a distant quarter is the second sign we have seen of his foreign origin; the first was the want of definiteness in his position of inferiority relatively to Zeus, as though he had been, elsewhere, without a superior.

So again there appears to be in the Outer or Phœnician system an elemental sea-god, Phorcūs, who is called ruler of the sea, and after whom a harbour in Ithaca is named[4].

Prayer appears only to be addressed to him, within the Greek world, in the neighbourhood of the sea, as by the Envoys in the Ninth Iliad; and by his own descendants, as Nestor in the Third Odyssey, who likewise worships by the shore[5]. He can assume the form of any man; can blunt the point of a spear; can carry off his friends, or envelope his opponents in vapour[6]. He can inspire vigour into heroes; not immediately, however, but by a stroke of his staff[7]. Direct action on the mind appears to be beyond his range. The storms of the Poems, in the Greek or inner world, are not raised by Poseidon. Probably he had not the power to raise a storm, though he can break, as the sea does, fragments from the rocks of the coast[8]. Storms seem to have been regarded as belonging to the province of

---

[1] Il. xiii. 11.
[2] Od. i. 22, 25.
[3] Od. iii. 5.   Cf. Il. xi. 728.
[4] Il. xiii. 43, 215; xiv. 135; xiii. 562; xi. 752; xx. 321–329.
[5] Il. xiii. 59.
[6] Od. v. 283.
[7] Od. i. 72; xiii. 91; Il. ix. 183.
[8] Od. iv. 506.

the air-god.   They are imputed to him in a passage of
the Twenty-fourth Odyssey[1]; but it would not be altogether safe, perhaps, to rely on that Book, in a case where
it seems to vary from the usual order of the Poems.

If, however, Poseidon was less than the absolute lord
of water, he was also more.

1. His possession of the Trident (triaina) could
hardly be due to a purely maritime sovereignty.

2. His relation to the horse, which is very perceptible, though not of primary rank, in Homer [2],
and which became almost paramount in the later age,
cannot be adequately explained by any comparison
between that animal and the ship, or the wave.

3. Poseidon is the building-god.

4. Poseidon stands in close relation to the giants
and other rebellious personages, who troubled both
gods and men.

The existence of these associations for Poseidon,
inasmuch as they cannot be explained by virtue of his
place in the Olympian system, again urges us to look
for the signs of his origin abroad.   The key to the
inquiry is to be found in the Outer world of the Odyssey.   For

1. It is plain that the materials of the narrative, so
far as the scene of the poem is laid in that Outer world,
must have been derived by the Poet from the Phœnicians, who alone frequented the waters beyond the
Ægean and the Greek coasts.

2. In the western portion of the Outer sphere, Zeus
practically disappears from the governing office, and
Poseidon becomes the supreme ruler.

We have seen that the subordination of Poseidon to

[1] Od. xxiv. 110.   [2] Il. xxiii. 277, 306, 534.

Zeus rested on juniority. If Zeus were the chief god
of the Pelasgian worship, and Poseidon came in with
the Phœnicians, this poetical arrangement is suitably
explained; and it exhibits a skilful adaptation to the
conditions under which the Olympian system was constructed. His rebellion against Zeus, in concert with
Herè and Athenè, appears to show that, as new immigrants arrived in Greece, bearing with them their own
religion, the older system was for a time brought into
question and endangered as a whole. The delivery of
Zeus from this rebellion will be considered in connection with the goddess Thetis[1].

The Greek legends relating to Poseidon are just such
as we might expect with reference to the god of a nautical people, touching at many points about the coast
of Greece. He contends with Helios for Corinth, with
Athenè for Troizen and Athens, with Herè for Aigolis,
with Zeus for Ægina, with Dionusos for Naxos. Even
in the Greece of Homer we find spots specially consecrated to him in Bœotia, in Eubœa, and in Aigialos.

Let us now turn to the Voyage of Odysseus in the
Outer world; which begins with the Lotos-eaters, and
ends with the Phaiakes of Corfù. Mure[2] suggests that
their name is a parody of the name Phoinikes: Homer
paints them as a wealthy, unwarlike people, singularly
expert in navigation. This apparent incongruity falls
in with the case of Corfù, if it was then inhabited, as
it has been in later times, by a stationary, gentle,
indolent peasantry, and at the same time held by a
dominant settlement or colony of foreigners, ruling
it through maritime power. Mure cites Phaïk as a

---

[1] *Infra*, sect. xxi.   [2] Lit. Hist. of Greece, vol. i. p. 510.

Semitic word for 'magnificent,' and Scher, as meaning
'an emporium.'

In this Phœnician or Outer world, Athenè, who had
constantly tended Odysseus while in Troas, and who
resumes the regular charge of him in Ithaca, systematically abstains from helping him; and wholly disappears
until Poseidon has, in the Fifth Odyssey, voluntarily
receded from the scene[1]. She declares that respect to
her uncle was the motive for her own disappearance[2].
The presumption then is that this Outer world was a
sphere in some way so specially his own, that Athenè,
whose power and prerogatives in Homer are so extremely lofty, was unwilling to offer him any opposition there.

Accordingly, we have direct evidence that, in relation
to the Outer world, Poseidon exercised prerogatives
which seem not to have belonged to him within the
Greek sphere. He raised the storm which wrecked
the raft of Odysseus; gathering the clouds, which was
the special function of Zeus, and causing the winds
to blow[3].

Moreover, in the lay of Arès and Aphroditè, it is evidently Poseidon who presides in the Assembly of the
gods, and who consequently negotiates with Hephaistos for the relief of Arès from the net of steel. And
just as, at the beginning of the Second Iliad, the other
gods were sleeping, but Zeus[4] (who was responsible)
slept not, so here, while the other deities were laugh-
ing, Poseidon did not laugh[5]; as we may suppose, for
the same reason. And while, on ordinary occasions,
we are always told that the gods assembled in the

---

[1] Od. v. 380.   [2] Od. xiii. 341.   [3] Od. v. 291.
[4] Il. ii. 1.   ·..   [5] Od. viii. 344.

χαλκοβατὲς δῶ of Zeus, here the words 'of Zeus' are omitted[1].

Undoubtedly the name of Zeus appears from time to time in those Books of the Odyssey which describe the wanderings of Odysseus; but his governing office disappears until, in the end of the Twelfth Book, he acts at the instance of Helios (the Sun), and on behalf of the Olympian Court. It is not the abstract, but the working supremacy of Poseidon, which the Poem seems to show. At the same time, the question might be raised whether, as in the later and extraneous tradition the name Zeus was often united with that of Poseidon (as much as to say 'Zeus the supreme deity, in the form and under the name of Poseidon'), so here the word may not improbably have the general force of 'god,' rather than the personal meaning of a particular god. Even in Homer, Aïdoneus is called the Zeus of the Underworld; and so Poseidon may be the Zeus of the sea and the sea-regions. And it is very notable that in Od. v. 302–304, Odysseus ascribes to Zeus that very storm, which we are expressly told that Poseidon had raised.

We have therefore very strong indications from the text of Homer that Poseidon was the god, or the chief-god, of the Phoinikes; and if he was, then, upon their arrival in Greece, he could only be incorporated into the Greek system by some such method as Homer has adopted, in giving him at once a parity and a disparity with Zeus.

Thus the Outer geography affords us the strongest evidence of the Phœnician origin of Poseidon. It

---

[1] Od. viii. 321.

shows us more than this, as will be seen when we
treat of the position of Helios in Homer.

The view now taken is in harmony with the evidence supplied from other sources respecting Poseidon.
Herodotus, deriving the names of the other Greek gods
from Egypt, excepts Poseidon. History shows abun-
dantly the prevalence of Poseidonian worship among the
Phœnicians and their colonial progeny. Diodorus[1]
says an altar to Poseidon was built at the northern
extremity of the Red Sea, where was a promontory
called Poseideïon, and a grove of palms (Phoinikes).
In the war with Gelon, Hamilcar, general of the Car-
thaginians, offered to Poseidon a magnificent sacrifice,
with a view to success in what were mainly land operations. Again, while sacrificing a boy to Kronos, he
threw into the sea a crowd of victims in honour of
Poseidon[2]. Later in the historic period, when Scipio
attacks *Carthago Nova*, he assures his army that he
has the favour of Poseidon made known to him in a
dream[3]; that is to say, that the foe was deserted by
his own national and proper god. Pausanias, again,
shows us the worship of Poseidon practised in parts of
Greece, whither it never could have come had he been
regarded as a mere sea-god; and nowhere more than
in Arcadia. Manifestly, if he were the chief and distinctive god of the Phœnician nationality, it is probable that, as that acute race penetrated for traffic into
Greece, they would carry with them their worship as
they went. And again, in many of the local legends
related by that author, which afford evidence of a
very trustworthy kind, we find Poseidon possessed of

[1] Diod. Sic. lli. 41.   [2] Ib. xl. 21; xill. 86.
[3] Polyb. Bk. x. 11. 7; 14. 12.

attributes which, in the established religion of Hellas, belonged properly to Zeus[1].

Let us now endeavour to examine the special and separate attributes of Poseidon, already enumerated, in the light of his Phœnician associations.

With respect to the Trident, an instrument so unsuited to water, it appears evidently to point to some tradition of a Trinity, such as may still be found in various forms of Eastern religion, other than the Hebrew. It may have proceeded, among the Phœnicians, from the common source of an older tradition; and this seems more probable than its direct derivation from the Hebrews, with whom, however, we know that the Phœnicians had intercourse.

Though the relation of Poseidon to the horse is not explained by his connection with Phœnicia, yet, as this connection points to his supremacy, and thus gives him wider associations than those of a merely maritime deity, it opens a field from which the true explanation may yet be gathered. I have suggested elsewhere a solution of the problem[2].

Reference to what has been already said of the Phoinikes will show that the relation of Poseidon to them at once explains his character as the building-god.

Lastly, with regard to the giants and monsters. The facts are as follows.

The Cyclops, a godless race, are his children[3]. The impious giants are declared to be of the kindred of the gods[4]: this is probably through Poseidon. By the

---

[1] See 'Phœnicia and Greece,' in the Quarterly Review of Jan. 1868.

[2] *Supra*, Phœnicians, chap. v.   [3] Od. ix. 275, 412.

[4] Od. vii. 205, 206.

daughter of their king and arch-tempter Eurumedon, he was the father of the royal house of Scheriè[1]. These giants the wicked and cruel Laistrugones are said to resemble[2]. By Iphimedeia, he was the father of Otos and Ephialtes, those monster-youths[3] who heaped up the mountains, and perished by the hands of Apollo. He was also the father of Briareus (called likewise Aigaion), who, however, took part against him[4].

The effort of the two youths recalls the traditions of the Tower of Babel, and of the War in Heaven.

Two considerations may be noticed, which tend to account for the place of Poseidon as the Phœnician god, in relation to many rebellious and unruly spirits.

First, the rough manners of a sea-faring and buccaneering people. Down to the time of Cicero and of the Roman Empire, a rude and ruffian-like character was called Neptuni filius.

Secondly, and in possible connection with what has just been said, Syria was inhabited by Canaanites; and it has been observed that the names given in Scripture to that race indicate great stature and physical force, which became the basis of a tradition that they were a race of giants[5]. To the Greek mind this would very naturally convey that they were children of Poseidon as the Phœnician god. In a word, the Phœnician origin of Poseidon, and that only, appears to supply a key to his position and attributes, such as they are shown in the Olympian system.

---

[1] Od. vii. 56-60.   [2] Od. x. 120.   [3] Od. xl. 305-320.
[4] Il. i. 401-406.   [5] Le Normant, vol. ii. p. 144.

Section IV. *Aïdoneus.*

The figure of Aïdoneus, or Aïdes, is one of the most obscure in the whole Homeric mythology. Yet here too there is, as I think, a reward for patient observation; and a clue is to be found which may enable us to trace him home to his origin, as a Nature-Power of an older theogony, rather than what he might at first sight appear to be, little more than a shadowy creature of the Poet's imagination.

The particulars respecting him in the Poems are but few.

He was one of the deities who suffered at the hand of man: namely, of Heracles[1]. Now the associations of Heracles in Homer are Hellenic, as we may perceive from the co-operation of Athenè with him; and therefore this legend, so far as it goes, tends to place Aïdoneus beyond the line of pure Hellenic tradition. It is true, that Heracles also assaulted Herè: but the enmity between them was special, and founded on the jealousy of the goddess in favour of the ruling house of the Perseids.

Heracles shot this god in the shoulder with an arrow at Pulos, not of Messenia but of Elis, according to Pausanias[2]; and laid him prostrate among the dead, huge as he was. He rose, went to Olympos, and was cured by Paieon[3].

Though a deity of the Underworld[4], he is the brother of Zeus, having shared in the partition of the universe by lot. He is therefore adopted, like Posei-

---

[1] Il. v. 395.
[2] vi. 25. 3.
[3] Il. v. 398–402.
[4] Il. xv. 187, 191.

don, into the Olympian Court, and becomes entitled
to appear in the Hellenic heaven, though supposed
usually to abide in the Shades.

His action in the Poems is singularly faint; an
arrangement of which we shall see the probable reason.
During the battle of the gods, he trembles[1] lest the
earth-shaker Poseidon should split the ground, and exhibit the nether region, where he is lord (*anax*), through
the chasm. This shuddering may be said to be the
single action ascribed to him in the Poems.

We have, however, passages illustrative of his character and functions. Stern and inexorable, he is to
men the most hateful of all the gods[2]. This declaration is curiously illustrated by the after history of the
Olympian system. In all Greece, says Pausanias[3],
there is no single temple of Aïdes, except at a single
spot of Elis, where, according to tradition, he fought on
the side of the Pulians against Heracles. And this
temple was opened once a year[3]: 'I suppose,' adds
Pausanias, 'because men die but once.' This perhaps
would have been a more apt reason if men had died
once a year.

He is also called the strong[4], the hateful or loathsome (στυγερός[5]), the gate-closer[6], and in a recurring
formula, the horse-famous (κλυτόπωλος[7]).

Though he is the king of the world below, he seems
to exercise no active power there: throughout the Eleventh Odyssey, the duties of government are in the
hands of Persephonè, who also has, by the shores of
Okeanos, the grove of worship. Odysseus, indeed,

---

[1] Il. xx. 61.   [2] Il. l. 158.   [3] Paus. as already cited.
[4] Od. x. 534; xi. 47, 276.   [5] Il. viii. 368.
[6] Il. viii. 367.   [7] Il. v. 654; xi. 445; xvi. 625.

offered to him prayer and sacrifice, together with her,
in the Underworld[1]: but there is no sign of his having
any established worship upon earth.

The helmet of Aïdes was used by Athenè[2] to make
herself invisible to Arès. We hear of this helmet in
Hesiod, as worn by Perseus[3]. It appears to be a symbol
of darkness.

Twice, however, this deity comes before us in the
legend of Phœnix. In the war of Caludon, Althaia,
invoking woes on Meleagros, beats the earth with her
hands, as she calls on Aïdes and Persephonè; and she
is heard and answered from beneath by the Erinüs[4].
In the other passage the process is reversed. The
father of Phœnix calls upon the Erinüs, and 'the gods'
fulfil his imprecation, 'and Zeus of the Underworld,
and Persephonè the awful;' perhaps meaning this, that
these are the gods to whom he refers.

Of this dualism in the exercise of the penal office I
shall speak elsewhere. But the name here given to
Aïdes is very remarkable: he is the Zeus of the Underworld. How comes he by this title? At first sight it
indicates some very close relation between him and
the traditions of Zeus in some one of their forms; for
Poseidon is never called the Zeus of the sea, although, as we have seen, he carries strong marks of
supremacy in the Outer world.

The part he takes at Pulos seems to mean that he
was the old god of the country, and the patron of the
inhabitants in their struggles against the invading
Heracles. The epithet 'huge' further tends to associate him with the old Nature-Powers. The con-

[1] Od. xi. 43-46.   [2] Il. v. 845.
[3] Scut. Herc. 227.   [4] Il. ix. 563-572.

tinuance of his worship at Pulos in the historic period, when it had disappeared in all other places, is probably to be taken as an indication, that Elis was even in the earliest times a religious centre for Greece, and that Pulos was the head-quarters of the system, so far as Aïdoneus was concerned.

We shall see that, in the worship of Dodona, there was a Dionè, associated as queen with the Pelasgian Zeus. This Dionè, to make room for Herè, disappears from active relations to mankind, and becomes a sort of lay-figure in Olympos.

Was there, then, a residuum of the tradition of the Pelasgian Zeus, after the Olympian Zeus had been fully conceived and established? And, as Gaia, or Demeter, or both, represent such a residuum in the case of Herè, does Aïdoneus represent it in the case of Zeus[1]?

This would be an adjustment in full analogy with Homer's general method. And it would at once account for the extremely faint outline which he has given to the figure of his Aïdoneus, and for his giving the executive office in the Underworld to Persephonè. As he keeps back Demeter, that she may not compete with Herè, so he would keep back Aïdoneus, that he might not compete with Zeus.

Plutarch[2] has preserved a tradition, which seems to supply a missing link, respecting an Aïdoneus, who was king of the Molossians; and he thus connects the name with the neighbourhood of Dodona. This Aïdoneus releases Theseus, his prisoner, at the request of Heracles : a transaction afterwards transferred to the nether world. Thus one great Hellic personage obtains from him the

---

[1] Kreuzer, Symbolik, iv. 477.   [2] Thes. c. 35.

release of another, which accords with the idea of his priority in time.

Althaias's beating the earth would lead to the conclusion, that Aïdoneus must have sprung from some tradition of an earth-god, and not an air-god. Hesiod, the Pelasgian poet, directs the husbandman to pray to him, as well as to Demeter, to prosper the fruits of the earth[1].

It is, I suppose, possible that at some period the rude religion of the Pelasgians, not yet having arrived at the Egyptian idea of Air and Earth, as representing respectively the active and the passive principle, may have conceived of Earth as its own supreme deity. At any rate the relation of Aïdoneus to the Zeus of Dodona appears to rest on probable evidence.

And if so, then the argument for considering Aïdoneus as an earth-Zeus, rather than as an air-Zeus, is certainly recommended by various probable suggestions. The general appearance of the aggregate phenomena of Nature- or Element-worship in Homer, and also in Hesiod, is by no means such as to fall into a single consistent whole, and appears to imply that more than one theogony, or scheme of deity and religion, had preceded the Olympian system. It is almost certain, that a plurality of such schemes must have presented discrepancies one with another.

Moreover, when we regard Zeus as an air-god, he stands in the relation of the active Nature-Power to Earth as the female and passive one. Now this was the notion embodied in the Egyptian system, which may have been carried, in accordance with the report

---

[1] Opp. 436; Döllinger, Heid. und Jud. p. 80.

of Herodotus, and either directly or mediately, from
Egypt to Dodona. But it is an idea implying a certain
refinement, an action of the speculative mind in the
discernment of cause and effect. An entirely rude
people might perhaps be more likely to associate its
idea of a God with the earth, of which the surface constantly tells them a tale of life, while from
its bosom spring the stores that sustain their bodily
existence.

SECTION V. *Leto.*

I think that every one who carefully examines the
text of Homer with reference to the picture there given
of Leto, must be struck alike by the slightness and by
the dignity of its outline; and, I may add, by the
absence (as far as I know) of any satisfactory attempt
to find for her an origin in any pre-existing tradition,
either of the Pelasgian Nature-worship, or of the Assyrian or Egyptian systems. Without origin, without
function, she seems to be a mother, and nothing more
than a mother; yet she is elevated into a commanding
position in the Homeric system by the transcendant
dignity of her son Apollo.

The only epithets given to Leto in the poems are of
a character entirely general: glorious [1], right-glorious [2],
lovely-cheeked [3], lovely-haired [4].

Her action in the poems is extremely circumscribed.
She appears in the temple of Apollo, as his minister,
with her daughter Artemis, to nurse and tend Æneas [5].

[1] Od. xl. 580. [2] Il. xiv. 327. [3] Il. xxiv. 607.
[4] Il. i. 36. [5] Il. v. 447.

She never performs any governing office of any kind, either upon nature or upon man; though she looks with delight upon Artemis sporting in the wild wood[1]. When she appears in the Theomachy on the Trojan side, and we are in hopes of finding a link to connect her with some definite prerogatives, we find the Poem so contrived, that the door is at once closed upon our curiosity by her release from the necessity of combat.

With this blankness and faintness, let us now compare the high ascriptions of her dignity. It is a great note of honour, that this inactive and hindward deity should find a place in the Theomachy, from which Demeter and Aphroditè are excluded. Hermes is her opponent. But when the time for action comes, he declines the fight: he will not lay hands on the spouse of Zeus: he gives her free leave to proclaim that she has worsted him. She makes no reply[2]. Again, it is the insult to Leto as the mother of only a pair, that is so fearfully avenged on Niobè and her children[3]. And Tituos, the son of Gaia, is tortured in Tartaros, because he sought to offer her violence as she was proceeding to the Pythian temple of her son[4]. In the ascending scale of the mothers of his offspring, she is placed by Zeus after Demeter and next to Herè[5].

Hesiod marries her to Zeus before Herè; which, considering the supreme rank of Herè in Olympos, appears to be the mark of some very old tradition. She is junior, among the consorts he assigns to Zeus, only to Metis, or the Spirit of Counsel. She is there made the

1 Od. vi. 106.   2 Il. xxi. 497-501.   3 Il. xxiv. 607.
4 Od. xi. 580.   5 Il. xiv. 327.

daughter of a Titan; and, in the Hymn to Apollo, she appears as a sister of Zeus, and a daughter of Kronos himself. But, colourless as she is in her own being, all this seems to be a marked reflection from the dignity of Apollo.

Some have explained this mute yet lofty personage in conformity, as they think, with the etymology of the name; and they regard Leto as the impersonation of Night, and Night as the mother from whose womb Day, or the Sun, is produced. The etymology appears to be uncertain: yet there may be no great difficulty in supposing an affinity between Leto and lateo, and a derivation from the root lath [1]. Nor is it any conclusive objection to this theory, that we have already a goddess of Night in Homer [2]. For this might be the obsolete Nature-Power, standing in the same relation to an impersonated Leto, as Gaia, or as Demeter, to Herè. The idea that the Night is the mother of the Sun, and also is the Moon, does not seem to be an idea much more likely to commend itself to the Greek mind than to represent Chaos as the parent of Cosmos, anarchy of order. At the same time it is conceivable that such an idea might find place in a scheme of Nature-worship. Nor was Apollo united with the Sun in the Olympian scheme of Homer. But, when we perceive the immense reverence accorded to a personage who is without any attribute or office in the poems except motherhood, we cannot but refer to the motherhood the dignity itself.

It is quite possible, though it is not proved, that there may have been in the Pelasgian or in some other mythology, a personage who may be the base of the

[1] Liddell and Scott, in voc. λανθάνω.   [2] Il. xiv. 261.

Homeric Leto, just as there are deities who form the base, or a base, of his Apollo. But as the properties attaching to his Apollo appear to be of an order too high to be justly accounted for by anything we find in mere mythology, so, and even more, we are driven to seek outside the limits of the system a mode of accounting for the majesty and reverence, with which the Leto of Homer is surrounded.

But if in Apollo there are exhibited, together with other matter, the features of that tradition of a Deliverer, divine, and yet in human form, which was handed down through the line of Patriarchs, and enshrined in the Sacred Scriptures, we have to bear in mind that this Deliverer was emphatically described as the Seed of the Woman. Whether by the woman was meant His mother, or Eve, the general mother of our race, is immaterial to our present purpose. What appears obvious is that, if such a tradition imparted its glory to the character of Apollo, it could hardly fail to shed a portion of collateral lustre upon the person, in whom the human descent was signified and foreshadowed. And it would be no matter of wonder, if the human figure of such a person were elevated to the Olympian Court, whose manifold orders made such admission easy, and whose anthropomorphic principle tended to efface or weaken the lines of separation between its divinities and mortal man.

I conclude, therefore, that in Leto we have a record, and a sufficiently clear indication, whether wrought into the texture of any current mythological legend, or otherwise, of the Hebrew tradition respecting the Woman, of whose seed the Deliverer of mankind was to be.

SECTION VI. *Demeter.*

The text of Pausanias exhibits by its enumeration
of temples and remains, though it does not explain,
the widespread prevalence and the great local importance of the worship of Demeter in Greece. And this
picture stands in marked contrast with her insignifi-
cance in the action of the Homeric Poems, and in the
Olympian system. We may safely assign to her one of the twenty
chairs or thrones [1], wrought for the Assemblies of Immortals in the palace of Zeus. But she nowhere
appears as taking part in those Assemblies. She has
no place in the Theomachy or in the War. She is never
mentioned in the Poems except incidentally.

The actual Homeric evidence concerning Demeter
is as follows :—

1. Ground corn, or meal, is called Δημήτερος ἀκτή, as
fire (or flame) is called φλὸξ Ἡφαίστοιο [2]. This is one
of the proper associations of a Nature-Power.

2. She is the companion of Zeus in one of the connections, which he relates in Il. xiv. 326. Her child
is not named by the Poet either there or elsewhere.
But, in the later tradition, we find associated with her
in local worship, under the name of Corè, the Damsel,
a great and even awful personage, who thus fills the
gap indicated by Homer, and who probably is represented by his Persephonè, queen of the Underworld.
Certainly the two have a marked correspondence in
character.

[1] Il. xviii. 373.   [2] Il. xiii. 322 ; xxi. 76.

3. She has a τέμενος at Purasos in Thessaly[1], and these land-endowments, as far as we can discern from Homer, were Pelasgian.

4. She is termed ἐϋπλόκαμος and ξανθή, fair-haired, and golden-haired, doubtless with reference to the idea beautifully expressed by Tibullus[2]: '*Deponit flavas annua terra comas.*'

5. She felt and gave way to a passion for a son or descendant of Iasos; and this took place among the fields[3]. The name of Iasos is obscure, but seems to be certainly older than the Hellenes. Hesiod enlarges the tradition, and says this event came about in Crete, a country at least partially marked with strong Pelasgic features[4]. This powerful element of lust in her character tends further to detach her, as a goddess, from Hellenic associations.

6. She presides over the operation of winnowing; and threshing-floors are consecrated to her[5].

The later tradition, testifying to an extensively established worship of Demeter, places the most noted seat of it in Attica, which is an eminently Pelasgian district, with Eleusis for its head-quarter.

In the Hymn to Demeter, she herself founds that worship; and reports herself as having come thither, but unwillingly[6], from Crete. This tradition may point to the epoch when the Phœnicians acquired the dominion of Crete. It certainly points to some decisive change tending to displace her worship.

Pausanias[7] states, that there was in his time a temple of Demeter Pelasgis at Corinth.

Diodorus[8] reports that she merely represents the cha-

---

[1] Il. ii. 696.　[2] ii. 1. 48.　[3] Od. v. 125.　[4] Theog. 971.
[5] Il. v. 499-502.　[6] v. 123.　[7] ii. 22. 2.　[8] i. 13.

racter of Isis in the Egyptian mythology; that is to say, as earth-goddess and inventress of cultivation.

We have indeed three Homeric personages, all of whom appear to be related to the old tradition of Nature-worship, which made Earth a deity, and a female deity [1]. The share of Demeter in that tradition is established by her attributes in connection with food, and by her name of Γῆ μήτηρ, Mother-earth.

Detached as this is from Hellenic associations, we cannot be surprised at our not finding her among the Hellenising divinities of the War. Nor is it very difficult to conjecture a reason, why she could not conveniently appear among those who were allies of Troy: namely this, that in Greece her personality had been sufficiently severed from that of Gaia, the Earth-goddess proper, by the relegation of Gaia to the Underworld, and probably by the prevalence of her local worship, to allow her a place in Olympos; but in Troas it would seem that this severance may not have been effected, and that the Earth-goddess was worshipped under her own name, like, and together with, the Sun [2].

Perhaps the same line of thought may carry us to the reason, why Demeter appears to us without a daughter, and Persephonè, the Awful, without a mother. For Persephonè is the queen of that dark region in which Gaia dwells: but, as being an Hellenic deity, she cannot have a Pelasgian Nature-Power for her mother. Neither can she be made by Homer the daughter of Demeter, because Demeter herself bears many signs of character which associate her with Gaia, but which are wholly absent from the picture of Persephonè.

We find in the Albanian language the same form

---

[1] See *supra*, p. 239.   [2] Il. iii. 104.

for the Earth as in Demeter, *deon*[1] : though it is combined with a form not found in that tongue, which
gives us *memme*, and other like forms, for mother.

The Demeter of Homer, then, seems to be a figure
partially Hellenised, principally of Pelasgian conception, and having parts of its material in Eastern
tradition.

In Athens, and in Olympia, her statue stood by that
of Zeus[2] : and, according to Herodotus, the Scythians
treated her as his consort. This is probably no more
than the mythological impersonation given to the earth
as the female or passive principle, subjected to the
action of air, light, and sky.

SECTION VII. *Dionè.*

We find Dionè present in Olympos, when Aphroditè
arrives there after her wound, and is received as her
daughter[3]. She was therefore one of the wives of
Zeus, who expressly owns Aphroditè as his child[4] : and
she, again, expressly names herself as one of the
Olympian gods[5]. To console Aphroditè, she relates
how Arès had suffered at the hands of Otos and Ephialtes, Herè and Aïdes at the hands of Heracles. But
there is nothing in the passage to throw light upon the
origin of Dionè herself; and it is the only passage of
Homer, in which she appears.

We learn however from Hesiod[6], that Dionè was
one of the daughters of Okeanos and Tethūs. These
daughters were sisters to the Rivers. Pherecydes, an

[1] Hahn, Alb. Stud. Lexicon.   [2] Ib. p. 251.
[3] Il. v. 371, 373.   [4] Il. v. 428.   [5] Il. v. 383.
[6] Theog. 353.

Athenian logographer of the fifth century before Christ,
represented her as one of the Nymphs of Dodona[1]. The
coins of Epiros show the head of a Zeus of Dodona,
the Pelasgian Zeus, crowned with oak-leaf[2], an association sustained by that passage of the Odyssey which
refers to the oak, from which the oracles were delivered[3]. Together with the head of Zeus on these
coins is a crowned female head, which cannot be the
head of Herè, as she belongs only to the Hellenic
traditions. Strabo[4] says that Dionè shared the temple
of Zeus at Dodona.

By combining together the fragments of this information, we may come with reasonable evidence to the
conclusion, that Dionè was of the family of Nature-
Powers; and that in this character she was associated
with the elder Zeus of the Pelasgians, the air-god, as
his wife. Some will have it, that she was the mother
of Persephonè. In Homer, the line between the deities of the Underworld and of Olympos is broad, 'and
not easily crossed: but Dionè is the mother of Aphroditè, and the traditions of Aphroditè, of Persephonè,
and of Artemis, undoubtedly intermix. Upon the case
of Dionè, we may make the general observation, that
Homer does not pursue an uniform method of dealing
with the divinities of all the old Theogonies. The darker
and grosser of them, related to the earth, pass into the
Underworld. But Okeanos remains, I suppose, in the
Ocean-River; and Nereus, we know, inhabits the sea-
depth, with his family. The water of rivers is bound
by the epithet Diipetes to the realm and to the idea of
the air-god: and of the rivers Dionè was the reputed

---

[1] Creuzer, Symbolik, iv. 157.   [2] Ib. iv. 156.
[3] Od. xix. 297.   [4] Strabo, b. vii. p. 329 C.

sister. Therefore, like the air-god himself, she perhaps
was sufficiently ethereal in her composition to pass,
though but as a dimly-drawn and unimportant personage, into the Olympian court.

SECTION VIII. *Athenè and Apollo.*

These two are by far the most remarkable personages
who adorn the Olympos of Homer; and the features,
which they possess in common, are so much more
numerous and significant than any by which they may
be separated, that it will be convenient to treat them
together for the purpose of bringing those common
features into view. Such differences as subsist between
them are much more in function, than in character.

But I speak only of their features as shown in the
Homeric text. It is perfectly possible that they may
severally represent in singleness groups of traditions
which either had been, or which afterwards became, the
property of more than one mythological personage. The
names of these may be wholly distinct, and their places,
outside the Homeric mythology, far apart. But the
self-consistency of each of them, upon the page of Homer,
is scarcely less remarkable than their mutual relation;
a relation which at one and the same time both
associates them with one another, and severs them from
most of the other members of the Olympian Court.

Their action, however, in the Poems is so extensive
and multiform, that it will not be possible to exhibit all
its particulars: nor is there the same need for such an
operation as in cases where the evidence is scanty.

Still, it is the more needful to make a comprehensive

and accurate survey of their attributes and offices, because upon the cases of these two deities will mainly
turn the answer to be given to the interesting and important question, whether there is or is not any sensible
infusion into the Homeric system of the ideas related to
the redemption of mankind, which have been preserved
in the Holy Bible and among the Hebrews, and which
may be termed for convenience Messianic. To their
case, however, that of Leto is an important auxiliary.

1. Unless we explain their position in the Olympian
system by the aid of the Hebrew traditions, it offers to
our view a hopeless solecism. The Olympian gods are
arranged generally in two generations. The really
great governing powers are given to the elder of the
two, to Zeus, Poseidon, and to Herè; with a parity of
dignity, though not of influence, to Aïdoneus. All the
three first, in one way or other, are representations of
some conception of the Supreme Being which had prevailed elsewhere, or at an earlier epoch. But Athenè
and Apollo present no such character; and, standing
as they do in the junior line, we are obliged to ask, why
do these two junior deities alone, and in a manner
which cannot be mistaken, share and exercise the prerogatives of supreme deity and government? Inferior
only in some respects to Zeus, they show no inferiority .
in any, and in some a marked superiority, to Herè or
Poseidon.

It is true indeed that both Athenè and Apollo recognise the rights of the Uncle, as the Senior, in Poseidon.
And, if I am right in considering him as having been the
supreme god of a foreign mythology, who was afterwards
naturalised in the Hellenic system, we may readily
understand why, notwithstanding the coarse material

of his being, he, too, is always shielded from palpable dishonour. Yet neither is he suffered to inflict any disgrace or shame on Athenè or Apollo. In the case of Apollo, the two part without fighting[1]. In the case of Athenè, Poseidon withdraws when Odysseus is about to pass beyond the special sphere of that god[2]; and the goddess then resumes the conduct of the affairs of the hero, and guides them to a happy issue. And when, in the disguise of Mentor, she attends the sacrifice of Nestor, and offers prayer to Poseidon, the Poet adds, ' so she prayed; and of herself accomplished all the prayer[3].'

Yet more notable is the relation of rank as between Herè and Athenè. Once Athenè appears, namely in the Debate of the First Book, as the messenger of Herè, to prevent the wrath of Achilles from bursting into flagrant violence[4]: as though Herè had a title to employ her services. Yet, even in this case, Herè, it should be remarked, supplies no instructions; and Athenè frames her discourse after her own will, and with no regard to the special inclination of Herè for Agamemnon. But elsewhere Homer has not scrupled to give to Athenè the first place. Twice the goddesses descend together from Olympos to the field of battle, in the chariot of Herè. It is Herè who yokes the horses, and acts as charioteer: Athenè not only mounts as the warrior beside her, but bears the Aigis of supreme power[5].

When Thetis arrives at Olympos, in the Twenty-fourth Iliad, she receives the honours of a guest, and is placed by the side of Zeus, Athenè giving way to her.

[1] Il. xxi. 468.	[2] Od. v. 380.	[3] Od. iii. 55-62.
[4] Il. i. 195.	[5] Il. v. 711-752; viii. 381-396.

She probably held the second seat of rank on the left side, the first being, as we need not doubt, given to Herè.´ It is Herè, again, who sends the Sun to his repose[1]. On the whole, an ingenious division of ascriptions seems to be carried through, by means of which Herè has the higher place in the internal relations of Olympos, but Athenè far excels in all that immediately touches the government of men.

And now as to the dignity of Apollo.

In the ancient Hymn to this god, cited by Thucydides, it is told that the gods rise from their seats as he comes near[2].

The superiority thus awarded to Apollo cannot be accounted for by anything in the mere order of Olympos, which it seems, indeed, to contravene. The child of Leto the obscure is preferred to the child of great Herè. In a time of wild men and deeds, a god presiding over peaceful functions infinitely outshines the god of war. We must seek for the reason, then, in traditions flowing from another source.

2. In the Fifth Iliad, Homer appears to inform us, that Athenè was born of Zeus without a mother[3]: a statement afterwards developed in the legend, which represents her as having sprung full-grown from his head. Now if the Hellenes had preserved the tradition of the Logos, it was impossible to clothe it, for the purposes of their system, in a more appropriate form. If they had not, how comes it that we have this one only exception made to the accustomed method of parentage?—a method so deeply ingrained in the Greek ideas, that even for Zeus a father must be found.

But Apollo is the child of Leto; and Leto, if we can

---

[1] Il. xviii. 239.   [2] Hymn, 2-4.   [3] Il. v. 880.

give the word a meaning, means darkness or oblivion. If Apollo be considered as the Sun, the name of his mother may signify his birth from Night. But the Apollo of Homer's Olympos is not the Sun; and of his functions a very large portion have no relation to the Night whatever. But if Homer saw in his Apollo a son of his Zeus, whose filial relation rested upon traditions anterior to any which the current mythologies supplied, and if the word Leto expressed such an obscurity, this surely appears to supply a rational and consistent explanation.

Thus the differences between the birth of Athenè and that of Apollo, according to Homer, correspond with the differences between the two forms of the Messianic tradition represented respectively in the Logos, and the Son of the Woman.

3. But while the rank and the power of these deities were traceable to those of Zeus in the Olympian system, it is plain that their dignity, their sanctitas, was greater than his. They were regarded with a more unmixed reverence, as if the traditions relating to them had been kept more free from earthy elements. These propositions do not rest merely on the general mode of handling them in Homer, but upon distinct and well-defined notes. They are never exhibited in the mood of sensual passion, like Zeus and Herè, to say nothing of lesser deities. This is true, without the least qualification, of Athenè. Apollo is stated to have carried up Marpessa the bride of Ideus[1]; and he enters into the ribald jesting of Olympos in the Lay of the Net[2]. But the latter story, as has already been observed, is conceived in the spirit of a foreign myth-

[1] Il. iv. 559-564.   [2] Od. viii. 334.

ology; and with respect to Marpessa, it may be remarked, that the numerous intrigues of the mythical
gods in Homer are never accompanied with violence,
but are invariably made to appear as connections voluntarily accepted; while again they are always attended
with the birth of children. In both particulars this story
differs from them, and it much more resembles that of
Ganymede[1], who was carried up to be cup-bearer in
heaven. Perhaps we are to understand that she was
taken for the service of the deity at the neighbouring
shrine of Delphi, where a priestess so long officiated.

But again, these deities, and these alone, are never
subjected to disparagement in any other form. Herè,
as we have seen, had once been wounded, and Zeus
had been, or was about to be, enchained; but to these
two no violence is ever offered. Further, Zeus is on
the very verge of open conflict with Poseidon; but in the
Theomachy, the battle between Apollo and his uncle is
avoided, while Athenè inflicts a terrible reverse on her
huge opponent Arès. Again, Zeus himself is, for the
time, completely baffled and outwitted by the stratagem
of Herè; and the Hellenising Poseidon is enabled to
take the field against his orders. But neither Athenè
nor Apollo are ever deceived or visibly put to shame.

Nor will this appear an easy matter to arrange, when
it is borne in mind that these two are the great agents
of the two great Olympian deities respectively. It is,
however, carefully contrived that they shall never come
into actual collision one with the other. Apollo interferes against Patroclos; but Athenè is absent. Athenè
interferes against Hector; but Apollo is absent. Again
he is absent, in the Doloneia, while she conducts to a

[1] Il. xx. 234.

prosperous issue the night-expedition of Diomed and
Odysseus[1]. In the Chariot-race of the Twenty-third
Book, where the contest for the first place is between
Eumelos and Diomed, Apollo, the partisan of Eumelos,
throws the whip of Diomed out of his hand[2]. Athenè
restores it, apparently when Apollo has departed, and
by breaking the chariot-yoke of Eumelos secures the
victory of her favourite. Apollo here, though saved as
far as the Poet's art can do it, comes off second best;
but only as against Athenè. A second instance occurs,
where he is brought to suggest, at a time when the
Greeks[3] were losing ground, in lieu of the general conflict, a personal challenge, from Hector which was sure
to be to their advantage. To appreciate the importance of this consideration, we must observe how other
deities are liable to be foiled and worsted : Arès by
Athenè in the Fifth Iliad, and by Hephaistos in the
Eighth Odyssey; Herè and Aïdoneus by Heracles;
Artemis by Herè in the Theomachy; Aphroditè by Diomed; Demeter[4], and Herè too[5], by Zeus. Zeus himself was delivered from a conspiracy by extraneous aid.

There is a manifest difference to be observed as to the
relations of will and affection with Zeus, between these
two and the other deities. These alone he calls by the
epithet ' dear[6].' The case of Apollo stands alone as an
exhibition of entire unbroken harmony with the will
of Zeus, which in all things he regards. When he
remonstrates, it is with the body of the gods, not
with Zeus personally[7]; and Herè, rebuking him for his

---

[1] Il. x. 515.   [3] Il. xxiii. 384.   [5] Il. vii. 20.   [6] Od. v.
[4] Il. xv. 18.   [2] Il. viii. 39, xxii. 183; and xv. 221, xvi. 667.
[7] Il. xxiv. 33.

interference, is at once checked by Zeus[1]. Though he seems to be the habitual organ for accomplishing his father's designs, he is never so employed in any purpose which is about to fail; such, for instance, as would have been the defence of Sarpedon. Zeus himself is by no means so carefully shielded, in great providential matters, as Apollo.

The necessities of the Poem place Athenè in antagonism to Zeus, and she goes all lengths in the prosecution of her purposes. But, if in opposition to the chief deity, she is on the side not only of justice, but of the Olympian decree, to which Zeus himself, his personal partialities leaning one way, and his governing responsibility another, has felt it right to yield. She exposes herself, together with Herè, to his threats; but his anger, in her case, is on account of her threatening him on a special and rare occasion[2], while Herè ever leads him an uneasy life[3]; and he seems anxious to take the first opportunity of reassuring her[4] as his beloved daughter.

We have, then, in the case of Apollo, an uniform identity of will with the chief god, and in the case of Athenè only an exceptional departure from it. This is a very remarkable feature. In Herè and Poseidon, it is wholly wanting. In Hermes and Iris we find the obedience of messengers, but not the unity of counsel and of mind. In general, such harmony can no more broadly be asserted of Olympos, than of a kingdom or court on earth. No traditions known to me appear in any way to account for it, except those of the Hebrew race. It

---

[1] Il. xxiv. 69.   [2] Il. viii. 406-408.   [3] Il. i. 561-563.
[4] Il. viii. 39.

is evidently the very picture for which they are calculated to furnish the materials.

The Hellenic religion represents Apollo as the defender of Heaven, and the Deliverer of the Immortals, in some great peril or struggle of contending spirits. He destroyed Otos and Ephialtes, the hugest, and after Orion the most beautiful, of all beings reared on earth, at the critical time when they are about to scale heaven by piling the mountains.

This function has no natural connection with the mythological offices of Apollo, great and varied as they are. Neither as physician, harper, poet, prophet, archer, nor angel of death, can he appear entitled to claim the honour thus awarded to him. There is also in Homer a glance at a general rebellion of the Giants and at their fall in consequence of their impiety[1]. The later tradition retains, down to the Augustan age, this account of Apollo with a diversity of accompaniments. In Homer, as the account is by no means to be explained through his Olympian offices, it appears to represent some older tradition, according to which this bright and lofty person, intimately associated with, and specially executing on earth, the divine will, had likewise put down in actual battle a rising of rebellious spirits in the Upper world.

To Athenè there is assigned by Homer no function resembling this. But the specialties of a certain divine supremacy are in a manner divided between them. Athenè takes a peculiar jurisdiction in the Underworld; and it is the more remarkable because, while she uses it in aid of Zeus, it does not come by derivation from him. She declares[2] that but for her, Heracles, when

[1] Od. vil. 36, 60.   [2] Il. vlil. 362-369; cf. Od. ii. 623-626.

he went to fetch Cerberus, never would have escaped
the dire streams of Styx. This seems to mean that
Zeus could not have delivered him.

Lastly, we cannot fail to observe how the powers
and offices of these two deities encroach upon and
cut across the provinces of other recognised divinities,
with a total absence of any reciprocity in regard to
what may be called their special function. Athenè,
as the goddess of war, not only rivals Arès, but excels
him. She is the goddess of art, like Hephaistos, with
some distinction, indeed, as he operates upon metals
with the aid of fire, and she ordinarily on tissues. Yet
not so as to limit her power; for she, together with
Hephaistos, instructs the silversmith in all the departments of his art[1]; and moreover teaches mensuration
to the carpenter[2]. She presides over industry and over
cunning, like Hermes; and she shares with this deity
his special function as conductor of the dead[3]. Again,
in parts of her relation to Polity, as Ἀγελείη[4], λαοσσόος[5], ἐρυσίπτολις[6], she approaches to the office of Themis[7]: who summons and dissolves assemblies, thus
discharging subordinate functions apparently on behalf
of the primary political deity.

Apollo, as the healer, discharges the office of Paieon.
But while Paieon[8], who is somewhat strongly marked
as a deity of the Egyptian system, heals with the
hand[9], Apollo has too high a dignity to be thus represented. He simply deposits the stunned Æneas
in his temple, where Leto and Artemis proceed to treat

---

[1] Od. vi. 233, xxiii. 154.   [2] Il. xv. 412.   [3] Od. ii. 626; cf. xxiv.1.
[4] Ἀγελείη = Spoil-driver, or Folk-leader.
[5] λαοσσόος = Folk-stirrer.   [6] ἐρυσίπτολις = City-warder.
[7] Od. ii. 69. Il. xx. 4.   [8] Od. iv. 231.   [9] Il. v. 401.

him[1]: or, in answer to the prayer of Glaucos, heals from afar the wound of that gallant warrior[2].

Apollo, as the musician, is supreme in the province of the Muses; who are purely poetical and Hellenic impersonations, sometimes one in number, sometimes nine[3]. His concern is with the instrument, theirs with the voice; but they perform together at the Olympian banquet[4], and have, probably, a community of relation to the Bard.

Apollo, as the agent of Zeus, moves in the same province as Hermes and Iris, especially the latter: but the highest offices are always reserved to him, in which the Divine intention is to take effect. It is left to Hermes to conduct Priam to the presence of Achilles, when the object is only that of a go-between, and the result depends upon the will of the hero.

In the 'Studies on Homer' I called by the name of Secondaries[5] the deities who are thus placed, even in their own departments, below Apollo and Athenè. Perhaps the name is not appropriate, since these personages have in general independent traditions of their own. The main point is that we should observe the approach to a divine universality of office and power in Apollo and Athenè, which can in no respect be accounted for by the formation of the Olympian family or its laws.

Let us now turn to points connected with the human and terrestrial relations of these great deities.

They are jointly invoked, together with Zeus, in a solemn but often-repeated formula expressing keen desire; as when Achilles prays, 'Father Zeus! and

---

[1] Il. v. 445–447. [2] Il. xvi. 527–529. [3] Od. xxiv. 60.
[4] Il. i. 603, 604. [5] Vol. ii. p. 59.

Athenè! and Apollo! would that every Trojan should perish, and every Greek[1].'

And they are placed at the climax of honour in another formula[2]:

'Were I honoured as are honoured Athenè and Apollo.'

This line suggests the question whether, in the time of Homer, some visible form of worship may possibly have been paid to these two deities, as the agents of a Supreme God, presumed to be less accessible than they, and was at the same time not accorded to others. Be this as it may, they are the only deities whose temples are unequivocally named to us in Homer: the temple of Apollo[3] at Chrusè, on Pergamos, and at Putho: the temple of Athenè[4] at Athens, on Pergamos, and in Scherìè.

Again, we do not find any local limit to the worship of these deities within the sphere of Greek knowledge and experience. Athenè, the most Hellenic deity, is the patroness of Pelasgian Attica, and is also the object of the supplicatory procession of Trojan women in the Sixth Iliad. She is worshipped at Pulos, in Ithaca, in the Greek camp. Apollo, the great Trojan deity, has his priest among the Kicones, his temple at Pytho, his altar in Delos, his grove and festival in Ithaca; and he is the fountain-head of the prophetic gift, which pervades all parts of Greece. He is connected with Killè, with Lycia in the south, and with the Lycian Trojans in the north of Asia Minor. Seers, whom he always endows with vision, are found[5] even among the Cyclops. He feeds the horses of Admetos in Picrìè,

---

[1] Il. xvi. 97.   [2] Il. viii. 540; xiii. 827.
[3] Il. i. 39; v. 445; ix. 404.
[4] Il. ii. 549; vi. 88, 297. Od. vi. 320–322.   [5] Od. ix. 508.

claims the daughter of Marpessa in Ætolia, and slays the children of Niobè near Mount Sipulos. In truth, he seems scarcely less universal than that scourge of Death, to which he stands in so near and solemn a relation.

No deity of the Poems, except Zeus, can at all compete with Apollo and Athenè in this respect.

Next, Apollo and Athenè are independent of all the limitations of place: another point in which no other deity, but Zeus, appears to resemble them.

Athens, indeed, appears to be indicated in the Odyssey as the abode of Athenè[1]. Apollo has no abode directly assigned to him. But the sign of omnipresence in both is, that prayer is addressed to them from all places indifferently. Only four times[2] do we find actual petitions to Apollo, and all these in Troas. But we may observe this essential point; that, as in the two last of these for example, he is presumed to be present, and to hear it as a matter of course, without reference to any special residence or function. To Athenè we have no less than twelve prayers given in the Poems, in Ithaca, Scheriè, Pulos, Troy, and the Greek camp; and always to her as an universal not a local power. But even Poseidon, great as he is, never has prayer offered to him, except near the sea, or by his own descendants.

In truth, but a small number of deities in Homer are made the subjects of actual invocation. For example, there is no invocation anywhere to Aphroditè, Arès,

---

[1] Od. vii. 80, 81.

[2] Il. i. 35–43; 450–457; iii. 100–103, 116–131; xvi. 513–529. Add, however, the references in Il. xi. 363, 364, and i. 65, 473.

Hermes, Hephaistos, Demeter, or even Herè. Artemis[1] and Poseidon are invoked: the first in connection with function, the latter with place. We have also addresses from mortals to the deities presiding over the Oath, or ruling in the Underworld. But general prayer is addressed only to Zeus, Pallas, and Apollo.

Again, these favoured deities are exempt from physical or other infirmity or need in general. They are never excited by mere personal passion. Neither of them individually eats or drinks; as Hermes, for example, does, at the dwelling of Calypso[2], or as Iris fears lest she should lose her share of the Ethiopian hecatomb[3]. Neither of them sleeps, or is weary, or is wounded, or suffers pain. They are never introduced as delighting in sacrifice apart from obedience. Artemis sends the boar to Caludon because she had been forgotten in the offerings[4]: but Apollo's wrath, in the First Iliad, is not for the want of prayer or hecatomb, it is on account of the shame and wrong done by Agamemnon to Chruses his priest[5]. Diomed and Odysseus are dear to Pallas: but she never asks or commends their bounty at the altar, as Zeus commends that of Hector, and of Odysseus himself[6]. When sacrifice is offered to Apollo, in the First Iliad[7], after the restitution, his pleasure is not stated to have been in the savour of it, but in the hymn of praise which was addressed to him. Zeus can accept the victims even while he frustrates the petition[8]: but when Athenè in like manner declines a prayer of the

[1] Od. xx. 61.   [2] Od. v. 94.   [3] Il. xxiii. 207.
[4] Il. ix. 536.   [5] Il. l. 65, 93.   [6] Il. xxiv. 68. Od. l. 66.
[7] Il. l. 473.   [8] Il. ii. 420.

Trojans, she is not stated to accept the offering[1];
and the idea that when offended she can be appeased
by mere offerings is thus practically repudiated[2].
Again, attributes of bulk stand at the bottom of the
scale of excellence. They are indirectly assigned to
Pallas by the weight of the Aigis which she carries[3].
This is possibly on account of the direct competition
which subsists between the huge Arès, as a god of war,
and herself, presiding over the same province[4]. Bulk
is never ascribed to Apollo.

Again, as to locomotion. Apollo and Athenè move
without the use of any instruments, such as wings,
chariots, or otherwise. Their journeys are usually
undistributed and instantaneous. They set out, and
they arrive[5]. On one occasion only, Athenè employs
the foot-wings[6] which were used by Hermes. But there
are details and steps in the movements of Hermes,
Poseidon, and Herè[7].

The ordinary Olympian deity, when offended by
mortals, most commonly makes his appeal to Zeus
for redress. Thus Poseidon acts with respect to the
Greek rampart; Aphroditè, tacitly, after her wound
by Diomed; Arès, in the same condition; and Helios,
after his oxen have been devoured by the crew of
Odysseus[8].

But the retributive action of Apollo, in the Plague of
the First Iliad, is wholly independent, and is the more
remarkable since he wastes the army of the Greeks to
the great peril of an enterprise promoted by such

---

[1] Il. vii. 311.   [2] Od. iii. 143-147.   [3] Il. ii. 443.
[4] See Il. xviii. 519.   [5] Od. i. 102-103. Il. xv. 150.
[6] Od. i. 96.   [7] Od. v. 50-58. Il. xiii. 17-31; xiv. 225-230.
[8] Il. v. 869, 426; vii. 445. Od. xii. 377, 387.

powerful divinities. In the Third Odyssey[1], on the
return of the Greeks, we are told that Zeus designed
evil for them by reason of their crimes, wherefore
many perished by the wrath of Pallas; that she could
not be appeased, and that Zeus suspended calamity over
them. There is no sign here of an appeal to Zeus,
but rather of an identification of the two agencies in
the providential government of the world.

Again, Apollo and Athenè administer powers which
are otherwise the special or exclusive property of Zeus.

The air-functions of that deity are sometimes,
indeed, exercised by Herè. This may reasonably be
accounted for by her relation to him as wife. No
kindred reason is available for the selection of these
two among his children for an office so elevated.
Athenè, with Herè, thunders in honour of Agamemnon[2]: and she can cause the winds to cease, or to
blow[3]. So he too sends for the Greek ship a toward
breeze[4]. But the most significant of all the partici-
pations of the supreme power is confined to Athenè
with Apollo. Both of them in turn carry the Aigis
in the Fifth and Fifteenth Iliads respectively[5]. And,
in truth, these two deities seem throughout the Iliad
to share with Zeus the function of Providence; the one
as towards the Trojans, the other as towards the
Greeks[6]. Indeed, in the Odyssey more especially,
they fill the very highest offices of divine government
over the minds of men; which appear to be conducted
by Pallas, much more than by Zeus himself.

---

[1] Od. lii. 132 seqq.
[2] Il. xi. 45.
[3] Od. v. 109, 382-385, *et alibi.*
[4] Il. l. 479
[5] Il. v. 735-742; xv. 229.
[6] See Studies on Homer, Olympos, pp. 115-122.

There is a very peculiar function attaching to the divine supremacy, in the signification of coming events to men by the flight of birds, and by atmospheric signs. This power, being connected with the future, is distinguished from the general power over external nature. It is shared with Zeus principally by Apollo, but also by Athenè. He sends the Kirkos, or wheeling falcon, to Thrace, as an omen of success to Telemachos[1] : she, a heron to cheer Odysseus and Diomed in the Night-excursion of the Tenth Iliad[2]. She stupefies and bewilders the Suitors as their ruin approaches : but his agent, Theoclumenos[3], announces, and he therefore may be considered as supplying, the portents which beset the Hall of the Palace before the final catastrophe.

Nägelsbach observes, that the power of signs is confined to Zeus, Herè, Apollo, and Pallas[4]. But the signs exhibited by Herè, the thunder of the Eleventh Iliad, and the gift of speech to the horses of Achilles, involve no knowledge or signification of the future. The prediction delivered by the horse Xanthos appears to be his own, and not the gift of the goddess.

It may be affirmed generally, that both these deities, but especially Athenè, exercise a power over external nature almost without limit. Assuming the human form, they can make themselves visible to one person only among many[5]. They, and none but they, frame images of human beings which can speak or fight[6] : Pallas alters at will the figures and features of

---

[1] Od. xv. 526.
[2] Il. x. 274.
[3] Od. xx. 345-371.
[4] Hom. Theol. Iv. 16 ; p. 147.
[5] Il. i. 198, and (apparently) xvii. 321-324.
[6] Il. v. 449. . Od. iv. 796, 826.

Odysseus, Penelopè, and Laertes; having command, apparently, of some organic power over matter and vital force. While Athenè's jurisdiction as to storms is unlimited, Apollo diverts rivers from their beds, and makes them converge upon a point[1]. In like manner they act upon the mind of man by infusing fear, courage, counsel, as the case may be. These operations are never assigned to any deity except those of the first order in Olympos.

But when Poseidon breathes valour into the two Ajaxes, he does it by striking them; just as when he has to convert the ship of the Phaiakes into a rock, he drives it downward with a blow of his hand[2]. On the other hand, Apollo infuses courage into Hector and Glaucos, and heals also the wounds of the latter chieftain[3], without any outward act. Most of the corporal changes effected by Athenè in the Odyssey are similarly brought about. Only in the case where she effects a total transformation of Odysseus, she touches him with her wand[4].

This exception, as a rule, from the use of instruments in giving effect to their will, is a sign of a high conception, on the part of the Poet, with respect to their divine power. In the Kestos of Aphroditè, in the wand of Hermes, an intrinsic virtue resides, apart from the will of those personages respectively. These are not mere symbols: they are causative seats of power. That Apollo and Athenè do not use any such vehicle, is a sign of force, essential, independent, and supreme, over matter.

---

[1] Il. xll. 24.
[2] Il. xlii. 58. Od. xiiL 164.
[3] Il. xvi. 528.
[4] Od. xiiL 429; xvi. 172, 455.

Yet once more, as to the common features of these extraordinary personages.

Their moral standard is conspicuously raised above that of the Olympian family in general.

Athenè has the purity of Artemis, whom in all other points she eclipses. This prerogative is expressly acknowledged in the ancient Hymn to Aphroditè[1]. No such statement can be made of any other among the active goddesses: not of Herè, Thetis, or Demeter; much less of Aphroditè herself.

So we have in the Poems sons of Zeus, of Poseidon, of Arès, of Hermes; all of them the fruit of their intrigues with women; but no son of Apollo. Hephaistos, indeed, is exempt from the charge, probably on account of his personal deformity. Down to the time of Æschylus[2], Apollo retained the epithet of 'the pure.' Later still, it had been lost[3]; and the legend of Marpessa, which by no means requires such a construction in Homer, had been read in the light of the later tradition, and had descended to the common level. His share in the scene described by the Lay of Demodocos may perhaps be accounted for by the fact that the subject belonged to a foreign theology, though it may have been one which was already beginning to act upon Greece.

I do not however attach to the term 'purity,' in an inquiry of this nature, its full Christian sense; in which it appears as one portion of the panoply of a complete and almost seraphic virtue, and is elevated as well as sustained by the spirit of the marvellous religion to which it belongs. The moral characters of Apollo and Athenè are lofty, if measured by the Olympian standard, although they will not bear the tests which

[1] vv. 8, 16.   [2] Suppl. 221.   [3] S. Clem. Alex. p. 20, B.

the Christian system would apply. Apollo descends from his height, in the scene where he strikes Patroclos from behind, and knocks his armour off, so as to bring the Greek hero into that unequal position in which even the keen national feeling of the Poet would allow him to be conquered by a Trojan. And Pallas undertakes a mean office when she incites Pandaros to a breach of the Pact. Counsel, with her, certainly degenerates at times into craft and fraud[1]. But these drawbacks are in both cases exceptional. Speaking generally, the two are beautiful and majestic delineations; and Athenè in particular has many of the characteristics of the Eternal Wisdom, which came forth from the bosom of God. .

The distinctive functions of Apollo, which sever him from Athenè, are many. The highest are these four: that he is familiarly employed by Zeus, with whom he has a perfect conformity of will, as his agent in the government of human affairs; that he is the champion of Zeus and of heaven against the rebellious powers; that he is the minister of death; and, finally, that to him alone there seems to be committed an absolute knowledge of the future, and the administration of that prophetic gift which Calchas, though acting in and for the Greek army, held from him[2]. Athenè, on the other hand, is occasionally the agent of Zeus, with whose will, however, she is less uniformly associated[3]. Apollo has also, besides the gifts of the bow, of healing, and of song, a special association with the light.

The ministry of death, exercised by Apollo for men as by Artemis for women, is most of all remarkable

---

[1] Il. iv. 86—92. Od. xiii. 299.   [2] Il. i. 72.
[3] Il. iv. 70. Od. xxiv. 539-545.

on account of its twofold aspect. It is sometimes
penal, as with Ariadnè[1]; or even a terrible vengeance,
as with the children of Niobè[2]. It is sometimes a
tranquil and painless deliverance from the burden of
the flesh, as in the island of Suriè[3]. Another peculiarity
of this prerogative is, that it refers to death produced
without second causes. All other deaths whatever in
the Poems, natural or violent, appear to be referred to
second causes. There is a mythological impersonation
of Death (Thanatos) provided by the Poet, to which to
refer them. The death brought about by Apollo and
Artemis is an exceptional death, in the point of being
directly due to their supreme will and special ministry.

And this is at least a wonderful phenomenon in the
Olympian system, especially when we consider how
gloomy and repulsive, in the view of Homer and his age,
was the extinction of our mortal life, and the prospect
of the region that lay beyond it. Here is, as matter of
fact, a tradition of a Power that was to take away the
sting from Death, preserved for the time, but for the
time only, among a people who surrounded death in
general with associations of a wholly different character.
Even if it stood alone, we should be driven surely to
treat it as derived, through whatever channel, from
some ancient and signal promise of a Deliverer for the
human race. It does not however stand alone, but
forms part of a multitude of varied testimonies, all
converging upon the same point.

Athenè, besides her great special prerogatives of War,
Policy, and Industrial Art, is invested generally with
yet greater power than Apollo, and rises to a still
higher grade of moral majesty. She seems also, by

[1] Od. xi. 324.   [2] Il. xxiv. 606; cf. vi. 205.   [3] Od. xv. 407.

virtue of a latent partnership in the divine supremacy, to partake of or represent something analogous to several of his peculiar gifts. She enters into his knowledge of the future; for in the Ithacan cave she foretells to Odysseus all that he has yet to suffer[1]. And if he is the champion of the gods in Olympus (an office which she shared with him in the later tradition), she, as I have above observed, possesses a jurisdiction in the Underworld[2], which appears to cross and over-ride that of its appointed rulers. Though she cannot avert death from a mortal, she can afterwards extricate him from its grasp[3].

The limits of this work forbid me to pursue the mythological history of Athenè and Apollo through the later literature of the Greeks and Romans. They continue, it may be said generally, to hold positions of great splendour, but the distinctive character of their features as a whole is gradually enfeebled and effaced.

Even the hasty reader of Homer cannot fail to be struck with it; but it is only by a minute and careful observation of particulars that the whole case can be brought out. It then becomes fully manifest that, by not one, but a crowd of attributes and incidents, they are severed from the general body of the Olympian deities of Homer, and closely associated together, though very far from being even substantially identified, far less confused. These attributes are partly intellectual, partly moral. The general result is to render their position grossly anomalous and wholly inexplicable, if the explanation of it is only to be sought in the laws of the Olympian system, or in such traditions as the

---

[1] Od. xiii. 306.   [2] Il. viii. 362-369. Od. iv. 790-793.
[3] Od. iv. 752, 753.

older nature-worship, or the Egyptian, or Syrian, or Phœnician mythologies could supply.

But when we turn to the Hebrew annals, we find there a group of traditions, belonging to what may be termed the Messianic order, which appear to supply us with a key to the double enigma. The general characteristics of the Messianic anticipations are in marked conformity with the common prerogatives of Pallas and Apollo. And the distinctions of the two deities fall in, not less clearly, with the twofold form in which those anticipations are presented to us; the one, which pointed to a conception more abstract, and less capable of being confounded with mere humanity; the other, to a form strictly personal, and intimately associated with our nature.

In these resemblances, there appears to be found a very strong presumption, that the Hellenic portion of the Aryan family had for a time preserved to itself, in broad outline, no small share of those treasures, of which the Semitic family of Abraham were to be the appointed guardians, on behalf of all mankind, until the fulness of time should come.

It is obvious that such traditions, when cut off from their fountain-head, supplied a material basis for that anthropomorphic character which distinguished the Greek religion from first to last, and associated it so closely with the whole detail of life. For, according to their tenor, the conception and representation of deity in human form were no idle fancy, but were the great design of the Almighty God for the recovery of an erring, suffering, and distracted race.

On the importance of these propositions I need not dwell. The more they are important, the more it is to be desired that they should be strictly noted. The intention of these pages is both to invite, and somewhat to assist, all such as shall be disposed to undertake the pains of such an investigation.

Section IX. *Hephaistos.*

Hephaistos bears in Homer the double stamp of a Nature-Power, representing the element of fire, and of an anthropomorphic deity, who is the god of Art, at a period when the only fine art known was in works of metal produced by the aid of fire.

As Homer gives us faint traces of the elemental god of air in endios, and as his Nereus is still represented in the nero of modern Greek for ‘water,’ so he actually employs the name Hephaistos in one passage undeniably for fire[1], if he does not also mean the flame of fire in other passages where he mentions ‘the flame of Hephaistos.’ This deity is worshipped in Troas, where he has a wealthy priest[2].

Hahn finds in the fouki-a of the Albanian tongue, signifying force, the root of the word Vulcanus[3]; and quotes Varro, ‘ab ignis vi et violentiâ Vulcanus est dictus.’ Schmidt connects the name with fulgere and fulmen[4].

Hephaistos is not one of the seven astral deities of the East, who stood in relation to seven metals.

It is doubtless in a double or plural tradition that we are to seek the explanation of our finding Hephaistos, on the one hand, bearing the marks of antiquity which belong to a Nature-Power, and, on the other

[1] Il. ll. 426.	[2] Il. v. 9.	[3] Alban. Studien, p. 252.
[4] Beckmann, Inventions, Art. Metals.

hand, made known to us as an infant, the offspring of
Zeus and Herè, whose mother sought to hide him, that
is to put him out of the way, on account of his lameness: a sure sign that, in the view of Homer, he was, so
far as regards his higher character of Art-master, a deity
of more recent introduction. This part of the traditions can relate to no mere fire-god. He is saved by
Thetis, the grand mediatress of the Theogonies, and
Eurunomè, the daughter of Okeanos; and hid by them
in a submarine cavern, where, with the tidal flood of
ocean ever gurgling in his ears, he spends his time for
nine years in working clasps, and necklaces, and other
trinkets. Such an assemblage of images is highly Phœnician, that is to say Eastern, in its colour.

The combination in this place of Thetis, a sea-god-
dess, and the ocean-deity, is remarkable; and stands, I
think, alone in Homer. I understand it to betoken
the dual course of tradition relating to Hephaistos. The
Okeanos of Homer is the sire of gods, or their source[1].
This may indeed relate to the Nature-Powers, rather
than to the Olympian gods, from whom Okeanos stands
somewhat widely apart. If so, Eurunomè has her
share in the transaction as a representative of the
older dynasty of gods, and Thetis as a personage who
has the *entrée* to the newer circle. But it seems more
probable that as Okeanos, the father of Persè, and
father-in-law of Helios, has strong Eastern associations, Eurunomè represents the newer and higher
character of Hephaistos imported from the East, and
that Thetis, according to her own stock, befriends him
as a Nature-Power.

Both the water of Ocean, and the connection of fire

[1] Il. xlv. 201.

with fine art in metals, probably attach Hephaistos to
the channels of Phœnician, in its widest sense of
Eastern, tradition: while he may have represented the
simple element of fire in the Pelasgian systems of
religion.

The latter relation accounts for his being worshipped in Troas, even while he is one of the deities
who, following his chief bent, takes decidedly, though
not passionately, the Greek part in the quarrel. And,
accordingly, it is under the rude conception of mere
fire that he is matched, in the Theomachy, with the
river Xanthos, whom he exhausts by drying up the
stream, and thus sorely afflicts, until Herè intercedes.

Through all his other marked operations in the
Poems, Hephaistos, instead of resolving himself into
the element, remains entirely anthropomorphic, although
he is so far from satisfying the Greek ideal of a god in
respect of form. He is such in the Olympian banquet
at the close of the first Book, at the smithy or forge in
his own palace, and again in the lay of Demodocos.

Married to Aphroditè in the Odyssey, he appears in
the Iliad as the husband of Charis[1]. Now Aphroditè
is a real member of the mythological system, whereas
Charis is loosely and faintly delineated, and seems
almost to hover between an idea and a person. Some
have treated these two representations as discrepant,
and have used them in support of the theory, which
separates the authorship of the two Poems. Others
(myself included) may have suggested modes of reconciliation between them, which are insufficient[2]. Having
now arrived, I think, at adequate proof of the Eastern
or Phœnician character of the mythology, as well as

[1] Od. viii. 269; Il. xviii. 382.   [2] Studies, vol. ii. p. 257.

the scenery, of the whole sphere of the Voyages, I find
in this fact the simplest explanation of a difference,
which, instead of any longer impeaching, rather tends
to sustain the unity of authorship. Hephaistos and
Aphroditè, as husband and wife, owe that relation probably to a Syrian or Syro-Phœnician source. Hephaistos
and Charis, in the sense of the Hellenic mythology,
together represent, with a perfect propriety, the strength
and the grace, the beauty or charm, which require to
be combined in works of Art. Nägelsbach, accordingly,
treats this marriage as allegorical[1].

The Poems, however, establish a relation, be it allegorical or not, between the Charites and Aphroditè;
for the Charites receive her on her return from the
scene of the Net to Cyprus, where they bathe, anoint,
and vest her. One junior of their band, promised by
Herè as a wife to Hupnos, or the god of sleep, in Lemnos, is named Pasitheè. Two handmaids of Nausicaa
in Scheriè draw their beauty from the Charites. There
is therefore some evidence to give them a personality
beyond that which the single mind of the Poet can
confer. Their relation to Eastern personages suggests
that they may have had a place in Eastern tradition;
while it seems that they acquired with time a recognised character and worship in Greece[2]. Professor
Max Müller derives their name, as well as that of
the Harits or horses of the Sun, from the Sanscrit root
ghar, to glitter, to render brilliant by oil[3].

The deity of Hephaistos is matchless within the
sphere of his own art. It is in concert with Athenè, that

[1] Hom. Theol. p. 114.
[2] Welcker, vol. i. p. 696. Dr. Schmidt in Smith's Dict. *sub voc.*
[3] Lectures on Language, ii. 373, 375.

he grants to mortals the gift of manual skill[1]; but his own
works are the most wonderful recorded of any god.   In
addition to every charm of grace and splendour, they
have the actual gift of life.   In Olympos, the metal
handmaids of the limping god both think and speak[2];
and in Scheriè, the porter-dogs of Alkinoos[3] have perpetual existence, and perpetual youth.   Even in the
inanimate Shield there are varied signs of life[4].   A certain kindliness of nature marks the intervention of
Hephaistos, in the first Book, to stop a quarrel[5] between his parents; and that he was endowed with
warm affections is evident from the recital he there
gives of a former effort made by him to save Herè
from the wrath of Zeus, which entailed on him a fall
from heaven to earth[6], as well as from the warm gratitude[7] he displays towards Thetis for the benefit she
had conferred on him.   His conduct respecting Herè
is the more praiseworthy, in proportion as her attempt
upon his deformed infancy had been unnatural[8].   In
the lay of the Net, under the heaviest provocation,
his conduct is not vindictive.

Hephaistos is the architect of the palaces of the gods[9],
as well as the artificer of the most conspicuous works of
Art mentioned in the Poems[10].   He made a lock for
Herè which not only no man, but no god could open[11].
Lemnos appears to be his chosen abode, as a volcanic
isle: of other similar islands or spots, in the later
mythology, we find the like recorded.

[1] Od. vi. 233; xxiii. 160.   [2] Il. xviii. 417.
[3] Od. vii. 91-94.   [4] *Infra*, p. 488.   [5] Il. i. 571-589.
[6] Il. i. 590-594.   [7] Il. xviii. 395.   [8] Il. xviii. 395-397.
[9] Il. i. 607; xiv. 167, 338.   [10] Il. viii. 195; Od. iv. 617.
[11] Il. xiv. 167, 8.

Out of his own art, he carries no signs of divinity in Homer; he does not act on general nature, or on the human mind, unless in a case where the sons of his own Priest are concerned; and these he merely conceals in a cloud of vapour, a power which even Aphroditè seems to exercise on behalf of the body of Hector. His powers of perception are so limited, that, in the lay of Demodocos, he is ignorant of what takes place, during his absence, in his own house, until the Sun informs him, whom he again employs as a spy; nor, in the Twenty-first Book of the Iliad, is he aware of the danger in which Achilles stands from the united Rivers, until Herè informs him, and bids him act[1].

Section X. *Arès.*

The Arès of Homer, like his Poseidon, exhibits that idea of deity which both rises above man, and sinks much below him: in point of strength divine, in point of mind and heart simply animal. He is a compound of deity and brute.

But Arès is greatly inferior to Poseidon in that class of conceptions, to which both, in a marked manner, belong. Glory and awe surround the one, from his unfailing might, and his high origin. Arès represents a huge mass of animal force; but he is so exhibited in the action of the Iliad, as to fall into much of the contempt (in a certain sense) which is evidently meant to attach to Aphroditè.

It seems safe to assume that a god, and more especially a god of war, whom Homer represents as wounded

[1] Il. xxi. 328-333.

and disabled by a Greek warrior, could not, in the time
of Homer, have been a deity of acknowledged worship
and renown in Greece. Nor is there found in the Poems
any trace of such worship. No prayer or sacrifice is
offered to him: he has no general command over the
mind of man, or over external nature. It is said, indeed, that he entered into Hector while that chieftain
was engaged in putting on the armour of Achilles[1]; but
this appears to treat him simply as a passion, just as in
other places his name becomes a synonym for war, or for
a spear. None of the five great gods of the Poems are
ever said thus to enter into (as if it were to be contained in and circumscribed by) the spirit of a man;
the highest divine agents effuse, so to speak, and inspire a temper, but do not impart themselves. He has,
however, a special relation to the martial spirit, which
he stirs in Menelaos[2], and which he confers as a gift
in the Odyssey upon the Pseudodysseus; but only in
conjunction with Athenè[3]. This may be taken, however, as a sign that he was known to some extent within
Greece; in Crete, for example. In Greece, too, he is
the father of Ascalaphos and Ialmenos[4]; and the wall
of Thebes is the teíchos Areion[5]. Lünemann[6] observes, that Arès represents the idea of raw courage.
He does not represent courage as Homer conceived it.
He has no skill, resource, or even perseverance in war,
whether against Athenè or against Diomed; but rather
a stupid insensibility, which rushes on the spear's point[7].
And, when he has felt it, he flies off, and howls under
the pain: two operations never (I think) permitted by

---

[1] Il. xvii. 210.   [2] Il. v. 563.   [3] Od. xiv. 199, 216.
[4] Il. il. in voc.   [5] Il. iv. 407.   [6] Wörterbuch in voc.
[7] Il. v. 859-863.

Homer to a wounded Greek; perhaps not even to a wounded Trojan. He groans again after his discomfiture by Athenè in the Theomachy[1].

In battle with the Solumoi, Arès is said to slay Isandros, the son of Bellerophon. This may mean no more than that Isandros fell in the war[2].

Represented as dwelling in Olympos, he is unaware of what has taken place on the battle-fields of Troas; he learns by accident the death of his son Ascalaphos; and when rushing forth to avenge it, he is arrested by Pallas, who strips off his armour, scolds him sharply, and replaces[2] him in his seat[3]. She habitually, indeed, to use our homely phrase, bullies him[4].

Thus inferior in action to Athenè, he only divides with her the prerogative of presiding over war. On the Shield of Achilles, the two are represented[5] as the patrons respectively of the two opposing hosts; and in a variety of passages[6] besides that already referred to, their common, or rather rival, possession of this field of action is exhibited. For example, in the Twentieth Iliad[7], while Athenè shouts to urge on the Greeks, Arès does the like for the Trojans.

In the Fifth Iliad[8], he envelopes the fight in darkness: but, as if to account for so powerful an operation by a deity of his secondary rank, the Poet goes on to say that he was fulfilling the orders of Apollo, who had bid him incite the Trojans.

He was overcome and bound by the youths Otos and Ephialtes (whom Apollo conquered); and he would have

---

[1] Il. xxi, 417.   [2] Il. vi. 203.   [3] Il. xv. 110-142.
[4] Il. v. 766.   [5] Il. xviii. 516.
[6] Il. v. 430, xvii. 398, xx. 350.   [7] 48-53.
[8] 505-511.

perished in his bonds, had not Hermes released him, after an imprisonment of thirteen months [1]. Immortal he is [2]; but, it appears, only just immortal. He is thirsty, not of sacrifices in the ordinary way, but of human blood [3]. According to Ammianus [4], the Thracians of history propitiated him by sacrificing the lives of prisoners.

So limited are his perceptions, that Pallas, by putting on a particular helmet, can prevent his recognising her [5].

His flesh is tender, like that of all the gods: but he is described principally by bulk and mass [6]. When Athenè smites him to the ground, he extends over nine pelethra, or about seven hundred feet [7], in length.

On escaping from the net, in the Eighth Odyssey, he repairs to Thrace. From thence, with his ideal son Terror, he comes forth to make war upon the Ephuroi (a race whom their name appears to associate with the Greeks), or with the Phleguai. In Thrace clearly was his home. Thrace appears to have been known by the name of Aria [8]. Berkel connects the two names together.

If, on the one hand, Arès was not fully established as an Hellenic deity, still he is a son of Herè, in the Olympian family, and there is a lack of special links between him and the Trojans. It appears that he wavered between the two parties: nay, even that he had promised to take part with the Greeks, and had then changed his mind. He is accordingly called turn-

---

[1] Il. v. 385-391.   [2] Ib. 901.   [3] Ib. 289.
[4] xxvii. 4.   [5] Il. v. 845.   [6] Il. li. 478; vii. 208; viii. 349.
[7] Il. xxi. 407.   [8] Steph. Byzant. in voc. Thrakè.

coat (alloprosallos), and is a special object of the wrath of Herè, who makes known in Olympos the death of his son Ascalaphos, with the hope that he may avenge it on the Trojans, and so change sides again. This he is evidently about to do, in despite of the prohibition of Zeus, when Pallas stops him, lest more trouble should arise from the wrath of the Sire. When he suffers defeat in the Theomachy, Pallas tells him it is because the Erinues of his mother Herè pursue him [1]. The whole nation of the Thrakes, however (as we now understand Thrace), with whom he is specially associated, are among the allies of Troy in the War [2].

It is difficult, from the materials afforded by Homer, to trace the god Arès up to his origin. But his prominent place in the Italian mythology renders it probable, that his worship may have prevailed among the Pelasgian forerunners of the Hellenic race. Welcker thinks that he had had a divine cultus at an early date among some race alien to the Greek, from which the Hellenic gods proper displaced him, and that there are traces of him as a Nature-Power [3]. Both ideas would be verified if he could be tracked to a Pelasgian or quasi-Pelasgian source; and this too would give a propriety to his siding with Troy; which, however, poetical necessity went far towards exacting, in order to give even the faintest show of equality to the Trojan party in Olympos.

[1] Il. xxi. 412.   [2] Il. ii. 844-846.   [3] Gr. Götterlehre, i. 414.

SECTION XI. *Hermes.*

The part played by Hermes in the Iliad is secondary. His only important manifestation is when, in the Twenty-fourth Book, he appears by order of Zeus to Priam, under the semblance of a young prince; and attends him, with amiable care, on his way to and from the scene of his arduous errand. But this mission is neither political nor military. It is only social and domestic. It is eminently illustrative of the peculiar function of Hermes, which is, to be the god of expedients, resource, and help; the accommodating and genial god [1]. This character is expressed alike in his epithets, such as eriounios [2] and akaketa [3], and in his conduct. His agency is, as a rule, beneficial to those with whom he deals: hence he is chosen to be the guide of Priam : hence he assures Calypso that he has come to her unwillingly at the command of Zeus, cautiously alleging, however, the length of way and want of provision on the journey, as his reasons [4]. He is the person employed to admonish Aigisthos [5] not to commit the meditated crimes : a warning, which aimed at saving him from vengeance.

Hermes is the son of Zeus and Maias [6]. He is the giver of increase, dōtor eaōn [7] : and it is perhaps in this capacity that Eumaios, the swineherd, consecrates to him a seventh portion, at the meal-sacrifice in his hut, on the arrival of Odysseus [8]. Like the majority of the other gods, he has one or more human children

---

[1] Il. xxiv. 334.   [2] Rare helper.   [3] Never harmful.
[4] Od. v. 99–102.   [5] Od. i. 38.   [6] Od. viii. 335; xiv. 435.
[7] Od. viii. 335.   [8] Od. xiv. 435.

born clandestinely[1]: but, whenever we hear of him,
it is as the giver of some gift, or renderer of some
service. Yet the idea of concealment inheres in his
functions. When the question is raised in Olympos
as to delivering the body of Hector, the first expedient
is, that Hermes should steal it[2]. Again he steals Arès
out of his confinement[3]. His prerogatives however
embrace not only thievery, but also perjury, as it was
he who conferred both these gifts on Autolucos[4]. Yet
perhaps, considering his general character of usefulness
without hurt, we may possibly presume that these ob-
jectionable faculties were only given for some defensive
or beneficial end. In Homer, he has no relation to
industry, or skill in manufacture: these belong to
Athenè and Hephaistos. But he seems to be the agent
or envoy of the Olympian assembly: and his office as
the god of increase, together with his relation to pilfering, place him in connection with the business of
exchange, at a period when commerce, so beneficial in
itself, is notwithstanding a near neighbour not only to
fraud on the one hand, but to violence on the other.

He never hates, or punishes, or quarrels, or is in-
censed with any one. Nor is he troubled with self-
love. Though ranged on the Greek side in the poem,
and in the Theomachy, he declines the contest with
Leto, his appointed antagonist, as a wife of Zeus, too
great for him to cope with: and tells her she may give
out that she has worsted him[5].

In the Fourth Iliad, Zeus chooses Athenè for the
mission to Pandaros, to persuade him to break the
covenanted truce[6]. This office would have seemed

---

[1] Il. xvi. 181.   [2] Il. xxiv. 24.   [5] Il. v. 390.
[4] Od. xix. 369.   [3] Il. xxi. 497-501.   [6] Il. iv. 69.

every way more suitable to Hermes. The reason that
it is not committed to him may probably be, that he
was unknown in Troy. In the Twenty-fourth Book,
he describes himself to Priam as a Myrmidon and an
esquire of Achilles, nor does he announce himself as
a god until it becomes necessary that he should depart,
and leave the old King alone within the cantonment
of the formidable hero. Priam does not then in any
manner recognise him personally, or address him in his
divine capacity.

The functions discharged by Hermes appear to point
to a connection with the Phœnicians, as the great merchants of the time. The name of his mother Maias
is not connected by Homer with Phœnicia, except by
the negative evidence that, like Dionè the mother of
Aphroditè, she does not appear in the list of the attachments of Zeus given in the Fourteenth Iliad, where all the
intimacies have their scene laid or supposed in Greece,
Greek traditions alone appearing to be admitted. In
the Hymn to Hermes the gap is supplied, and Maias
is declared to be the daughter of Atlas, who is with
Homer a personage entirely Phœnician.

Again, Hermes manifestly has a personal relation
with Calypso[1], who welcomes him as αἰδοῖός τε φίλος τε[2];
terms, which are much beyond the limit of ordinary
courtesy; which are employed in the very special case
of Zeus and Thetis[3]; and which Herè flatters herself
she shall deserve at the hands of Okeanos and Tethūs,
provided she shall succeed in bringing them together
again[3]. Calypso was the daughter of Atlas: and it
is probable that Maias was her mythological sister,

[1] Od. v. 88.   [2] Revered and loved.
[3] Il. xxiv. 111. Cf. Il. xviii. 394.   [4] Il. xiv. 210.

and Hermes her nephew. We have another sign of
the ties between him and Calypso in this, that Odysseus obtained from her the account of the proceedings
in Olympos about the oxen of the Sun, and that she
had had it from Hermes. This could hardly be on
any other footing than that of a mythological relationship, really indicating an ethnical affinity. He was
systematically worshipped by the people of Scheriè
before retiring to rest [1].

We find him yet again employed, within the circle
of the Phœnician traditions [2], to instruct Odysseus as
to the means, by which he may safely encounter Kirkè
and her enchantments. I again use the word Phœnician
as including, for Homer, what was Egyptian or Eastern.

Other remarkable incidents are recorded of him.
It was he who, together with Athenè, conducted Heracles in safety, with the formidable dog, out of Hades [3]:
and he likewise escorts the souls of the Suitors from
Ithaca to the Underworld [4]. He, moreover, carried to
Pelops, from Zeus, the sceptre which Hephaistos had
wrought [5].

Hermes is an agent rather than a mere messenger:
and, as a messenger, he is pretty clearly distinguished in
this vital respect, that he goes not, like Iris, upon the
personal errand of Zeus or Herè, but he carries the
collective resolution of the Olympian Court [6]. His
general office is best represented by the word diactoros
or agent, hers by angelos or messenger. He may be
called the god of intercourse.

His very marked name, Argeiphontes, is nowhere

---

[1] Od. vii. 137.   [2] Od. x. 275-307.   [3] Od. xi. 623-626.
[4] Od. xxiv. 1-14.   [5] Il. ii. 104.
[6] Od. i. 38, 84. Cf. Il. xxiv. 24.

explained in Homer; or in Hesiod; or in the Homeric
Hymn. It is discussed fully by Welcker[1]: and the
constructions put upon it tend to connect him with
the East, and with the astronomic worship. In the
system of the Persians, as stated by Origen, the seventh
or mixed metal is assigned to him[2]. The first verse
of the Twenty-fourth Odyssey connects him with Arcadia through Cyllenè. Hahn finds in the Albanian
language words capable (chermes, tourme,) of relation to his name. It is quite possible that two or more
streams of mythological traditions may meet in him;
but his dominant relations are evidently Eastern.

But as this deity, of great importance and highly
diversified attributes in the later mythology, is of secondary consequence in Homer, I pass on.

Section XII. *Artemis.*

We must not be discouraged if, especially in the
case of a deity of the second order like Artemis, we
find much difficulty in discerning the precise channel
through which she reached her actual place in the
Hellenic mythology, as daughter of Leto, and sister
of Apollo, with the other attributes attaching to her.

On the whole, however, it seems that there is much
truth in the observation of Müller, who says she was
worshipped 'as it were a part of the same deity[3]' with
Apollo. She is in the main a reflection of her brother,
much in the same manner as, saving the substitution

---

[1] Gr. Götterlehre, vol. I. pp. 336 seqq.
[2] Beckmann, Hist. of Inventions, Art. 'Metals.'
[3] Müller's Dorians, vol. iL ch. 9. The chapter contains much
information on the worship of Artemis.

(as it may be called) of the sisterly for the conjugal relation, Herè is a reflection of Zeus. The relation of atmosphere to earth, which had been recognised outside of the Olympian scheme, became, under the anthropomorphic law of that scheme, the relation of King and Father Zeus, to Queen and Mother Herè. The affinity of Sun to Moon, acknowledged already as divinities in eastern, and probably also in Pelasgian, systems of religion, undergoing a like transmutation, appears in the Olympian scheme as the relation of the brother Apollo to the sister Artemis. For we have already seen the reasons for supposing that in Troy itself the Sun was worshipped as the far-darting Apollo. If there was a Sun-worship there, so in all likelihood there was a worship of the Moon. But Olympian laws seem not to allow an acknowledgment in the action of the Iliad of the relation between Apollo and the Sun; nor, by parity of reasoning, can they recognise any relation of Artemis to the Moon.

That such a relation subsisted out of Greece, we may readily suppose. The traditions, on which Homer had to employ his plastic power, varied and heterogeneous, were on that very ground the more elastic and flexible, partly in things, but especially in names. Identity is as hard to follow in them, as it is easy in human life. They seem to form, disform, and re-form before us, like the squares of coloured glass in the kaleidoscope as it is turned about by the hand. One group of these traditions, which when associated compose a *nebula*, appears before us in severalty, divided between the three individualities of Artemis, Persephonè, and Aphroditè. Another form of the severance, wholly Greek in spirit, comes before us in the double tradition of the celestial

and the earthy or sensual Aphroditè; and to the celestial Aphroditè the Artemis of Homer bears no small
resemblance. Indeed it seems likely that, as Homer
found or shaped the old Earth-tradition in several
forms, of which the portion least earthy, and most
sublimed, became his Herè, so probably there may have
lain before him a variety of forms of the tradition of
the Moon-goddess, in association with highly varied
ascriptions, the most ethereal and purest part of which
took, we may suppose, its place in the Olympian
system as his Artemis.

But the relations of wife and sister respectively, in
which Herè and Artemis are placed, are probably due
to the anthropomorphic principle, and to that method
of copying for heaven the things seen and known on
earth, according to which the Theo-mythology of Homer
is constructed. And the remarkable participation of
Artemis in the high prerogatives of Apollo is notably
like the participation of Herè in the prerogatives of
Zeus. In this participation, this greatness by reflection,
consists principally the dignity of each goddess. The
rude material, which as Nature-Powers they respectively offered to the hand, is thus lighted up with an
extraordinary splendour.

The Homeric signs of relation between Artemis and
the Moon are of the same kind with those of Apollo to
the Sun ; but fainter in proportion to smaller energies,
and a more confined activity. The terrible clang of
the arrows of Apollo is reflected in the rattle of those of
Artemis[1]. His golden sword is represented in her
golden distaff[2]. She is also golden-throned, and uses
golden reins[3]. These are epithets suitable to the moon.

[1] Il. l. 46 ; xvl. 183.   [2] Il. xx. 71.   [3] Il. vi. 205 ; ix. 529.

Hahn finds no root for the name Artemis in the Albanian tongue; and we cannot in this way trace it to the Pelasgian religion. But in 'Charnea,' meaning the moon, he detects the Anna Perenna of the Latins, of whom Ovid[1] says, 'Sunt quibus haec Luna est;' and likewise the Anath or Tanath of Egypt, who is taken by some to be the analogue of Artemis[2]. On the whole we seem to have a groundwork in the scheme of Nature-worship, on which the Homeric tradition of Artemis is built, and which places her on the Trojan side.

The great function which in Homer she shares with Apollo, is that of being the minister of Death, in the double sense of a deliverance or translation, and of an infliction penal in its nature. In the first capacity, Penelopè asks her aid, that she may be set free from the persecutions of the Suitors[3]: and in like manner she dismisses from life the women, and Apollo the men, of the happy island of Suriè, where want and sickness are unknown[4]. But she likewise slays Ariadnè, for her lapse from chastity in Diè[5]; and avenges on the daughters of Niobè (as does Apollo on the sons) the offence of their mother[6]. As the Huntress-queen, she is the destroyer of life in animals, and perhaps this office was committed to her as an inferior portion of the ministry of death, more suitably placed in her hands than in those of her brother Apollo; as if she had, so to speak, the leavings of his great offices.

The inferiority, indeed, of Artemis to Apollo is very strongly marked in Homer, although the relation of Moon to Sun was most suitably represented in an an-

---

[1] Fast. lii. 657.   [2] Hahn. Alban. Stud. pp. 250, 277.
[3] Od. xx. 61.   [4] Od. xv. 407.   [5] Od. xi. 324.
[6] Il. xxiv. 604-609.

thropomorphic religion by placing them as brother and
sister. In the Fifth Iliad, when Apollo carries Æneas
to Pergamos, and places the disabled chief in his own
temple, Leto and Artemis are found there[1], to nurse
and restore him; not in any shrine of their own, nor
in one common to the family. And again in the Theomachy, Artemis, contending with Herè, is subjected to
sad indignity, and actually whipped with her own bow
and arrows[2]. She is here treated with none of the
special respect that is given, not only to Apollo and
Athenè, but to Leto. This convinces me on further
reflection[3] that her Olympian relation to Apollo is
more probably based upon physical facts, than upon
participation in the higher traditions.

Her agency, however, is ubiquitous; perhaps in
virtue of facts belonging to the same order; yet it
would be singular, if her worship obtained among Hellenes earlier than that of the Sun. So, however, it
seems to have been. A generation at least before the
War, Artemis is worshipped in Caludon, and she sends
the Boar thither to avenge the lack of sacrifice[4]. We
are thus enabled to conjecture that in this instance,
even before the hand of Homer was applied to mythologic manipulation, the Hellenic mind had done its
work, and she was fairly impersonated in the capacity
which we find that she fills in the Poems. We meet
her in Troas, where she taught Scamandrios[5] to hunt;
she is invoked in Ithaca by Penelopè[6]; her part in the
legend of the daughters of Pandareos belongs probably
to Crete; and we have seen her agency in Suriè, and

---

[1] Il. v. 445. [2] Il. xxi. 489-496.
[3] Studies on Homer, vol. ii. pp. 110, 144. [4] Il. ix. 533-542.
[5] Il. v. 49-52. [6] Od. xx. 61, 71.

in Diè[1]. Again, in Ortugiè she took the life of Orion. And the Artemis of Homer has no relation to any one or more places in particular.

Apart from the ministry of death, and from this apparent attribute of omnipresence, her powers, in regard both to Nature and to the mind, are those of the lower or secondary order of the Olympian Court. But, in the matter of personal beauty, she is the rival of Aphroditè; and here she appears to absorb that part of the tradition, which afterwards went by the name of the heavenly Aphroditè. One most frequent illustration of great beauty is a comparison with Aphroditè the golden; and it is to her that Achilles refers[2] as the model of loveliness. But the incomparable Nausicaa, who appears to be the poet's ideal of youthful beauty combined with purity and excellence[3], is likened by Odysseus to Artemis in countenance, bearing, and stature. And again, in the case of the daughters of Pandareos, while it is Herè who confers upon them beauty of feature, and Aphroditè simply purveys food for them, it is Artemis who gives them stature, which I suppose to include all that relates to beauty of figure. It is noteworthy that stature is never mentioned (I think) in connection with Aphroditè, and I suppose it therefore to be in the province of Artemis.

While this attribute marks the point at which the traditions appropriated to her touch upon those of Aphroditè, on the other hand the epithet ἁγνή, the severely pure[4], seems to indicate her point of contact with Persephonè, the Queen of Hades. The two forms were, as we know, afterwards fused into one.

---

[1] Od. v. 123.   [2] Il. ix. 389.   [3] Od. vi. 150.
[4] Od. v. 123; xviii. 201; xx. 71.

SECTION XIII.   *Persephonè.*

Persephonè the Queen of Hades is called by Homer the ' severely pure' (ἀγνή), the ' majestic' (ἀγαυή), and the ' terrible' (ἐπαινή). And she represents what we might reasonably expect from her position as Queen in the Underworld: a mixture of Pelasgic and of Eastern traditions. Of the former, because all the Pelasgic Nature-Powers had been disposed of by carrying them into that nether sphere; of the latter, because the site of the Underworld of Homer was in the East, the entrance to it by the point of the rising of the Sun[1].

She is represented as ruling together with Aïdoneus, and by no means as merely his wife. Introduced together with him into the Legend of Phœnix by his father, and also by Althaia[2], she seems even to be charged in chief with the sovereignty. She gathers the Women-shades for Odysseus, and she disperses them. It is she who, as he fears, may send forth the head of Gorgo should he tarry over long; who may have deluded him with an Eidolon or shadow in lieu of a substance; who endows Teiresias with the functions of a Seer[3]. On the shores of Ocean, just before the point of descent in the far East, are the groves of Persephonè. Aïdoneus does no personal act in the Poems, except that with her he executes the imprecatory vow of the father of Phœnix[4]; and that he trembles lest the crust of earth should be riven by earthquake, during the battle of the gods[5].

---

[1] Od. xii. 1-4.   [2] Il. ix. 457-569.
[3] Od. xi. 226, 385, 634, 213; and x. 494.
[4] Il. ix. 456, 457.   [5] Il. xx. 61-65.

Notwithstanding his high rank as the brother of Zeus, she is the principal, and he is the secondary figure in the weird scenery of the Eleventh Odyssey.

It seems very probable that she represents that old Pelasgian tradition of the awful Damsel, which had, as we know especially from the mythological itinerary of Pausanias, such extraordinary longevity and power in the Greek religion. Together with this, we have to consider 1. her Eastern site, 2. her gift to Teiresias, alone among the dead; connecting her on the one hand with Apollo, the god of foreknowledge, but on the other with the Phœnicians, and with the Eastern associations of which they were the channels.

The name Persephonè appears to attach itself by etymology to other names in the Homeric Poems; all of which are Eastern in their associations. Persè, the daughter of Okeanos, is also the wife of Helios, and the mother of Kirkè, who dwells in Aiaiè. Each of the three points of contact thus established is a link to the East. Perseus, the founder of the dynasty which precedes the Pelopids, is the son of Zeus and Danae, a parentage which, as we have already found, we may properly consider as implying a foreign, and an Eastern, origin. In the person of Perseus, the son of Nestor[1], the name is continued in the Neleid House, which appears to have been of Phœnician extraction. The national designation of Achaians appears also not improbably to connect itself with the Persian race through the name Archaimenidai and otherwise[2], which may not improbably have contributed an element to the formation of the Greek nation.

Our first historical notice of that race is about the

[1] Od. iii. 414.   [2] See Studies on Homer, vol. i. p. 557.

middle of the ninth century before Christ[1], when Shalmaneser II found them in south-western Armenia. This point approximates to the region, in which the imagination of Homer placed the shadowy dwelling of Persephonè.

In the later tradition, she becomes united with Artemis, and so related to Apollo; a relationship of which perhaps we have a single Homeric trace in her command over the knowledge of the future.

Section XIV. *Aphroditè.*

The Aphroditè of Homer was a goddess, for she is the daughter of Zeus, and of Dionè, whose residence is in Olympos, and who belongs to the divine order[2]. She is also herself expressly stated to belong to it[3]. But it does not appear that she had as yet come to be a goddess of the Hellenic religion properly so called.

In order to estimate her position in the scheme of Homer, the following circumstances should be considered:—

1. There is no trace of her worship, or of any influence exercised by her over mortals, either in Greece, or among the Greeks.

2. She is never once exhibited by Homer in a favourable light; sometimes in a neutral one; more commonly in an odious or contemptible point of view.

3. Though herself a model of personal beauty[4], she was not the goddess of beauty, inasmuch as she had

---

[1] Rawlinson's Ancient Monarchies, li. 374; lii. 349.
[2] Il. lv. 370, 381, 383.   [3] Il. iv. 337–342; xx. 106.
[4] Il. ix. 389.

not the power to confer the gift. Beauty is not included in the properties[1] conveyed by the Kestos; and it is Herè who endows the orphan daughters of Pandareos with beauty, while Aphroditè has no other office assigned to her in their rearing, than supplying them with food, and preferring to Zeus, when they are grown up, the prayer that they may marry[2].

4. She is wounded by Diomed, and is apparently destitute alike of the powers of resistance, of vengeance, and of endurance. We can hardly suppose that a deity exhibited in a light so contemptible, as is Aphroditè in the Battle of the Fifth Iliad, was as yet an object of Hellenic worship[3].

5. Her helplessness after receiving her wound from Diomed is remarkable. While Arès rides spontaneously to heaven[4], Aphroditè is led out of the battle by Iris[5], and makes a petition to her brother Arès for the loan of his chariot and horses, that she may by their means be carried to Olympos.

In the Lay of the Net, she is reported as going from Olympos to Paphos without aid[6]: possibly because this is a descent, not an ascent; or more probably because in a Syrian episode her rank would be more fully recognised than in an Hellenic poem.

6. No place is assigned to her, even on the losing side, in the Theomachy, which determines or ushers in the issue of the Iliad. And this is the more remarkable, because a fifth deity is wanting to make up a number equal to the five deities of the Greeks; and

---

[1] Il. xiv. 198, 215.   [2] Od. xx. 66-75. Cf. Il. v. 429.
[3] Il. v. 311-380.   [4] Il. v. 864-870.   [5] Il. v. 353.
[6] Od. viii. 362.

Leto, who is elsewhere in the Poems a perfectly mute personage, is introduced in order to fill it.

7. The only place where she is named among the Olympian family, is in the Lay of the Net, a tale apparently of Phœnician importation, and of Syrian origin. She bears the name of Cypris; and her place of abode is Cyprus, where were her altars, and her glebe or domain [1]. She was therefore worshipped in that island; and we may trace her worship as far westward as Cythera, from the following circumstances: first, she is twice called Κυθέρεια [2]; and secondly, Κύθηραι are called ζάθεοι, an epithet which always indicates the special relation of the place to some deity. Her relation to Paris [3] proves that she was in some manner acknowledged in Troas; and the taunt of Helen respecting her supposed favourites in Meonia and Phrygia is to be taken as showing that she was also recognised as a deity in those regions. In effect she was an Asiatic deity; and her name and worship were crossing the sea by steps towards the Greek Peninsula. But she must have been of small account in Asia Minor, or she could hardly have failed to find a place in the Theomachy.

8. The power of this goddess over external nature is extremely limited. The greatest manifestation of it is where she 'with ease' draws Paris out of the fight, wrapping him in vapour [4]. In the Fifth Book, it is when she is slily dragging off Æneas, covered with her robe, that Diomed pursues and wounds her, 'knowing that she was an effeminate or strengthless deity [5].'

She is however invested with a certain superintendence of marriage in its physical aspect; and in this

---

[1] Od. viii. 362.　　　　　[2] Od. viii. 288; xviii. 192.
[3] Il. iii. 400-402.　　[4] Il. iii. 380.　　　[5] Il. v. 331.

capacity she sends to Andromache the nuptial gift of her hood or head-band[1].

Athenè, taunting her upon her wound, makes the supposition[2] that she got it in undressing some Greek woman that she had persuaded to elope with one of her beloved Trojans. ' Nay, Helen also bitterly reproaches her, advising her to cease altogether from pretending to divinity; and Aphroditè, in the Third Iliad, only overcomes her by the violence of her threats[3]. From these it appears, if indeed proof were wanting, that this character, odious on the side of lawless indulgence, has its base in simple appetite, and in no degree carries the softening accompaniments of gentleness or compassion.

In the Odyssey it is contrived that the Suitors, before they are put to death, shall offer gifts to Penelope; perhaps by way of partial requital for the waste of the substance of Odysseus. With this view, the Queen[4] issues from her chamber, like to Artemis or golden Aphroditè. Aphroditè is introduced here, because passion was the motive of the Suitors. But the deity, at whose suggestion Penelopè thus adorned herself, was Pallas. Had Aphroditè been worshipped in Greece, this office surely would have fallen to her. It is yet more noteworthy, that the whole design is executed by Pallas. Penelopè is lulled to sleep; and then Pallas applies ambrosion to her face, 'such as Aphroditè uses when she goes among the Graces.' But Aphroditè herself is excluded from the entire process.

Even in the Lay of the Net, apparently a legend of the Eastern mythology, the Poet seems to intend

---

[1] Il. v. 429; xxii. 470.
[2] Il. v. 422-425.
[3] Il. iii. 399-517.
[4] Od. xvii. 37.

to make the guilty pair ridiculous by sending them off, when released, so rapidly and in silence[1].

9. She is never invested with any of the higher attributes, such as foreknowledge, omnipresence, or command over the mind of man. Her only power seems to be that of stimulating passion[2].

10. We now know that the planetary worship of the Assyrians was brought by the Phœnicians into Greece, and that each deity was associated with a particular metal. We find in Cyprus, the land of copper, with a Phœnician colony, the worship of Aphroditè. We may safely then refer the origin of this Olympian personage to the Assyrian mythology.

The local indications of her worship, as proceeding from the East, are in accordance with the traditions which under the names of Astartè, Ashtoreth, Mylitta, Mitra, exhibit to us a similar character as held in honour there. The marriage with Hephaistos bears a similar witness; the more remarkable, because it is only recognised in the mythology of the Outer world, drawn from the Phœnicians, while in the Iliad he is the suitor of Charis. Aphroditè, however, is placed by Homer in relation with the Charites, Eastern personages, whose name corresponds with the Sanscrit Harits, meaning originally 'bright,' and afterwards the horses of the dawn[3]. In very late mythology, Aphroditè appears as the daughter of Poseidon[4], and thus acquires a new note of Eastern origin.

In historic Greece, we find the double tradition of the heavenly and the promiscuous Aphroditè. It would

[1] Od. viii. 360.   [2] Il. xiv. 215-217; xxiv. 30.
[3] Max Müller, Lect. on Language, Second Series, p. 370.
[4] Pausanias, Corinthiaca.

seem as though any elements of the former character, known to Homer, were assigned by him to his chaste Artemis, the rival in beauty of his Aphroditè. The pure tradition was, according to the view of Max Müller, the original basis of the character of Aphroditè; and he thinks that it was 'afterwards debased by an admixture of Syrian mythology[1].' He gives to this word his favourite meaning of the 'dawn.' Some old traditions however connect Aphroditè as Astartè with the Moon[2]. There has been therefore an intermixture of the traditions, which ultimately distributed themselves between Artemis, Aphroditè, and Persephonè; and there is a certain correspondence of the two first, as we find them in Homer, with the vulgar and the heavenly Aphroditè of later times respectively.

Of the name there seems to be no sign in the Albanian tongue, which brings down to us so much of the old speech of the Pelasgoi. But the root of the name Venus is found in the Gegian branch of the language[3].

Dionè, the mother of Aphroditè, resides in Olympos. Homer affords us no means of tracing her origin or functions; but from other evidence we have been enabled to interpret her as a Nature-Power of the Pelasgian worship. If this is so, then probably we are to consider her motherhood to be assigned to her, not in virtue of that Syrian character of Aphroditè, which we trace in the South, but of the place which Aphroditè (or

---

[1] Lectures, Second Series, p. 373.

[2] Hahn, Albanesische Studien, p. 250. 'Wir glauben diese Verbindung mit dem in so vielen Sprachen dem Hahnrei zukommenden Hörnern zusammen stellen zu dürfen.' p. 251. See Smith, Dict. Bibl., Art. Ashtoreth.   [3] Hahn, ibid.

Venus) appears to have held in the Trojan system, and therefore in the Pelasgian cultus of the Nature-Powers.

SECTION XV. *Dionusos.*

The traditions of Dionusos in Homer are as dark as they are slight. On the one hand he is the son of Semelè; and we have no case in the Homeric Theogony where a deity is born of a woman: but Semelè is mentioned in the list given by Zeus among the mortal mothers of his children, who stand separate from the goddess mothers. She comes between the unnamed mother of Minos, and Alcmenè [1]; and the birth of Dionusos thus appears to be parallel with that of Heracles. Dionusos is, however, called in this passage 'a joy to mortals;' which may of itself faintly seem to sever him from the race. Neither is there in the Poems any clearly divine act assigned to him. The Homeric Hymn to Hermes treats Semelè as the daughter or descendant of Kadmos [2].

But on the other hand there is a great resemblance between the good offices of Metis to him and to Hephaistos [3]. When the terrible Lucourgos attacks and scourges his nurses, he trembling takes refuge in the sea; and Thetis receives him in her bosom [4]. This is confirmed indirectly by the Odyssey [5], which represents him as the giver to that goddess of the golden urn which she used for the ashes of Achilles; doubtless in requital for her services, which are thoroughly in keeping with her character as the great

---

[1] Il. xiv. 323-325.   [2] v. 57.
[3] See *supra*, Sect. Hephaistos.   [4] Il. vi. 136.   [5] Od. xxiv. 74.

mediatress in matters respecting contrasted or competing worships.

The conclusive test however is found in this, that the recital concerning Lucourgos is offered to illustrate a class of cases where outrage is offered by mortals to deities; and the scourging of his nurses is treated as an offence to himself, for which, accordingly, not however by him, but by Zeus, Lucourgos was smitten with blindness, and then cut off prematurely[1]. Homer must therefore be understood to include him in the phrase 'gods of heaven.'

In the Odyssey we have a probable sign of his worship. Ariadnè is put to death in Diè, supposed to be Naxos, by Artemis, when Theseus is carrying her to Athens. Artemis does this 'upon the testimony of Dionusos[2].' The only probable construction of these words which offers itself is, that Theseus landed with Ariadnè in Naxos, as Paris had landed with Helen in Cranaè, and that Dionusos procured the intervention of Artemis to avenge a meditated profanation; which presumes that the island, or some place in it, was sacred to him. It is also likely, that the epithet ἠγάθεον applied to the Nuseïan mount, means that it was sacred to him as a god.

Nägelsbach observes[3], that Homer places neither him nor Demeter in Olympos by any distinct recital or declaration. But in both cases the recognition of deity, coupled with the personal relation to Zeus, appears to make good the title.

At the same time, I have pointed out an inconsistency which I do not know how to rectify. The traditions are not closely pieced together.

[1] Il. vi. 129-140.   [2] Od. xi. 321-325.   [3] Hom. Theol. p. 115.

What is most clear about Dionusos in Homer is, first, that his worship was extremely recent; secondly, that it made its appearance in Thrace[1], to which belongs the Nuseïan mountain; thirdly, that it was violently opposed on its introduction, a fact of which we have other records, as for example, in the Bacchæ of Euripides.

Lucourgos, who resisted and punished it, was the son of Druas; and Druas was alive and a warrior in the youth of Nestor. Consequently, Dionusos was an infant, that is, his worship was in its infancy, not more than two generations before the War of Troy. The Hymn addressed to Dionusos describes how Tursenians found him on the shore, and brought him over sea. The colouring of this legend is Phœnician; as is that of the legend, if such there were, that gave him the isle of Naxos as the seat of his worship. It is also on the sea shore that he appears, according to Homer; and it is in Thrace, where there would seem to have been Phœnician manufactures of metal. Again, he obtains a work of art, probably Phœnician, from Hephaistos[2], just as does Phaidimos, the king of the Sidonians[3]. And the name of Semelè[4] itself, according to general traditions, supports the Phœnician association thus established at a variety of points.

We cannot perhaps treat the Dionusos of Homer as the discoverer of wine, and father of its use, in Greece; for it is universal and familiar, while he appears to be but local and as yet strange. The novel feature, which connects itself with his name, seems to be the use of wine by women; and the effect produced, in an extra-

[1] Nägelsbach, p. 9.   [2] Od. xxiv. 74.   [3] Od. iv. 615-619.
[4] Hymn to Dionusos, v. 37.

ordinary and furious excitement, which might well justify not only jealousy, but even forcible resistance to demoralising orgies. It seems, then, as if this usage was introduced by immigrants of a race comparatively wealthy and luxurious, and was resisted by, or on behalf of, the older and simpler population.

The later account of Hesiod makes Dionusos the husband of Ariadnè, who was the daughter of Minos. The poet of Ascra thus places him within the circle of Phœnician traditions.

Though Homer has represented this personage as a god, and though, as we see, traces of his worship are not wanting, yet the human maternity might possibly indicate that we should do best to regard him as a deified mortal, rather than as a god from the beginning of his existence. In this case, we are to suppose that the fascination of the usage he introduced not only proved so powerful as to overrule all opposition, but likewise generated a halo which was reflected on his birth, and caused his deification by a process more rapid than that which took effect upon Heracles or the Tyndarids. In the later time, greater consistency was given to the legend by a parallel deification of Semelè, his mother.

Homer has attached no ennobling epithet or circumstance of dignity to the name of Dionusos, unless we so regard the eulogy of Zeus [1] under an excess of excitement. The Poet acts in this case as in the cases of Arès and Aphroditè; since he has no reverence for either drunkenness, or violence, or lust.

[1] Il. xiv. 325.

SECTION XVI.   *Helios, or the Sun.*

It is sometimes stated, that Helios, or the Sun, does
not appear as a god in the Iliad, but only in the
Odyssey. This is not so. As far as the Odyssey is
concerned, he appears only in the Outer, not in the
Inner, world. In the Iliad his personality is undeniable, though very faint. The Sun hearing all, as well as
seeing all, is certainly a person [1].

Again, all will remember the long day of the Iliad,
with the close of which the successes of the Trojans
were to end. When the appointed moment came, at
the command of Herè the Sun went, unwillingly [2], to
his rest beside the Ocean stream.

Here then he is a person, though in the background.
In the Odyssey, he reappears with more marked effect.
In the Lay of Demodocos, it is he who first makes
known to Hephaistos the intimacy of Arès with Aphroditè [3], and then undertakes to act as spy upon the
guilty couple. The Island of Thrinakiè, placed by
Homer not far from the entrance to the Euxine, is
his island [4]. Here are his oxen, and his sheep, tended
by the care of his daughters, whose mother was
Neaira, and who were called Phaëthusa and Lampetiè [5].
These animals the crew of Odysseus had been warned
on no account to molest. Under the direst pressure
of famine [6], however, they at length slew certain of
the oxen; having first vowed that on their return to

[1] Il. iii. 277.   [2] Il. xviii. 239.   [3] Il. xviii. 204, 270.
[4] Od. xii. 261, 274.   [5] Od. xi. 132.   [6] Od. xii. 330, 353.

Ithaca [1] they would build a temple to the Sun and store
it richly; a sign, it may be remembered, that such an
edifice would be a novelty in the island. Portents,
such as we nowhere else encounter in the Poems, wait
upon the deed; the hides of the animals creep about,
and the flesh, even when roasted, lows upon the spits [2].
Notwithstanding the Sun's all-seeing function, it is
Lampetiè who carries him the news. It seems possible,
however, as Odysseus was asleep, that we are to understand the deed to have been done by night. The god
makes his complaint in the court of the Immortals,
to which he is thus proved to belong [3]; and he demands reparation for the loss of his oxen, with whom
'he disported himself night and morning.' Failing it,
he declares that he will thenceforward shine in Hades.
Zeus at once promises to destroy the crew at sea, which
is done accordingly [4].

The extraordinary sanctity ascribed to these oxen is
wholly alien to the genius of the Greek mythology.
But when we turn to the East, and observe that Phœnicia
was impregnated with Egyptian traditions, we find the
sacredness of the ox, and its relation to the Sun, indicated in the consecration of Apis to Osiris; while the
function of the ox in agriculture also falls in with the
earlier form of the religion, which appears to have
regarded Isis as the land, or passive principle, and
Osiris as the Nile-god, who taught to the Egyptians the
use of the plough.

And again, we find in the temple of Jerusalem, for
the erection of which Solomon called in the aid of
Phœnician workmen, the forms of twelve oxen [5], sup-

---

[1] Od. xii. 345.   [2] Od. xii. 394.   [3] Od. xii. 377.
[4] Od. xii. 403-419.   [5] 1 Kings vii. 24, 25, 44.

porting a brazen sea[1]. These were made by King
Hiram of Tyre; and they symbolise at once the Egyptian religion, with other Oriental forms of fable, and
the maritime pursuits of the Phœnicians.

It is also remarkable, that the use of the ox for meat
appears to cease in the Outer world of the Odyssey.
In the land of the Cyclops, we find only sheep and
goats. And it is with mutton only that Kirkè stocks
the vessel of Odysseus.

All these indications agree together. In other respects, too, Helios is marked as an Eastern god. He
is the father of Aietes, and of Kirkè, dwelling near the
Eastern Okeanos[2]; and the island of Aiaiè is indicated
as the place of his rising[3]. The fact of his sporting
with the oxen night and morning goes far to show that
Homer did not think the earth a plane, but round,
perhaps as upon a cylinder, and believed that the West
and East were in contact. But only in the East does
he give the Sun a dwelling. Aietes, the son of Helios,
carries the exclusively Phœnician epithet of ὀλοόφρων.

Further, we may notice that, as long as the Voyage of
Odysseus is in the West and North, we hear nothing
of the Sun. Poseidon rules in the land of the Cyclops,
stirs the northern sea into a tempest, and is supreme
in Scheriè. It is in Aiaiè, and Thrinakiè, that we are
brought into contact with this deity, and both these
islands appear to lie in Homer's East.

Thus the Sun, by many concurrent signs, is marked
out to us as an Eastern deity. There is not in the
Odyssey the faintest trace of his identification with
Apollo. The traditions respecting him were doubtless
conveyed by the Phœnicians; but we cannot say that

[1] 1 Kings vii. 13.   [2] Od. x. 137.   [3] Od. xii. 4.

they were Phœnician in themselves. The division of
regions to which I have adverted, seems to point to
Poseidon as the god of Phoinikes proper, and to Helios
as the god of the Canaanitish population of Syria to
the Eastward. Among them it is not improbable that,
at the period represented by Homer, the Egyptian
belief extensively prevailed, but Assyrian elements may
also enter into this conception.

In the Iliad, though not in the Odyssey, we have
a sign of the process which finally incorporated the
traditions of Apollo with the Sun; while the humanitarian spirit of the Olympian system of Homer seems
to have resisted the operation. The plague of the First
Book can hardly represent anything else than the
miasma rising from the marshes of the Troad, and
the arrows of Apollo are the rays of the sun causing
the moisture to evaporate. We find a family of epithets applied to Apollo, which evidently glance at the
solar properties: Hekaergos, Hekatebolos, Heke-
bolos. It is somewhat remarkable that these epithets,
which are only used twenty-five times in the other
forty-seven books of the Poems, are met twelve times
in the First Iliad alone. It is also likely that the
epithet Phoibos may glance at the relation between
Apollo and the Sun, already recognised beyond the
borders of Greece, and possibly also in the old Pelasgian
religion of the Peninsula. Again we have the term
Lukabas applied to the year. It is probable that in the
religion of Troy, where Nature-worship seems to have
prevailed more largely, Apollo and the Sun were identified, and that this union made it convenient for the
Poet to place Apollo on the Trojan side in the war.
Whilst Poseidon built the walls of Troy for King

Laomedon, Apollo fed his oxen ; and we have seen the close relation between these animals and the worship of the Sun. And this interpretation accounts for what otherwise would be most difficult to'explain : I mean the fact that Helios does not appear in the Theomachy, nor does he under that name take part in the war, though his inclination towards the Trojans is plainly declared. Troy was probably a sort of meeting-point for Greek and Asiatic systems. But in the Phœnician or Syrian mythology of the Outer world, Apollo and Helios can appear together, because the Eastern conception of the latter ran no risk of being confounded in the Greek mind with the purely anthropomorphic idea of the true Homeric Apollo.

Section XVII.   *Hebè.*

Hebè is a deity, whose offices are very clearly set forth, but whom we can scarcely consider as having a perceptible root in any tradition beyond the circle of the Greek mythology.

She is the Cup-bearer, who pours out nectar for the gods[1]. She puts together the parts of the chariot of Herè, though Herè herself yokes the horses to it, before her descent to the field of battle[2]. She performs the offices of the bath for Arès, after he has been healed by Paieon[3]. Again, we find her in the Eleventh Odyssey, as the celestial bride of Heracles, and in an obelised verse, as the daughter of Zeus and Herè[4].

Her offices are exclusively Olympian; and she is

[1] Il. iv. 2.   [2] Il. v. 722, 731.
[3] Il. v. 905.   [4] Od. xi. 602-604.

nowhere brought into relations with our mortal state; one sign among many that she is probably to be regarded as a purely ideal conception.

Her name in Greek expresses youth adult, or full age just attained. Her marriage with Heracles appears to signify that the divine gift of an unending youth is imparted to him when he reaches Olympos[1]. Homer assigns to her the epithet callisphuros, prettily ancled, which he only gives to those who are to be understood as youthful persons; Danae, Ino, and Marpessa[2].

She may well be conceived as the daughter of Zeus in that general sense, according to which he is the father of divinities in general; and thus it must be, in all likelihood, that the Muses, the Hours, and the Nymphs in general are his daughters. But these personages are not daughters of Herè, who has but few children, and those due apparently to special traditions. In truth she expresses the idea of youth[3], and is perhaps but a thought seized and personified. There is no note in Homer of her worship on earth, which however is mentioned by Strabo and Pausanias: and Hahn finds no trace of her in the Albanian language.

It is the distinct and clear, though simple, account given by Homer of her functions, which seems to give her a place in the Olympian court upon one of the twenty thrones of Hephaistos.

---

[1] Hes. Theog. 944-955. Ov. Met. ix. 400.
[2] Il. xiv. 319; ix. 553. Od. v. 333.
[3] Nägelsbach, Hom. Theol. p. 41.

SECTION XVIII. *Themis.*

Slightly as her outline is drawn, we cannot refuse
to reckon Themis among the ordinary members of the
Olympian Court, for the simple reason that we find
her actually installed there. When, in the absence of
Zeus, Herè enters the company of the Immortals, and
they rise in honour of her[1], it is from Themis, who
came first to meet her, that she accepts the cup of
greeting. This is evidently because she had been presiding: for Herè, who is troubled at the view, invites
her to continue to preside[2].

Again, in the Twentieth Iliad, all the deities, including the minor Nature-Powers (whom Homer probably recognises as divine because they continued to
hold their ground in local worship), are invited to the
Great Assembly which is to decide finally the fate of
Troy: and it is Themis who summons them[3].

In the Second Odyssey, Telemachos describes himself
as making his prayer to Zeus, and to Themis, who
collects and dissolves public assemblies generally.

Nevertheless, I apprehend we are not to look for
her origin in any foreign traditions, but simply to regard her as a creation of the Hellenic mind[4], and
probably of the mind of our Poet himself. Like Hebè
she represents, in the main, the deification of an impersonated idea[5].

In reference to terrestrial affairs, the name Themis
signifies civil right, and is the basis on which are

---

[1] Il. xv. 85. [2] Il. xv. 95. [3] Il. xx. 4.
[4] Od. ii. 68, 69. [5] Welcker, Gr. Götterlehre, i. 700.

founded the relations of the whole political and social order. If Olympos was to be fashioned into a quasi-commonwealth, such a personage could hardly be dispensed with in its formation, among a race with whom the political spirit was so strong as among the Greeks of the heroic age.

Even Hestiè, who represents the principle of the family order, in the same way as Themis represents the groundwork of the State, though she is not impersonated by Homer, yet is at the least on her way to impersonation, and attains fully to it after his time. She was less necessary to the theogonic scheme of the Poet ; for, though the family is involved in the Olympian arrangements, it does not embrace the whole of them, whereas Olympos gives the complete picture of a Court and a Polity.

Hahn[1] derives the name of Themis from θεμ, 'I speak,' and observes that the statue of this deity was placed over against the bema of the orators in Athens.

Section XIX. *Paieon.*

In the Fifth Iliad, Dionè recites that when Aïdes, wounded by Heracles, repaired to Olympos, Paieon (or Paian) applied anodyne drugs to his shoulder, and healed him[2]. It is evident that the presence of this deity there, as the healer, was regarded by the Poet as habitual; for when Arès has been wounded by Diomed, and appears in the palace of Zeus, his father, after rebuking him, commands Paieon[3] to heal him, which accordingly is done forthwith, as by one at hand.

[1] Alban. Studien, p. 253.   [2] Il. v. 395-402.   [3] Il. v. 399.

In the Fourth Odyssey, Helen, after using the drug, which produces the effect of opium, and may indeed be opium, states that she obtained it from the Egyptian Poludamna, wife of Thon[1]; and adds that every Egyptian is eminently a physician, since they are of the race of Paieon.

Apollo is a healer as well as Paieon: but while Paieon heals by instrumental causes after the manner of a man, Apollo heals Glaucos immediately, as by a divine action[2].

The Phaiakes are called angchitheoi, near to divine, because the royal house of Alkinoos is descended from Poseidon. Something like this may be meant with respect to the Egyptians and Paieon: or just possibly they may be called children of Paieon for no other reason than their medical skill, without actually implying that the traditions relating to the person of ·Paieon were Egyptian.

But the word Paieon, which is the name of this deity, is also twice used in the Iliad for a hymn: first for the hymn of purgation, addressed to Apollo, after the offence of the First Book has been expiated; secondly for the hymn of triumph sung by the Greek soldiers over the lifeless body of Hector[3].

A singular relation is thus established between Paieon and Apollo, somewhat like that between the Sun and the same deity; as though Homer had not been willing to treat as amalgamated, or even had actually severed into two personages traditions which had already, and elsewhere, been combined; for the reason that parts of them did not seem to be of sufficient elevation to

[1] Od. iv. 227 seqq.   [2] See *supra*, sect. viii.
[3] Il. I. 473; xxii. 381.

suit the rest, and to be proper for the equipment of so gorgeous a figure as his Apollo.

The name pa ia n became subsequently the established name of those Hymns to Apollo, which were sung in connection with victory and deliverance, especially, as it seems, upon a completed act of purification[1].

Welcker observes that, even down to a late epoch, the separate personality of Paieon had not altogether been submerged, as Cicero mentions a statue to him[2].

It is however possible that he may be, like Hebè, a purely ideal personage, not rooted in former or in foreign tradition, and representing in a physical way the office of healing in Olympos itself, as Hebè represents the faculty of youth among the divine race.

Section XX. *Iris.*

Iris, constantly introduced in the Iliad as the ordinary messenger between Olympos and mankind, and likewise among the gods themselves, is nowhere mentioned in the Odyssey. Yet the name of Iros is given to Arnaios the vagrant, because it naturally fell to him to circulate messages and news; and it is evidently derived from, or from the same source with, the name of this deity[3].

Her office in the Iliad is not exclusive. Themis is the pursuivant who summons the gods to the great assembly[4]; and Hermes is the envoy or agent who, in

---

[1] Müller's Dorians, vol. i. pp. 319, 320. (Transl.)
[2] Welcker, Gr. Götteslehre, vol. i. p. 695.
[3] Od. xviii. 7.
[4] Il. xx. 4.

consequence of the general resolution of the gods respecting the body of Hector, is employed to conduct Priam to and from the presence of Achilles[1].

In the Odyssey, Zeus does not act in his individual capacity, but only as head of the Olympian Court; and Iris is his personal messenger rather than the agent or envoy of the Olympian Court. There is therefore no obvious place for her in a poem where the conduct of affairs rests, in the Greek sphere, with Athenè, and beyond that sphere either with Poseidon, or with the collective body of the gods.

The name of Iris is also the Greek name for the rainbow; and the correspondence is very remarkable between her office of messenger from heaven to man, and the traditional function of the rainbow as a sign that the great covenants of Nature remain undisturbed[2]. As it is only by the tradition recorded in Scripture that the rainbow has this meaning, and not by any obvious natural significance, it appears hard to explain how Homer came to combine the two ideas, except by supposing that his race drew the association from the same early source from which Moses and the earlier descendants of Abraham obtained it.

It is true that Homer nowhere recognises the relation of the Messenger-Goddess to the rainbow. He does not, even on any high occasion, assign to her an epithet of colour. But this is precisely of a piece with his manner of separating the deities of his anthropomorphic system from the mere Nature-Powers of other theogonies: his Zeus from the Air, his Apollo from the Sun, his Artemis from the Moon. Iris as the Rainbow would have been wholly out of place in Olympos.

[1] Il. xxiv. 333 seqq.   [2] Genesis ix. 12-15.

This separation from the older deities he has marked, in the case of Iris, after a most curious fashion. In the Twenty-third Iliad[1], she carries to the palace of Zephuros the prayer of Achilles for a Wind to consume the pyre of Patroclos. She finds the Winds at table, and they eagerly solicit her to sit and feast with them. She answers that she has not time: if she tarries, she will lose her share of a banquet which the Ethiopians are just about to provide in their country for the Immortals. This want of time is evidently an excuse devised by good manners: in truth, the higher deity of the Olympian order will not stoop to keep company with the mere agents of Nature. And this, although Homer has given them animation, for Boreas is the Sire of the Trojan mares[2]. His impersonation, then, was not a human one, like that of the Olympian system.

In the case just mentioned, the prayer of Achilles is addressed to the Winds. But apparently the Poet does not allow them the faculty of hearing when they are invoked; for it is Iris who, spontaneously it appears, charges herself with the supplication, and in the character of metanggelos, inter-messenger, carries it to them.

In one[3] other case, when she appears to Helen, and exhorts her to repair to the Wall of Troy, no one is named as sending her; but as she has here the title of messenger expressly attached to her name, it is probable that we are to understand she is despatched by Zeus.

When, however, Aphroditè is wounded by Diomed, in the Fifth Iliad, Iris comes to her assistance[4], and

----

[1] 198-212.   [2] Il. xx. 223.   [3] Il. lii. 121.
[4] 353, 365.

here, without doubt because her action is spontaneous, she is not called messenger. She drives the chariot of Arès, which carries the wounded goddess to Olympos.

Though Iris hears prayer, she does not appear to be an object of worship, and her spontaneous action is confined to the business of the gods. It serves perhaps additionally to mark her Hellenic character that, when she appears to Achilles, she is without disguise, and is addressed by him in her proper character[1]; but when she addresses[2] Priam it is with the voice of Polites, and she comes[3] before Helen in the character of her sister-in-law Laodike. When she carries the order of Zeus to Priam, in the Twenty-fourth Book, she announces herself as the messenger of Zeus, but there is no proof or even sign of his being acquainted with her personally[4].

Her mission to Achilles is remarkable, because she is sent by Herè. In this instance alone, she obeys the order of a deity other than Zeus[5]. It is one of the instances in which Herè exhibits a command over aerial phenomena, apparently in virtue of her wifehood ; and it bears an independent witness to the connection between Iris and the rainbow.

In every other case (I think) Iris is sent personally by Zeus, from the message for Priam in the Second Book of the Iliad, to those for Thetis[6] and Priam in the Twenty-fourth.

By much the most important errand with which she is intrusted is the mission to Poseidon in the Fifteenth Iliad, where she carries the order for his withdrawal from the field of battle. Supporting it with skill and

[1] Il. xviii. 182. [2] Il. il. 791. [3] Il. iii. 121.
[4] Il. xxiv. 173. [5] Il. xviii. 268. [6] Il. xxiv. 77.

persuasiveness, she by these means induces him to obey [1].

SECTION XXI. *Thetis.*

Thetis is not to be regarded as properly an Olympian deity in the restricted sense of the phrase; yet by reason of her great influence in the Iliad, she is entitled to a marked position of her own.

The origin of Thetis in Homer is elemental only, and her attributes as a goddess are feeble. She does not act upon the course of Nature; she does not influence the mind: her powers of knowledge and vision are limited; she deplores her own lot among the Immortals; she is subject to weeping; she was married to Peleus much against her will. In no single instance throughout the Iliad does she exercise any divine power: nor is there in the Poem the faintest sign of worship as paid to her in any place.

But while her power, strictly so called, is thus bounded, her influence and consequence are immense. She is the pet deity of the Poet; or rather the engine he has chosen to carry through his theurgic process. It is her request to Hephaistos, that in a moment sets him to work upon the arms for Achilles; and when, in answer to the summons of Zeus, she repairs to Olympos, she is received with an extraordinary respect. But the chief act performed by her is the exercise of influence over Zeus in the First Book, where she overcomes his undisguised reluctance to act, growing out of his fears of a conjugal quarrel; and obtains his assent to her petition or demand, that the Trojans may prevail in the war,

[1] Il. xv. 157-219.

until the Greeks shall have made full reparation to her son Achilles[1].

This is termed *ἐξαίσιος ἀρή*[2]; a prayer lying outside the provisions of destiny and the moral order, or one which caused them to vary from their course. The meaning of the phrase is not hard to discover. The cause of the Trojans in the war was radically unjust. The moral law required their discomfiture. In this channel ran the main stream of justice and of Providence. The request of Thetis was not in itself unjust, for her son, who had so powerfully fought for the just cause, had been deeply wronged by Agamemnon, the head of the Greeks. But it tended to delay the consummation of a greater justice in a world-wide quarrel; and for a time it set aside the moral purpose of divine government. Interposing a secondary obstacle, it deflected the current from its course; and an immense influence must be supposed to have been possessed by Thetis, who, and who alone, by her personal intervention, produced this extraordinary effect.

While she is thus a deity of far greater importance than her rank in the preternatural order would lead us to suppose; there is no personage, either sublunary or celestial, that appears to bear more or deeper marks of the moulding hand of the Poet. Some find in her only a transposition of the primitive but obsolete deity Tethūs, the wife of old Okeanos. Her name Thetis also appears to be found in the dēti of the Albanian tongue, meaning the sea[3]. On the other hand, as one of some thirty or forty daughters of Nereus, himself an elemental god, though practically superseded by Posei-

---

[1] Il. i. 505-510.   [2] Il. xv. 598.
[3] Hahn, Alban. Studien. p. 252.

don, there is really no regular place for her in Olympos. She has all the appearance of a character shaped and turned to account for the purposes of the Poem: while, at the same time, there are functions ascribed to her which seem to imply a higher parentage than that assigned to her, and to support the hypothesis which makes her a reflection, as it were, of an older deity. For though, of the regular Olympian divinities, Aphroditè is among the lowest, she is expressly declared to be of a higher order than Thetis[1].

In her marriage to Peleus, there is nothing that resembles the clandestine or lawless and transitory connections with mortals, that are ascribed to Demeter, to Aphroditè, and to the Nymphs. It is the result of solemn divine Counsel[2], and it is celebrated by the whole Olympian Court. She had habitually sat[3] as Queen in the palace of Phthiè, and in the discharge of her motherly cares she had supplied Achilles with a chest of garments for the war[4]. Though at first sight the birth of Achilles may seem to be the counterpart of that of Æneas, they are really opposed in every feature: the one is lawful, solemn, permanent wedlock, the other occasional and secret lust. Thetis herself, indeed, appears to have been reluctant at the time to marry Peleus; and she rendered obedience only to an order of the gods in general.

The purpose of the Poet in giving this high and unexampled sanction to the union, is not difficult to trace. For her agency is the hinge on which turns, in the first place, the reconciliation of the old and the new Theogonies; in the second, of the Pelasgic and the Hel-

---

[1] Il. xx. 106.
[2] Il. xviii. 85; xxiv. 59.
[3] Il. i. 396; xvi. 574.
[4] Il. xvi. 221-224.

lenic nationalities; in the third, of the rival purposes of the gods (so far as the general scheme of Homer admitted them) with regard to Troy. I think we may find, that the marriage of Peleus to Thetis signifies and records the union, both on earth and in Olympos, of the Pelasgian and Hellenic systems.

The worship of Zeus, as we know, was Pelasgian, and therefore pre-Hellenic. The revolt of the three great deities of the new scheme, Herè, Athenè, and Poseidon, against him, seems to signify the tendency of the new worship, with its anthropomorphic or humanising forces, to effect the overthrow of the former creed, cherished by the older but less intelligent and less powerful population. And the pure Nature-Powers indeed disappear; but Zeus, whose relation with Nature is in its most refined region, that of air, and who represents, too, the central principle of Theism, survives the change. The agency employed for his relief is that of the hundred-handed giant, called Briareus by the gods, that is, in relation to the old religion, but Aigaion by men, that is, under the new[1]. It seems to be in virtue of his being a giant that he is the son of Poseidon; but his having a place both in the old and the new Theogonies evidently fits him to be the reconciler, and his being under the influence of Thetis, which is shown by his obeying her call, harmonises with her double relation.

That relation is again indicated by her good offices to the child Hephaistos, whose adoption into the Hellenic Theogony, notwithstanding his Pelasgian associations and his leaning to an elemental character, she seems to have procured[2].

[1] Il. i. 403.   [2] Il. xviii. 394-407. See sect. ix. Hephaistos.

z

And in·yet a third instance do we find her discharging a like office. Such were the troubles excited by the introduction of the worship of Dionusos, that it seems to have been all but cast out of the country; but, as we have already seen, she gave him a refuge, which he appears to have requited with the gift of a golden (or gilded) amphora, the work of Hephaistos [1].

For this office of reconciler between the creeds and ideas of the two nationalities, she has been carefully prepared by the fancy and skill of the Poet. Independently of the apparent association with Tethūs, she is rooted in the Pelasgian system by her owning Nereus for a father. An ample counterpoise, however, has been provided, and in part by a most curious contrivance. She is the mother of Achilles, who is himself the highest specimen of the pure Hellenic type, and whose Phthian country is, in a pre-eminent sense, already the land of Hellenes and Achaians.

Something, however, is added, that the transition may not be too abrupt, and that an Hellenic colour may be made to attach even to the extraction of the great hero. In the Eighteenth Iliad [2], when his mother issues from the depths, she is followed by a long train of sisters; and the names of no less than thirty-three of them are given in a string. No catalogue of names approaching to this length is to be found anywhere in Homer. The nearest to it is in the Eighth Odyssey, where he describes his Phaiakes repairing to their Games [3]. Here he gives in rapid succession the proper names of sixteen youths of Scheriè. On examination, we find that every one of them has relation to ships and navigation. It is

---

[1] Il. vi. 136. Od. xxiv. 73.   [2] Il. xviii. 39-49.
[3] Od. viii. 111-116.

therefore evident that the long list has a meaning. He desires to illustrate the especial, if not exclusive, devotion of the people to nautical pursuits. Now, on examining in a similar manner the catalogue of Nereids, we find that their names, instead of being, as is often the case with his Immortals, of an etymology that cannot be ascertained, are in nearly every instance pure Hellenic appellations, and that they even include the name Doris [1]. It is extremely difficult to suppose that Homer should have deviated so widely from his usual practice as to these lists, without a reason. And the reason seems to be obvious; namely, his desire to give a sort of Hellenic character to the family of Nereus, (whose name he never introduces except once in the patronymic,) as the maternal ancestry of Achilles.

From the obligations thus conferred, Thetis is in a condition to use urgency, though not authority, with Zeus; and honour is done to her son at the expense of the Greek army, notwithstanding the murmurs and devices of the Hellenising deities. In like manner, she has no difficulty in obtaining from Hephaistos, on a similar ground, the gift of the Arms. In each case it is not a mere act of grace and favour, but the requital of a benefit received. In the case of Zeus, it is the more noteworthy, because the prayer of Thetis is declared to be in the nature of a deviation from the appointed course of destiny [2], which had long ago fixed the downfall of Troy [3]. And again he signifies his attachment to her, when, though most of the gods recommended that the body of Hector should be removed by stealth, he arranges that she shall have an opportunity of giving

[1] Il. xviii. 45.   [2] Il. xv. 598.

[3] Il. ii. 305-330.

glory anew to her son, by advising him to accept the ransom [1] which is to be offered by Priam.

The other principal particulars given us respecting Thetis are as follows.

During the action of the Poem she habitually resides with 'the old man her father,' in the depths. We may suppose that this was because she was now released from any direct maternal duties in the house of Peleus.

Here was her nurse; and was the special designer of the marriage [2]. Here again we observe the meeting of Hellenic and Pelasgic elements. The undisguised reluctance of the bride [3] may have been due to her prevision of the time when Peleus her husband would be overtaken by old age; but I rather think it may have been inserted by Homer in order to separate the case of Thetis broadly from those of Demeter and Aphroditè.

She has an union of strong human affections with the fainter attributes of deity. Besides what we have already seen, she hears from beneath the prayer of Achilles, but then he offers it from the shore, and looking seawards [4]. She also hears his wail over Patroclos; but it was an awfully loud one [5]. She herself joined in the audible lament [6]. She was aware of his appointed destiny [7], but was under the necessity of applying to him to know the cause of his grief. So at least she asserts, though her own son seems to contradict her [8]. She suggests to him to seek comfort in sensual indulgence [9]. In his sorrow, however, she

---

[1] Il. xxiv. 107–111.   [2] Il. xxiv. 60.   [3] Il. xviii. 434.
[4] Il. i. 348–351.   [5] Il. xviii. 35.   [6] Il. xviii. 37, 71, *et alibi.*
[7] Il. i. 416–418; xviii. 95.   [8] Il. i. 363, 365; xviii. 63.
[9] Il. xxiv. 130.

watches over him night and day, besides inspiring him
with courage for the field [1]. And when summoned to
Olympos in the matter of Hector's ransom, she appears
there in deep mourning [2].

Upon entering the divine Assembly, she is received
with the utmost deference, Athenè yielding her place
by Zeus, which Thetis takes [3]. This may be a proceeding of delicate courtesy, having reference either to
her sorrowing state, or more probably to the honourable
customs of hospitality.

On repairing to Hephaistos to obtain the Arms, she
dispatches her sisters to inform old Nereus of what had
happened [4]. When the gift is ready, she herself, descending like a falcon from Olympos, carries the Arms
to the tent of Achilles [5].

The point of the sea, at which she dwells with her
father, is between Samothrace and Imbros [6].

She came once more to the camp on the yet more
sorrowful occasion of the death of Achilles [7]. She then
appointed the great contest between Ajax and Odysseus
for the arms of the departed hero [8]. She supplied the
famous urn, to receive his ashes; which was the work
of Hephaistos, and the gift of Dionusos. She also supplied the prizes for the funeral games [9], which she obtained from the other gods, more richly endowed, as is
probable according to the idea of the Poems, than herself.

The epithets applied to Thetis are generally connected with her marine extraction, and of these Argu-
ropeza, the silver-footed, is the most characteristic; or
else they relate to her good disposition.

[1] Il. xxiv. 72; xlx. 37.   [2] Il. xxiv. 93.   [3] Il. xxiv. 100.
[4] Il. xviii. 139–147.   [5] Il. xviii. 616; xix. 2.   [6] Il. xxiv. 78.
[7] Od. xxiv. 47, 55. .   [8] Od. xi. 556.   [9] Od. xxiv. 85.

She is plainly not an Olympian deity in the sense of belonging to the ordinary Assembly. Of this her reception as a guest in the Twenty-fourth Book appears to be a positive sign; and it is in harmony with all that we can see of her origin.

Most of the later tradition respecting Thetis appears to be but arbitrary comment and embellishment. The authentic *data* are few. She had a temple, according to Strabo, between Old and New Pharsalos, in Thessaly; doubtless owing to traditions of local worship, which had grown out of the distinguished honours assigned to her in the Poems[1]. Pausanias mentions a case in which, during the Messenian wars, a priestess of Thetis, named Cleo, was taken and found to have in her possession an ancient wooden statue of the deity. This appears to have been the only temple to her which existed south of Thessaly[2]; but there was a tale of a statue of her, planted by Menelaos over against Cranaè[3], on his return from his wanderings. It is not improbable that, after the Troica, there may have been tendencies to establish this worship, and that they were afterwards effaced from the want of a sufficient basis for such a divinity. Hesiod adds nothing to the Homeric account[4].

I cannot help leaning to the belief that, whether she is or is not a transformation of Tethūs, she is, in most of what we hear of her, a creation of Homer for the purposes of his work; and that, as the Poet of Greece, engaged in building up her nationality and religion, he has employed her as a most effective instrument for signifying that union of ethnical and theogonic elements,

---

[1] Strabo, ix. p. 431.   [2] Paus. iii. 14, 4.   [3] Paus. xx. 2.
[4] Theog. 244, 1006.

which he in part commemorated, and in part brought about.

With reference to the etymology of her name, it is perhaps worthy of remark that the only office of mediation at all resembling hers is ascribed to Tethūs, who, with her husband Okeanos, gives shelter and nurture to Herè[1], at the great crisis when Zeus was thrusting his father Kronos down to the Underworld[2].

---

[1] Il. xiv. 201–204.

[2] It would be matter of great interest to know how far, apart from any theory, the names of the Hellenic divinities are really derivable from the Sanscrit: and in the recent work of M. Jacolliot, *La Bible dans l'Inde*, a list of many of them is given with Sanscrit roots, in many cases seemingly appropriate. But for one ignorant like myself of that language, this etymology must rest upon authority: and the general propositions of M. Jacolliot's work are not sufficiently restrained and circumspect at once to inspire confidence in his judgments.

CHAPTER IX.

I. *Various Orders of Preternatural Beings.*

I HAVE dwelt largely on the Olympian Deities. The
goddess Thetis has received a separate supplemental
notice, on account, not of her mythological rank but of
her essential share in the machinery, both human and
theogonic, of the Iliad. Also it is essential to give
some attention to the deities or impersonations connected with Duty, Doom, and Justice. With respect to
all other preternatural figures appearing in the Poems,
it will nearly suffice to present their names according
to the classification which has been already stated.

    1. The Nature-Powers:—

        Okeanos: the source of deities (θεῶν γένεσις).
        Il. xiv. 201.

        Tethüs: the mother of deities. Il. xiv. 201.

    These two were married, but estranged. Il. xiv. 206.

It is probable that Homer intends by these expressions to represent Okeanos and Tethüs as the general
parents of the various dynasties of gods; and it can

only be from a supreme respect to Okeanos that, when
all other Rivers are summoned to the Great Olympian
Assembly, he alone is not called[1], because he could not
appear there in his proper place, as head and Sire of all.

Gaia. In the Underworld. The word means
Land, rather than Earth.

Nereus. In the sea. Never expressly named;
but only called 'the aged father of Thetis,'
and signified in the patronymic of Nereides.

Kronos and Rhea. In Tartaros. Welcker thinks
that Kronos (Time) is a mythical reflection
from the conception of Zeus, who alone has in
Homer the title of Kronides. Rhea he takes,
as kindred to Era[2], to be an Earth-goddess of
one of the old associated races of the Greek
Peninsula. Rhea is clearly placed in association with Okeanos and Tethüs, by her delivering over Herè to their care.

Amphitritè, the moaning sea ($\dot{a}\gamma\delta\sigma\tau\sigma\nu\sigma s$), is mentioned in the Odyssey; in a very faint personi-
fication. In later mythology, she becomes a
wife of Poseidon. The passages where she is
named, as well as the fact that she is only
named in this poem, well admit of our referring her to the circle of Phœnician traditions[3].

2. The Minor Nature-Powers:—

The Rivers: of whom are specially named—
    Xanthos or Scamandros. Il. xx. 74.
    Asopos. Od. xi. 260.
    Spercheios. Il. xxiii. 144.

[1] Il. xx. 4.   [2] Welcker, I. 143; Il. 216.
  [3] Od. iii. 91; v. 422; xii. 60, 97.

Alpheios.   Il. xi. 728.
Enipeus.   Od. xi. 238.
Axios.   Il. xxi. 141, 157.
The Nymphs—
    Daughters of Zeus.   Il. vi. 420.   Od. vi. 105.
    The Mountain Nymphs.   Il. vi. 420.
    The Grove Nymphs.   Il. xxi. 8.
    The Fountain Nymphs.   Il. xiv. 144; xx. 384; xxi. 9.   Od. xiii. 356.
    The Meadow Nymphs.   Il. xxi. 9.
    The Nymph Abarbareè.   Il. vi. 22.
    Worship of Nymphs.   Od. xiv. 435.
    Their Altar.   Od. xvii. 211.
The Nymphs mentioned thus far are named as having been summoned to the Great Olympian Assembly.
    The Nymphs of the Sun, Lampetiè and Phaëthousa.   Od. xii. 132.   Their mother is Neaira.   Od. xii. 133.
    The Nereids, sisters of Thetis, dwelling in the sea.   Il. xviii. 37.
The Winds: never admitted to Olympos; but worshipped; viz.
    Zephuros.   Il. xxiii. 195, 200, 208.
    Boreas.   Il. xx. 223; xxiii. 195, 208.
    (Notos and Euros are not mentioned as separate impersonations.)
    3. Mythological Personages of the Outer, or Phœnician Sphere.
    Helios, father of Aietes and Kirkè.   Od. x. 138.
    Kirkè.   Od. x. 136.
    Calypso, daughter of Atlas.   Od. i. 52.

Ino Leucotheè. Od. v. 333. A deified mortal.
Proteus. Od. iv. 385. Declared to belong to
Egypt.
Atlas, the Pillar-bearer, and sea explorer. Od.
i. 52.
Maias, mother of Hermes. Od. xiv. 435.
Thoosa. Od. i. 71.
Phorcūs. Od. i. 72. 'Ruler of the sea:' in
relations with Poseidon through his daughter
Thoosa.
Aietes, brother of Kirkè. Od. x. 137.
Persè, mother of Kirkè and Aietes. Od. x. 139.
Aiolos. Od. x. 2. A semi-deified mortal.
The Sirens: two in number. Od. xii. 52.

4. The Rebellious Powers are—
Kronos (probably). Il. xiv. 203.
Titans (perhaps). Il. xiv. 279.
The Giants. Od. vii. 59, 60.
Tituos. Od. xi. 576.
Otos and Ephialtes. Od. xi. 305 seqq.

But it is not easy to distinguish in all cases between
powers rebellious, and powers simply deposed or superseded.

Passages relating to the punishment of rebellious
powers, according to the Sacred or Hebrew tradition,
are to be found in Job xxvi. 5; Prov. ii. 18, xxi. 16;
cf. Gen. vi. 4, 5; in 2 Pet. ii. 4, 5; Wisd. xiv. 6;
Ecclus. xvi. 7; Baruch iii. 26, 28.

5. Ministers of Doom.
Atè.
Erinues.
Moira, Moirai, Aisa, Kataclothés.
These will be mentioned severally.

6. Poetical Impersonations.

The Muses, daughters of Zeus: their number is
only mentioned by Homer in Od. xxiv. 60.
The invocation is most commonly in the
singular. They are, however, nine in all.
The Fates (Kêrès, Cataclothes).
The Prayers (with Atè).
Ossa, Rumour. Il. ii. 93; Od. xxiv. 412.
Deimos, Terror. Il. iv. 440, ii. 37, xv. 119.
Probably son of Arès.
Phobos, Panic. Ibid. A son of Arès. Il. xiii. 299.
Kudoimos, Tumult. Attends upon Enno. Il.
v. 593.
Eris, Discord. Il. v. 740. See *supra*, Chap. VIII.
Oneiros, Dream. Il. ii. 6–54.
Hûpnos, Sleep. Il. xiv. 231.
Thanatos, Death. Il. xiv. 231, xvi. 454, 682.
Alkè, Might. Il. v. 740.
Iokè, Rout. Il v. 740.
Arpuiai: the Storm-winds. Od. i. 241; re-
peated xiv. 371, xx. 77; cf. 63. Of these
Podargè is named as the mother; who bears
to Zephuros the two immortal horses of
Achilles, Zanthos and Balios.

II. *The Erinues.*

There are three chief descriptions of preternatural
force recognised in the Homeric Poems.
1. The will and power of the Olympian deities.
2. The binding efficacy of Destiny.
3. The obligations of the moral order.
The first of them may be described, from its mixed

character of truth and fable, as the Theomythology of the Poet.

The second is his Necessitarianism.

The third is his Deontology.

But none of these are scientifically set forth or viewed; and no one of them has an exclusive sway.

In the first, a personal will is everywhere apparent; and though this will is largely used in sustaining moral ideas, yet with them are mixed mere propensities and partialities, and even passions and vices.

In the second and third, personality and will are thrown into the background. As his first rests on 'shall,' so the second is based on the idea we convey by ' must;' but the third is founded on 'ought.'

The second, if absolute, is perhaps among the most immoral and degrading of all philosophical systems; but those, who have given it a logical assent, have seldom adopted it as the rule of life; and in Homer it has only a very limited range. It is rarely held up to us apart from some reference either to the personal will of the gods, or to the moral order; and it never appears as the single, ultimate, overruling force.

The third corresponds with the second in its generally, though not invariably, impersonal character; and the ideas belonging to the two respectively are sometimes mixed in the words μοῖρα, which leans however to the idea of force, and αἶσα and δαίμων, which contains more of the moral element. There is also a relation between the idea of Zeus, and that of Fate, exhibited in the remarkable phrase Διὸς αἶσα, the fate of, that is, proceeding from, Zeus.

But in the rear of this law of the great Ought, or the moral order of the Universe, there is a personal agency,

which in Homer is principally charged with enforcing
its observance; that namely of the 'Ερινύες. With the
progress of time, and the growth of moral corruption,
the function of these venerable ministers of Right
comes more and more to be, not enforcing the observance, or repairing the breach, but simply punishing the
offender; and they themselves gradually assume the
power of Furies, dressed in every imaginable horror.
The later pictures of them are coarse and vulgar, compared with the awful yet noble figures of the Erinues
of Homer, in whom is really represented, more than in
Zeus himself, the idea of an ultimate Divine Judgment,
together with compensating and rectifying powers.

The action of the Erinues is to a certain extent
mixed with that of the subterranean or avenging gods.
When the father of Phœnix prays the Erinues to make
him childless, the imprecation is fulfilled by 'the gods,
and (or namely) the nether Zeus and the awful Persephonè:' and again, when Althaia invokes these two
deities for the punishment of Meleagros, it is the
Erinùs who from Erebos hears, and accomplishes, the
prayer[1]. The Erinues are invoked by Agamemnon to
witness to his asseverated oath concerning Briseis, as
punishers of the perjured; together with Zeus, Gaia,
and the Sun[2]. The Erinues of Epicastè haunt her
son Œdipus[3]. In his father's house, Telemachos ap-
prehends that, should he dismiss his mother, her Erinues
will come upon him[4]: and Odysseus, when the Suitor
Antinoos has hurled the stool at him, invokes upon
him 'if,' or, 'for surely,' 'there are such,' the gods and
Erinues of the poor[5].

---

[1] Il. ix. 449–457 and 565–60).   [2] Il. xix. 258–260.
[3] Od. li. 279.   [4] Od. li. 135.   [5] Od. xvii. 475, 476.

The functions of the Erinues are not confined to mortals. They affect also the gods. When Arès is laid prostrate in the Theomachy, Athenè tells him his fall is due to the Erinues of his mother Herè, whose side he had abandoned [1]. And, when Iris finds it difficult to induce Poseidon to obey the behest of Zeus by withdrawing from the field of battle, she reminds him that the Erinues are with the elder [2].

The horse Xanthos receives a voice from Herè, to warn Achilles of his fate: when he has done it, the Erinues arrest his speech [3].

When Agamemnon has to confess his ἄτη or sin in the matter of Briseis, he says, 'I however am not to blame, but Zeus, and Fate, and the Erinus that stalks in cloud [4].'

When the daughters of Pandareos have received all manner of gifts by the agency of the gods, and Zeus is being asked to find them husbands, instead of this, the Harpuiai or Hurricanes, who are either storm-blasts or subordinate ministers of vengeance, carry them off, and deliver them to the Erinues to deal with [5].

Thus far, in eleven cases out of the twelve in which Homer introduces these remarkable personages, they evidently appear as the champions and avengers of the moral order, in all forms, and against all persons whatever.

They are never subject to the order of any Deity. The gods indeed are subject to control, or even punishment, by them. Zeus is never mentioned in this relation: but their office expressly reaches to Poseidon. Their agency is wholly anterior to, and independent

---

[1] Il. xxi. 410–414.   [2] Il. xv. 202.   [3] Il. xix. 418.
[4] Il. xix. 87.   [5] Od. xx. 66–78.

of, all volition whatever. They represent Law in
action. But, besides punishing offenders, they actually
stop and repair infractions of the moral or settled
constitution of the world, as in the case of the horse
Xanthos. They therefore represent not only right as
opposed to wrong, but order as opposed to disorder:
and, in this respect, they supply a very characteristic
product of the symmetrical mind of the Greeks.

The Erinues of parents, of elders, of the poor, and the
like, are the sanctions of those great relations, in which
moral obligation has its roots for the mass of men.

In the case of the offence of Œdipus, will was not
concerned: yet it is enough for them that law was
violated; and they appear in order to avenge it.

In the case of the orphan daughters of Pandareos,
it is simply excess which they appear to resent. All
personal gifts, even their food, were conveyed to these
maidens by the direct agency of deities. This abnormal
provision, lying far beyond, was therefore in derogation
of, the established laws for the government of the world:
it left no space for human volition, effort, or discipline.
This is the probable ground for the remarkable intervention of the Erinues against the damsels.

The twelfth and remaining case represents the close-
sticking, or tenacious, Erinūs[1] (δασπλῆτις) as insinuat-
ing an Atè or offence into the mind of Melampous.
Neleus had made it a condition of obtaining the hand
of his daughter Pero, that the Suitor should bring him
certain oxen of Iphiclos. This Melampous undertook
to do, on behalf not of himself but of a brother; though
it entailed a year's imprisonment, which as a Seer he
must be supposed to have known beforehand. We

---

[1] Compare 'Post equitem sedet atra cura.' Hor. Od. 3. 1, 40.

have to ask, in what did the offence consist? Was it an imprudence or folly thus to expose himself? or was the theft an offence against the laws of good neighbourhood or guestship? In either case we do not escape this difficulty, that it was suggested by the Erinüs. This is a representation not easily brought into accordance with any of the other Homeric references to the Erinues: which, though severe beyond the limits of justice, nowhere else appear as the instigators of evil. It seems to be peculiarly strange, because of the habitual care of the Erinüs to maintain the established order, and not merely to punish the breach of it.

It is true that, in the Odyssey, Athenè is said to restrain the Suitors from discontinuing their evil deeds. But these are men who had long persisted in a profligate and cruel disregard of all the laws of duty[1]. No such consideration will apply to the case of Melampous. Agamemnon, indeed, blames the Erinüs for his own fault: but this is a mere excuse. The whole legend of Melampous is given in a form somewhat cramped; and, like other passages in the later books of the Odyssey, suggests that it had not been fully wrought out by the Poet. Possibly, but I cannot say more than possibly, this may account for the mode in which the Erinüs is introduced. We may also remark that here only she is called by the name of goddess; which appears rather inconsistent with her position.

Whether we are to regard the Erinüs as really capable of being a tempter or not, the conception deviates from the highest form of rectitude by ad-

[1] Od. xviii. 151, 346.

ministering punishment, in the case of Œdipus, to an
involuntary offence. But here the elements of good
greatly preponderate; and there is something noble as
well as awful in these beings, watching with so much
care over constituted laws, and maintaining or restoring
the equilibrium of the moral world. It is by an immense declension that these sublime Erinues become
the savage Furies of the Latin Hades [1].

The name of Erinüs is traced etymologically by
Professor Max Müller to the Sanscrit Saranyû, a name
of the Dawn [2]: which, as importing discovery by means
of light, would connect it with the office we have been
considering.

III. *Atè, the Temptress.*

The Atè of Homer, as a person, represents a Temp-
tress, who insinuates into the mind error or crime,
begun in folly, and ending in calamity. Among the
later Greeks it is Calamity simply, with a shadow of
Destiny hanging in the distance.

The Homeric Atè means and wishes ill to mortals;
but seems to have no power to hurt them, except it
be through channels wholly or partially opened to her
by their own erring or bewildered volition. Even
Deity is not exempt from her illusions: for, before the
birth of Heracles [3], she it is who leads Zeus to promise
what will, through Herè's craft, overturn his own most
dearly cherished plans. For this excess of daring, Zeus
seizes her by the hair, and hurls her from Olympos
to Earth [4], apparently taken to be her native seat.

[1] Æn. vi. 555, 571.   [2] Lectures on Language, il. 484, 516, 562.
[3] Il. xix. 95 seqq.   [4] Il. xix. 126-133.

For she [1] is his eldest daughter; his daughters too
are the Litai, or prayers, that lag behind her. She
is vigorous and nimble, prowling about for mischief.
They are limping and decrepit : they cannot see
straight before them [2]. In this allegory, we have man
ready and quick to err, slow to repent. We have
also a living power of Evil extraneous to him, and ever
soliciting him to his own loss and ruin. Here is a
picture in substance much resembling the Serpent of
the Book of Genesis, the Satan of Scripture, and the
punishment he has undergone.

The temptations of Atè are to acts, also called atai,
variously shaded between folly and sheer crime. The
most innocent atè of Homer is perhaps the sleep of
Odysseus in Thrinakiè, during which his crew consume
the oxen of the Sun [3]. He may, indeed, be regarded
as in some sort responsible for his comrades: yet he
had bound them by oath [4] not to commit the acts.

We cannot be surprised if occasionally we find moral
government in Homer out of joint, as in the case lately
observed, where the Erinüs is said to send an Atè [5].
Agamemnon complains that his Atè was sent to him
by Zeus, together with Destiny and Erinüs [6]; but this
is an exhibition of a weak and self-excusing character,
rather than a normal example of the thought current
in that age.

Besides the Atè of Zeus, of Agamemnon, and of
Odysseus, we have in Homer the following chief
examples:

Of Dolon, Il. x. 391.

[1] Il. xix. 91.

[2] Od. xii. 372.

[3] Od. xv. 234.

[2] Il. ix. 499–514.

[4] Od. xii. 303.

[6] Il. xix. 87.

Of Melampous, Od. xv. 233.

These are offences against prudence.

Of Paris, Il. vi. 356; xxiv. 28.

Of Helen, Od. iv. 261; xxiii. 223.

Of the Manslayer, Il. xxiv. 480.

Of the drunken Centaur Eurution, Od. xxi. 296-302.

These are moral transgressions.

The higher form of human wickedness, deliberate and self-conscious, is, as we shall see, not atè but atasthaliè.

IV. *Fate or Doom.*

The words used in Homer to signify Fate, Doom, and Destiny, are Kēr, also in the plural Kēres; Kataclothés; Moira; Aisa; and Moros.

Of these, Kēr approaches most frequently to a distinct impersonation ; has the faintest trace of any moral element, distinct from the mere machinery of an iron system of decrees; and is of the darkest colour, as it always implies doom or death, never a fated blessing. Kēr again is the destiny of an individual; not of law governing the world. It is, however, on no occasion eluded or contravened.

The Kataclothés or Spinners are only mentioned in Od. vii. 197. They are personal : and the epithet 'weighty' or 'oppressive' is attached to them. They partake of the character of the Kēres.

Neither of these touch the great questions, how far destiny overrules the human will, and how far it is separate from, or even superior to, the divine will.

The word Aisa means the destiny of a particular
person [1]: or the moral law for the government of
conduct [2]; or that moral law as proceeding from Zeus or
Providence personally, as the Dios aisa[3], daimonos
aisa: or lastly a separate power moving and ruling
affairs [4]. In this last and gravest sense, Aisa is not very
prominently used. Again, it is but rarely and faintly
personified; it contains more of the moral element,
more of *ought* than of *must*: though, when used to mean
Death it is irresistible, because the law of death cannot
be directly cancelled. Otherwise, it may be overcome.
In Il. xvi. 780, the Achaians gain the upperhand against
the Trojans, in spite of Aisa. But this particular Aisa
was no more than the decree of Zeus, which gave
that one day of success to the fortunes of Troy. The
dominant idea of Aisa generally is not blind command, but an ordained law of right: a law without
doubt very liable to be broken.

Moira, like Aisa, means an allotted share: but it
is less ethical, more contracted, and more sovereign
and resistless. Moira deals with each man: but we
scarcely hear of the Moira of a man. It may mean
good fortune, and has this sense in opposition to am-
moriè [5]: it requires a darkening epithet to give it the
adverse sense [6]. It is however often used for death.
It may be the divine will embodied, as we have the
Moira of the god, or the gods [7]; but never of any
named god, which seems to place it somewhat higher
than Aisa. Nothing in Homer is actually done con-

---

[1] Il. i. 416.   [2] Il. Ili. 59.   [3] Il. xvii. 321.
[4] Il. xx. 127; xvl. 441.   [5] Od. xx. 76.   [6] Il. xil. 116.
[7] Od. iii. 269; xxii. 413.

trary to Moira: but such things seem to be regarded
as not beyond the bounds of possibility [1].

It is not however incapable of receiving the moral
element. To speak generally, morsimos is destined,
aisimos is right. But when Antinoos is killed, he is
killed according to Moira [2], that is rightly: and the
term cata moiran connects it with the moral order, in
the sense of propriety [3].

In the order of action, then, Moira is above Aisa;
in the order of law, below it.

Moros in Homer is never personified. Referred
to an individual it seems to mean his death: and
etymologically it corresponds with the Latin *mors*. It
is never associated with the deity. But it is like Aisa
in receiving the sense of the moral law. And here it
corresponds with the Latin *mos*, *moris*. For mortals
bring calamity on themselves in defiance of moros,
and in similar defiance Aigisthos commits his crimes [4].
This can hardly mean that he was too strong for
Destiny; but he was too strong for Right.

In none of these forms does Destiny ever fight with
the gods; or, unless it be in the shape of Death, defy
them. The later Greek mind elaborated the idea of
a Fate apart from, and higher than, the gods [5]. But, in
Homer, not even the human will is controlled in such
a manner as to suggest or sustain the Necessitarian
theory. Indeed we find the gods helping Destiny against
man: as when, in the Second Iliad [6], the Greeks would,
against Moros, have returned to their country after the

[1] Il. xx. 335.   [2] Od. xxii. 54.   [3] Il. x. 169.
[4] Od. i. 34, 35.
[5] Æsch. Ag. 993; Herod. i. 91; Philem. Fragm. 86.
[6] Od. i. 155.

rush from the Assembly, had not Herè urged Athenè
to stay the torrent of home-sick emotion: and Apollo
entered Troy, lest the Greeks should take it, against
Moros, on the day of the fall of Hector [1]. Nor is the
Fate of Homer absolutely blind: on the contrary it
shows rather a tendency at times to grow into a sort
of rival Providence, as in 'The Fates have ordained
for man a hardy mind [2].'

And when, in order to obtain a comprehensive view
of the field of human action, we turn to the general
plan of the two Poems, we find that in each case they
work, not according to the impulsion of a blind and
occult force, but rationally, towards the fulfilment of
a divine or Olympian decree, announced at the outset,
and steadily pursued to the end [3].

V. *Animal Worship.*

Although Animal worship has played so considerable
a part in the religions of the East, the traces of it in
Homer are few, and, with one exception, they are
also faint.

That exception is the extraordinary sanctity attaching, in the Twelfth Odyssey, to the Oxen of the Sun,
which I have treated as belonging to the Phœnician
system, and as foreign to the Olympian religion [4].

Other traces seem to be rather dubiously discoverable,
as follows:

[1] Il. xxi. 517.   [2] Il. xxiv. 49.
[3] Il. l. 5; iv. 61–64. Od. l. 76–79.
[4] See *supra*, Helios, Chap. VIII.

(*a*) The introduction of the immortal horses, Xanthos and Balios; the gift of speech, conferred for the moment by Herè on Xanthos; and, what is of more weight, the gift of prevision, which enabled him to foretell his master's death. That gift he did not derive from the goddess. But, when he had thus spoken, the Erinũs interfered to arrest this violation of the natural order [1].

(*b*) The assumption by deities of the forms of birds: viz:—

> By Athenè, Il. vii. 59; Od. i. 320, iii. 372, xxii. 240.
> Apollo, Il. vii. 59.
> Hupnos, Il. xiv. 290.
> Ino Leucotheè (Phœnician), Od. v. 333.

(*c*) The horse in Homer generally has not only a poetical grandeur, but a near relation to deity, which I am unable sufficiently to explain: but which, it seems possible, may be the reflection or analogue of the place assigned to the ox in the East. Several circumstances, and among them the practice of describing a champaign country as one suited to feeding the horse [2], combine to show how completely, for the Greek, this noble creature stood at the head of the animal creation.

Some have pointed to qualities belonging to the brute creation as the possible groundwork of the extraordinary system of religion, which regarded animals as fit objects of worship: the unity and tranquillity of animal life, which makes it, as it were, a colourless medium for an inward spirit to inhabit: and the

---

[1] Il. xix. 404–418.
[2] Il. li. 287, and in fourteen other places.

singular instincts by which it appears in a manner
to apprehend the future [1].

For my own part, I am not able, even after reading
the argument of the learned and able Mr. Davison [2],
to escape from the belief that the hypothesis of a divine
command, given before the races recorded in Scripture
were multiplied and dispersed, affords by far the most
rational and satisfactory explanation of the wide extension of the practice of animal sacrifice, and of its
remarkable uniformity as between races such as the
Hebrews and the Hellenes, who had no communication
together, and little indeed of anything in common.
At the same time, it is an hypothesis only, and has
not been demonstrated.

But if mankind thus offered certain animals to their
gods, under what they esteemed a divine authority, it
is not difficult to perceive the chain of association by
which those animals might themselves, in process of
time, very easily be taken for symbols of the godhead,
and might again, from being mere symbols, grow to
be esteemed the real shrines of its glory, and thus to
attract the worship which is its due.

VI. *On the Modes of Approximation between the Divine and
the Human Nature.*

The anthropomorphic principle of the Greek religion
found for itself, in a spontaneous manner, several distinct forms or channels of development, for the closer
association of the races of gods and men.

---

[1] Döllinger, Held. u. Jud. vi. 130, p. 424.
[2] Inquiry into the Origin and Intent of Primitive Sacrifice.
London, 1825.

The deification of heroes and benefactors after death appears before us in Homer as begun, yet, at least in the Olympian mythology, as incomplete. No person, avowedly of human origin, has yet been advanced to the rank of deity with the full consequences both of an abode in heaven, and a worship on earth.

Yet the consummation of the process is imminent. All the materials are prepared; and all the steps taken, except the final one which combines them into a consistent whole.

The elements of what was soon to be a system are found in Homer principally as follows:—

1. The ascription of human forms, manners, affections, passions, and other qualities, to the gods in general, lying at the root of the Homeric mythology as an anthropomorphic system, firmly lays the ground for further assimilation and intercommunion of the two orders of being.

2. Divine beauty, strength, influence, and intellect, are ascribed freely in a long list of epithets and phrases, to the mortals most eminent for these properties: and even the epithet θεῖος, meaning simply 'divine,' is attached, in the two grand cases of the Protagonists Achilles and Odysseus, to the living personages of the Poems, and to a larger number of the most eminent among the dead. This second head of preparation is as it were the counterpart of the first.

3. Birth from a divine progenitor, and even from a divine father, is ascribed to many personages who are active in the Poems, as well as to many who were dead.

4. Passion for beautiful or distinguished men is freely ascribed to goddesses, in a number of instances.

Among these were some, especially Aphroditè and Demeter, who were already in part, and whom at a later date we find fully and unequivocally, adopted into the Hellenic religion. But it is remarkable that such passion is in no case throughout the Poems ascribed to any of those goddesses who were either the most elevated or else the most national : Herè, Athenè, Leto, Artemis. A higher and purer idea of woman was entertained among the Achaians, and reflected in their religion, than in the elemental or the oriental systems.

5. More closely to the purpose than anything that has yet been stated, are the instances of Ganymede and Cleitos, translated to heaven and the society of the Immortals for their beauty [1] : of Tithonos, taken up to be the husband of Eos or the morning ; possibly of Marpessa, whom Apollo 'snatched up' [2] : and of Ino Leucotheè [3], who locally, that is, in the great sea region, has from being a mortal risen to the honours and character of deity. Aiolos, too, may be considered as nearly approaching to the character of a deified Personage [4].

These, indeed, are all foreign, or extra-Hellenic, traditions. But of Hellenes, we have Castor, and Poludeukes or Pollux, who, even while on alternate days alive though not among men, and still in the lower regions, yet have by gift of Zeus had divine honours allotted to them [5]: and more still, we have Herakles [6], who, while his Wraith is in the Shades, himself dwells among the gods, and has Hebè, who is apparently a goddess proper, assigned to him for his mate.

[1] Il. xx. 233. Od. xv. 250.
[2] Il. ix. 564.
[3] Od. v. 333-335.
[4] Od. x. 1.
[5] Od. xi. 298-304.
[6] Od. xi. 601.

6. We have also the case of Dionusos, whom, as having been born of a woman, we must apparently take to have been at the outset a mortal, but who had, as is pretty clear, in the time of Homer already become an Olympian god.

7. Asclepios underwent a subsequent deification; but in Homer he is a mortal only, for his sons, Podalirios and Machaon, bear the title of Asclepiad[1], and no mortal in Homer ever derives a patronymic from a god.

8. To whatever inferences the case of Dionusos may lead, there is no other in which we find a trace or suggestion of worship in its proper sense, as paid to any deceased or translated hero. Yet there are two instances of what may be called initial worship, which must not be overlooked. Achilles, besides the fat of oxen and sheep, casts four horses, two dogs, and twelve Trojan youths, upon the funeral pyre of Patroclos[2]. This is, however, I think, to be interpreted purely as a gratification to the departed spirit. In the Eleventh Odyssey we advance a step further, though some may think the Oriental character of the scenery of the Poem in this part ought to be taken into account. Odysseus, by express order from Kirkè, besides making a libation, sacrifices a ram and a sheep on the spot, with invocation to the gods, of whom Aïdes and Persephone are named; and permits the dead successively to drink the blood, that they may tell him what he wants to know[3]. Here we see, dominant and unmixed, that idea of actual enjoyment by the objects of the sacrifice, which in the case of ordinary offerings to the gods is combined with other ideas more proper to the notion of worship. But

[1] Il. iv. 204.   [2] Il. xxiii. 171–176.
[3] Od. xl. 35, 44–47.

besides this, Odysseus is also enjoined to promise, and
he promises accordingly, that, on his return to Ithaca,
he will offer (and here the sacrificial words ῥέζειν and
ἱερεύειν are employed) a black sheep to Teiresias, and
a cow that has never calved to the dead in general [1].
This vow seems to come within a step, at least, of the
full idea of worship. We do not hear of its fulfilment
on his return home: but this may be because we are
not carried by the Poem to a perfect settlement of the
difficulties which he finds awaiting him. Prayers (εὐχαί
and λιταί) are here expressly mentioned as used in the
propitiation of the dead. But these are the entire
mass of dead, not selected spirits of the great or
brave.

One marked, and yet rather obscure, form of the connection between the gods and the human race in Homer
is that of divine filiation. It is with much diffidence that
I offer any explanation of this subject. A very large
number of cases are recorded by the Poet, in which the
parentage of a god is expressly assigned to some human
house or hero. In some instances it arises by inference; as when he calls Bellerophon, the son of Sisuphos,
descended from the god (θεοῦ γόνος[2]), which can only
mean, as Sisuphos was descended from Aiolos, that Aiolos
was the offspring of a god. So, again, in the Legend
of Nestor [3], we are told that the young heroes of the
line of Actor were saved from death by their ancestor
Poseidon. The Iliad enables us to trace this line up to
Azeus [4], who must either have been a reputed son of
the god, or may more probably have been an Aiolid,
and thus descended from him, like the heads of so many

[1] Od. xi. 29.
[2] Il. vi. 191.
[3] Il. xi. 751.
[4] Il. ii. 513, 621.

other great houses. Amphimachos, another Actorid, is
slain in the Thirteenth Iliad: whereupon Poseidon is
exceedingly vexed at heart for his υἱωνὸς or descendant [1].

To examine more thoroughly into this matter, let us
take first for consideration the case of the great Ancient
Houses, represented by their chiefs in and before the
Trojan war. We find expressly assigned to Zeus the
stocks of

1. Perseus,	4. Heracles,
2. Minos,	5. Minos,
3. Aiacos,	6. Dardanos.

And to Poseidon those of

1. Actor (probably through Aiolos),
2. Pelias,
3. Neleus,
4. Bellerophon, through Aiolos,
5. Cretheus, (and Eumelos,) through Aiolos.

Again it appears, upon examination, that Homer very
commonly characterises by the epithet ἀμύμων persons
of recognised divine descent. This epithet he gives to
members of the families of

1. The Pelopids,
2. Odysseus,
3. Telamon.
4. Portheus (ancestor of Meleager and of Tudeus),
5. Salmoneus and Augeias (through Aiolos,) with a
   very few others of less distinction.

But the question arises, why is Homer so reserved,
in many of these cases, with respect to the immediate
connection between the first ancestor and the divine
stock? The case, where we should have expected it to

----

[1] Il. xiii. 206.

be most clearly declared, is that of the great sovereign
house of Agamemnon. But not a word is said by him
expressly on the subject of the birth of the Pelopids;
and the sceptre comes first into the hands of Pelops [1],
whereas tradition names Tantalos as the first ancestor,
and this Homer in no way contradicts. In the case of
Dardanos, on the contrary, which is the counterpart to
that of the Pelopids, the line is traced straight up to
Zeus [2].

The natural explanation seems to be that, here as in
so many other cases, Homer's functions as Chronicler
were circumscribed by his feelings of nationality; and
that he acted on his usual rule of never knowingly referring, or providing means to refer, anything Hellenic
to a source admittedly foreign. Therefore, where the
oldest recognised ancestor is an undoubted Greek, as
in the case of Aiacos or Heracles, he gives the divine
parentage; but where the line ran up to some one,
who had not been completely or adequately Hellenised,
there no distinct declaration is given, and we are left to
form a judgment for ourselves, from slighter indications, or from the fact that there is a general representation of the Kings and Chiefs of the heroic age as
heaven-descended.   In the case of Dardanos, there
could be no corresponding motive for reticence.

It will be observed, that all the very ancient houses
in Homer, say those of from four to seven generations
back, as well as the most distinguished modern ones,
like those of Aiacos and Heracles, are referred either
to Zeus, the supreme god of the Pelasgians and Hellenes; or to Poseidon, who appears to have been the
supreme god according to the conception of the Phœ-

[1] Il. ii. 104.   [2] Il. xx. 215.

nician immigrants. So far, then, as these cases are concerned, it seems needless to travel far in search of an explanatory hypothesis. In fact, if there was a tradition, such as we find from the Scriptures to have prevailed among the Hebrews, and by which man in his first inception was viewed as standing in the relation of sonship to the Almighty, it is in accordance with all likelihood that, in process of time, this illustrious extraction should come in popular estimation to be confined to chiefs or ruling men.

This explanation is however principally available for the class of Kings and Princes, who are called Zeus-born and Zeus-nurtured; and for those individual cases, which are of the greatest antiquity, and where no name of a mother is preserved. When we find a maternal name, a new element of difficulty is introduced. This difficulty may be deemed secondary in cases like those of Minos and Perseus; because there the mother may be nothing more than an indication, supplied by tradition, of the national extraction of the son. The mother of Minos is simply ' the daughter of an illustrious Phœnician,' and Danaè has her counterpart in a local Phœnician name. But what are we to say of Alcmenè, the mother of Heracles[1]? of Laodamia, the mother of Sarpedon[2]? of Astuochè, the mother of Ascalaphos and Ialmenos[3]? of Polumelè[4], the mother of Eudoros? perhaps also, of Turo, the mother of Pelias and Neleus[5]? All these are women, having a place and an individuality as well defined as any other pre-Homeric women of the Poems.

[1] Il. xix. 98.
[2] Il. vi. 198.
[3] Il. ii. 513.
[4] Il. xvi. 180.
[5] Od. xi. 235, 254.

The explanation commonly given of these cases has been that they were cases of mere bastardy, covered with the illustrious names of deity. May it not however be said that, if this be true, then nowhere did those connected with the birth of illegitimate children take so amazingly high a flight as among the Greeks; since, not content with equality, they gave them a higher title, by extraction, than the lawful offspring of the family themselves enjoyed? Of bastardy, as commonly understood, we have plenty of examples in the Homeric poems. Sometimes, as in the case of Eudoros, a person born out of wedlock was reared upon the same footing as a legitimate child. But when this is done, it is always mentioned as a thing worthy of note, evidently because more or less exceptional.

I cannot help thinking that these singular cases of persons who had a known mother, and who supplied the want of a known father by claiming the parentage of a god, were not cases of common bastardy, but that they are rather to be explained by reference to the ancient customs of what may be called marriage by violent abduction, or violation without dishonour, practised in ancient times by the men of one tribe upon the daughters of another[1]. Of the traces of this custom, ancient history is full; and even modern manners, in certain cases, aye at our very doors, visibly retain them. It seems to me that where, in the incidents of a tribal raid, some noble maid or even some matron of high birth fell a victim to the lust of an invader, it was agreeable to likelihood, as well as to social justice, that a clear line should be drawn between such cases and cases of dishonour willingly or corruptly incurred; and

[1] See Maclellan on Primitive Marriage, Edinb. 1865.

that either the involuntary mother at the time of the
birth, or her offspring as he grew up, and went among
his fellows without having like them a father to point
to and to lean on, might exceptionally, and under
favouring circumstances, have contrived to imitate for
themselves the old tradition of the descent of kings
from gods. The choice of the deity might in such cases
be influenced by the particular worship in vogue among
the aggressive tribe.

The correlative cases, of legendary births due to the
passion of goddesses for men, may perhaps admit of a
similar explanation. The probable difference in the
facts being, that these would be instances where the
mother disappeared, and the child remained in the possession of the father. This remark may possibly apply to
Æneas, son of Aphroditè; to Aisepos and Pedasos, sons
of the Naiad Nymph Abarbareè; to Satnios, the son of
another Naiad; and to Iphition, the son of a third [1].

The birth of Achilles from Thetis will not fall into
either of these categories; since it is represented as
having taken place in regular wedlock. My conjecture
respecting this birth is, that it may possibly be a pure
invention, due to Homer himself, though perhaps suggested by the legends current in his day, respecting the
attachments contracted by goddesses to mortal men.
Such a fiction would be comparatively easy in the case
of one who, like Peleus, was a reputed immigrant into
the country which he ruled.

I sum up then by observing that we find, over and
above the use of language properly figurative, four main
channels of approach for the human nature to the
divine,

[1] Il. ii. 821; vi. 21; xiv. 444; xx. 384.

1. Translation.
2. Mixed Composition.
3. Affiliation.
4. Deification.

And affiliation again, if I am right, appears in at least four shapes,

(*a*) The ascription of a Divine birth or nurture to Kings and Princes as a class.

(*b*) The ascription of a particular god as ancestor to a sovereign house. This god is always either Zeus or Poseidon.

(*c*) More recent births from a divine father.

(*d*) Births of men from a goddess; few, and all recent.

VII. *The Homeric View of the Future State.*

The picture of the future state of man in Homer is eminently truthful as a representation of a creed which had probably fallen into dilapidation, and of the feelings which clustered about it; and it is perhaps unrivalled in the perfectly natural, but penetrating force, with which it conveys the effect of dreariness and gloom. It does not appear to be in all respects coherent and symmetrical; and, while nothing betokens that this defect is owing to the diversity of the sources from which the traditions are drawn, it is such as might be due to the waste wrought by time and change on a belief which had at an earlier date been self-consistent.

The future life, however, is in Homer used with solemnity and force as a sanction of the moral laws, especially in so far as the crime of perjury is concerned[1].

[1] Il. iii. 297; xix. 259.

The Erinues dwell in the Underworld, and punish perjurors. As the Erinues are invoked with reference to other offences [1], we may therefore presume them also to have been punishable in the Underworld. The world to come is exhibited to us by Homer in three divisions.

First, there is the Elysian plain, apparently under the government of Rhadamanthûs, to which Menelaos will be conducted, or rather perhaps translated, in order to die there; not for his virtues, however, but because he is the husband of Helen, and so the son-in-law of Zeus. The main characteristic of this abode seems to be easy and abundant subsistence with an atmosphere free from the violence of winter, and from rain and snow. Okeanos freshens it with Zephyrs; it is therefore apparently on the western border of the world [2]. Mr. Max Müller conjectures that Elysium (ἤλυθον) may be a name simply expressing the future [3]. The whole conception, however, may be deemed more or less ambiguous, inasmuch as the Elysian state is antecedent to death.

2. Next comes the Underworld proper, the general receptacle of human spirits. It nowhere receives a territorial name in Homer, but is called the abode of Aïdes, or of Aïdes and Persephonè. Its character is chill, drear, and dark; the very gods abhor it [4]. Better to serve for hire even a needy master, says the Shade of Achilles, than to be lord over all the Dead [5]. It reaches, however, under the crust of the earth; for, in the Theomachy, Aïdoneus dreads lest the earthquake of Poseidon should lay open his domain to gods and men [6].

---

[1] See Erinues, sect. iii. *supra.*   [2] Od. iv. 561-569.
[3] Lectures on Language, li. 562, n.
[4] Il. xx. 65.   [5] Od. xi. 489.   [6] Il. xx. 1. Comp. Od. xi. 302.

Minos administers justice among the dead, as a king would on earth. But they are in general under no penal infliction. Three cases only are mentioned as cases of suffering: those of Tituos, Tantalos, and Sisuphos[1]. The offence is only named in the case of Tituos; it was violence offered to the goddess Leto. Heracles suffers a strange discerption of individuality; for his eidolon or Shade moves and speaks here, while 'he himself is at the banquets of the immortals[2].' Again, Castor and Pollux are here, and are alive on alternate days, while they enjoy on earth the honours of deities[3]. Here, then, somewhat conflicting conditions appear to be combined.

Within the dreary region seems to be a palace, which is in a more special sense the residence of its rulers[4].

The access to the Underworld is in the far East, by the Ocean River, at a full day's sail from the Euxine, in the country of the cloud-wrapt Kimmerioi[5]. From this point the way lies, for an indefinite distance, up the Stream; to a point where the beach is narrow, and where Persephonè is worshipped in her groves of poplar and of willow[6].

3. There is also the region of Tartaros, as far below that of Aïdes, as Aïdes is below the earth. Here dwell Iapetos and Kronos, far from the solar ray[7]. Kronos has a band of gods around him, who have in another place the epithet of sub-Tartarean; and the name of Titans[8]. It does not appear whether these are at all identified with the deposed dynasty of the

---

[1] Od. xi. 576, 582, 593.
[2] Od. xl. 601–627.
[3] Od. xl. 300–304.
[4] Od. xl. 627, 635.
[5] Od. xi. 9–14. See Chap. XIII. sect. 3.
[6] Od. x. 506–512.
[7] Il. viii. 16, 479.
[8] Il. xiv. 274, 279.

Nature Powers, whose dwelling is in the Underworld [1];
and with whom the human Dead had communication,
for Achilles charges the Shade of Patroclos with a commission to the River Spercheios [2].

The line, therefore, between the realm of Aïdes and
the dark Tartaros is obscurely drawn; but in general
we may say that, while the former was for men, the
latter was for deposed or condemned Immortals. We
hear of the offences of Eurumedon and the Giants with
their ruler [3]; and, though their place is not named, we
may presume them, as well as Otos and Ephialtes, to
be in Tartaros, in addition to the deities already
named [4]. Hither it is that Zeus threatens to hurl
down refractory divinities of the Olympian Court [5].

This threefold division of the unseen world is in
some kind of correspondence with the Christian, and
with what may have been the patriarchal, tradition; as
is the retributive character of the future state, however
imperfectly developed, and the continuance there of the
habits and propensities acquired on earth.

VIII. *The Olympian System in its Results.*

The history of the race of Adam before the Advent
is the history of a long and varied but incessant preparation for the Advent. It is commonly perceived
that Greece contributed a language and an intellectual
discipline, Rome a political organisation, to the apparatus which was put in readiness to assist the propaga-

---

[1] Il. Ili. 278.   [2] Il. xxiii. 141-153.
[3] Od. vii. 60.   [4] Od. xi. 318. Il. v. 385, 407.
[5] Il. v. 897, 898; viii. 10; xvii. 401-406.

tion of the Gospel; and that each of these, in its kind, was the most perfect that the world had produced. I have endeavoured elsewhere to show with some fulness what was the place of Greece in the Providential order of the world [1]; and likewise what was the relation of Homer to the Greeks, and to their part of the Divine plan, as compared with the relation of the Sacred Scriptures to the chosen people of God [2]. I cannot now enter on that field at large; yet neither can I part without a word from the subject of the Olympian religion.

In the works of Homer, this design is projected with such extraordinary grandeur, that the representation of it, altogether apart from the general merits of the Poems, deserves to be considered as one of the topmost achievements of the human mind. Yet its character, as it was first and best set forth in its entirety from the brain of the finisher and the maker, is not more wonderful than its subsequent influence and duration in actual life. For, during twelve or fourteen hundred years, it was the religion of the most thoughtful, the most fruitful, the most energetic portions of the human family. It yielded to Christianity alone; and to the Church it yielded with reluctance, summoning up strength in its extreme old age, and only giving way after an intellectual as well as a civil battle, obstinately fought, and lasting for generations. For the greater part of a century after the fall of Constantinople, in the chief centres of a Christian civilisation in many respects degenerated, and an ecclesiastical power too little faithful to its trust, Greek letters and Greek thought once again asserted their strength over the

---

[1] Address to the University of Edinburgh, 1865.
[2] Studies on Homer, vol. ii. Olympos, sect. x.

most cultivated minds of Italy, in a manner which testified to the force, and to the magic charm, with which they were imperishably endowed. Even within what may be called our own time, the Olympian religion has exercised a fascination altogether extraordinary over the mind of Goethe, who must be regarded as standing in the very first rank of the great minds of the latest centuries.

The Olympian religion, however, owes perhaps as large a share of its triumphs to its depraved accommodations, as to its excellences. Yet an instrument so durable, potent, and elastic, must certainly have had a purpose to serve. Let us consider for a moment what it may have been.

We have seen how closely, and in how many ways, it bound humanity and deity together. As regarded matter of duty and virtue, not to speak of that highest form of virtue which is called holiness, this union was effected mainly by lowering the divine element. But as regarded all other functions of our nature, outside the domain of the life to god-ward, all those functions which are summed up in what Saint Paul calls the flesh and the mind, the psychic and the bodily life, the tendency of the system was to exalt the human element, by proposing a model of beauty, strength, and wisdom, in all their combinations, so elevated, that the effort to attain them required a continual upward strain. It made divinity attainable; and thus it effectually directed the thought and aim of man

'Along the line of limitless desires.'

Such a scheme of religion, though failing grossly in the government of the passions, and in upholding the

standard of moral duties, tended powerfully to produce
a lofty self-respect, and a large, free, and varied conception of humanity. It incorporated itself in schemes
of notable discipline for mind and body, indeed of a
lifelong education; and these habits of mind and action
had their marked results (to omit many other great-
nesses) in a philosophy, literature, and art, which remain
to this day unrivalled or unsurpassed.

The sacred fire, indeed, that was to touch the mind
and heart of man from above, was in preparation elsewhere. Within the shelter of the hills that stand about
Jerusalem, the great Archetype of the spiritual excellence and purification of man was to be produced and
matured. But a body, as it were, was to be made ready
for this angelic soul. And as when some splendid edifice is to be reared, its diversified materials are brought
from this quarter and from that, according as nature
and man favour their production, so did the wisdom of
God, with slow but ever sure device, cause to ripen
amidst the several races best adapted for the work, the
several component parts of the noble fabric of a Christian manhood and a Christian civilisation. 'The kings
of Tharsis and of the isles shall give presents: the
kings of Arabia and Saba shall bring gifts[1].' Every
worker was, with or without his knowledge and his will,
to contribute to the work. And among them an appropriate part was thus assigned both to the Greek people,
and to what I have termed the Olympian religion.

[1] Ps. lxxii. 10.

CHAPTER X.

ETHICS OF THE HEROIC AGE.

SECTION I.

In general outline, we may thus sum up the moral character of the Homeric Greeks, favourably regarded.

A high-spirited, energetic, adventurous, and daring people, they show themselves prone to acts of hasty violence; and their splendid courage occasionally even degenerates, under the influence of strong passion, into ferocity, while their acuteness and sagacity sometimes, though more rarely, take a decided tinge of cunning. Yet they are neither selfish, cruel, nor implacable. At the same time, self-command is scarcely less conspicuous among them than strong, and deep, and quick emotion. They are, in the main, a people of warm affections and high honour, commonly tender, never morbid: they respect the weak and the helpless; they hold authority in reverence. Domestic purity, too, is cherished and esteemed among them more than elsewhere; and they have not yet fallen into the lower depths of sensual excess.

The Greek thanks the gods in his prosperity; witness the case of Laertes. It is perhaps less remarkable that in his adversity he appeals to them for aid. If, again, he is discontented, he complains of them; for he harbours no concealed dissatisfaction. Ready enough to take from those who have, he is at least as ready to give to those who need. He represents to the life the sentiment which another great master of manners has given to his Duke of Argyle, in the 'Heart of Mid Lothian': 'It is our Highland privilege to take from all what *we* want, and to give to all what *they* want[1].' Distinctions of class are recognised, but they are mild and genial; there is no arrogance on the one side, nor any servility on the other. Reverence is paid to those in authority; and yet the Greek thinks in the spirit, and moves in the sphere, of habitual freedom. Over and above his warmth and tenacity in domestic affections, he prizes highly those other special relations between man and man, which mitigate and restrain the law of force in societies as yet imperfectly organized. He thoroughly admires the intelligence displayed in stratagem, whether among the resources of self-defence, or by way of jest upon a friend, or for the hurt or ruin of an enemy; but life in disguise he cannot away with, and holds it a prime article in his creed that the tongue should habitually represent the man[2].

From these facts, if taken alone, we might be tempted to suppose, that the Greeks of the Homeric age were an inhuman and savage race, who did not appreciate the value of human life. But this is not so. They are not a cruel people. There is no wanton infliction of pain

[1] Scott's Novels and Tales, 8vo. ed., x. 238.   [2] Il. ix. 312.

throughout the whole operations of the Iliad; no delight
in the sufferings of others, no aggravation of them
through vindictive passion. The only needless wounds
given, are wounds inflicted on the dead body of Hector[1].
It seems to be not a disregard of human life, but an
excess of regard for courage, which led them to under-
value the miseries incident to violence.

The character of Heracles, or Hercules, is one of
which we hear much more evil than good in the
Poems, if indeed we hear any good at all. The
climax of his misdeeds is in the case of Iphitos, the
possessor of certain fine mares. Heracles became his
guest, slew him, and carried off the animals[2]. Yet,
he is nowhere held up to reprobation. Indeed he seems
to be a sharer of the banquets of the gods, and has
Hebè for his wife; his Shade, or E i d o l o n, however,
dwelling in the Underworld[3]. If this passage be
genuine, we can only suppose his crimes to be redeemed, in the public judgment, by his courage, together with his divine extraction. And the passage is
supported by the application to him of the epithet
t h e i o s, which is given in the Poems only to the two
Protagonists, Achilles and Odysseus, among the living,
and to the most distinguished among the dead. Certainly, the indignation of the Greeks is against Paris
the effeminate coward, much more than Paris the
ravisher. The shame of the abduction lay in the fact
that he was the guest of Menelaos[4]. And the guilt of
Aigisthos finds its climax in this, that he slew Agamemnon by stealth, at a banquet, like a stalled ox[5]. Piracy,

---

[1] Il. xxii. 371.   [2] Od. xxi. 24-30.
[3] Od. xi. 601-604.   [4] Il. iii. 351-354.
[5] Od. i. 35-37; iv. 524-535; xi. 409-420.

again, was regarded, at the very least, with a moral indifference[1], which continued down to the time of Thucydides in many parts of Greece[2]. Even Odysseus, the model-prince, when he has destroyed the Suitors, and is considering how he can repair his wasted substance, calculates upon effecting it in part by occasional free-booting[3]. To the principle, then, he freely gives his sanction; although he probably attacked the Kicones as allies of Troy[4]; and he disapproved, as it appears, of the raid upon the Egyptians, which in one of his fables he imputes to his ship's company[5]. This act is denominated an outrage[6]; and some disapproval of pirates is implied in another passage[7]. But it is faint. Piracy was a practice connected on one side with trade, and on the other with fighting; and it seems to have been acquitted of guilt for the reason that the gains of the pirate's life were the fruit of bravery combined with skill, and were not unequally balanced by its dangers. And piracy seems to have been practised only upon foreigners; of course such foreigners only as did not come within the range of any bond of guestship.

Religion, however, had a considerable moral force.

The connection in the age of Homer between duty on the one side, and religious belief and reverence on the other, is well seen

(*a*) Negatively, by the faithlessness and ferocity of the Cyclops towards men, while he avows his contempt for Zeus and the gods[8].

(*b*) By the fact that the persons addicted to sacrifice and religious observances are with Homer the upright

---

[1] Od. iii. 72.   [2] Thuc. L 5.   [3] Od. xxiii. 357.
[4] Od. ix. 40.   [5] Od. xiv. 259 seqq.   [6] Od. xiv. 262.
[7] Od. xxiv. 111.   [8] Od. ix. 273-280, 356, 368-370.

and good men: such as Hector in the Iliad, and Eumaios in the Odyssey[1].

(c) As our word 'righteous,' founded on right, and embracing morality, extends also to piety, so in Homer the corresponding word d i c a i o s clearly embraces duty towards the gods[2]. The Abioi[3], an uncivilised nation, are with him 'the most righteous of men.'

(d) Conversely, the character of the theoudês, or god-revering man, is identified with that of the stranger-loving, and opposed to that of the insolent, the savage, and the unrighteous[4].

(e) The wicked man cannot by sacrifices secure the fruits of his crime. Aigisthos offers them in abundance: but the gods destroy him by the hand of Orestes[5].

(f) Though the outward act of sacrifice did not of necessity imply a corresponding frame of mind, yet it was of religious tendency. The ordinary offering, at the common meal, of a portion to the deity as the giver, may be compared with the 'grace' among Christians. In solemn celebrations, and sometimes indeed at the private meal[6], prayer and thanksgiving were commonly combined with the rite.

(g) The gods, as we have already seen, were thought, in a real though incomplete measure, to be rewarders of the good, and punishers of the bad.

(h) There was a strong general belief in the efficacy of prayer, testified by its practice.

We must not deny the reality of moral distinctions

[1] Il. xxiv. 68. Od. xiv. 420.
[2] Il. xiii. 6.
[3] Od. iii. 272-275; i. 35-43.
[4] Od. iii. 132-136.
[5] Od. vi. 120.
[6] Od. xiv. 423.

in Homer upon any such ground as that he sometimes
describes greatness and strength by names rather denoting virtue, and mentions, for example, the services
' which the inferior render to the good[1].' The language
even of our own day has not yet escaped from this
very improper confusion. . We still speak of the ' better
classes,' and of ' good society.' By him, as by us, the
error is escaped in other cases: for he calls the Suitor-
Princes ' very inferior men[2].' And the word a g a t h o s,
or good, has unquestionably in some passages a solely
moral meaning[3]: while it is never applied to any
bad man or action, however energetic or successful.

There was a voice of conscience, and a sentiment
ranging between reverence and fear, within the breast.
Sometimes this ascended to a point far higher than
the mere avoidance of crime. After his conquest of
the Hupoplakian Thebes, Achilles would not despoil
the body of the slain king Eetion, and burned it with
the precious armour on. He was restrained, not by
general opinion, but by the inward sentiment called
s e b a s[4]. To strip the corpse would have been the
usual course. Telemachos endeavours, of course in
vain, to arouse in the minds of the Suitors a nemesis[5]
of self-judgment, or sense of the moral law. To this
n e m e s i s (often inaccurately rendered as revenge)
Menelaos appeals, when exciting the Greeks to defend
the body of Patroclos[6] from insult. But the whole
matter is best learned from an address of Telemachos
to the Suitors, where he says (a) ' rouse within you of
yourselves a nemesis (or moral sense); and (b) an αἰδὼς
(a sense of honour, or regard to opinion of your fellow-

---

[1] Od. xv. 323.   [2] Od. xxi. 325.   [3] Il. vi. 162; lx. 341.
[4] Il. vi. 417.   [5] Od. ii. 138.   [6] Il. xvii. 254.

citizens); and (*e*) fear the wrath of the gods[1].' These
three principles were the three great pillars of morality.
The motive of αἰδώς may be stirred by the δήμου φάτις,
or public sentiment, which we find to have been an
engine of great power with Phœnix[2], and even with
Penelopè and Nausicaa. This aidōs is a sentiment
which has ultimate reference to the standard of opinion;
but it does not require that opinion to be in present
and immediate action. It is self-judgment, according
to the standard supplied by the ideas of others; as
nemesis is self-judgment by the inward law. This αἰδώς
ranges through a great variety of sub-meanings—deference, tenderness, scrupulosity, compassion, self-respect,
piety, bashfulness, honour, and every form of shame,
excepting false shame. Hesiod says in his iron, or
post-Homeric age, that αἰδώς, along with νέμεσις, had
vanished from the earth.

With respect to blood-shedding, the morality of the
Greeks of Homer was extremely loose. To have killed
a man was considered a misfortune, or at most an error
in point of prudence[3]. It was punished by a fine payable
to relatives, which it was usual to accept in full satisfaction. But fugitives from their vengeance were everywhere received without displeasure or surprise. Priam,
appearing unexpectedly before Achilles, is compared
to a man who, having had the misfortune to slay
somebody, appears on a sudden in a strange place[4].

The cases of such homicides are numerous in the
Poems. It may be enough to observe that Patroclos,
whose character is one of great gentleness, committed

[1] Od. ii. 64–67.   [2] Il. ix. 460.
[3] Il. ix. 632.   [4] Il. xxiv. 480–482.

one in his youth without premeditation [1], and was
therefore given over by his father Menoitios into the
honourable charge of Peleus: that Ajax had received
Lycophron after homicide, and 'honoured him as if
a beloved parent [2];' and that Telemachos receives
Theoclumenos, and gives him the place of honour,
when he had simply announced himself as a fugitive
from the vengeance of the powerful kindred of a man
whom he had killed [3], without stating anything about
the cause.

It is difficult however to trace in Homer the existence
of an universal law of relative duty, between man and
man as such. The chief restraints upon misdeeds were
to be found in laws, understood but not written, and
which were binding as between certain men, not between all men. These were

1. Members of a family.
2. Members of a State or nation.
3. Persons bound by the law of guestship.
4. Suppliants and those whom they addressed.

The weakest point of the Homeric system of ethics
is its tenderness (to say the least) for fraud under certain conditions. This has ever been indeed a difficult
chapter in the science of Ethics: it is probably one,
in which the human faculties will ever, or very long,
remain unequal to the task of drawing at once clearly
and firmly, in abstract statement, the lines of discrimi-
nation between right and wrong. In Homer, however, we seem to find the balance not doubtfully determined, but manifestly inclining the wrong way. Into
the mouth of Achilles, indeed, he has put the most

---

[1] Il. xxiii. 86.   [2] Il. xv. 429-440.   [3] Od. xv. 260 seqq.

powerful denunciation of falsehood ever uttered by
man[1]. Pope's rendering is not quite unworthy—

> 'Who dares think one thing, and another tell,
> My heart detests him as the gates of hell.'

· This, however, we may consider as in great part belonging to the single character of Achilles. It is a principle
worked out in his entire conduct, without a single flaw.
His soul and actions are sky-clear. Among the Homeric
deities, there is nothing that approaches him in this respect. Indeed it is especially in the region of the Immortals that we find the plague-spot planted. In Athenè, by
far the loftiest of his Olympian conceptions, we find
a distinct condescension not simply to stratagem, but
to fraud: and she, with Odysseus, finds a satisfaction,
when they respectively allow to one another the praise
of excelling all others within this department, she
among the gods, he among mortal men[2].

At this we may not be greatly surprised; for force
and energy already outweigh the moral element in the
whole conception of the supernatural: and the character
of Odysseus, with its many and great virtues, has a
bias in this direction. But we may be much more
surprised to find what we may fairly call a glorification
of cunning, if not of fraud, exhibited in the character
of that Greek chieftain, who, next to Achilles, may
be thought most to approximate to the ideal of Homeric
chivalry. Diomed meets the noble Glaucos on the
field: they explain, and recognise as subsisting between
them, the laws of hereditary guestship. The Greek
then proposes the exchange of arms, which Glaucos

---

[1] Il. ix. 312 (Pope, v. 412).   [2] Od. xiii. 294 seqq.

accepts: and Diomed obtains the value of a hundred oxen in return for the value of nine.

We may however observe, that Achilles, in whom comes out the bright blaze of perfect openness and truth, is not only the Coryphæus of the Greek band of heroes, but he is above all things the type of Hellenism; the model of that character, which Homer considered to belong to his race. And, as far as we can perceive, though there is a delight in the use of deceit as stratagem for a particular end, the general course of thought is unreserved and open: the Poems show us nothing like life in a mask.

The idea of sin, considered as an offence against the divine order, has by no means been effaced from the circle of moral ideas in Homer. It seems to be strongly implied in the word ἀτασθαλίη, which is applied to deep, deliberate wickedness; to sinning against light; to doing what, but for a guilty ignorance, we must know to be wrong. For, when it is intended to let in any allowance for mere weakness, or for solicitation from without, or for a simply foolish blindness, then the word ἄτη is used. And I doubt whether, in any one instance throughout the Poems, these two designations are ever applied to one and the same misconduct. It is certainly contrary to the general, and almost universal, rule. The atasthaliè is something done with clear sight and knowledge, with the full and conscious action of the will: it is something regarded as wholly without excuse, as tending to an entire moral deadness, and as entailing final punishment alike without warning and without mercy. Nothing can account for the introduction into a moral code of a form of offence conceived with such intensity, and ranked

so high, except the belief that the man committing it
had deliberately set aside that inward witness to truth
and righteousness which is supplied by the law of our
nature, and in the repudiation of which the universal
and consentient voice of mankind has always placed
the most awful responsibility, the extremest degree of
guilt, that the human being can incur.

The wicked man, thus hardened in his deliberate
wickedness (ἀτασθαλίη), is then driven on by the deity,
that is, as we should say, by a divine order and dis-
pensation, in his mad career. Of this penal mechanism
Athenè is, in the Odyssey, the instrument. When the
stool has been hurled at Odysseus disguised in his own
house, and the insolence of the Suitors has reached its
height, Telemachos tells them 'ye are mad with
excess of food and wine: some deity now drives you¹.'
Before this we are told 'Athenè would not let the
haughty Suitors stop in their biting insolence².' And
when Amphinomos has received the friendly but very
solemn warning of Odysseus³, he is shaken inwardly,
and a presentiment of calamity presses on him. Here
the Poet goes beyond that 'hardening of Pharaoh's
heart,' with which a comparison is naturally suggested,
and indicates that, even while he was suffering this
pain, which may almost be construed into a state of
indecision, Athenè held him entangled inwardly in the
meshes of his guilt, that he might be conquered by
Telemachos⁴. The subsequent attempt of Amphinomos
to restrain outrageous excess appears to show, that he
was still at this time halting between two opinions.
The sentiment of the Poet, usually so just, appears here

---

¹ Od. xviii. 406.   ² Od. xviii. 346.   ³ Od. xviii. 125-150.
⁴ Od. xviii. 155.

even to tremble on the verge of a dark fatalism. But this belongs to ulterior and later processes of thought. What we have here to notice is, how very deeply the idea of moral guilt was engraven in the mind of the Poet, and therefore probably of his age.

The peculiar word atasthaliè is chiefly used by Homer to describe the prolonged and hardened wickedness of the Suitors. The weakest case of its application is to the obstinate folly of Hector in refusing the counsel of Poludamas, and thus ruining the Trojan cause[1]: but here it is applied by the hero himself, not by any one else to him.

The view of patience in the Ethics of Homer is a very noble one. It is with him a prime virtue. Indeed, the characteristic merit of one of the Protagonists, Odysseus, is to be patient (πολύτλας), as his distinguishing intellectual endowment is to be πολύμητις; resourceful, elastic, versatile. This patience of the Homeric hero is as far as possible from being a mere acquiescence in fatality, or a cowardly retirement from the battle of life in order to put the soul to sleep. It is full of reason and feeling; it involves and largely partakes of self-restraint; it might almost be defined as moral courage. It is an active, not a passive function of the mind. Its action, indeed, is generally confined to the inward sphere. Yet it is not always so confined[2]. And it is always on the verge of, and ever capable of being developed into, the most heroic energy.

The sense of justice is also very strong in the Poems. Agamemnon indeed is unjust, as well as rapacious; but, notwithstanding his sense of responsibility, and his fraternal affection, Agamemnon is not a character

---

[1] Il. xxii. 104.   [2] Il. xxiv. 505.

towards whom Homer intends to attract our sympathies.
The Greek chieftains seem never among themselves to
deviate from fairness, except in the case of the chariot-
race. It is singular that three thousand years ago, as
now, horse-racing should have been found to offer the
subtlest temptations to the inward integrity of man.
The winning positions of Diomed[1] and Eumelos in the
race are reversed by a divine intervention, which throws
Eumelos into the very last place. And it seems to be from
a sense of substantial justice that Achilles proposes to
commit what would have been a technical breach of it
by giving him the second honour. But Antilochos, who
has gained the third place against Menelaos by a sheer
trick, remonstrates; and Achilles, with his supreme
courtesy, introduces for Eumelos an additional prize to
avoid even the semblance of wrong. Then comes the
turn of Menelaos, who vehemently protests against the
proceeding of Antilochos. The young warrior, who
had been greatly excited against Eumelos, at once
acknowledges the justice of the complaint, and offers to
give Menelaos not only the prize in question, but anything else that he possesses, rather than offend him.
Upon this Menelaos, not to be outdone in the contest
of high manners, and without doubt recollecting that all
his competitors are suffering in the war on his behalf, at
once surrenders the second prize and takes the third. Thus,
notwithstanding the device effected in the race itself,
a strong sense of right predominates in the whole scene
of the distribution, and governs the final adjustment.

The high estimate of the virtue of justice, thus observable, perhaps connects itself with that strong political genius which had already found development

[1] Il. xxiii. 373-402.

among the Greeks, inasmuch as justice is to political society as its vital spark. But again, justice is moral symmetry; and in it the exact spirit of the Greek would, on this ground, find at least a strong speculative satisfaction, which would help to determine the habits of the mind and life.

The idea of self-restraint, which seems to admit only of a limited application to the order of deities, is exceeding strong in the Homeric man, where he at all approaches excellence. Hence we find, in various forms, excess among the Immortals, such as would not have been tolerated in the Achaian circle. The howling of Arès[1] in pain when wounded, his loss of all power of reflection on learning the death of his son[2], and the licence which prevailed among the gods, with only few exceptions, in matters relating to sexual passion, are striking examples. But the same observation may be made in lesser matters. Inextinguishable laughter is excited in the Olympian Court, when the gods see Hephaistos limp about to minister the wine. But the Achaians never laugh with violence. If there could be a case warranting it at all, it would be one like that of Oilean Ajax, when he slipped and fell amidst the ordure[3]. Even here, however, self-control is not lost. They only smiled, or laughed mildly or gently (ἡδὺ γέλασσαν), at the strange predicament[4].

The self-command of heroes, which is thus observable in minor matters, extends also to the greatest. When we find any virtue prominently exhibited in the two Protagonists, we may without more ado be certain that Homer intends to give it a very high place. And by

[1] Il. v. 860.   [2] Il. xv. 115.   [3] Il. xxiii. 777.
[4] Il. xxiii. 784.

far the greatest instances of self-command are given us
in these two characters. On this basis is founded the
singular courtesy of Achilles, in the midst of his resentment, to the heralds who came by order of Agamemnon
to remove Briseis[1]. When he was in danger of losing
himself for the moment, on the occasion of the First
Assembly, a divine interposition took place to enable
him to hold his equilibrium. And many times, when
he feels the tide of wrath rising within him, he seems
to eye his own passion as the tiger is eyed by its
keeper, and puts a spell upon it so that it dare not
spring. When, for example, he is sensible that the
incautious words of Priam[2] are kindling within him
a fire that might blast the aged suppliant, he seizes the
moment, and, ere it is yet too late, bids him to desist.
Whenever, after the death of Patroclos, his mind goes
back upon the thought of Agamemnon and the wrong,
he breaks sharply away from the subject[3]. So it is with
this tempestuous character. But not less remarkable
is the self-command of Odysseus. This extends to all
circumstances: it suffices alike for the cave of Poluphemos; for enforcing silence in the body of the wooden
horse; for bearing in his disguise the insults of the
Suitors. But most of all in point is that wonderful
speech in answer to the insolence of Eumalos, the
Phaiakian prince, which teaches us more than any composition with which I am acquainted, up to what a
point emotion, sarcasm, and indignation can be carried
without any loss of self-command.

The fiery Diomed also offers us, in his submission to
the reproof of Agamemnon, a fine example of this great

[1] Il. i. 329-336.   [2] Il. xxiv. 560.
[3] Il. xvi. 60; xviii. 112; xix. 65.

quality[1]. But in truth it extends to the army, that is, the nation. We see it in their stern silence on the march, and in the battle-field. And their manner of applause in the Assembly is always described by a term different from that which the Poet uses to describe the corresponding indication of feeling among the Trojans. The Greeks usually shouted (ἴαχον) their applause; the Trojans rattled or clattered it (ἐπικελάδησαν).

In truth, there lies at the root of the Homeric model of the good or the great man, in a practical form, that which Aristotle has expressed scientifically as a condition of moral virtue; a spirit of moderation, a love of τὸ μέσον, or the mean. There should be moderation in sorrow[2], moderation in wrath, moderation in pleasure. Not a mean between extremes of mere quantity; but a true mean, an inward equipoise of the mind, and in the composition of mental qualities, abhorring excess in any one of them, because it mars the combination as a whole, and throws the rest into deficiency. This sentiment is conveyed by Homer in a multitude of slight and fine shadings of expression, like that insensible action of the hand in driving which keeps a straight instead of a fluctuating line. We trace it in the frequent expression οὐδὲ ἔοικεν: in ἐναίσιμος: in the πυκινὸν ἔπος: in the φρὴν ἔμπεδος: in the censure implied by μέγα ἔργον, and in a multitude of other expressions.

This being so, it follows that one of the qualities most unequivocally vicious in Homer is an absolute implacability; that state of mind towards which Achilles for a time appears to lean; first, with regard to the Greeks, secondly, with regard to Hector; to both the living and the dead. It is a sin against Nature, rather

---

[1] Il. iv. 411-418.   [2] Il. xxiv. 419.

than one of mere infirmity; because the very first requisite of such a feeling, to give it even colourable justice, is that the person entertaining it should himself be without fault, or weakness, or shortcoming of whatever kind.

This law, of moderation in quantity, was bodily as well as mental. Homer sings the praises of wine; but he reprehends even that mild form of excess which does no more than promote garrulity[1]. When the Greeks are about to suffer calamity in the Return, he lets them go in a state of drunkenness to their Assembly[2]. Elpenor dies by an accidental fall from drunkenness, and his character is accordingly described in terms of disparagement[3]. A legend is introduced to show the mischief of this vice, which even the Suitor Antinoos condemns[4]. No character esteemed by the Poet ever acts in any matter under the influence of liquor. It was for him the dew, not the deluge, of the soul; and it was nothing more. The gods indeed sit by the bowl the livelong day[5]; but for men it is not seemly to tarry for hours at the sacred (that is regular and public) feast. And this, not only in cases like that of wine, where the truth is obvious, and the excess repulsive; but in instances where it would less be expected. 'Do not go to bed too soon: excess of sleep is itself ἀνίη, a trouble[6].' 'Do not admire,' says Odysseus, 'or wonder at your father to excess[7].' 'I disapprove,' says Menelaos[8], 'of excess, either in attachments or in aversions: better to have all things in

---

[1] Od. xiv. 463-466.
[2] Od. x. 552-560; xi. 61.
[3] Il. ix. 69.
[4] Od. xvi. 202, 203.
[5] Od. iii. 139.
[6] Od. xxi. 293-304.
[7] Od. xv. 394.
[8] Od. xv. 70.

moderation.' The exact word is αἴσιμα, according to
αἶσα, which may be said to signify the moral element
of measure, order, just proportion, in fate.

This general disinclination to excess is happily ex-
emplified in relation to excess of wickedness.

The extremest forms of human depravity are unknown to the practice of the Greeks in the Homeric
age. We find among them no infanticide; no cannibalism; no practice, or mention, of unnatural lusts:
incest is profoundly abhorred, and even its uninten-
tioned commission in the case of Oidipous and Epicaste
was visited with the heaviest calamities. The old age
of parents is treated with respect and affection. Slavery
itself is mild; and predial slavery apparently rare.
There is no polygamy; no domestic concubinage; no
torture. There are no human sacrifices; and even
down to the time of Euripides the tradition subsisted
that they were not a Greek but a foreign usage [1]. The
legend of the seizure of Ganymedes, which was afterwards deeply tainted with shame, is in Homer perfectly
beautiful and pure. Adultery is detested. The lifelong bond of man and wife does not wholly yield even
to violence: absence the most prolonged does not shake
it off: and there is no escape from it by the at best
poor and doubtful invention of divorce.

There is undoubtedly something savage in the wrath
of Odysseus against the Suitors, as there is in the
wrath of Achilles against Agamemnon and the Greeks.
Neither of these two are represented to us as faultless
personages. But when they err, it is in measure and
degree; in the exaggeration of what, as to its essence,
virtue justifies, and even requires. But an exceeding

[1] Eurip. Iphig. in Aul. ἔθος μὴ πάτριον.

nobleness marks the rebuke of Odysseus to the Nurse
Euruclcia, when she is about to shout in exultation
over the fallen Suitors. 'It is wrong,' he says [1], 'to exult
over the slain, who have been overthrown by divine
providence, and by their own perverse deeds.'

So again, while Hecuba wishes she could find it in
her heart to eat Achilles, Achilles [2] utters a similar
wish with regard to Hector. But the wish is that he
could prevail upon himself to perform the act; which
accordingly he cannot do. From these passages, as well
as from the case of the Cyclops, we may learn that
cannibalism was within the knowledge, though not
the experience, of the nation; that it might even come
before them as an image in the hideous dreams of
passion at seasons of extreme excitement, but never
could enter the circle of their actual life.

Indeed, the manifestations of mere personal revenge
in the Poems are almost wholly among the divinities,
not the mortals. The vengeance of Achilles has reference not to an arbitrary or imaginary code, but to a
gross breach by Agamemnon of the laws of honour and
justice. The vengeance of Odysseus vindicates not
merely the duty of political obedience, but the violated
order of society, against depraved and lawless men.

The point, however, in which the ethical tone of the
heroic age stands highest of all is, perhaps, the strength
of the domestic affections.

They are prevalent in Olympos; and they constitute
an amiable feature in the portraiture even of deities
who have nothing else to recommend them. Not only
does Poseidon care for the brutal Poluphemos, and Zeus
for the noble and gallant Sarpedon, but Arès for As-

[1] Od. xxii. 412.   [2] Il. xxii. 346.

calaphos, and Aphroditè for Æneas.   In the Trojan royal family, there is little of the higher morality; but parental affection is vehement in the characters, somewhat relaxed as they are in fibre, both of Priam and of Hecuba.   Odysseus chooses for the title, by which he would be known, that of the Father of Telemachos [1]. The single portraiture of Penelopè, ever yearning through twenty years for her absent husband, and then praying to be removed from life, that she may never gladden the spirit of a meaner man, could not have been designed or drawn, except in a country where the standard, in this great branch of morality, was a high one.   This is the palmary and all-sufficient instance. Others might be mentioned to follow, though none can equal it.

Perhaps even beyond other cases of domestic relation, the natural sentiment, as between parents and children, was profoundly ingrained in the morality of the heroic age.   The feeling of Achilles for Peleus, of Odysseus for his father Laertes and his mother Anticleia, exhibits an affection alike deep and tender.   Those who die young, like Simoeisios [2] by the hand of Ajax, die before they have had time to repay to their parents their threptra, the pains and care of rearing them.   Phœnix, in the height of wrath with his father, and in a country where homicide was thought a calamity far more than a crime, is restrained from offering him any violence, lest he should be branded, among the Achaians, with the stamp of parricide [3].   All this was reciprocated on the side of parents: even in Troy, as we may judge from the conduct and words of Hector [4], of Andromache [5],

[1] Il. ii. 260.   [2] Il. iv. 473-479.   [3] Il. ix. 459-461.
[4] Il. vi. 476.   [5] Il. xxii. 483-507.

of Priam[1]. While the father of Odysseus pined on
earth for his return, his mother died of a broken heart
for his absence[2]. And the Shade of Achilles in the
Underworld only craves to know whether Peleus is still
held in honour; and a momentary streak of light and
joy gilds his dreary and gloomy existence, when he
learns that his son Neoptolemos has proved himself
worthy of his sire, and has attained to fame in war.
The very selfish nature of Agamemnon does not prevent
his feeling a watchful anxiety for his brother Menelaos[3].
Where human interests spread and ramify by this
tenacity of domestic affections, there the generations
of men are firmly knit together; concern for the future
becomes a spring of noble action; affection for the
past engenders an emulation of its greatness; and as
it is in history that these sentiments find their means
of subsistence, the primitive poet of such a country
scarcely can but be an historian.

We do not find, indeed, that relationships are traced
in Homer by name beyond the degree of first cousins[4].
But that the tie of blood was much more widely recognised, we may judge from the passage in the Second
Iliad, which shows that the divisions of the army were
subdivided into tribes ($\phi\tilde{\upsilon}\lambda\alpha$) and clans ($\phi\rho\acute{\eta}\tau\rho\alpha\iota$)[5].
Guestship likewise descended through generations:
Diomed and Glaucos exchange arms, and agree to avoid
one another in fight, because their grandfathers had
been xenoi[6].

The intensity of the Poet's admiration for beautiful
form is exhibited alike with reference to men, women,

---

[1] Il. xxii. 424.
[2] Il. x. 234-240.
[3] Il. ii. 362.
[4] Od. xi. 196, 202.
[5] Il. xv. 419-422, 525, 554.
[6] Il. vi. 216, 226-231.

and animals. Achilles, his greatest warrior, is also his most beautiful man : Ajax, the second soldier, has also the second place in beauty according to Odysseus [1]. Nireus, his rival for that place, is commemorated for his beauty, though in other respects he is declared to have been an insignificant personage[2]. Odysseus, elderly, if not old, is carried into rapture by the beauty of Nausicaa[3]. Not Helen alone, but his principal women in general, short of positive old age (for Penelopè is included), are beautiful. He felt intensely, as appears from many passages, the beauty of the horse. But this admiring sentiment towards all beauty of form appears to have been an entirely pure one. His only licentious episode, that of the Net of Hephaistos, he draws from an Eastern mythology. He recounts it as sung before men only, not women; and not in Greece, but in Scheriè, to an audience of Phœnician extraction and associations. It is in Troy that the gloating eyes of the old men follow Helen as she walks[4]. The only Greeks, to whom the like is imputed, are the dissolute and hateful Suitors of the Odyssey. The proceedings of Herè in the Fourteenth Iliad are strictly subordinated to policy. They are scarcely decent; and a single sentiment of Thetis may be criticised[5]. But the observations I would offer are, first that all the questionable incidents or sentiments are in the sphere of the mythology, which in several important respects tended to corrupt, and not to elevate, mankind. Secondly, how trifling an item do they contribute to the great Encyclopædia of human life, which is presented to us in the Poems. Thirdly, even among the great writers of the

[1] Od. xi. 550. [2] Il. ll. 676-680. [3] Od. vi. 151-169.
[4] Il. lil. 156-158. [5] Il. xxiv. 130.

Christian ages, how few will abide the application of a rigid test in this respect so well as Homer. And lastly, let us observe the thorough rectitude of purpose which governs the Poems: where Artemis, the severely pure, is commonly represented as an object of veneration, but Aphroditè is as commonly represented in such a manner as to attract aversion or contempt: and when, among human characters, no licentious act is ever so exhibited, as to confuse or pervert the sense of right and wrong. The Poet's treatment of Paris on earth, whom he has made his only contemptible prince or warrior, is in strict keeping with his treatment of Aphroditè among Immortals.

With regard to anything which is unbecoming in the human person, the delicacy of Homer is uniform and perhaps unrivalled. In the case of women, there is not a single allusion to it. In the case of men, the only allusions we find are grave, and admirably handled. When Odysseus threatens to strip Thersites, it is only to make him an object of general and unmitigated disgust[1]. When Priam foretells the mangling of his own naked corpse by animals[2], the insult to natural decency thus anticipated serves only to express the intense agony of his mind. The scene in which Odysseus emerges from the sea on the coast of Scheriè, is perhaps among the most careful, and yet the most simple and unaffected, exhibitions of true modesty in all literature. And the mode, in which all this is presented to us, suggests that it forms a true picture of the general manners of the nation at the time. That this delicacy long subsisted in Greece, we learn from Thucydides[3]. The morality of the Homeric period is that of the

[1] Il. II. 262.   [2] Il. xxii. 74-76.   [3] I. 6.

childhood of a race: the morality of the classic times belongs to its manhood. On the side of the latter, it may be urged that two causes in particular tend to raise its level. With regular forms of political and civil organization, there grows up in written law a public testimonial on behalf, in the main, of truth, honesty, and justice. For, while private conduct represents the human mind under the bias of every temptation, the law, as a general rule, speaks that which our perceptions would affirm were there no such bias. But further, with law and order comes the clearer idea and fuller enjoyment of the fruits of labour; and for the sake of security each man adopts, and in general acts upon, a recognition of the rights of property. These are powerful agencies for good in a great department of morals. Besides these, with a more imposing beauty, but probably with less of practical efficacy, the speculative intellect of man goes to work, and establishes abstract theories of virtue, vice, and their consequences, which by their comprehensiveness and method put out of countenance the indeterminate ethics of remote antiquity. All this is to be laid in one scale. But the other would, I think, preponderate, if it were only from the single consideration, that the creed of the Homeric age brought both the sense and the dread of the divine justice to bear in restraint of vice and passion. And upon the whole, after the survey which has been taken, it would in my opinion be somewhat rash to assert, that either the duties of men to the deity, or the larger claims of man upon man, were better understood in the age of Pericles or Alexander, of Sylla or Augustus, than in the age of Homer.

Perhaps the following sketch of Greek life in the heroic age may not be far wide of the truth.

The youth of high birth, not then so widely as now separated from the low, is educated under tutors in reverence for his parents, and in desire to emulate their fame; he shares in manly and in graceful sports; acquires the use of arms; hardens himself in the pursuit, then of all others the most indispensable, the hunting down of wild beasts; gains the knowledge of medicine, probably also of the lyre. Sometimes, with many-sided intelligence, he even sets himself to learn how to build his own house or ship, or how to drive the plough firm and straight down the furrow, as well as to reap the standing corn [1].

And, when scarcely a man, he bears arms for his country or his tribe, takes part in its government, learns by direct instruction, and by practice, how to rule mankind through the use of reasoning and persuasive power in political assemblies, attends and assists in sacrifices to the gods. For, all this time, he has been in kindly and free relations, not only with his parents, his family, his equals of his own age, but with the attendants, although they are but serfs, who have known him from infancy on his father's domain.

He is indeed mistaught with reference to the use of the strong hand. Human life is cheap; so cheap that even a mild and gentle youth may be betrayed, upon a casual quarrel over some childish game with his friend, into taking it away. And even so throughout his life, should some occasion come that stirs up his passions from their depths, a wild beast, as it were, awakes within him, and he loses his humanity for the time,

[1] Od. xviii. 366-375.

until reason has re-established her control. Short, however, of such a desperate crisis, though he could not for the world rob his friend or his neighbour, yet he might be not unwilling to triumph over him to his cost, for the sake of some exercise of signal ingenuity; while, from a hostile tribe or a foreign shore, or from the individual who has become his enemy, he will acquire by main force what he can, nor will he scruple to inflict on him by stratagem even deadly injury[1]. He must, however, give liberally to those who are in need; to the wayfarer, to the poor, to the suppliant who begs from him shelter and protection. On the other hand, should his own goods be wasted, the liberal and open-handed contributions of his neighbours will not be wanting to replace them.

His early youth is not solicited into vice by finding sensual excess in vogue, or the opportunities of it glaring in his eye, and sounding in his ear. Gluttony is hardly known; drunkenness is marked only by its degrading character, and by the evil consequences that flow so straight from it; and it is abhorred. But he loves the genial use of meals, and rejoices in the hour when the guests, gathered in his father's hall, enjoy a liberal hospitality, and the wine mantles in the cup[2]. For then they listen to the strains of the minstrel, who celebrates before them the newest and the dearest of the heroic tales that stir their blood, and rouse their manly resolution to be worthy, in their turn, of their country and their country's heroes. He joins the dance in the festivals of religion; the maiden's hand upon his wrist, and the gilded knife gleaming from his belt, as they course from

---

[1] Od. xiii. 252-270.   [2] Od. viii. 5-11; xiv. 193-198.

point to point, or wheel in round on round[1]. That maiden, some Nausicaa, or some Hermionè of a neighbouring district, in due time he weds, amidst the rejoicings of their families, and brings her home to cherish her, 'from the flower to the ripeness of the grape,' with respect, fidelity, and love.

Whether as a governor or as governed, politics bring him, in ordinary circumstances, no great share of trouble. Government is a machine, of which the wheels move easily enough; for they are well oiled by simplicity of usages, ideas, and desires; by unity of interest; by respect for authority, and for those in whose hands it is reposed; by love of the common country, the common altar, the common Festivals and Games, to which already there is large resort. In peace he settles the disputes of his people, in war he lends them the precious example of heroic daring. He consults them, and advises with them, on all grave affairs; and his wakeful care for their interests is rewarded by the ample domains which are set apart for the prince by the people[2]. Finally, he closes his eyes, delivering over the sceptre to his son, and leaving much peace and happiness around him[3].

Such was, probably, the state of society amidst the concluding phase of which Homer's youth, at least, was passed. But a dark and deep social revolution seems to have followed the Trojan war; we have its workings already become visible in the Odyssey. Scarcely could even Odysseus cope with it, contracted though it was for him within the narrow bounds of Ithaca. On the mainland, the bands of the elder society are soon wholly

---

[1] Il. xviii. 594-602.   [2] Il. Ix. 581; xii. 313.
[3] Od. xxiii. 281-284.

broken. The Pelopid, Neleid, Œnid houses, are a
wreck: disorganization invites the entry of new forces
to control it; the Dorian lances bristle on the Ætolian
beach, and the primitive Greece, the patriarchal Greece,
the Greece of Homer, is no more.

SECTION II.

We must not dismiss the subject of Ethics or morals
without considering what is both a criterion and an
essential part of it, namely, the position held by
Woman in the heroic age[1].

Within the pale of that civilisation, which has grown
up under the combined influence of the Christian
religion as paramount, and what may be called the
Teutonic manners as secondary, we find the idea of
Woman and her social position raised to a point higher
than in the Poems of Homer. But it would be hard to
discover any period of history, or country of the world,
not being Christian, in which women stood so high as
with the Greeks of the heroic age.

I will here very briefly illustrate this proposition
under several heads; and first, that of marriage with
its accessories.

The essence of Homeric marriage seems to have
lain in cohabitation, together with a solemn public
acknowledgment of the relation of the parties as man
and wife, and with an attendant ceremonial such as
is represented on the Shield of Achilles. This might

---

[1] For a fuller exposition, see Studies on Homer, Olympos,
Sect. 9. See also Mr. Buckle's Lecture on Woman, in Frazer's
Magazine.

apparently be preceded by cohabitation with the intention of marriage. Hence Briseis is called by Achilles his wife[1]; yet in the very same speech he speaks of himself as open to marriage with another woman; and Briseis, in her lament over Patroclos, says[2], ' Thou wouldst not let me weep, but saidst thou wouldst make me the wife of Achilles, and take me by ship to Phthiè, and feast (i. e. celebrate) my marriage among the Myrmidons.' So that the full accomplishment of the union was apparently to follow the expected return; and she was in the meantime a wife-designate.

It is in the interest of the woman that the law of marriage should be strict, and that marriage should be single. Among the Homeric Greeks we have not the slightest trace of polygamy; or of a woman taken from her husband, and made the wife of another man during his lifetime. The Suitors always urge Penelopè to re-marry, on the ground that Odysseus must be dead, and that there is no hope of his return. A shorter period of absence, than that assigned to him, is recognised by the law of England as making re-marriage legal. A presumption of death brought near to certainty must, under the conditions of human affairs, be taken to suffice; for, says Butler, with a sweep of comprehensive wisdom, ' Probability is the very guide of life[3].' But in the case of Agamemnon, there was no presumption of death; and, accordingly, the act of Aigisthos, is described by Zeus as a double outrage, made up of two crimes; the last part of it being

---

[1] Il. ix. 340 seqq.
[2] Il. xix. 295 seqq. I omit the word κουριδίην, which would require a discussion.
[3] Introduction to the Analogy.

the murder, but the first the simple fact of the marriage[1].

Even the violent bodily abstraction of the wife, as in the case of Helen, does no more than destroy the marriage for the time. When she is recovered, she resumes her domestic place. There is no such thing as a formal and final dissolution of a marriage, except by death. In the narrative, and by the Trojans, as well as by herself, Helen is called the wife of Paris; yet we never find this acknowledgment in the mouth of a Greek. Nay, Hector even calls Helen the wife of Menelaos[2]: but this may mean the past wife. Menelaos never treats what had occurred as setting him free from his obligations to Helen. And the long resistance of Penelopè, presented to us in the Odyssey as a central object of our interest and admiration, could not have been chosen for this purpose by the poet, unless it had been in conformity with the actual Greek idea of a genuine and lofty virtue.

Concubinage is practised by some few, and as far as we are informed only by few, of the Greek chieftains before Troy: yet this also is single. Of actual domestic concubinage we have no example. But Agamemnon threatens to take Briseis home with him[3]. This, however, is done under angry excitement. In the Assembly, he thinks it necessary to give the reason of a proceeding, which he apparently perceived would require a justification; and it is, that he prefers her in all respects to Clutaimnestra. But we have no trace, in the Return, of any chief's carrying a concubine home with him. The wife of Amuntor adopted an extreme measure to prevent her husband from falling into a

---

[1] Od. l. 36.   [2] Il. ill. 53.   [3] Il. l. 29, 113.

lawless connection[1]; and Laertes, from an apprehension of conjugal trouble, respected the maidenhood of his young bondwoman[2]. These instances, if they show that the man was not exempt from passion, bear very emphatic testimony to the position of the wife.

The relations of youth and maiden generally are indicated with extreme beauty and tenderness in the Iliad[3]; and those of the unmarried woman to a suitor, or probable spouse, are so pourtrayed, in the case of the incomparable Nausicaa, as to show a delicacy and freedom that no period of history or state of manners can surpass[4]. On her return home, Alkinoos, far from reproving her, thinks she should have shown more forwardness to entertain the shipwrecked stranger. We often hear of a parent, who gives or promises a daughter in marriage: but like expressions[5] are applied to sons. The very fact that the profligate and violent Suitors always confine themselves to a moral pressure, and profess to submit to the choice of Penelopè, is of itself a probable witness to the recognised free-agency of the woman of the period.

In that early state of society we hear of no such personage as an elderly bachelor or spinster. Nor, within due limits of age, could there, I presume, be a prolonged widowhood. The apparent connection of Helen with Deiphobos[6], after the death of Paris, should probably be read in the light of Trojan usage. But whenever Penelopè, or others in her name, contemplate the death of Odysseus, and her consequent release, that

---

[1] Il. ix. 51.
[2] Il. xviii. 567, 593; xxii. 127, 128.
[3] Il. ix. 394. Od. iv. 10.
[4] Od. i. 433.
[5] Od. vi. 275-288.
[6] Od. iv. 276.

change is always treated as the immediate preface to another crisis, in the choice of a second husband.

Marriage, in Homer, is the very pivot of life. War is the deadly enemy of woman. On the capture of a city, her lot is exile, and the conqueror's bed. The familiarity of this idea renders it remarkable that we should not hear much more than we do hear of concubinage among the Greeks of Homer. Of professional prostitution, we have no trace at all.

As the restraints imposed upon marriage are in general among the proofs of its high estimation, I proceed to observe that the Greeks regarded incest with horror, even when, as in the instance of Oidipous and Epicastè, it was involuntary. Passing on from extreme cases, we may observe, that the connection of Phœnix with a woman at once presented an insurmountable bar to the unlawful passion of his father for the same person. It appears however probable, though not certain, that Diomed was married to his mother's sister[1]. In Scherìè, the king Alkinoos had his niece for his wife[2]: but this is in the Phœnician circle. In Troy, Iphidamas marries the sister of his mother[3].

It is observed that, in the classical period, the law of incest in Greece, instead of being tightened, was relaxed[4]. The older sentiment about it is the more remarkable, because of the extreme looseness of the code applied to supernatural beings[5].

A series of words for the different relationships by affinity, includes the word e i n a t e r for the husband's brother's wife, to which we have no correlative in

---

[1] Il. iv. 131.   [2] Od. vii. 65, 66.   [3] Il. xl. 220-226.
[4] Friedreich's Realien, iii. 2.
[5] Il. iv. 441; xvi. 432. Od. x. 2.

English; and the terms, in which these relationships are spoken of, testify to the definiteness and solidity of the marriage bond.

We have a single case of a woman who attempts the breach of her own marriage-vow. It is Anteia, the wife of Proitos; but the family was Phœnician.

Thus, then, we have in the Poems a picture of Greek marriage as to its unity, freedom, perpetuity; as to the restraints upon it, and as to the manner in which breaches of it, and substitutes for it, were regarded. This picture, so striking in itself, becomes yet more so by comparison with Eastern manners, even as they were exhibited in the Hebrew race. It is also in glaring and painful contrast with the lowered estimate of woman among the Greeks of the classical period, and with their loathsome immorality.

More important, however, than any particulars is the general tone of the intercourse between husband and wife. It is thoroughly natural: full of warmth, dignity, reciprocal deference, and substantial, if not conventional, delicacy. The fulness of moral and intelligent being is alike complete, and alike acknowledged, on the one side and on the other. Nor is this description confined to the scenes properly Hellenic. It embraces the conversation of Hector with Andromachè, and is nowhere more applicable than to the whole character and demeanour of Nausicaa—delineations probably due rather to the Hellenic experience of the Poet, than to any minute observation either of Phœnician or of Trojan manners. Of rude manners to a woman there is not a real instance in the Poems. And to this circumstance we may add its true correlative, that the women of Homer are truly and profoundly feminine. As to the intensity of conjugal love, it has never passed the climax which it reaches in Odysseus and Penelope.

Presents were usually brought by the bridegroom; dowries sometimes given with the bride. With a wife returning in widowhood to the parental home, the dowry returned also[1]. On the other hand it would appear, from the Lay of the Net, that a fine was imposed upon the detected adulterer[2], as well as on the manslayer. In some instances, personal and mental gifts serve in lieu of possessions, as recommendations in suing for a wife.

Lastly, with respect to the employments of women.

It appears to be at least open to question whether they were not capable of political sovereignty[3]. The suggestion of the text seems to be that Chloris was queen in Pulos when Neleus married her ; and the mention of Hûpsipulè with Jason is best accounted for by supposing, conformably to tradition, that she reigned in Lemnos[4]. On the departure of Agamemnon Clutaimnestra was left in charge, with the Bard as an adviser[5]; and in Ithaca Penelopè had a similar regency, apparently with the aid of Mentor[6].

Priesthood appears not to have existed among the Hellenes of the Homeric age ; but in Troas, where we find it, a woman was priestess of Athenè. This was Theano, the wife of Antenor; and she is said to have been appointed to her office by the Trojans. The seizure of Marpessa, or Alcuonè, by Apollo, may have had reference to some religious ministry at Delphi.

---

[1] Od. il. 132.
[2] Od. viii. 329.
[3] Il. vii. 468, 469. Od. xi. 281—285.
[4] Il. vii. 469.
[5] Od. iii. 263 268.
[6] Od. ii. 225-227 ; xix. 317 ; xx. 129-133. Il. vi. 297-300.

The domestic employments of women are pretty clearly indicated in the descriptions of the Palaces of Kirkè and of Odysseus. The outdoor offices were performed in Ithaca by men, who likewise prepared the firewood, killed, cut up, and carved the animals, and carried to the farm the manure that accumulated about the house. The Suitors also had male personal at-·tendants. The women performed the indoor operations generally, including the fetching of water and the grinding of flour.

Another employment discharged by women has given rise to misunderstanding; namely, their waiting on men for purposes connected with the bath. Damsels of the highest rank performed this duty for strangers. But the delicacy of the early Greeks, with regard to any undue exposure of the person[1], was extreme; and, though they may have differed from our merely conventional usages, it cannot be imagined that they departed from propriety in a point where a people far less scrupulous would have respected it. The error has lain principally in failure to observe that in the words used for washing, bathing, and anointing, the actual operation is described by the middle voice[2], and the words louô, chriô, niptô, in the active, in general signify supplying another person with the means of performing these offices for himself[3]. The same rule I believe to hold good with respect to the word which describes dressing after the bath (ballô).

---

[1] Il. II. 260-264.

[2] So Wakefield. See Il. I. 572-577; Od. vi. 96, 219, 220, *et alibi.*

[3] Od. vi. 210, 218, 222; vii. 296. Even Od. x. 361 need not be an exception.

CHAPTER XI.

POLITY OF THE HEROIC AGE.

THE Poems of Homer are the seed-plot of what is best and soundest in the Greek politics of the historic period. Nor are we, the moderns, and, as I think, the British in particular, without a special relation to the subject. In part we owe to these ancient societies a debt. In part we may trace with reasonable pleasure an original similitude between the Homeric picture and the best ideas of our European and our British ancestry. What are those ideas? Among the soundest of them we reckon the power of opinion and persuasion as opposed to force; the sense of responsibility in governing men; the hatred, not only of tyranny, but of all unlimited power; the love and the habit of public in preference to secret action; the reconciliation and harmony between the spirit of freedom on the one hand, the spirit of order and reverence on the other; and a practical belief in right as relative, and in duty as reciprocal. Out of these elements, whether in ancient or in modern times, great governments have been made. The Homeric Poems exhibit them all, if not in methodical development, yet in vigorous life.

Even war required a basis of right, perhaps rudely defined; and retribution a *corpus delicti.* Hence the readiness with which the offer of Paris[1] to decide the war by single combat is accepted; and hence it may be that when Agamemnon anticipates the death of Menelaos from his wound, he judges also that, on that event, the army will return home.

Personal reverence for sovereigns is undoubtedly a powerful principle in the governments of the heroic age. There is for them a kind of divinity that doth ' hedge a king.' Odysseus, wishing to arrest the sudden impulse of the army to return, furnishes himself with the famed Sceptre of Agamemnon, as a token of his title to be heard. This principle, which has survived almost every modification of political forms, could not but be lively at a period when probably no great number of generations had passed since the exchange of nomad for settled life. For society, in the nomad stage, has something of the organization of the army; and it is still either in view or in actual experience of the time when the family, forming itself around its head, had not yet grown into the tribe; much less the tribe into the people.

But, while this reverence existed under all social forms, the characteristic difference of the Homeric states is to be found in the qualifications by which on every side it was hindered from passing into excess. The monarch was controlled by the princes or chiefs assembled in the council (βουλὴ); an institution which the Odyssey mentions in Scheriè, and the Iliad (informally) in Troy; so that we must presume it to have been in the view of the Greeks not a merely local

[1] Il. lil. 96-112.

institution, but a prime element of human society.
The mass, however, of the free citizens were also
called together in the Agorè, or Assembly, to consider
any matter of cardinal importance; and appeal was
made to their reason in speeches which, for aptitude
and force, to this day extort the admiration, and
perhaps defy the rivalry, of the moderns.

It is upon a just balance of forces that good government now mainly depends. In the Homeric age, there
were no detailed or even defined provisions to secure this
balance. Even the name of law (nomos) is unknown,
though the name of public right (themis) is familiar
and revered. Into the Greek Constitutions, described by
Aristotle, a multitude of expedients for that purpose
had been introduced by human ingenuity. Yet those
constitutions were subject to frequent and most violent
changes, usually attended by the absolute ejectment of
the defeated party from house and field. And even
when not under disturbance they commonly exhibited
a strong bias towards excess in one quarter or another.
To the Troic period, too, revolutions were not unknown. But the idea of government, which then prevailed, was perhaps both more strongly fortified by
religious reverence, and likewise better founded in
reciprocal duty, than that of later times. The separation and conflict of interests between the different
parts of the community had not become a familiar
idea; particular classes did not plot against the whole;
we hear little of the tyranny of kings, or the insubordi-
nation of subjects. A worse era was about to follow.
As in the case of the Crusades, so during the War of
Troy, the absence of the rulers prepared the way for
social convulsion. And Hesiod, living at a time later

probably by some generations, looks back from his iron age with an admiring envy on the heroic period.

'The early monarchies,' says Thucydides, 'enjoyed specified[1] prerogatives;' and Aristotle assures us that they were monarchies[2] upon terms, and depended on a voluntary allegiance. The threefold function of the King among the Hellenes was (*a*) chiefly perhaps, though not exclusively, to administer justice[3] between man and man; (*b*) to command the army, and (*c*) to conduct the rites of religion. Sometimes the sovereignty was local, or subaltern; sometimes, as perhaps in the case of Minos[4] and of Priam, and even of Peleus, but clearly and broadly in that of Agamemnon[5], it was a suzerainty over other Kings and princes, as well as a direct dominion over territory specially appropriated, and perhaps also over an unclaimed residue of minor settlements and communities. Besides the towns, which supplied Agamemnon with his division of the army, he claimed to dispose of the sovereignty of other towns, which lay in the south-west of the Peloponnesos[6].

The Homeric Kings, however, constitute in the Iliad a class by themselves. The greater part of the chiefs do not bear the title of Basileus, but had probably that of anax, prince, or lord. Some of these were like Phoinix under Peleus; but most of them in no other subordination than to Agamemnon. The only duty to the suzerain of which we hear is that of military service. His superior rank[7] is acknowledged; so that both he, and apparently Menelaos, on account of his

---

[1] i. 13.   [2] Arist. Pol. lii. 14, 15, ver. 10.   [3] Il. ii. 204-206.
[4] Thucydides, i. 4, says that Minos appointed his sons to be local or deputed Governors.
[5] Il. ix. 483; xxiii. 25-90.   [6] Il. ix. 149-153.   [7] Il. i. 186.

relationship, are termed 'more kingly¹' than the other
Kings. These gradations in the order may perhaps be
compared to those of a modern Peerage or Noblesse.
The King, as such, stands in a special relation to
deity. The epithet theios, divine, is only applied to
such among the living as have this relation. The King
is also Diotrephes, or reared by Zeus, and Diogenes, or
born of Zeus; and these titles are given rarely below
the kingly order even to a prince or ruler, if of inferior
degree or eminence. It is expressly declared that
Kings derive the right to rule² from Zeus, from whom
descended, by successive deliveries, the sceptre of
Agamemnon. In the Greek army the Kings alone
seem to constitute the council of the Generalissimo.
Scarcely on any occasion does a ruler of the second
order appear there. The Kings are called Basilées, or
Gerontes (elders), or perhaps Koiranoi; but the
leaders at large are Archoi, or Hegemones, or
(ἀριστῆες) the aristocracy.

In the Catalogue, the command of some of the divisions is held as it were in commission; or, in other
words, rests with two or more persons jointly and
severally, on a footing of parity between themselves.
But wherever there is a King, he either appears alone,
in his capacity of General, as Agamemnon, Menelaos,
Odysseus, Nestor, Achilles, the greater and the lesser
Ajax; or with other leaders who are distinctly under
him, as Diomed³ and Idomeneus⁴. These nine persons

---

¹ Il. ix. 160; x. 239.   ² Il. ii. 101, 205.   ³ Il. ii. 563-566.
  ⁴ The Catalogue, Il. II. 645-652, might leave doubtful the position of Meriones; but it is fixed by the terms θεράπων and
ὀπάων, applied to him in Il. x. 58, xxiii. 113, *et alibi;* which,
though perhaps more than Squire, means less than Colleague.

are the only undeniable Kings of the Iliad, as may appear from comparing together Il. ii. 404-409, Il. xix. 309-311, and from the transactions of Il. x. 34-197. Particular phrases or passages might raise the question whether four others, Meges, Eurupulos, Patroclos, and Phoinix, were not viewed by Homer as being also Kings. Probably his idea of the class was not so definite as ours; but on the whole the line, which excludes these and all the other chiefs from the kingly rank, is drawn with considerable clearness. The King, as viewed in the Iliad, must be a person combining three conditions: first, he is subordinate to none but Agamemnon; secondly, he has in all cases marked personal vigour and prowess; thirdly, if his dominions are small, he must either be of surpassing strength of body at least, like the Telamonian Ajax, or of vast powers of mind as well as limb, like Odysseus.

Among the bodily qualities of the Kings, one is personal beauty. This attaches peculiarly to the Trojan royal family, and it is recorded even of the aged Priam in his grief[1]. At the head of all stands Achilles. Odysseus has this endowment, though in a less marked degree. Ajax, in the Odyssey, appears to compete with Nireus, in the Iliad, for the second place. It is never predicated individually, I think, of any single man below the princely station, although when the crew of Odysseus were re-transformed, at Aiaiè, into human shape, they are collectively said to have been by far larger and more beautiful than before[2].

Personal vigour is also a condition, not only of assuming, but almost of continuing in, the exercise of

---

[1] Il. xxiv. 631.   [2] Od. x. 396.

sovereignty[1]. Laertes quitted his throne at a time anterior to the departure of Odysseus for the war, long before the period of decrepitude[2], and probably when his activity had but begun to diminish. Achilles, in the Shades[3], inquires whether Peleus still occupies the throne, or has retired from it on account of his years. Nestor, indeed, yet occupies the royal seat; but perhaps it is on account of his notable talents, combined with the greenness of his old age. The word aizēos, which signifies a man in his full strength, when joined with Diotrephes, or royal, is applied to princes as a class, and thus testifies to the custom I have described[4]. Telemachos was the proper heir to his father's throne[5]; but he was only coming to, though close upon, full age, and he had not yet assumed its privileges at the point where the action of the Poem begins.

Over and above the work of battle, the Prince is peerless in the Games. Of the eight contests of the Twenty-third Iliad, seven are conducted entirely by the Kings and chiefs. The exception is the boxing-match. And Epeios, the winner in this match, himself declares[6] that he does not possess the gifts necessary for distinction in battle; an indication by the way, among many, of the immense value set by Homer upon skill as compared with mere strength[7]. The prizes, too, which are given in the boxing-match appear, when compared with the other rewards, to show the reputed inferiority of this accomplishment.

So likewise with the gifts of music and song. Usually, of course, we look for them to the Bards.

---

[1] Grote, Hist. Greece, vol. ii. p. 87.   [2] Od. xi. 174, 184.
[3] Od. xi. 495.   [4] Il. li. 660. Comp. Il. xvi. 716.
[5] Od. L 386.   [6] Il. xxiii. 670.   [7] Comp. Il. xxiii. 315-318.

Upon the Shield, in the procession of youths and maidens who bear the grapes from the vineyard, a boy attends them to play and sing, probably because it did not comport with the dignity of the Bard to exercise his art while in bodily motion; for presently we come to another scene, where he plays, without moving, to the dancers[1]. There are but two certain indications of (so to speak) amateur song and playing. The lyre which Achilles used was among the spoils of the city of Eetion, and may possibly have belonged to that King himself[2]. On this lyre Achilles himself played during his retirement. And our other musician is Paris[3].

But the kingly character in Homer is also all-comprehensive; and it sometimes embraces even the manual employments of honourable industry. Odysseus, in the Island of Calypso[4], is a wood-cutter and ship-builder: Odysseus on his throne was the carpenter and artisan of his own bed[5], so elaborately wrought: Odysseus, in disguise, challenges Eurumachos the Suitor to try which of them would soonest mow a meadow[6], and which drive the straightest furrow down a four-acre field.

Such were the corporal accomplishments of the Homeric King. He was also, in the exercise of higher faculties, Judge, General, and Priest. In addition to all these, and as binding them all together, he was emphatically a gentleman. In Agamemnon, indeed, there is a half-sordid vein, which mars the higher type; though he corresponds in general to the eulogy of Helen[7], as a good King and a valiant soldier. Nestor, Diomed, Menelaos, are markedly gentlemen in their

---

[1] Il. xviii. 569, 604.   [2] Il. ix. 186-188.   [3] Il. iii. 54.
[4] Od. v. 243, 261.   [5] Od. xxiii. 195-201.
[6] Od. xviii. 366-375.   [7] Il. iii. 179.

demeanour. The character of Odysseus, caricatured and debased by the later tradition, abounds in Homer with similar notes. Quick in the sense of undeserved reproof from his chief, he appeals only to the confutation which his conduct in the field will supply[1]. When grossly insulted by Eurualos, his stern and masterful rebuke is so justly measured as to excite the sympathy of strangers[2]. But the best exhibition of the profound refinement inhering in the character of Odysseus is, perhaps, afforded by the scene in which he first appears before Nausicaa[3], after his escape from the devouring waters.

It is, however, in Achilles that courtesy reaches to its acmè. In the First Iliad, he hails with a genial kindness the heralds who came on the odious errand of enforcing the removal of Briseis, and he at once reassures them by acquitting them of blame[4]; though as we know

> 'The messenger of evil tidings
> Hath but a losing office.'

In the Ninth Book, while still in the Wrath, we find him bidding the envoys of Agamemnon a hearty welcome. In both cases he anticipates the new comers with a speech, of which the promptitude is itself a delicate stroke of the best manners. The most refined, however, of his attentions is perhaps that shown to Agamemnon, after the reconciliation, on the occasion of the Games. It was difficult to exclude the chief King from the sport of Kings; inadmissible to let him be worsted; impossible either to make him conquer those who were his superiors in strength, or to place

---

[1] Il. iv. 349-355.   [2] Od. viii. 165, 396.   [3] Od. vi. 115 seqq.
[4] Il. I. 334.

him in competition with secondary persons. Achilles
avoids all these difficulties by proposing a ninth, or
supernumerary match, with the sling; and then at once
presenting the prize to Agamemnon with the observation that, as his excellence is known to be paramount,
there need be no actual trial[1].

Yet these great chiefs, so strong in every form of
power, bravery, and skill, can upon occasion weep like a
woman or a child. A list of the passages, in which the
tears of heroes flow, would probably by its length cause
astonishment even to those who are aware that a susceptible temperament prompted them, and that a false
shame did not forbid them, thus to give vent to their
emotions[2]. Every one of them, unless it be the aged Nestor, would be included: we should find there even Agamemnon, whom we may probably consider as the prince
least richly furnished in this department of our nature.

Thus far we have spoken mainly of the persons.
The office, which these persons bore, was hereditary,
in the line of the eldest son. Yet though the practice
prevailed, the definition was, in this and in other cases,
not so sharp as ours. Menelaos, the brother of Agamemnon, partakes in a certain limited degree of his
dignity: is specially solicited, with him, by the priest
Chruses[3]; receives, jointly with him, the presents
offered by Euneos[4] for leave to trade with the army;
and is held more royal than the other chieftains[5].
Probably when Thuestes succeeded Atreus, it was on
account of the childhood of Agamemnon, which prevented his fulfilling the conditions of strength and
vigour necessary for holding the monarchy.

[1] Il. xxiii. 884-897.   [2] Comp. Juv. Sat. xv. 131-133.
[3] Il. i. 16.   [4] Il. vii. 470.   [5] Il. ii. 32 and 239.

The case of Telemachos supplies us with an express declaration of the title of the son to succeed his father[1]. But Antinoos the Suitor, at a time when Odysseus was supposed to be dead, states his hope that Zeus will never make the youth king of Ithaca. The answer is far from claiming that unconditional right to the throne of the islands, which it asserts to the estates of Odysseus[2]; and leaves room for the supposition, that the succession was liable to be more or less affected by personal qualifications, and by the assent or dissent of the nobles, or even of the community. Even at this time, however, Telemachos assumed in the Assembly the seat of his father.

Telemachos, indeed, is an only son. But, in the case of the Pelopids, Agamemnon appears to succeed to the paternal throne, and Menelaos to govern Sparta in right of his wife. Of the two brothers, Protesilaos and Podarkes, in the Catalogue, the former, who is the elder, commands the force from Phulakè and its sister towns[3]. He was, however, we are expressly told, braver, as well as older. The position of Antilochos in the Iliad as the eldest son of Nestor, and of Thrasumedes, after his death, in the Odyssey, appear to be sufficiently marked[4]. In four cases of the Catalogue, pairs of brothers are named as in command, without any distinction formally drawn between them.

The Olympian arrangements bear, perhaps, the most emphatic testimony to the higher dignity and authority of the elder brother. For it is only in that capacity, that the superiority of Zeus is confessed by his juniors[5].

---

[1] Od. i. 387.   [2] Od. i. 396.
[3] Il. ii. 695-708.   [4] Od. iii. 402, 439-446.
              [5] Il. xv. 204-207. Od. xiii. 142.

They are not, however, excluded from inheritance; and the respective provinces are taken by lot.

On the whole, we seem to have the custom or law of primogeniture sufficiently, but not over-sharply, defined.

The Homeric King, decked out with attributes almost ideal, appears before us, so far as Greece is concerned, in not a threefold only, but a fourfold, character; besides being Priest, Judge, and General, he is also, as King, a great Proprietor.

Priesthood is a function touching the daily course of life. Besides the solemn and public sacrifices, the meat of each meal is an offering; the word 'to sacrifice,' hiereuein is used as meaning ' to kill;' the animal ready to be killed is hiereion, a sacrifice. Yet there appears to be no professional priest among the Hellenes. We hear of many priests in the Poems: but of none of them can we positively assert that they were Greek. The priest is referred to, together with the prophet and dream-teller, in the first Assembly of the Iliad: but the Greeks are there[1] in a land of priests; and as Achilles plainly points to the prophet Calchas, who immediately afterwards rises to speak, so it is probable that he may point to the priest Chruses, who had already visited the camp. Among the chief professions of a Greek community, enumerated in the Odyssey[2], the priest does not appear. Though priests are wanting, prophets are not; and in this important passage, the class of prophets is the first named. One passage only speaks of priests within the local limits of Greece[3]: it refers to a generation before the War; and it is quite possible that, both then and subsequently, there may have been priests in Greece of Pelasgian institution. Wherever there was a

[1] Il. i. 62.   [2] Od. xvii. 385.   [3] Il. ix. 575.

temenos, or glebe, probably there was a priest to
live upon the proceeds. But the only sacred glebes
of which we hear in Greece are (I think) the glebes of
Spercheios and of Demeter[1], both of them old Pelasgian
deities.

In conformity with this view, we find that among
the Hellenes, in the public and solemn sacrifices, the
priestly office is performed by the King. Moreover,
the assistants are termed n e o i[2], young men. This
supports a conjecture suggested to me by the resemblance of the words, that hieros and gerōn have been
originally identical in root. In Greece down to the
present day the monk is called calo-gero (the French
caloyer). It was to the Father, as such, that in the
origin of society the offices both of King and Priest
generally accrued. To the Father, in the time of
Homer, the ordinary consecration or offering of the
meal appertains, as he presides at the domestic
board.

The office of the Judge seems to be, more than any
other, proper to the King. It probably constituted his
only official employment which was at once permanent
(that of war being occasional), and of a nature[3] to
weigh upon the mind. But it should be understood
as including all deliberative work. On the Shield[4],
the trial of a cause is conducted by the Elders; perhaps
in the character of delegates. Causes must have been
conducted by natural equity, or by what in Ireland was
called Brehon, that is judge-made, law. Probably
custom had already established some rules with respect

---

[1] Il. xxlii. 148; li. 696.   [2] Il. l. 463. Od. iii. 460.
[3] Il. l. 237; il. 204; ix. 98; xvi. 386.   [4] Il. xviii. 506.

to fines for homicide and adultery, if not for other offences.

The duty of the King as General is best exhibited by the whole plan of the Iliad. Here the King, if in full vigour, assumes the captain's office as a matter of course, and quits his house and throne to discharge it. Peleus[1], the father of Achilles, remains at home, because he is disabled by old age. Nestor, retaining more of his bodily vigour, goes to war, but acts in the camp chiefly as a counsellor, and at no time actually handles arms.

Never has the idea of regal duty and responsibility, both in general and with respect to war in particular, been more nobly set forth than in the speech of Sarpedon to Glaucos[2], in the Twelfth Iliad; before the high-souled speaker proceeded to execute what was, on the Trojan side, by far the greatest exploit of the War.

Lastly. In consideration of the duties and burdens of his office, the King was a great Proprietor. A domain[3] (temenos) was set apart for him out of the common stock of territory (from temnein, to cut, to carve out). The class had apparently two other sources of revenue. They received presents from merchants, for leave to trade; of which we find an example also in the Book of Genesis[4]. The practice of offering such gifts is probably to be regarded as the germ of Customs-duties, or taxes on the import and export of goods. The other was from fees on the administration of justice[5]. Of these, we have the

---

[1] Il. xxiv. 487. Od. xi. 497.   [2] Il. xii. 310-328.
[3] Il. xii. 313; vi. 194; ix. 574; xx. 184.   Od. vi. 293; xi. 184; xvii. 299.
[4] xliii. 11.   Il. vii. 467-475.   Od. vii. 8-11.
[5] Il. ix. 155.

earliest rudiment represented on the Shield; where lay two talents of gold, to be awarded to the judge whose sentence in the cause should be most approved[1]. In time of war, too, Agamemnon was charged with appropriating a very large share of the prizes to himself[2].

But the King was expected to be liberal in his official entertainments, so to call them, to his chiefs and nobles, over and above the general duty of hospitality[3]. This, probably, was the excuse of the Suitors for devouring the substance of Odysseus. It appears, at any rate, that friends of the royal house frequented the table at the palace, as well as its enemies, though perhaps not so constantly[4].

The King might also obtain private property. Laertes lived, in his old age, on an estate thus acquired[5]. And, in the First Odyssey, we find a distinction between the house of Odysseus with the lands about it, to which Telemachos was to succeed as of right, and the kingly dignity with whatever might attach to it[6].

Such was the position of the King. Agamemnon, however, was a King of Kings: more or less resembling what we now call a Suzerain, or the highest feudal superior of the middle age. Thucydides is of opinion that the fear of him[7] had more to do than good will, or than the oath of Tundareus, in the formation of the confederacy which undertook the war of Troy. National sentiment, and the hope of booty, might also contribute powerfully to this extraordinary effort. We have, however, no

---

[1] Il. xviii. 508. [2] Il. ix. 333. [3] Il. ix. 70. Od. vii. 49, 108.
[4] Od. xvii. 68.   [5] Od. xxiv. 206.
[6] Od. i. 397, 402.   [7] L 9.

means of tracing in the Poems any interference of the
Suzerain, beyond his own proper dominions, in the
ordinary government of the country; or any duty owed
to him, except in war.

The general reverence for rank and station, the safe-
guard of publicity, and the influence of persuasion, are
the usual and sufficient instruments for governing the
army, even as they governed the civil societies, of
Greece. The few words quoted by Aristotle[1] from
some text of the Iliad which was current in his day and
place, signifying that Agamemnon had a right of life and
death, cannot reasonably, without a context, be made
to convey a theory of military discipline out of harmony
with the tone and analogies of the poem, and belonging
to the definite ideas of the present rather than to the
free life of the older time. Moreover, as these words
(πὰρ γὰρ ἐμοὶ θάνατος) afterwards disappeared from the
text of the Poem, the most natural inference seems to
be that they were not finally approved as genuine.

It is in the Assemblies, that the great transactions of
the army are decided. There, arises the quarrel with
Achilles; there, the tumultuary impulse homewards;
there, that impulse having been checked, it is deliberately resolved to see what can be done by the
strong hand against Troy. There it is settled to ask
a truce for burials, and to erect the rampart. There
the second proposition of Agamemnon to return to
Greece is made, and is summarily overruled[2]. There
the Council is appointed to sit, which despatches the
abortive mission to Achilles. There Agamemnon con-
fesses and laments his fault, and the reconciliation with
the great chief is sealed. There, finally, arises the

[1] Aristot. Pol. lil. 14. 15.   [2] Il. ix. 26-28, 50.

dissension of the two sons of Atreus, after the fall of Troy[1].

The ranks traceable in the army are:

1. The Kings: Basileis or Koiranoi.
2. The Leaders under the rank of King.
3. The officers of minor command.

Both these last come under the name of hege-mones. The ships had each her kubernētēs or pilot, who probably commanded as well as steered: and there were a number of tamiai, or stewards, whom we may regard as the commissariat of that day[2].

The privates of the army are called by the names of laos, the people; demos, the community; and plethûs, the multitude. But no notice is taken, throughout the Poem, of the exploits of any soldie below the rank of a high officer. Still, all attend the Assemblies. On the whole, the Greek host is not so much an army, as a community in arms.

On the nature of the arms employed by the bulk of the force, it is not easy to pronounce with con-fidence. There were heavy-armed, who fought with spear, sword, axe, and stone; javelin-men, who used a lighter dart; archers; and hippeis, those who fought from the chariot. Though the art of riding, in our sense of it, was known, it was not used in battle. One passage appears to speak of the Trojans as at-tacking with javelins and arrows, and of the Greeks as resisting with the weapons proper to the heavy-armed[3]; another distinctly describes the first in the same manner[4]: and on the whole I judge that the Greek soldiery, with its solid march, were combatants,

---

[1] Od. III. 139.
[2] Il. xix. 42-45.
[3] Il. xv. 707-712.
[4] Od. xvlii. 264.

in the main, using weapons of weight; the Trojans somewhat less so. Only the Trojans distinguish themselves as archers, in the persons of Pandaros and Paris: but there were bowmen in the Greek army also [1].

Two modes of fighting were in use: the open battle of main force, without strategy or tactics, and liable to panic. The other was the lochos, or ambuscade. As a severer trial of nerve and moral fortitude, this latter was held in higher estimation, and was reserved to the chiefs [2]. We must not say that Achilles would have been inferior to any man in any act of martial skill or daring: but in the Poems, as they stand, Odysseus has been chosen as the prince of ambush [3].

The Council was composed of chief persons, who bore the name of gerontes [4], or elders: a name which was probably in its origin personal, and had by degrees become, like that of Senator in later times, official. In the Council of the Army, Nestor is old, Idomeneus near upon old age: Odysseus might be called elderly, though still in the perfection of strength [5].

In the Second Book, the Boulè or Council is summoned by Agamemnon, to prepare for the Assembly [6]. The same persons meet before the solemn sacrifice [7], without being called a Council. They meet again, as a Council, by appointment of the Assembly, in the Ninth Book [8]; and send the Envoys to supplicate Achilles. In the Seventh Book, this body plans the truce and the rampart [9]. It is spoken of as an institution

[1] Il. ii. 720; iii. 79.
[2] Il. xviii. 509; xiii. 20, 276-286; i. 226.
[3] Od. iv. 277-288.   [4] Il. ii. 52.   [5] Il. xxiii. 791.
[6] Il. ii. 52.   [7] Il. ii. 404-408.   [8] Il. ix. 10, 89.
                    [9] Il. vii. 344, 382.

evidently familiar [1]. The disorganised society of Ithaca
does not afford scope for a regular Council; but a place
is set apart for the elders in the Agorè [2], and Odysseus
in his youth had been sent on a mission by Laertes and
his Council [3]. In Scherиè, Nausicaa meets her father [4]
on his way to the Boulè. The members of the Army-
council contend freely in argument with Agamemnon;
and Nestor takes the lead in that body, and observes
to Agamemnon that it is his duty to listen as well as
to speak, and to adopt the plans of others when they
are good [5]. This institution was one utterly at variance
with anything like absolutism in the command.

In the Homeric ideas upon Polity, perhaps the most
remarkable of all is the distinction accorded to the
power of speech. The voice and the sword are the
twin powers, by which the Greek world is governed;
and there is no precedency of rank between them.
The power of public speech is essentially a power over
large numbers; and, wherever it prevails, it is the surest
test of the presence of the spirit and practice of
freedom. The world has repeatedly seen absolutism
deck itself with the titles and mere forms of liberty,
or seek shelter under its naked abstractions; but from
the use of free speech as the instrument of governing
the people, it has always shrunk with an instinctive
horror. The epithets and incidental passages with which
Homer honours it, show much of his mind [6]. But the
most emphatic testimony to its importance, and to the
state of things which it betokens, is the free, signal,
and varied excellence of the Homeric Speeches.

[1] Od. lii. 127.   [2] Od. ii. 14.   [3] Od. xxi. 51.
[4] Od. vi. 53-55.   [5] Il. ix. 100-102.
[6] Il. i. 490; ix. 438-443. Od. xi. 510-516; il. 150; viii. 170-173.

In the case of speakers, Homer is less chary of
description than his wont: and he has exhibited to us
in action too a great variety of manners. There is
Thersites, glib, vain, and saucy [1]. There is Telemachos,
full of the gracious diffidence of youth, but commended
by Nestor for a power and a tact of expression beyond
his years [2]. Menelaos harangues with a laconic ease [3].
We have the Trojan elders, whose volubility, and their
shrill thread of voice, Homer compares to the chirp of
grasshoppers [4]. Nestor's tones of happy and benevolent
egotism flow sweeter than a stream of honey [5]. Phoinix
would, in unskilful hands, have been a pale reflex
of Nestor's garrulity without his sagacity; but his
speaking is redeemed by his profound and absorbing
affection for Achilles, which gives him as it were
a different centre of gravity. Far above all these soars
Odysseus, who when he first rises, with all his energies
concentrated within him, seems to give no promise of
display; but when his deep voice issues from his chest,
and his words drive like the flakes of winter snow, then,
says the Poet, for mortal to compete with him is
hopeless [6].

But yet there is another speaker who, when he rises
to his noblest, seems as though he were scarcely mortal.
Homer leaves the eloquence of Achilles to stand self-
described. That chief modestly pronounces himself to
be below Odysseus in the use of oratory. It seems to me
that his speeches may challenge comparison with all that
we find in Homer; and with all that the ebb and flow
of three thousand years have added to our records of
true human eloquence. Even here, Homer's resources

---

[1] Il. ii. 212.   [2] Od. iii. 23, 124.   [3] Il. iii. 213.
[4] Il. iii. 150.   [5] Il. i. 243.   [6] Il. iii. 216–223.

are not exhausted. The decision of Diomed, the irre-
solution of Agamemnon, the bluntness of Ajax, are all
admirably marked in the series of speeches allotted to
each respectively. Scarcely anywhere is mediocrity to
be found; and perhaps the greatest example on record
of a perfectly simple nobleness is to be found in the
speech of Sarpedon to Glaucos on the duties of Kings[1].

With respect to the power of speech, and the capacity
of being moved by it, the performances of the Poet are
truly the best picture of the age itself. Unlike great
poems, great speeches cannot be made, except in an
age and place where they are understood and felt. The
work of the orator is cast in the mould offered him by
the mind of his hearers. He cannot follow nor frame
ideals at his own will; his choice is to be what his
time will have him, what it requires in order to be
moved by him, or not to be at all.

If the power of oratory proper is remarkable in
Homer, so likewise, and perhaps yet more, is the
faculty of what in England is called 'debate.' In
Homer's discussions, every speech after the first is
commonly a reply. It belongs not only to the subject, but to the speech that went before; it exhibits,
given the question and the aims of the speaker, the
exact degree of ascent and descent, of expansion or
contraction, which the circumstances of the case, in
the state up to which they were brought by the preceding address, may require. The debate in the Assembly
of the First Book, and that in the Encampment of
Achilles[2], are, as oratorical structures, complete and
consummate.

A people cannot act in its corporate capacity without

[1] Il. xii. 310-328.   [2] Il. ix. 225-655.

intermission; and the King is the standing representative of the community. But though he be the pivot of its functional and administrative activity, the Agorè, or Assembly, is the centre of its life and vital motion. The greatest ultimate power possessed by the King is that of exercising an influence upon his subjects, there gathered into one focus, through the combined medium of their reverence for his person, and of his powers of persuasion. There is no decision by numbers; the doctrine of majorities is an invention, an expedient, of a more advanced social development. In Olympos, a minority of influential gods carry the day against the majority, and against their head, in the great matter of the Trojan war.

The interference of Thersites in the Debate of the Second Iliad, and his attempt to bring the Assembly back to the impulse of returning home, were followed by sharp corporal chastisement, and by the menace of the last degree of personal disgrace. But the very attempt to interfere by suggesting such audacious proposals, and these from a person so contemptible, may perhaps be taken as an indication that freedom of debate generally prevailed.

In one of the scenes represented on the Shield of Achilles, new evidence is afforded us, that the people took a real part in the conduct of affairs. An Assembly is sitting. A criminal suit is in progress. The parties plead on either side, and challenge a decision; and the people, taking part some one way and some the other, encourage them by cheering. The heralds keep order, and stay the interruptions when the time arrives for the judges to speak[1]. This applause of itself asserts

[1] Il. xviii. 502. Cf. ii. 211.

the recognised interest and participation of the people; for it contributes both to the decision, and to the spirit and efficacy of the means of persuasion, by which that decision is to be influenced. Not only so; but it seems to have been by popular vote that the two talents were to be awarded, which lay on the floor, and were to be given to the Elder who might pronounce the soundest judgment [1]. Finally, in the Assembly of the Seventh Iliad, Idaios arrives from Troy with an offer to restore the stolen property, but not Helen herself. Diomed repudiates it, and his opinion is echoed back in the cheers of the army. Agamemnon then addresses himself to the herald, 'Idaios, you hear the sense of the Achaians, how they answer you; and I think with them.' Thus the acclamation was also the vote [2].

That which we do not find in Homer is, the submission of the minority to the majority in any public or deliberative meeting. This without doubt is an expedient of much later date. But where difference of opinion prevails, the Assembly breaks into opposing factions. So it was in the drunken Assembly mentioned in the Odyssey [3]; and the minority which then set sail was afterwards again divided [4]. In like manner, of the Ithacan Assembly in the Twenty-fourth Odyssey, the majority determined on neutrality, but the minority took arms. And, throughout the Voyages, we see how freely the crews of Odysseus both spoke and acted, when they thought fit, in opposition to his views. These illustrations might be yet further extended.

The truth is, that everywhere among the Greeks of

---

[1] Il. xviii. 508.   [2] Il. vii. 381.   [3] Od. iii. 139.
[4] Od. iii. 162.

Homer we find the signs of an intense corporate or
public life, subsisting, and working side by side, with
that of the individual. Of this corporate life, the
Agorè is the proper organ. If a man is to be described
as great, he is always great, in debate and on the field:
if as insignificant, then he is of no account either in
battle or in council. The two grand forms of common
and public action are taken for the tests of the individual man.

When Homer wishes to describe the Kuklopes as
living in a state of barbarism, he says, not that they
have no kings, or no towns, or no army, but that they
have no Assemblies, and no administration of justice [1].
The source of life lay in the community, and the community met in the Agorè. So deeply imbedded is this
sentiment in the mind of the Poet, that it seems as if
he could not conceive an assemblage of persons having
any kind of common function, without their having, so
to speak, a common soul too in respect of it.

Of this common soul, the organ, in Homer, is the
Tis or 'Somebody:' by no means one of the least
remarkable, though he has been perhaps the least
regarded, among the personages of the Poems. The
Tis of Homer seems to be what in England we
now call Public Opinion : the immediate impression
created in the general mind by public affairs, or by the
conduct of the chiefs. We constantly come upon occasions, when the Poet has to tell us what was the
prevailing sentiment of the Greek army. He might
have done this didactically, or by way of narrative.
He has adopted a method more poetical and less ob-

[1] Od. ix. 112.

trusive. He proceeds dramatically, through the medium of a person and of a formula, 'Hereupon, thus spoke somebody:'

Ὧδε δέ Τις εἴπεσκεν.

This would be sufficiently noteworthy if we found it only among the Greeks in war, and again in peace: for, when Odysseus causes music and dancing in his palace, with a view to producing an impression on the people of the town of Ithaca, it is Tis who tells what it was[1]. But it is not only in a normal state of things among his own people, that Tis is found. When Greeks and Trojans meet for the purpose of the Pact, there is a Tis for the Trojans also[2]. The Suitors, again, are a body of dissolute and selfish youths, and are competitors with each other for a prize which but one among them can enjoy. Yet in some sense they are bound together by a common interest of iniquity; and, although we are introduced to many of them individually by their speeches, yet they too have a Tis[3] who expresses their general sentiment on occurrences as they pass. Too broad to be confined to Greece, this conception is not even restricted to mankind: and Tis appears in Olympos, expressing the common or average sentiment of the assembled gods[4].

This remarkable and characteristic creation remains, I believe, the exclusive property of Homer. But perhaps we may discern in the Homeric Tis the primary ancestor of the famous Greek Chorus. Like Tis, the Greek Chorus is severed from all mere individuality, and expresses the generalised sentiment of the body or

---

[1] Od. xxlii. 148-152.
[2] Il. iii. 319.
[3] Od. li. 324.
[4] Od. viii. 328.

people to which it belongs, in the highest and best sense which their prevailing standard will allow.

Except in the mouth of the scoundrel Thersites, nothing like political discontent appears in any part of the Poems of Homer. The popular sentiment adverse to Odysseus on his return to Ithaca is probably a personal resentment, not only for the death of the Suitors, but for all the crews of his good ships lost in the War and on the Voyage. There is no invidious distinction between class and class, nor any of the social feuds which might be its result. No recognised portion of the community is imagined to require repression or restraint from the government. The King, or Chief, is uplifted to set a high example, to lead the common counsels to common ends, to conduct the public and common intercourse with heaven, to decide the strifes of private persons, which might bring danger to the common weal, and to defend the borders of the common territory from invasion.

For the chief component parts of Greek society, we have first the King and his family. Round him are his Kerukes, serjeants or heralds, his only executive government: his Bard, ever giving delight, and receiving respect: his Seniors, who assist in council, and in judgment: his Nobles, the only wealthy of the period. From them the Prince or King seems to be in general pretty broadly distinguished; for the rule is that the legitimate son, the heir-apparent, contracts marriage beyond his own borders. But Megapenthes, the serf-born son of Menelaos, marries in Sparta itself[1].

Under the name of demioergoi[2], which includes both the professional men and the skilled labourers of

---

[1] Od. iv. 5, 10, 797; xl. 87; *et alibi*.   [2] Od. xvii. 383.

the community, Homer includes the prophet, the physician or wound-healer, the carpenter or wright, and the Bard [1]. The fact that the worker in metals is not included, tends to show, in accordance with all the other evidence of the Homeric text, that this kind of labour had not attained to any great degree of development in Greece.

That the pursuits of manual labour were not below the notice even of princes, we find from the case not only of Odysseus, but of Paris [2], who joined in the building of his own palace; and of Lucaon, who was cutting young wood for his chariot, when, for the first time, he fell into the hands of Achilles [3]. Bards, heralds, and seers, are all persons of general influence and importance [4]. We hear of merchants only within the Phœnician circle: as Mentes of the Taphians, and again from the mouth of Eurualos in Scheriè [5]. We have also in Scheriè aisumnetai, or masters of the ceremonies, who make the arrangements needful for the dance [6].

There are inferior professions of partially skilled hand-labourers; among whom it is interesting to notice the drain-digger; the fisherman, named only in Ithaca [7]; the charioteer, and the woodman, for both of whom, says the Poet, as well as for the pilot, skill avails far more than force [8].

But the persons named in connection with special employments are rather classes, distinguished from the general body of the community, than the parts which make up the aggregate. They seem all to be picked

---

[1] In another place he adds the herald, Od. xix. 135.
[2] Il. vi. 314.   [3] Il. xxi. 35.
[4] Od. iii. 267; xvii. 263; xxiv. 439.   [5] Od. i. 183; viii. 161.
[6] Od. viii. 258.   [7] Od. xxiv. 418.   [8] Il. xxiii. 315–318.

men. Considering on the one hand the position of the masses in the Assemblies, and the appeals there made to them, on the other, the absence, in both the Poems, of anything like an extended personal following attached to the kings or chiefs, I come slowly to the conclusion, as most agreeable to the evidence, which is far from demonstrative, that the bulk of the community were probably small or peasant proprietors, tilling their own lands. The mode of their equipment as heavy, not light, armed soldiers, tends to sustain this conclusion. Even the sons of the slave Dolios appear to put on the ordinary armour [1]. We have then probably before us, in the composition of early Greek society, that mixture and gradation of fortunes, which so much contribute to the unity and strength of a community: the eminent men leading because they were the best, and the mass content to follow them for the same good reason.

The representation of the state of society and of opinion in Ithaca, contained in the Odyssey is extremely curious. The term Βασιλεὺς, so carefully limited in the Iliad, is here extended to the chief nobles ; as it is in Scheriè to the twelve principal persons who were counsellors of Alkinoos: and, along with it the epithet Διοτρεφὴς undergoes a similar enlargement. Since Homer drew from hearsay his materials for treating of Scheriè, we cannot reason confidently upon its institutions in their minute detail. But, when he speaks of Greek society, the case is different. And, in effect, what the Poet shows us in the dominions of Odysseus is, a great political change, brought about by the absence, through a prolonged period, of a powerful influence much more personal than traditional. King-

[1] Od. xxiv. 596.

ship subsisted at that period in virtue of the strong
mind and strong hand of the King. Only the aizēos,
the man within the flower of his manhood, was equal
to it. Laertes from his age, Telemachos from his
youth, Penelope as a woman, and thus open to the access
of suitors, were unequal to the charge. In the absence,
then, of the true King, each minor personage of the
order of nobles apparently set up as king. Moreover
local attachment prevailed over central influences ; and
the people, at least of the town, were with the opponents of Odysseus. Except on his own estate, the
influence of his family, after a course of years, was
gone. Telemachos can only say that by no means are
the whole of the demos[1] or people averse to him.
The Suitors, shut within the palace for the terrible
assault of Odysseus, feel that, if they could but get
out into the town, so as to give the alarm, they should
be safe. After the fact, Odysseus proposes by a stratagem to arrest any rumour of the slaughter[2]. On
finding Laertes, he declares, 'we have no time to
lose[3].' He had quitted the town at once, evidently
as having no hope there. A civil war is the sequel
to the return of the legitimate Sovereign, who has only
to rely, after the favour of the gods and his own
powerful mind, upon a mere handful of dependents.
Odysseus calls the Suitors, whom he had destroyed, the
stay or strength[4] of the community ; and the Shade
of Agamemnon recognises them as the flower of men[5].
Doubtless their party was strengthened by their King's
having lost all his comrades, and by the biting appeal[6]

---

[1] Od. xvi. 114.   [2] Od. xxiii. 137–140.   [3] Od. xxiv. 324.
[4] Od. xxiii. 121.   [5] Od. xxiv. 106–108; cf. 429.
[6] Od. xxiv. 428.

they were thus enabled to make to the relatives of the
dead. His sources of aid seem to have lain in Pulos and
in Elis[1]. Of the Ithacan Assembly, near half[2] went
to take arms against Odysseus; while the others stood
neuter. The great Chief had on the moment but twelve
men in all to resist them: three of his family, nine
serfs.

A flood of light is thrown, from this picture in
miniature, upon the structure of society, and the nature
of political power among the Hellenes of the heroic,
or the immediately post-heroic, age.

Laws can hardly exist without writing; and, in the
age of Homer, writing, or what stood in its place, was
at most no more than the secret of a few families of
Phœnician extraction. It was certainly unavailable
for any purpose of general interest. A Greek word for
'law' is not to be found in Homer. With him, νομός
means a tract of pasture[3]. We find however (*a*) δίκη
and δίκαι, (*b*) θέμιστες. The latter appear to be the
principles of right; the former, those principles of right
put into action by judicial proceedings, when they have
become matter of contention; the two[4] are clearly
enough to be distinguished.

In the absence of law, strictly so called, the Oath was
of peculiar importance. It was so solemn, that the only
special offence, expressly marked out for punishment in
the other world, is the offence of perjury[5]. And it was
so effectual, as not only to bind man to man, but deity
to deity[6]. The river Styx was the great Oath of the

---

[1] Od. xxiv. 430, 436.   [2] Od. xxiv. 463.   [3] Od. ix. 217.
[4] Od. ix. 215.   [5] Il. iii. 279.
[6] Il. xiv. 278; xv. 36-46.

gods[1], evidently implying their liability, not indeed to
death, but to deposition; and the possibility that they
might exchange bright Olympos, as the older dynasties
of Nature-Powers had exchanged it, for the dreary
Underworld. The Trojans break faith and oath in
the Fourth Iliad: the Greeks never. Yet Autolucos,
the father of Penelopè, had received from Hermes[2] the
gifts of pilfering and perjury; and thus moral corruption had begun to distil from depraved belief.

The xeinos or xenos, in the largest sense, com-
prehends and brings together three very different
classes.

1. The itinerating beggar[3], ptochos pandemios,
who, in days when money did not exist as a circulating
medium, sought relief in the form of hospitality, relief
in kind; and in some sense paid for it by carrying
news[1].

2. The Suppliant (hiketês), who may be of station
high or low, but who appears with a suit for shelter,
subsistence, or other aid, under the pressure of some
peculiar necessity or calamity.

3. The xeinos proper; the guest, whose need arises
simply out of the fact that, being away from home, he
has not his resources at hand, and therefore seeks to
have them supplied in the home of another.

Slavery is not a prominent feature of Greek society
in the Homeric age. It would appear to have been
nearly or perhaps wholly confined to the establish-
ments, in-door and out-door, of the chiefs. The language of Achilles in the Underworld, 'rather would I
serve for hire even with a poor employer,' seems to

[1] Il. xv. 37.   [2] Od. xix. 369.   [3] Od. xviii. 1.
[4] Od. xviii. 7.

imply that hire was the ordinary basis of service. If Odysseus had had very numerous slaves, without doubt he and Telemachos would have been represented in the Odyssey as having raised and armed them against the party of the Suitors; which they did with the mere handful at their command. The slaves appear to have been few, in comparison with the number of the community. The demos or free people, who constituted the Assemblies, seem also to have composed the mass of the population of cultivators.

The two sources named for supplying slaves are

1. War;
2. Kidnapping.

In all cases this kidnapping is of single individuals. We hear of it as practised by the Phœnicians, the Taphians (a branch of the Phœnicians), and the Thesprotians. Not by the Greeks; though Melanthios, the goatherd in the Odyssey, without doubt a serf, as he was the son of a serf[1], among his other insolences, threatens to carry away Eumaios, and sell him[2].

We do not hear of any physical want or suffering in connection with the condition of slaves; nor ought we to interpret too rigidly the prophecy of Hector concerning Andromachè, as proving that they were treated with rudeness[3]. But Homer saw both the enfeebling and the depressing effect, the moral blight, of even a mild slavery, and has recorded it in golden words. With Homer, a slave is but one half of a man[4].

Slaves, from the circumstances of the case, were often of birth and manners not unequal to those of

---

[1] Od. xvii. 212; iv. 737.   [2] Od. xvii. 249.
[3] Il. vi. 454-463. Comp. Il. xxi. 484-507; where not slavery, but orphanhood, is supposed.   [4] Od. xvii. 213.

their masters. Eumaios was the son of the ruler of his
country; and was brought up together with Ctimenè,
the daughter of Laertes[1].

The slavery of Homer's time is a mitigated slavery.
It nowhere appears in association with wanton cruelty
or oppression. The slave may be familiar with his
master: Odysseus, on the Return, is kissed by his slaves.
The slave may acquire property, may be the master of
other slaves, as Eumaios was of Mesaulios[2]; finally, he
is trusted with arms. A good master is expected to
supply his slave with a wife.

The absence of the chiefs and army from Greece for
a lengthened period, without any danger arising from
this source, of itself appears to prove, that slaves must
have constituted an element numerically insignificant
in that country. Another reason for this belief is to
be found in the fact, that no distinction appears to have
been drawn, as in after times, of a nature to make
laborious manual employments dishonourable. As it
was part of the prized accomplishments of a King like
Odysseus to be able to drive the plough, we may be
almost sure that field-labour could not have been, either
universally or generally, intrusted to the hands of
slaves.

The general picture presented to us is, that of free
self-governing agricultural societies under mild aristocratic rule, the mass living in a self-sufficing independence; and only a comparative handful, it is probable,
dependent in any degree, however small, on the assistance of slaves for the management of their households
and estates. At the same time, as between the serf
and the thês or labourer for hire, it is material to

[1] Od. xv. 413, 363.   [2] Od. xiv. 449.

remember that, in the Homeric period, wages could only be paid in kind, as there was no currency available. This being so, the hired freeman, if without other resource, might perhaps, as to material comforts, be in no better position than the bondman.

We have no trace of slavery in the Greek army, nor of any large or numerous class of slaves anywhere. The probable inference again, is, that slaves constituted but a limited proportion of the community.

It is possible that gold and silver may to a very trifling extent have been used as a common measure of commodities, or medium of exchange. For gold is frequently mentioned as a constituent part of stored wealth; and we can hardly suppose that it was so stored simply for use in the manufacture of commodities for the owners by gilt plating or otherwise. But, on the other hand, other commodities are not valued in gold or in silver. Only the payment of the Judge's fee, or prize, in gold, on the Shield of Achilles, approaches to a case of the use of gold money. It is like the semata or signs on the tablets of Proitos, the germ of a practice rather than the practice itself.

The arms of Glaucos and of Diomed, the tripod which is the first prize for wrestlers in the Games, and the skilled captive woman who was the second, are all valued or priced in oxen[1]; and the ox is the commodity which represents in Homer what we now term the measure of value, as far as it can be said to be represented at all. The captive Lucaon fetches for Achilles the value of a hundred oxen[2]: Eurucleia is sold to Laertes for the value of twenty[3]. The Suitors promise

---

[1] Il. xxiii. 702-705.   [2] Il. xxi. 79.   [3] Od. l. 431.

to Odysseus the value of a hundred oxen each, as ransom[1]. The most detailed account in the Poems of a commercial transaction is in the Seventh Iliad, where Euneos gives wine in exchange for slaves, hides, copper, iron, and oxen. The four first-named commodities he might well carry away from a camp for sale elsewhere. As to slaves, for example, the skilled woman of the Iliad is worth only four oxen: Eurucleia in Ithaca worth twenty. They represent respectively the prices of an exporting market with a glut, and of a market of import with a demand from over sea scantily supplied. The oxen which Euneos took, he possibly took from those who were overstocked, and sold again on the spot to such as chanced to want them[2].

Thus we can understand why Æschylus represents the ox as the earliest sign impressed on money[3].

Among the leading political ideas exhibited in the Homeric Poems will be found the following:—

Authority to rule is derived from heaven, and the abuse of this authority, the corruption and the crimes of rulers, are marked by divine judgments on a land.

Equality is not dreamt of; but liberty is highly prized.

A strong sense of responsibility weighs upon the mind of any ruler not utterly corrupt.

The possessions and honours of kings are not unconditional, but are held by them in trust for the performance of public duties; among these, in order that they may set an example to the people in time of danger.

The gravest matters affecting the public interest are debated and decided in the Assemblies of the people.

[1] Od. xxii. 57–59.   [2] Il. vii. 467–475.   [3] Agam. 37.

Discussion is conducted in general by persons enjoying weight from their age, station, birth, or ability; in a word, by the class possessed of leisure and social influence; but the deliberation and assent of the Assemblies are free.

A public opinion readily forms and freely circulates among the people, approving or condemning the acts of those in authority.

Publicity attends all judicial and deliberative proceedings; but a council of chiefs often privately prepares matter for the Assembly.

The will of the Assembly takes effect in the Act of the Executive[1].

Speech is the great accomplishment of man; and is the main instrument of government in peace, as the sword is in war. These two powers, representing moral and martial force respectively, stand in a position of honour peculiar to themselves.

These political ideas are traceable in the Olympian, as well as in the human, society; but their application and development are less satisfactory in that upper region.

The bond that held Greek society together in the Homeric time, and that secured the basis on which it was to be organised and developed, was fivefold; and the strands of this well-knit rope are represented respectively by single words.

1. Θεός, the Deity, and the worship of Immortal and unseen Beings in all its various forms.

2. Θέμις, the principle of social right and duty, chiefly as between neighbours and fellow-citizens.

---

[1] Od. v. 99.

3. Ὅρκος, the ultimate sanction of good faith.

4. Ξεῖνος, representing the basis of kindly and friendly relation, and of good offices among men, beyond the limits of polity and of class.

5. Γάμος, the great institution of marriage, determining the relation between the two varieties of human kind; constituting the family, and providing for the continuance of the species.

The one great creative and formative idea which runs through the whole of these is Reverence, that powerful principle, the counter-agent to all meanness and selfishness, which obliges a man to have regard to some law or standard above that of force, and extrinsic to his own will, his own passions, or his own propensities.

The five given above are the main channels into which the stream is distributed. But they have many subdivisions or specific forms, such as—

Reverence for Parents;

Reverence for Kings;

Reverence for the old;

Reverence for beauty; of which perhaps the very noblest example ever given is the manner in which Odysseus is struck by Nausicaa. One much lower, and more Asiatic, is that of the Trojan δημογέροντες, or Elders, when Helen goes forth to the Wall [1];

Reverence for the opinion of fellow men [2];

Reverence for the dead;

Reverence for the weak and poor.

These emotions and habits of reverence were to the

---

[1] Od. vi. 149 seqq. Il. iii. 154-158. [2] Il. ix. 459-461.

Greek mind and life what the dykes in Holland are to the surface of the country; shutting off passions as the angry sea, and securing a broad open surface for the growth of every tender and genial product of the soil.

CHAPTER XII.

THIS subject, which has been treated with some detail in the 'Studies on Homer[1],' will now be touched on only so far as to present its main heads.

Sufficient reason has perhaps been given for the belief that there is a double ethnical relation between the inhabitants of Troas and of Greece. The common soldiery appear to correspond, without any sensible inferiority of the Trojans, who, however, appear to have been in greater proportion lightly armed; and all that we learn of the people tends to associate them, in blood and language, with what we may largely call the Pelasgian and more archaic element in Greece. The ruling houses, again, are connected in the bonds of hospitality, as appears from the visit of Paris to Menelaos. The son of Anchises resided in Greece[2]. Diomed has the xenial relation with the Lycian Glaucos. Relations to the line of the personage termed Aiolos, so powerful in Greece, are visible in the Dardanian royal family.

[1] Vol. iii. Ilios, pp. 145-247.   [2] Il. xxiii. 296.

When we turn to language, a near relation, perhaps that of substantial identity, seems probable. A Greek name, Astuanax, lord of the city, is expressly stated to have been given by the Trojans to the son of Hector. The Trojan army, indeed, is stated to have spoken various tongues; but this is placed in immediate connection with the presence of the Epicouroi or allies[1], one race of whom, the Carians, are called speakers of a barbarous, meaning probably a wholly foreign, language.

In the matter of religion there is little, if any, difference between the mere names of such gods as are brought prominently forward. As the great controversy was to be fought out in Olympos, no less than on earth, Homer was in a manner compelled to find a meeting-point for the mythologies of the respective parties. We find mentioned expressly the worship in Troas of Zeus, Athenè, Apollo, and Hephaistos. Leto and Artemis attend in the temple of Apollo on Pergamos. Arès must have been known as a god to those, for whom he fights. Aphroditè was eminently Trojan, as we see from her favour for Paris; her passion for Anchises; her marriage-gift to Andromache; her ministerial charge over the body of Hector[2]; and from the biting taunts of Pallas, of Helen, and of Diomed[3]. Hermes is said to give increase to the flocks of Phorbas[4]; yet does not appear to be recognised as a known Trojan deity by Priam, when he gives his name, and specifies in addition that he is an immortal god[5]. Poseidon had a deadly quarrel with Troy, but was in

---

[1] Il. ii. 803-806.
[2] Il. xxiii. 184-187.
[3] Il. lii. 400-402; v. 348-351, 420-425.
[4] Il. xiv. 490.
[5] Il. xxiv. 461.

close and friendly relations with the Dardanian branch[1]. Herè is named as the wife of Zeus, and as slighted in the Judgment of Paris[2].

Now, a great River—not the humanised spirit of a River, but the River itself—the Scamandros, or Xanthos, of the Ilian plain, appears in the Theomachy, and fights on the side of Troy against Hephaistos. Here is an indication, which cannot be mistaken, that a Nature-worship, alien to the Olympian system, prevailed in Troas. We have other signs of this great and, probably, fundamental distinction of the two religions. While Herè is so faintly sketched, her Pelasgian prototype, Gaia, is an object of ordinary worship in Troas, although in Greece she is banished to the Underworld. And the Sun (Helios) of the Iliad sympathises with the Trojans, while the Apollo of the First Book shows signs of affinity with that luminary, that are rooted perhaps in his name Phoibos, but that are not allowed any place or recognition in the Olympian scheme. Of all single passages, that which most gives the key to the distinction is the speech of Menelaos before the Pact[3], where he proposes a joint act of religion to be performed on behalf of both parties. The Greeks are to offer a single lamb to Zeus; and the Trojans two, one of them to the Earth, the other to the Sun. Eōs, the morning, another Nature-Power, is made known to us as the bride of Tithonos, and may therefore be set down among the deities of Troy. It does not seem clear that she was in any way impersonated in Greece.

It is very probable, that Hephaistos and other deities may have been known under forms of tradition variously

---

[1] Il. xx. 290–292.   [2] Il. x. 329; xiii. 827; xxiv. 29.
[3] Il. iii. 103.

modified, in Troas and in Greece respectively; and,
indeed, in different portions of one and the same
country. These forms, however distinct or discordant,
the plan of Homer required him in some manner to
amalgamate.

So much for abstract belief. As to the modes of its
development, they would appear to have been on the
Trojan side sacerdotal, on the Greek imaginative. In
the Greek system, besides the great Olympian deities,
we have the gods of the older dynasty, and of the
Underworld; the Giants; the Nymphs, and other personages, anthropomorphically conceived, and presiding
over groves, rivers, meadows; the great ethical figures
of the Destinies and the Erinues, of Atè and the
Prayers; and a multitude of purely poetical impersonations, such as Terror, Rumour, and the like. In Troas,
we seem to find none of this large and varied apparatus, except the names of certain Nymphs, who are
mentioned as mothers of human children. Indeed,
even the future state seems to have been feebly conceived in Troy[1]; and the oath of Hector to Dolon[2]
makes no allusion to the penalty of perjury, which, as
we see, was incurred by Pandaros without shame or
hesitation. Not only do we still hear of the illustrious
Shade of Patroclos after death, but the passage of the
souls of the Suitors from Ithaca is vividly described in
the Odyssey[3]; but of the Trojans nothing is ever told
us beyond the grave, except one or two repetitions of
the mere formula that they went to Hades. A ma-
terialising religion is not favourable to the retention
of the belief in a future state; and human experience
seems to have established widely, up to the present

[1] Il. vi. 422; xxii. 482.   [2] Il. x. 339.   [3] xxiv. 1-10.

point of the history of the race, the connection between such a belief and the repression of perjury.

But when we turn to sacerdotal institutions and ritual forms, again the contrast is a striking one.

The three subjects of priesthood, temples, and glebes, seem to be closely connected; especially the first and third: for where there was an estate, we may be pretty sure that there was some official person, namely the priest, to live upon the proceeds.

Now we never hear of a temenos, or consecrated glebe-land, for any deity, except four times. There is the temenos of Zeus in Gargaros[1]; of Demeter in Thessaly[2]; of Aphroditè at Paphos[3]; and of the River Spercheios in Thessaly[4]. The first is in Troas; the third in Cyprus; the other two stand in evident connection with the old or Pelasgian worship.

Let us next look to the Priests of the Poems. We have Chruses, the priest of Apollo in Troas; Maron, a priest of the same deity at Ismaros, among the Kikones, allies of Troy; and again in Troas, Dares, priest of Hephaistos; Dolopion (arētēr, literally pray-er) of Scamandros; Theano, priestess of Athenè; Onetor, priest of the Zeus of Ida. But neither in the Greek army, nor in Greece itself, have we any mention of a priest contemporary with the Poems. Especially in the case of Ithaca this negative evidence is strong. I refer back to what has been already said on this subject in the description of the kingly office.

Besides the Priests, there is the separate order of Prophets. These are fully known in Greece under different names, and are recognised as one of the

---

[1] Il. viii. 48.   [2] Il. ii. 696.   [3] Od. viii. 362.
[4] Il. xxiii. 148.

regular standing professions in a community at peace,
while Calchas is the mantis or prophet of the army.
These organs of the deity interpret sometimes from
signs and omens, sometimes without them. There
was some degree of approximation between the two
characters. A prophet, or seer, might be an inspector
of sacrifices, though he did not offer them[1]. On the
other hand, a priest was supposed to be capable of
interpreting the divine will[2]. But distinctions of the
social state serve sufficiently to manifest the separation
of the two characters, even independently of the fact
that the seer or prophet never offers sacrifice. For the
last-named personage is distinguished from the rest of
the community only by the possession of his gift; whereas
the priest appears to be wholly exempted from military
service, and a kind of sanctity attaches to his character,
as is most of all clearly shown by the fact that the
offence of Agamemnon, which brought the Pest upon
the Greek army, consisted only in his refusal to take
ransom for the captive daughter of a priest, an act
which he probably might have ventured with impunity
in the case of the child even of a prince. Yet the
teaching office, as far as we can trace it at all, seems
to lie less with the priest, than with the prophet[3].

With respect to temples, it is plain that Apollo had
a temple at Putho, and probable that Pallas also had
one at Athens. No temple is named in Ithaca. They
seem to have abounded in Troas: and, in the Sixth
Odyssey, the building of temples[4] is named as one of
the elements of the construction of a city. It does not
follow that these temples were in all cases roofed

[1] Il. xxiv. 221. Od. xxii. 318.   [2] Il. i. 62.
[3] Od. xxii. 313-315.   [4] Od. vi. 10.

buildings: they may have been in some instances no
more than consecrated inclosures. Even in the Greek
camp, there was a central place for Assemblies, and for
Suits: and here were the altars of the gods[1]. We
are not entitled to infer from the existence of a temple
in any particular place, the existence of a priesthood.

The grove (alsos) appears to have been a common
form for the site of religious worship, both in and out
of Greece.

In Troy, we hear of a statue or image of Athenè[2],
to which was offered the Robe, presented by the Trojan
women in their solemn procession. And on the Shield
of Achilles there are delineated figures[3] of that goddess
and of Arès respectively, together with those of the
armed bands under their several patronage. But
no sanctity attends these figures; they are simple
representations of Art. We have no trustworthy trace
of a statue used in worship, except the solitary case
just named in Troy. And the common expression of
Homer, that the disposition of events lies in the lap
of the gods, is perhaps sufficiently explained by the
anthropomorphic character of the Olympic scheme, if
indeed it requires even that explanation.

Lastly, the Trojans appear to be distinguished[4] for
punctuality and liberality in sacrifice. But we hear of
much neglect of this matter on the part of the Greeks.
Menelaos, one of the best and purest characters among
the Greek chieftains, was punished for his omission to
offer up the proper hecatombs, by a long and trying
detention in Egypt[5]. A like neglect was the cause
of difficulties in the general Return of the Greek

---

[1] Il. xl. 806–808.   [2] Il. vi. 303.   [3] Il. xviii. 516–519.
[4] Il. iv. 48.   [5] Od. iv. 351–353.

army[1]. And before Troy, in the hasty construction of
the trench and rampart, the whole of the army forgot the
proper hecatombs[2]. The Trojans, then, much excelled
their enemies in religious observance. It seems also
true that, as between Greek and Greek, the pious
observers of the law of sacrifice were the better men.
But we can in no manner claim for the Trojans a
morality superior to that of their opponents.

Rather, indeed, the reverse. In the War of Troy,
justice is plainly with the Greeks. Of course I speak
of the delineation of the case such as we have it in
Homer, and do not inquire how far the Poet may have
caused the scale to incline on behalf of his country by
the weight of his own thoughts and wishes. The crime
of Paris would have been gross, had it been merely an
elopement. But it was an abduction; and an abduction too, attended with mere thievery of goods. These
features in our eyes are aggravations; probably, in
those of Homer and his contemporaries, they may have
tended to mitigate the offence, by imparting to it some of
the features of war[3]. And, in those days, abduction was
probably not regarded as criminal in itself. But there
always remains the grave offence of violated hospitality.
And accordingly, while Helen shows marks of aversion
for Paris, the Trojan people hate him like black death[4].
He contrives to hold his place by effrontery, and by
bribes[5]; and he is the object of sharp rebuke from
Hector[6]. With the exception of Menelaos, we find
much less indignation among the Greek chiefs, than

[1] Od. iii. 141–145.   [2] Il. vii. 450.
[3] Compare the case of Heracles and Iphitos, Od. xxi. 22–30.
[4] Il. iii. 428–436; vi. 352.   [5] Il. vii. 354–364; xi. 123.
[6] Il. iii. 46–53.

we might have expected. Perhaps we may reasonably consider that in this, as in many later cases, the original causes of the quarrel were to a great extent lost and absorbed in its following incidents. Christian ideas, again, would fix a deeper guilt on Paris, especially under the actual circumstances, according as his adulterous connection was more prolonged. But the offence of Paris is regarded in Homer as arising from want of self-control, rather than from hardened wickedness. It is always treated as an a t è, into which weakness enters, and not, like the conduct of the Suitors, as an atasthaliè, which is purely deliberate and hardened. The evil act once perpetrated, Paris had a marriage of fact with Helen, who was installed into the family of Priam: and of this marriage, odious as his character must be held, he is in some sort the defender. It was not wholly unlike the stealing of a birthright; which, once acquired, was valid. So the offence of Helen did not lie in living with a man who was not her husband, so much as having taken one husband in exchange for another.

It is not unlikely that a more base and less manly morality among the Trojans may help to account for the patient endurance of so much privation and calamity for the sake of a man, who did not even redeem his vices (so to speak) by personal courage, or by refinement of manners [1]. This conjecture is certainly sustained [2] by the remark of the Senators on the wall. In Ithaca the same idea is ascribed to the dissolute Suitors [3]. But much of the cause must, I think, have lain in a difference of institutions. The outward forms

---

[1] See the whole of Il. iii.   [2] Il. iii. 156.

[3] Od. xviii. 160-217.

of polity were not, indeed, broadly different. We have
on both sides a King; a Council, or Councillors at the
least; and an Assembly. But we have no indications
of that spirit of freedom in the Trojan community,
which found such noble scope in masculine debate,
and even in positive action, among the Greeks. On
both sides we find the germ of after-history: the
Trojans bearing in many points the more Asiatic, the
Greeks the more European stamp. The one type leans
to fraud, where the other inclines to force. King Laomedon defrauds Poseidon and Apollo; Anchises steals
from Laomedon, Paris from Menelaos: when Pandaros
most grossly breaks the public faith, there is no
reproach: Euphorbos wounds Patroclos in the back.
The mild Menelaos declares, that the sons of Priam
cannot be trusted [1]. Though a single passage in the
Odyssey places flat perjury, as well as theft, under the
patronage of Hermes [2], the Greeks appear, throughout
the Iliad, to pursue an honourable course of conduct.

A tendency, again, to sensual excess appears to run
in the royal line of Troy, under much less of restraint
than we find in the Greek houses. This is especially
remarkable in the mythology. Aphroditè and Eôs,
goddesses markedly Trojan, and Demeter, who is at
least Pelasgian, condescended to irregular relations
with men [3]. So it is with the Naiad nymphs of
Troas [4]. But about the goddesses recognised by the
Homeric Greeks, Pallas, Artemis, Persephonè, and
even Herè, we hear nothing of the kind.

The polygamy of Priam is wholly without counter-

[1] Il. iii. 105.   [2] Od. xix. 369.   [3] Od. v. 121-127.
[4] Il. vi. 21; xiv. 444; xx. 384.

part in Greece. It seems, however, to be not that of
a dissolute man, but of the head of a family regularly
organised: not personal, but traditional. He had fifty
sons, nineteen of them from the single womb of
Hecuba[1]; and twelve daughters. Besides Hecuba,
who was the principal queen, there were other
recognised wives; and behind them again were concubines, or else, which seems less probable, women
in no permanent relation whatever to the King. As
ten sons of Antenor (besides one spurious son) are
mentioned in the Iliad, all within the fighting age,
and as his wife Theano is still blooming (καλλιπαρῆος),
it seems highly probable that he, too, may have had
more wives than one.

Again, while the guilty act of Paris appears to have
been regarded without moral disapproval in Troy, the
first act of Aigisthos, the corruption of Clutaimnestra,
was regarded by the gods as a crime[2], even apart from
the murder of Agamemnon: and their sentiment probably expresses the average moral judgment of the
country. Again, it was the main part of the guilt
of the Suitors, which drew down so terrible a retribution, that they sought to wed Penelope while her
husband might still be supposed to be alive[3].

The prevalence of polygamy, even in the highest
families, is obviously adverse to the rule of an hereditary succession to the crown. And it seems more
than doubtful, from the Poems, whether this rule was
observed on the Trojan side as fully as in Greece.
Sarpedon and Glaucos are both called Kings: yet they
belonged to the same kingdom, and they were cousins.
Again, Sarpedon evidently had the chief place: yet

---

[1] Il. xxiv. 496; vi. 248.   [2] Od. i. 35.   [3] Od. xxii. 37.

Glaucos was the representative of the royal house in the male line, Sarpedon only in the female. Among the Greeks the title of King is only given to one person in one country, who must be either in possession, or heir-apparent.

In the recital of the genealogy from Dardanos, Æneas does not give a precedence of superiority to either branch; and he leaves[1] us to doubt, or to inquire from some other sources, which line was the senior, the Trojan or the Dardanian. Again, Achilles expressly taunts that chieftain as a candidate for the succession in Troy after the death of Priam[2].

Further, it appears open to much question, which of the sons of Priam himself we are to understand to have been the eldest. The whole responsibility of command evidently lay upon Hector; and there can be no doubt, even if it were only from the name given to his infant son by the people, that he was already the king-designate in the public view. But that name would have had little special significance, had Hector been sure of the succession by mere seniority. While the ability and value of Hector are of themselves sufficient to account for his prominent place, it is very difficult, except upon the supposition that seniority was more or less the competing element with merit, to account for various features in the position of Paris. Alone among the children of Priam, he enjoys the title of Basileus or King, which is never given to Hector. Although utterly insignificant as a warrior, he is the chief in command of the second among the five

[1] Il. xx. 231-240.   [2] Il. xx. 178-183.

divisions of Trojans in the great battle of the Twelfth
Book, as Hector is of the First[1]. Except Hector, Paris
is the only prince who has a separate dwelling of his
own on the hill of Pergamos. The other princes all,
married as well as unmarried, sleep in the palace
of their father. His expedition to Greece does
not absolutely imply his being the eldest son; but
perhaps best accords with that otherwise far from improbable supposition.

Again; Paris, according to the representation of the
Iliad, had been in manhood for at least twenty years.
But Hector had one child only, a babe in arms. The
word h e b è, which expresses a full-grown, but still a
blooming, manhood, is applied to Hector[2], but not to
Paris. It is applied indeed to Odysseus in Scheriè;
but this is when he had been preternaturally beautified
under the restoring hand of Athenè; and also in the
complimentary speech of a host[3]. We cannot suppose
Hector to have been very different in age from
Andromachè: but she must still have been young,
for her own grandfather had been alive during
the War[4]. And finally, in her lament over her
husband, she distinctly calls him young[5]. So much
as to the apparent seniority of Paris; and, with this,
for the less defined and more lax law of succession
in Troy.

The relation of Priam to the districts or countries,
which supplied the several contingents of his force, is
but indistinctly conveyed to us. Yet it is probable
from the arrangement and expressions of the Trojan

[1] Il. xii. 93.   [2] Il. xxii. 363.   [3] Od. viii. 135.
[4] Il. vi. 426–428.   [5] Il. xxiv. 725.

Catalogue, and from minor circumstances, that, besides his kingdom of Ilion, he exercised over Dardania, and at least three other districts, an authority more or less like to that of Agamemnon over the Greek chieftains. However this may be, even the ancients justly described the Trojan war as the conflict of the Eastern with the Western world. And it foreshadowed other yet greater conflicts, down to our own day.

Within the kingdom of Troy, we can more clearly discern the inferior compactness of political society, and its lower spirit of intelligence and freedom. We have every sign that the Trojan Elders did not act collectively as a Council[1]. This is an important defect in such a body with reference to the means of moral influence. But Assemblies met. There Antenor proposed, and Paris refused, the surrender of Helen: popular discontent was expressed; and we are expressly told, that he was able to procure the defeat of other such proposals only by corruption[2]. An Assembly agreed to ask a truce for the burial of the dead. In an Assembly, Hector somewhat curtly put down the opposition of Poludamas as a stranger[3].

But we have to remark, in the Trojan Assembly, as follows:—

1. That there is no sign of its having been guided by men of wisdom and valour, but only by age and rank.

2. That oratory does not seem to have been employed in it as an instrument of persuasion.

3. That the Elders, who assist Priam in public affairs, are simply the old men, and not, as with the

[1] Il. ii. 788, 789.   [2] Il. vii. 379.

[3] Il. xii. 211-214.

Greeks, the chief and able men, belonging to the high families of the State.

4. The Trojan Assembly does not clearly appear to have been convened on special occasions: but perhaps rather to have sat in permanence, in the sense of having only consisted of such persons as might chance to be present, at any given moment, in the places of public resort [1].

There seems in Troy—as in the institutions we now term Asiatic—to be nothing to stand between royalty and the people. There was thus less balance of forces, less security against precipitate action; a state of facts in all likelihood accompanied by less respect for public morality, less security for private rights.

The Poet has given us, evidently of set purpose, a minor indication of Trojan inferiority, in the contrasts he presents of the silence and self-possession of the Greeks, with the din and buzz of the Trojans, as they marched to battle. At the burying of the dead, both armies wept and were silent: but the silence of the Trojans was because great Priam forbade a noise [2]. A Trojan Assembly is uneasy and excitable [3]: never a Greek one. Even for the expressions of approval, different words are used: the Greeks were eager and vehement, the noise of the Trojans was promiscuous and tumultuous. In a word, all through the Poems, the Greek mind is evidently endowed with a finer sense, and a higher intelligence.

---

[1] Il. ii. 788; vii. 414.   Studies, pp. 237 seqq.
[2] Il. vii. 426-432.   [3] Il. vii. 346; iii. 2, 8; iv. 429, 436.

H h

CHAPTER XIII.

THE GEOGRAPHY OF HOMER.

SECTION I. *The Catalogue.*

THE Catalogue of Homer is a great attempt to construct what may, for those times, be justly called a cadastral account of Greece; together with an outline of the Trojan force, sufficient for the purposes of the Poem.

In 348 lines, it contains 501 proper names, spread over diverse and very irregular tracts of country, and including many which belong to personal history and genealogy. To recite this part of the Poem with accuracy evidently required a great effort of memory. To write it, would have required no more effort, perhaps indeed less, than the average tenour of the Iliad. Now the Invocation to the Muses at the commencement, the most formal and elaborate which the Poems contain, clearly shows that the Bard was about to undertake a weighty task. Thus the Catalogue, together with its introduction, becomes a powerful piece of evidence to show that the Iliad was not written but recited.

Next; the Genealogies of the Greek Catalogue, eleven in number, testify in a remarkable manner to the historic aims of the Poet, which led him to connect all his leading personages with the past, at the very time when he was securing to them a deathless heritage in the future. Again, the Poet has avoided the error of confounding his primary with his secondary leaders. The greater chiefs have their descents traced singly, in various parts of the Iliad, so as to give them due prominence. But in the Catalogue a number of secondary genealogies are massed together.

In his performance of this operation, where a reciting Bard was to lose the aid commonly afforded him by the natural continuity of his subject-matter, Homer has sought for a substitute in a kind of mental figure-drawing. He divides the whole territory of Greece and the Islands into three circles, more or less regular and perfect; with a fourth figure of the nature of a zigzag.

The first circle begins with the Bœotians and ends with Mycenæ; containing nine contingents[1].

The second is a zigzag, beginning with Lacedæmon, and ending with the Aitoloi; and comprises seven contingents[2].

The third is part of a circle of islands, beginning with Crete, and ending with Carpathos and other small islands. This portion gives four contingents[3].

In the fourth, or Thessalian portion[4], it is more difficult, and in some cases hardly feasible, to identify the sites; but, as far as may be, the Poet appears to adhere

---

[1] Il. ii. 424-580. [2] 581-644. [3] 645-680.
[4] 681-759.

to the same circular arrangement. Here also we have nine contingents.

In each, then, of these four divisions of the territory, the Poet makes his figure his guide, and proceeds from each district to the one lying next to it on the proper line, until the figure is completed. Water sometimes intervenes; but no territory seems to be skipped over.

Thus there is a clue all along, except indeed at the points of transition from one division to another. For these, also, he seems to have provided. In each case he ends with a district, the neighbour to which, according to the line of his figure, has already been disposed of. Thus in the first, were he to go beyond Mycenæ, he would find himself among the Bœotians again. So that he is as it were reminded, by this contrivance, to re-commence.

In the Trojan Catalogue, I find but two genealogies; and one of them is that of the Pelasgian leader. Now the Pelasgian blood, it will be remembered, seems to be the common bond between the masses on each side.

In the Greek Catalogue, Homer specifies the respective amounts of the contingents of force supplied from the different portions of the country. This is evidently meant to give to each chief and district his due position, relatively to the rest. In Troas he pursues no such arrangement; for he had no such object. And among the Epicouroi, or Allies[1], there was another difficulty; as they came and went in successive reliefs, whereas the Achaians were a permanent force.

Generally, I cannot but think that the comparison

----

[1] Il. ii. 816-839

of the two Catalogues is highly unfavourable to the
theory which regards Homer as an Asiatic Greek: a
theory which, in my opinion, should also be repudiated
upon more comprehensive grounds. The Greek Catalogue is charged throughout with what I may call
local colour and with visual epithets: epithets which
imply some personal familiarity, and raise up a prospect or scene before the mental eye of a reader or
a hearer. In the fifty-two lines of the Trojan Catalogue, it would be difficult to point out more than
eight of these: the precipitous tops of Tereïè and
Mucalè; the fertile Larissa; the wide-flowing of the
limpid Axios; the eddying Xanthos; the dark water
of Aisepos; the lofty Eruthinoi; the wooded hill of
Pïtheiroi[1]. Four only of these come from Asia Minor
to the south of Troas, with which Homer is supposed
to be so familiar. On the other side of the Ægean,
ten at least of such epithets are found within the thirteen lines that describe the places, which supplied the
Bœotian contingent.

[1] Il. ii. 825, 829, 841, 849, 855, 868, 869, 877.

Section II. *The Plain of Troy*[1].

The leading topical points in the plain of Troy are as follows:—

1. The Scamandrian plain[2], near the river Scamandros, forming the northern and western part of the Trojan plain, and reaching up to or near the Encampment.

2. The Ileïan plain[3], near the city, lying south and perhaps east from it.

3. The Scaian Gates[4], north of the city, the ordinary way of exit to the plain. Near them is the phēgos[5].

4. The Dardanian Gates, south of the city, communicating with Dardania on the hill. Il. xx. 216-218.

5. The junction of the rivers. Il. v. 774.

6. The ford of Xanthos, and the monument of Ilos near it. Il. xxiv.

7. The ἐρινεὸς, or wild fig-tree, near this ford (346-353 and 692-694), and the tomb of Ilos. Here was a σκοπιὴ or place convenient for observation, and a waggon road. All these are near the city. Il. vi. 433; xi. 166, 167; xxii. 145.

8. The Θρωσμὸς, or roll, of the plain near the northern extremity, and the Encampment of the Greeks. Il. x. 160; xi. 56; xx. 3.

9 The Mound of Aisuetes, near enough to the Encampment for observations. Il. ii. 793.

10. The hillock Bateia, in the southern part of the plain, at some distance from the city. Il. ii. 813.

---

[1] Of this subject, no notice was taken in the 'Studies on Homer.'   [2] Il. ii. 465   [3] Il. xxi. 558.
[4] Il. iii. 145, *et alibi.*   [5] Il. vi. 237.

11. The two fountains of Scamandros. Il. xxii. 147.

12. The mouths of the two rivers, distinct one from another. See Il. xii. 21.

13. The quarters of Achilles and of Telamonian Ajax respectively, marking the extremes east and west of the Greek Encampment by the shore. Il. xi. 5-9.

The chief questions which arise are two.

1. In what manner can the description given by Homer of the several parts be combined into a self-consistent whole?

2. In what manner can that description be reconciled with the actual geography of the plain of Troy under stood, as it best may, from its present condition?

The first of these two questions presents no in surmountable difficulty.

We have to imagine an irregular oblong lying north and south; the north end formed by the coast and the Greek line of ships and cantonments, from that of Achilles on the west to that of Ajax on the east, running along it; the eastern side, by Simoeis; the western by Scamandros, with rough and steep banks above, and with marshy lands near the mouth. The southern part of the plain is closed by the roots of Ida; and in the south-western corner lies the city with a gate southwards towards the hill, and towards Dardania which lay within its recesses; also a gate (the Scaian Gate), with the ground descending towards the plain northwards.

Passing from the north towards this gate, and having on the right hand the river, we come along a waggon-road to the wild fig-tree, where is the mound or tomb of Ilos, used apparently as a place of observation, like Batieia and the tomb of Aisuetes[1], at the other end of

[1] Il. Il. 793.

the plain. This is hard by the river. We then have
the Scaian Gate on the left; and farther on are the
two fountains of the Scamandros, near to which Hector
passes, in making the circuit of the city.

It is plain, that there was a communication between
the rivers; but probably one dry in summer; and we
may take notice that it was not in the fierce Scamandros, but in Simoeis, that there lay both heroes and their
spoils; and this in the dust, not in the waters, as Virgil
has vividly, but carelessly, represented [1].

The ford of Xanthos we must understand to be a
ford leading to the westward, not one crossed between
the city and the camp. With these suppositions, the
topography of the plain appears to be self-consistent.

The best examination I have been able to make of
the second question leads me to the conclusion that
the description of Homer cannot be accurately fitted to
the natural features of the plain, as they now are, or
even as we can probably suppose them to have been
some three thousand years ago.

There is no site near the two fountains, on which
the city can have been placed, of such a nature as to
allow of the threefold circuit ascribed to Hector flying,
and to Achilles pursuing him.

The general idea conveyed by the Iliad of the distance between the city and the encampment is, that it
was short. After the second Battle, in Book viii.
Hector holds an Assembly. The Trojans had pressed
upon the Greek entrenchment, and their gathering is
away from the ships, νόσφι νεῶν (v. 490); but this
seems to be explained by what follows as meaning
simply clear of the field of battle, whereon lay the dead

[1] Æn. i. 100.

bodies. And it is expressly called 'near' (ἐγγὺς) that is, near the ships, in Il. ix. 232. But Hector proceeds to give directions for fetching oxen and sheep, with wine and corn, from Ilion for the immediate repast; and herewith the wood for cooking and for watchfires (505-507).

Again, in Il. viii. 532, Hector says, 'to-morrow we shall see whether Diomed will drive me from the ships to the wall (evidently of the city), or whether I shall slay and spoil him.' Now the idea of the pursuit from the ships to the wall and the corresponding movement of the armies, are wholly inapplicable to a distance of five or six or more miles.

On the whole, the length of the plain, and the distance of the two fountains from the shore, are not in harmony with the descriptions of the forward and retrograde operations of the armies which took place on the great day of battles, ending with the unwilling retirement of the Sun in Il. xviii. 239. Other inconsistencies of a like nature might be pointed out.

On the other hand, the number of the natural features pourtrayed, and the actual correspondence of most of them, when taken individually, with those we now discern, establish the general authenticity of the scene. They also lead to the conclusion that Homer may have seen it 'in person; or may, by the power of a vigorous imagination, have conceived its general character, and the relative position of the points, from the narratives of eye-witnesses.

But it seems plain, that he did not sing either on the spot, or to persons minutely acquainted with the topography; and not unlikely, that he generalised his materials, and used them with a certain licence, as a poet, for the purposes of his art.

Lastly: I cannot but observe the analogy between this loose placement of objects, each of which singly had been vividly conceived, and the indefinite method of handling geographical points on a large scale, in the Outer Voyage of the Odyssey. In the latter case we are morally certain that he spoke at secondhand; and this tends to diminish the unlikelihood that the Song of Troy was composed without personal experience of the spot to aid the work.

SECTION III. *The Outer Geography.*

The geography of Greek experience, as exhibited by Homer, is limited, speaking generally, to the Ægean and its coasts, with the Propontis as its limit in the North-east, with Crete for a southern boundary, and with the addition of the western coast of the peninsula and its islands, as far northward as the Leucadian rock. Respecting that rock, and respecting the conformation of Corfù (Scheriè) and the shape of Ithaca, Homer had some accurate information. But a visit to that region in 1858-9 convinced me that the Poet, who described the view of Corfu[1] from the north as lying on the sea like a shield, never could have seen it; that he was not personally acquainted with the topography of Ithaca; that he guessed at, and over-estimated, its size; and, as is demonstrable from several passages in the Odyssey[2], that he has given it a wrong relative position.

[1] Od. v. 281.
[2] Especially Od. iv. 844-847 and Od. ix. 25-26; lines which it has in vain been attempted to force into conformity with actual geography.

Beyond the limits I have named, all ordinary navigation was conducted by the Phœnicians; and upon these mariners, possibly in a few cases on their settlers or colonists in Greece, Homer must have depended for his information. At any period, such information could only give rise to very inaccurate geographical results. But we cannot even expect a resemblance to the actual face of earth, in a case where not only are the points described by those who would naturally seek both to excite and to deter, but where they could be nowhere arranged and digested, except only in the brain of the Poet, ideally compounding in the mind what fell upon the ear.

It appears to me, that interpreters have been wholly wrong, when they have laboriously strained their endeavours to fit the Outer Geography of Homer to the actual surface of the globe. Unwilling to recognise error in his descriptions, they have closed their eyes to much really indisputable evidence of it that the text supplies; and have, after a sort, assigned to him geographical knowledge which he did not possess, at the expense of that mental self-consistency, and that plastic power, with both of which he was endowed in a degree never surpassed among the sons of men. It was no reproach to him, if he believed in a great sea, connecting the Adriatic and the Euxine; but it would have been at variance with all the rules of his mental action, if he had spoken without any definite meaning, when he treats of sailing and floating distances, of the direction of the wind, or of the position of the stars: if he had forgotten his distinction between land of the continent and island, or if he had placed the sunrise in the West.

No doubt his descriptions are very vague in some

cases, and especially as to the Island of Calypso. The
fact seems to be, that he was misled not only by falsehood, but by truth. When informants, speaking of the
same region, described it as one of all but perpetual
day, and also as one of night all but perpetual, although
both these statements were true, he had not the key to
their truth in the annual revolution of the earth combined with the declension of its axis from the perpendi-
cular; and thus he could only seek refuge in vagueness
from contradiction. Again, when he heard of great sea-
currents, which set through the Bosphorus, the Straits
of Messina, the Straits of Yenikalè, and the Straits of
Gibraltar respectively, what means could he possess,
considering the palpable points of resemblance, of effectually separating each one of these from the others?
Hence it is, as we shall find, that he carries his Thrinakiè (or Sicily) to the immediate vicinity of the Bosphorus, consecrates it to the Sun, and places there the
Oxen and the Nymphs belonging to that deity.

The proper object of our search is, not a forced accommodation of Homer's conceptions to a basis of fact
with which he was unacquainted, but simply a copy, if
we can get it, of the map, which he constructed in his
brain from the materials supplied by Phœnician discourse or legend. And the proper mode of search must
be, to take for our primary authority his own statements of distance, direction, and physical features; and
then, but only in subordination to this rule, to see
where and how far they fit any portion of what actually
exists; moreover, whether they so correspond with it as
it is situate in its proper place, or as he has arbitrarily
transplanted it to some other.

There are fractions of border-land, between the Inner

or home, and the Outer or wholly foreign sphere, which
receive somewhat of a mixed treatment. To this group
Scheriè belongs: and the land of the Lotos-eaters possibly
may be but another phase of Egypt. Epirus again, and
the country of the Glactophagoi and other nations, over
whom Zeus directs his view at the outset of the Thirteenth Iliad[1], belong to this zone, as does Phœnicia,
if not Cyprus.

Our data for constructing an Homeric map of the
Outer Geography seems to be chiefly as follows :—

1. The points of the horizon, marked for morning
and evening respectively, connect themselves with two
of Homer's winds. His Zephuros is akin to zophos,
and knephas, the darkness[2]: his Euros to eôs[3] the
morning, and perhaps to his euroeis, an epithet used
by him four times only, and in each case to describe
the Underworld. Sunrise and sunset, with him, verge,
though not perhaps with uniform precision, to the
south of East, and to the north of West respectively.

2. And such are the directions, from which Zephuros
and Euros blow. But it is plain, as Zephuros blows
from Thrace upon the Ægean[4], that his range also
approximates to the north pole on the western side :
and further, that, as Boreas blows from the same
quarter, he takes up the next arc of the horizon, and
may be defined as a north-north-east wind ; a title which
the same wind, as far as my memory serves me, still
bears in the Adriatic. Again, Euros and Notos, the third
and fourth of Homer's winds, are associated together as
a pair, raising the Ægean from the South nearly as

---

[1] Il. xiii. 3-6.   [2] Buttmann, Lexil. in voc. κέλαινός.
[3] Liddell and Scott, in voc.   [4] Il. ix. 4.

Boreas and Zephuros catch it from the North. The greater portion however of the arc covered by the southern pair is to the east of the Pole, by the northern pair to the west. It is not probable that Homer had names for winds from all points of the compass, or that he did more than mark inartificially the directions from which the winds of his actual experience principally blew. Notos may probably be a South wind, blowing from near that pole on either side: Euros is between Notos and the east.

3. Next to these, we have to mark Homer's measures of sea distances. Of extended land distances, he has no measures at all; a separate proof of the very limited range of the land experience of the Greeks.

(*a*) Homer measures the time of a voyage from Troas to Phthia; and from Crete to Egypt [1]. The result of these measurements is, to give some ninety miles as a good average day's journey of a ship using sails or oars, under favourable circumstances. With peculiar good fortune, that distance might be exceeded.

(*b*) In a floating or drift passage on the waves, we can trace Homer's idea of what was possible by the supposed transit of Odysseus from a point near Crete to the Thesprotoi. It appears to be about half the rate of a ship's motion, or two miles an hour.

(*c*) The floating of a raft may probably be taken at a little more, or two and a half.

Thus we should have ninety-six miles, forty-eight miles, and sixty miles a day as our results respectively.

These are, of course, but rude measures, yet they are not unimportant aids in our inquiry.

(*d*) The rate of a Scherian ship is described by com-

[1] Il. Ix. 362. Od. xiv. 257.

parison with a bird's flight, or a four-horse chariot
scouring the plain. 'It would go,' says Alkinoos, 'to
Euboea (or perhaps to Euboea and back) in a day.' We
cannot, I think, put it at less than thrice the speed
of the ordinary ship.

The key to the great contrast between the Outer
Geography and the facts of nature lies in the belief
of Homer, that a great sea occupied the space, where
we know the heart of the European Continent to lie.
Proofs and indications of this belief are to be found,
such as to place it beyond denial or even doubt.

(*a*) For example, we find one of these in the voyage
of the Phaiakes to Euboea, which was certainly not
supposed to take place round the whole coast of the
Greek Peninsula, for the Phaiakes are supposed to hang
as strangers on the outer skirt of the Greek world, not
to traverse all its chief waters[1]. It must therefore
have been a passage by a supposed northern sea.

(*b*) When Hermes travels from Olympos to the Island
of Calypso, he passes over Pieria, and then sweeps
down upon the sea[2]. That sea must therefore have been
in the north or north-east. The journey of Herè over
Pieria to Emathia and Lemnos[3] shows the acquaintance of the Poet with the general direction of those
countries.

(*c*) The Shades of the Suitors, on their way to the
Underworld, take a northerly direction, past the Leucadian rock, in a journey towards the stream of Ocean,
and the gates of the Sun[4]. Can there be a clearer
declaration than this that they were to pass into the

---

[1] Od. vii. 19-26.   [2] Od. v. 43-58.
[3] Il. xiv. 225-230.   [4] Od. xxiv. 11-14.

east along the Adriatic—apparently avoiding the known land of Greece on their journey?

Next, Homer appears to have compounded into one group two sets of Phœnician reports concerning the entrance from without to the Thalassa or Mediterranean: one of them referring to the Straits of Messina, with their Scylla and Charybdis; the other to the Bosphorus and its Planctai. It is also very easy to believe, that with each of these narrow passages he associated another strait beyond it at a distance of several hundred miles, namely the Straits of Gibraltar with the first, and the Straits of Yenikalè with the second: and the striking resemblance of these last to one another, in the cardinal point of presenting at all times an inward flowing current, would tend to favour the confusion. The Ocean was, in Homer's system, the feeder of the Sea: he tells us in the Odyssey distinctly enough of one sea-passage to the Ocean, but he nowhere glances at the existence of any second access.

This Ocean mouth, to which he conducts Odysseus, is unequivocally placed in the East, near the island of Aiaia, and the rising Sun. To the left and North, lie the people of the Kimmerians hid in fog, for which the Black Sea is even now said to be remarkable. Kirkè is the daughter of Aietes, to whose country Jason had sailed through the Bosphorus. And giving the darkness a place near the dawn is a proceeding necessary to complete the idea of morning. The mouth of the Underworld is farther southward, inasmuch as Odysseus is carried to it by the Wind Boreas, up the Ocean-Stream. The whole of his voyage, up to this point, is accomplished without his being obliged to traverse any dangerous narrows. But, pursued by the vengeance of Poseidon, who rules

the outer or Phœnician Thalassa, he eschews returning by the same open, lengthened, and menacing
route. Kirkè accordingly apprises him of a short
passage, by which he may soon find himself once more
within the margin of the Greek or Ægean waters.
This is the Bosphorus; near which the Poet plants
Thrinakiè, an island evidently projected in his mind
on the basis of ideas derived from Sicily, and with it
the Scylla and Charybdis of the Straits of Messina.

This transportation of western features to the East
is further illustrated by the Homeric treatment of
Atlas. For, associated though he be in general tradition with the coast of Africa, and the Straits of Gibraltar, he is with Homer the Father of Calypso, whose
island plainly lies in the northern and eastern waters,
since it seems to be Boreas who brings Odysseus from
thence to Ithaca.

The general result of this blending is, that the supposed
Ocean mouth in the Euxine gets the benefit of the open
sea-route which really leads to the Straits of Gibraltar;
and the real Ocean mouth at Gibraltar has credit for
being placed in a northern latitude and a distant eastern
longitude ; while the Faro and the Bosphorus, in
consequence of this identification, are brought near to
one another : each group of reports thus throwing
its own separate attributes into the common stock.

The Bosphorus must be considered not as belonging
to the Greek world, but yet as fast linked to it, and
therefore as a point fixed by practical experience, and
not to be removed. And even if we could not give
probable ground for Homer's having placed the Faro
near it, the fact would still be undeniable from the
evidence of the text, and must be recognised in any

transcript of the Outer Geography which we may attempt.

The island of Calypso, again, must be in the north:

(*a*) From the direction taken, as we have seen, by Hermes.

(*b*) Because fire is kept burning there, which indicates a climate requiring it. Kirkè has none in her island [1].

(*c*) Because it is the omphalos[2], or central point of a vast sea, spreading on all sides, with which nothing to the east, west, or south of Greece corresponds either in nature, or in the ideas of Homer.

(*d*) Because the meaning of her name, the Concealer, and the length of the voyage back to Scheriè, indicate her dwelling as belonging to a region wholly untravelled and unknown to the Greeks.

(*e*) Because Odysseus [3] is apparently carried to it by Notos. And the general rule of the Wanderings is, that southerly winds bear Odysseus away from home, while northerly ones carry him towards it.

Again, the association of Calypso with the Eastern mythology prevents us from placing her in the Northwest, where lies the country of the Laistrugones; and keeps her in relation with the east rather than the west of North.

The island of Aiaiè is bound to an eastward position by the name and character of Kirkè; by its relation to Aietes, and thus to Jason, and his voyage; by the names of Helios, the father of Calypso, and of her mother Persè, an appellation savouring, in Homer, of the far East, to which the Persians of that day belonged [4];

---

[1] Od. v. 60; x. 210 seqq.   [2] Od. i. 50.

[3] Od. xii. 426, 447.

[4] Rawlinson, Anc. Monarchies, vol. iv. p. 349.

by its being the point of Sunrise; and by the residence of Dawn.

All particular conjecture respecting any position for these islands is, however, vague: the several points of the scheme of Homer in the Outer Geography were determined by relation to each other broadly conceived, and by directions generally taken, rather than by any attempt at exactitude even in mental measurement.

With these *data*, I now proceed to note the several stages of the Voyage of Odysseus.

1. From Troy to the Kikones on the north coast of the Ægean; in a region strictly belonging to the Inner Geography[1].

2. From the Kikones, Boreas (N. N. E. wind) carries Odysseus to Cape Malea, prevents him from rounding it, and drives him out to sea, where nine days of bad or plaguy winds (olooi anemoi) bring him to the land of the Lotos-Eaters, which appears to be like an Egypt in a new dress. As five days[2] drive a ship from Crete to Egypt, we must suppose that nine imply some considerable westing, and place the Lotos-Eaters on the African coast along the Syrtis Major. We are now in the Outer Sphere[3].

3. From the Lotophagoi to the Kuklopes, we have no direct guide afforded by the text, except that it was a voyage onward, and that the Kuklopes live on a mainland[4], not an island. From this mainland they had, at an earlier date, displaced their neighbours the Phaiakes, who, being a nautical people, passed over and settled in Scheriè. Therefore we are probably to

---

[1] Od. ix. 39.
[3] Od. ix. 67, 80-84.
[2] Od. xiv. 253.
[4] Od. vi. 4-8.

place them in Iapugia, the heel of Italy, over against Scheriè [1].

4. From the land of the Kuklopes, perhaps called by Homer Hupereiè [2], Odysseus proceeds to the island Aioliè [3], and Aiolos gives him a Zephyr (N. W. wind) which would carry him home to Ithaca. Therefore the island of Aiolos (whether related to Stromboli as its prototype or not) lies to the north and west of Ithaca, with a clear sea-passage between [4]. Then a tempest drives him back to Aioliè, after nine days of Zephuros, and when the ships were in full sight of Ithaca [5]. Thus we have a very good measurement from the direct evidence of the text: and Aioliè lies at sea and at from eight hundred to a thousand miles from Ithaca, in a north-westerly direction.

5. From Aioliè, Odysseus comes, in seven days of rowing, to Laistrugoniè, the city of Lamos, evidently far north, as it is the land where one day runs into another [6]. We are now seventeen days from Ithaca in a direction north and west. There can be little doubt that the prototype of this place was supplied by a tradition brought from the north-western main. The very marked description of the harbour, and the epithet (a i pu) applied to the city, correspond closely, I am told, with one or more of those on the south Devonshire and south Cornish coasts. But the site in the open sea, and the description of the continuous day, might more properly be taken from the Faro Islands. The size of the people, especially of the women [7], suggests a Scandinavian race; the want of cultivation [8] a position

[1] Od. ix. 105.   [2] Od. vi. 4.   [3] Od. ix. 565; x. 1.
[4] Od. x. 25, 46.   [5] Od. x. 28, 54.   [6] Od. x. 80-83.
[7] Od. x. 113.   [8] Od. x. 98.

in the far north, and with a climate suited for pasture, not for tillage.

6. From Laistrugoniè we pass, without indication, to Aiaiè[1]. I have already shown that this island is absolutely fixed, according to the mind of Homer, in the East, as Aioliè is in the West. It cannot be in the remote North, because no fire is used. It is not very likely to lie to the south of East, because of the neighbourhood of Kimmerian fog. This is a difficulty for Homer, since his Dawn ought to be somewhat to the south of East. He tries (it may seem) to escape, like some of his Trojan heroes, in a fog; for he declares that, on arriving here, Odysseus could make out nothing about his position relatively to the Dark and the Dawn, the Sunset and the Sunrise[2]. This difficulty of course cannot wholly be removed: but it rather bears upon latitudes, than on longitude or distance eastwards. I place Aiaiè at a spot near the Colchis of Aietes; adding that we are by no means to assert positively that the island lies to the northward of East, even though the balance of evidence may lie in that direction.

From Aiaiè, one day's favouring wind takes Odysseus to the Ocean-mouth, hard by the Kimmerian darkness[3]. It is Boreas that carries him southward, or up the stream, it is hard to say which[4]. After landing, the party pursue the course of the shore, in the same direction, to the entrance of the Underworld; we know not at what distance. Thence they return to Aiaiè. No fresh indication is given.

7. From Aiaiè to the Island of the Sirens. No

[1] Od. и. 133-135.   [2] Od. x. 189-192.
[3] Od. xi. 1-19.   [4] Od. i. 507.

specific indication is afforded us; except that apparently
the passage is a short one. We are now within the
virtual limits of the eastern and southern Euxine [1].

8. From the Sirens, by Scylla and Charybdis, leaving
the (neighbouring) Planctai aside, to Thrinakiè. This
evidently is also a short passage [2]. Odysseus is here
detained by Notos (S. S. W.) chiefly, but also by Euros;
both of them blowing from the southern hemisphere.

9. From Thrinakiè, Notos having ceased to blow, he
is able to pursue the homeward route. The ship founders
in a violent gale from the North-west [3]. Notos
carries him back in one night to Scylla and Charybdis,
which he traverses in safety [4] after great peril; and
then, drifting on, apparently with the same wind, he
reaches, on the tenth day, Ogugiè, the Island of
Calypso, the quasi-central point of the great (northern)
sea [5].

10. From Ogugiè to Scheriè; never called an island,
but called the land of the Phaiakes, which may be on
account of its size, for the Poet appears to have considered it as an island [6]. This is a raft voyage, and the
eighteenth day brings him within view of Scheriè. Then
comes the storm, with a hurricane of all the winds [7].
The raft founders [8]; and Odysseus drifts, with a wind
(Boreas) sent by Athenè, to Scheriè, where he arrives
on the third day [9].

In this passage he is ordered to observe the stars,

[1] Od. xii. 149-154, 165-167; also 39, and xxiii. 326.
[2] Od. xii. 201, 261, 262; xi. 166, 167; xxiii. 327-329.
[3] Od. xii. 403.   [4] Od. xii. 424, 427-430, 442-446.
[5] Od. xii. 447, 448; xxiii. 333; l. 50.   [6] Od. vi. 204.
[7] Od. v. 263, 278, 293, 331, 345.   [8] Od. v. 370.
[9] Od. v. 382-398.

and to steer with Arctos looking over against, or opposite, his left[1]; that is to say, on his right. The
exact phrase used is not a common one in Homer, and
it has usually been translated 'on his right.' If this were
correct, the island of Calypso must lie in the north-
west. This would not so well agree with the winds
indicated, though not expressed; namely, Boreas for
the passage home, and Notos for the passage from the
Bosphorus to Ogugiè. Nor would it agree as well
with the time allowed for reaching Ogugiè from the
Bosphorus. Besides, we have to keep in mind the fact,
that all other associations draw Calypso eastward.

11. From Scheriè to Ithaca; a passage of some sixteen or eighteen hours in the hawk-ship; beginning
early in the day, and ending before the next dawn[2].

Allowing for the rapidity of the voyage, it is plain
that Homer placed his Scheriè farther north than the
original Corfù, which may be eighty miles from Ithaca.
Eighteen days of raft voyage, with an allowance for
the distance of Scheriè, when first seen, will place
Ogugiè at more than eleven hundred miles from Ithaca.
Ten days of floatage from the Bosphorus will give five
hundred miles, or thereabouts, from that point. We
have already found that Laistrugoniè is near seventeen hundred miles from Ithaca. All these routes are
over the open sea. Speaking generally, Homer gives to
the voyage of Odysseus all the world he knows of,
lying from South, round by West and North, and then
far to the East of Greece; except only what in terms
of slight outline he gives to the tour of Menelaos,
between the East and South[3]. The two routes diverge

---

[1] Od. v. 277.   [2] Od. xiii. 18, 78, 86, 93–95.
[3] Od. iv. 80–85.

at the Malean promontory[1]. Perhaps it is because the
real Phœnicia lies on the border of the Outer world, in
the south, that he has given us an idealised Phœnician
people upon the border-line towards the north, and the
name Scheriè is possibly Suriè (Syria), travestied for
the ear, as the Phaiakes are the Phoinikes.

The general arrangements of Homer show that he
thought the Earth and Sea had a great extension northwards, but give no idea of great distances in the longi-
tudinal line, or from east to west. How far he carried
it to the south, we have no means of judging. We
know that the Shield of Achilles represented the form
of the Earth, with the River Okeanos for its rim[2].
Now a shield in general is sometimes compared with
the moon by Homer; but he does not say the full moon:
and the prevailing epithets for the shield would tend to
show an oval form, or one adapted to cover the entire
figure[3]; the same form as that indicated in the formula
of the Spartan mother for a soldier son: 'bring it, or be
brought upon it.' The natural shape of the hide, of
which the name is often applied to a shield, likewise
seems to favour this belief. And such a form of the
shield apparently agrees with the figure which the descriptions of the Outer Geography tend to give to the
Earth, in conjunction with the representation of the
Shield of Achilles.

The noble conception of a great circumfluent River
was probably founded on a combination of a double set
of reports; the one, of great currents setting into the
Thalassa, or Mediterranean Sea, and seeming to feed
it, such as those of Yenikalè, the Bosphorus, Gibraltar;

---

[1] Od. lii. 318.   [2] Il. xix. 374.
[3] Il. xi. 32; xxv. 646; and xiii. 130; ix. 537; x. 15.

the other, of Outer Waters, such as the Caspian, the
Persian Gulph, and probably the Red Sea.

The name Kimmeria is derived by some from the
Arabic *kabm*, black; Maiotis from *maneth*, meaning
death[1]; and Tartaros is taken to be the reduplication
of the *tar* in *tarik*, the Persian word for darkness.
The seeming contradiction of perpetual light and perpetual darkness in the north is of course removed for
us, who know that both reports are true, but for different
seasons of the year.

[1] Welsford on the English Language, pp. 75, 76, 88.   Bleek,
Persian Vocab. (Grammar, p. 170).

CHAPTER XIV.

PLOTS, CHARACTERS, AND SIMILES.

SECTION I. *The Plots of the Poems ; especially of the Iliad.*

THE works of Homer are not constructed upon
speculative models. His is the fresco painting of
poetry. He is a man singing to men, and to men
immensely his inferiors. He is perhaps more under the
conditions of the orator, than of the modern poet. He
cannot store up or record his thought ; there is but one
depository for it, upon the living tablets of the heart,
and within its deep recesses. Hence, in both the Iliad
and the Odyssey, we have that rush and exuberance of
life, which result from the common action between the
Bard and his hearers, the separate currents of whose
existences seem to be thrown into one great volume,
never exhausted, though gently slackened from time
to time to meet the conditions of our nature.

He is also an artist, living by his art ; addressing
himself by his genius to universal nature, but by his
circumstances to his country, and to the several squares
of that tesselated nation, each with its local patriotism
and limited traditions, as well as with its portion in
the common inheritance of Hellenism.

Viewed in the light of considerations such as these, the plot of the Odyssey is simple, without knots or breaks of texture, and generally well-devised if not uniformly sustained; but that of the Iliad is, as far as I may presume to judge, in the main a consummate work of art. The mechanism is double throughout. But the train of action on Olympos never clashes with that in Troas, and nowhere impairs the free, natural, and thoroughly human character of that part of the business, which is in the hands of mortals. At the same time, it is so contrived as to assist the Poet in overcoming one of his greatest difficulties; which was, to maintain a clear and ample martial superiority on the part of the Greek chieftains, and yet to give them in Troy a thoroughly worthy and sufficient object for their prowess. What in this respect was lacking in the Trojan leaders, has been supplied by the Theotechny, or divine movement of the Poem.

The most favourite topic of objectors to the plot of the Iliad has been the length of time during which Achilles is kept out of sight. From the Second to the Eighth Book inclusive, and again from the Twelfth to the Fifteenth, he does not appear upon the stage.

Now it is by this withdrawal of Achilles that Homer obtains scope for his other heroes, who were dwarfed by the presence of that colossal figure. The moment he appears they become insignificant; they are almost invisible in the blaze of his light. But, by means of his absence, Diomed, Ajax, Agamemnon, Idomeneus, and likewise Odysseus in the Doloneia, and Menelaos in the Seventeenth Book as well as in the Third, have each their opportunities of distinction. In this manner a double object is gained. First, satisfaction is given to the local sentiment of the parts of Greece, with which these heroes are severally connected. In the second place, by this series of personages, embodying the idea and practice of martial prowess as it was commonly understood, Homer constructs, as it were, a platform, on and from which he can build upwards the astonishing figure of his Achilles, for which the reader has been prepared by a *propaideia*, or preliminary course of greatness, on the scale on which it commonly (as far as it is common at all) appears among men.

But perhaps the most emphatic confutation of such objections is to be found in the total failure of all attempts to combine the ideas of the objectors into anything like one positive sense or view, or to improve the Iliad by the process of excision. While this negative criticism treads its hopeless and dreary circle of doubt without progress or achievement, the Poem itself confirms and enlarges, from generation to generation, its hold upon civilised mankind; and the translations in which it is (of necessity so imperfectly) represented, but which carry it beyond the limited circle of Greek scholarship, multiply in this nineteenth century of ours, and in the very focus of its keenest activity, at a rate beyond all precedent.

The main steps of the action of the Iliad seem to be these. Upon the Wrong perpetrated by Agamemnon arises the Wrath, and thereupon the Secession, of the prime hero, in whose marvellous character the Greek nationality is to find its supreme satisfaction. And this character, not the fate of Troy, is the true central thread of the great epic. On the absence of Achilles, the Greeks, after a panic and recovery, decide upon doing as well as they can without him. Though their

superior prowess is fully maintained, they are losers on
the whole; and they seek the aid of a rampart, which
previously they had disdained. Here is the first marked
triumph of the Wrath. Driven back upon their works,
they are themselves threatened with a siege. The
infirm spirit of Agamemnon gives way, and he a second
time utters counsels of flight, to which the chivalrous
spirit of the other chiefs will not submit. A mission
to the tent of Achilles is substituted, offering splendid
gifts and the maid Briseis; a reparation morally imperfect, for there is no confession of the wrong. To the
inflamed and inexorable spirit of Achilles they afford
matter for fresh exasperation, and the Envoys return
baffled in their aim. Here is the second triumph of the
Wrath. Not till the ships are about to burn, will he
entertain the thought to interfere.

The Greeks fight again; and, a second time, with
martial superiority, yet with an unfavourable issue.
The rampart is broken by the brave Sarpedon, a chief
be it remarked of Greek associations, and apparently
the best warrior fighting on the side of Troy. Fire
reaches the fleet. But Achilles does not go forth. In
his towering pride, he will even now only send Patroclos, a semblance of himself; and this, too, with the
vindictive wish that they two, all else having perished,
may alone dash down the sacred battlements of Troy[1].

This, the third great triumph of the Wrath, seems
also to mark the point of its overflow into excess; and
the moral[2] order must avenge itself, in the divine de-

---

[1] Il. xvi. 97–100.
[2] See a fuller discussion on the Plots of the two Poems in
Studies on Homer, vol. iii. Aoidos, Sect. 5.

crees, and through the persons of men. By divine intervention, after acts of might unsurpassed by the other
chiefs, Patroclos is slain, and Achilles receives a punishment, in recesses of his nature more profound even
than those penetrated and possessed by the Wrath; those
recesses, wherein dwelt his intense affection for his
friend. That which was to have been the last triumph
of his wounded pride, namely, that not he but his
deputy should repel the attack which all the other chiefs
had failed to baffle, now becomes the cause of an agony
so intense, as by far to surpass, both in duration and
in intensity, the emotions he had suffered from anger.

The remainder of the fiery current, thus diverted
from the Greeks, he turns upon the Trojans. When he
goes forth as a warrior, we seem to feel as if we had seen
or heard of no warriors before. The King repents, and
makes restitution. Hector is slain. The Greeks have
been punished for the wrong which they did, or allowed.
Achilles has been punished for allowing indignation
to degenerate into revenge. The mutilation and dis-
honouring of the body of his slain antagonist now
became to him a second idol, stirring the great deep of
his passions, and bewildering his mind. Thus, in
paying off his old debt to the eternal laws, he has
already contracted a new one. Again, then, his proud
will must be taught to bow. Hence, as Mr. Penn has
well shown[1], the necessity of the Twenty-fourth Book,
with its beautiful machinery.

On the other side, the death of Hector opens the
way for the retribution due to the great guilt of Troy.
The recovery of his remains is a tribute to his personal

[1] Primary Argument of the Iliad, pp. 241-273.

piety; and, after the fierce excitement of the action
of the Poem, sheds a softened light upon its close. If
the plot of the Iliad is to be condemned, where is the
epic that can claim either admiration or acquittal?

Section II.   *Some Characters[1] of the Poems.*

1. Achilles.

The character of Achilles, as I view it, differs from
that of all other heroes of poetry and romance in these
respects: it is more intense; it is more colossal in
scale; it ranges over a wider compass, from the borders
of savagery to the most tender emotions and the most
delicate refinements. Yet all its parts are so accurately
graduated, and so nicely interwoven, that the whole
tissue is perfectly consistent with itself.

The self-government of such a character is indeed
very partial. But any degree of self-government is a
wonder, when we consider over what volcanic forces it
is exercised. It is a constantly recurring effort at rule
over a constantly recurring rebellion; and there is a
noble contrast between the strain put upon his strength,
in order to suppress his own passion, and the masterful
ease with which he prostrates all his enemies in the
field. The command, always in danger, is never wholly
lost. It is commonly re-established by a supreme and
desperate struggle; and sometimes, as in the first
Assembly after the intervention of Athenè[2], we see

---

[1] The reader should, on the Greek characters of Homer, consult Col. Mure's History of Greek Literature, vol. I.

[2] Il. I. 219-346.

the tide of passion flowing to a point at which it resembles a horse that has gained its utmost speed, yet remains under the full control of its rider.

Ferocity is an element in his character, but is not its base. It is always grounded in, and springing from, some deeper sentiment, of which it is the manifestation. His ferocity towards the Greeks grows out of the intensity of his indignation at the foul wrong done, with every heightening circumstance of outward insult, not merely to him, but in his person to every principle of honour, right, and justice, in the matter of Briseis; as well as to the real attachment he felt for her. His ferocity towards Hector is the counterpart and recoil of the intensity of his passionate love for the dead Patroclos.

Magnitude, grandeur, majesty, form the framework on which Homer has projected the character of Achilles. And these are in their truest forms; those forms which contract to touch the smaller, as they expand to grasp the greater things. The scope of this character is like the sweep of an organ over the whole gamut, from the lowest bass to the highest treble, with all its diversities of tone and force as well as pitch. From the fury of the first Assembly, he calms down to receive with courtesy the pursuivants who demand Briseis. From the gentle pleasure of the lyre, he kindles into the stern excitement of the magnificent Debate of the Ninth Book. From his terrible vengeance against the torn limbs of Hector he melts into tears, at the view and the discourse of Piiam. The sea, that home of marvels, presents no wider, no grander contrasts, nor offers us an image more perfect according to its kind in each of its varying moods. Foils,

too, are employed with skill to exalt the hero.
The half-animated bulk and strength of Ajax (who was
also greatly beautiful[1]) exhibit to us the mere clay of
Achilles, without the vivifying fire. The beauty of
Nireus[2], wedded to effeminacy, sets off the transcendant, and yet manful and heroic, beauty of Achilles;
and the very ornaments of gold, which in Nastes the
Carian[3] only suggest Asiatic luxury and relaxation,
when they are borne on the person of the great Achaian
hero, seem but a new form of tribute to his glorious
manhood.

2. ODYSSEUS.

The high quality of Homer's portraitures is in no
way better apprehended, than by the clearness of the
distinctions between the personages who most approximate. Odysseus receives in the Odyssey a development,
which raises him, as a protagonist, almost to the level
of Achilles; but in the Iliad, while he is separated from
Nestor by some twenty years of juniority, these two
characters bear a resemblance which some might mistake for repetition. But, in truth, they are radically
distinct, both in speech and action. Nestor's eloquence
is gentle and flowing, with a decided flavour of egotism
and of garrulity. That of Odysseus is masculine and
compressed: when he refers to himself, it is only to
enhance his own obligation, in a great crisis, to act
as it demands[4]; and he never wastes a word. The
sagacity of Nestor is addressed to questions where calm
judgment, and the weight given by age and great ex-

---

[1] Od. xi. 469.   [2] Il. ii. 671.   [3] Il. ii. 872.
[4] Il. il. 259–264.

K k

perience, are alone required; the interpositions of
Odysseus are in cases, where vehement impulses and
strong passions are to be encountered, and where
the presence of mind, which can face a crisis, is indispensable. He checks and recalls the whole army from
its tumultuous rush homewards; he undertakes the
burden of the remonstrance and petition to Achilles.
But the interposition of Nestor, in the great Debate of
the First Book, is only employed by the Poet when
the matter has already, by the direct interposition of
Athenè, been reduced to an issue of words alone. To
untie a knot is the office of Nestor; to stem a torrent,
or scale a frowning barrier, is the business of Odysseus.
Again, and more generally, Nestor heals differences by
a soothing interposition, and offers suggestions: Odysseus constructs wider plans, but the specialty of his
case is this, that he executes what he designs. He has
touched that period of life when the faculties of the
mind are fully ripened, and the bodily powers are consolidated, but not yet decayed. Nestor belongs to one
more advanced; when the mind, without acquiring
vigour, in the main retains it, but when the province
of bodily action is narrowed by comparative infirmity,
and the person becomes as it were a head without a
hand, a dependent instead of a self-subsistent organism.

The character of Odysseus, as a whole, is admirably
balanced between daring and prudence, both of which
are carried in him to the highest degree. The picture is
however diversified by two occasions, on each of which
he records his having failed in his usual circumspection.
On visiting the cave of Poluphemos, his companions ad-
vise him to be content with carrying off a supply of cheese,
and retiring; but he determines to remain and see the

monster [1]. And after the escape from the cave and the
re-embarkation, while his men try to keep him quiet,
he persists in exasperating the Cyclops with his stinging
addresses [2]. In both these cases we may discern a
fault; yet not a fault alone, but the irresistible aspira-
tion of genius to measure itself with danger, and to
pierce boldly into the unknown.

Odysseus is represented as somewhat wanting in one
element of the beauty of the Homeric hero; namely,
amplitude of stature. Menelaos is taller by the head
and shoulders [3]; and the Cyclops despises him for his
deficiency in height [4]. But that his frame was otherwise well developed and powerful is manifest, as he
was more majestic than Menelaos when they sate
down [5]; and also from his wrestling on equal terms
with the huge Ajax [6], and from his extraordinary feats
of strength and endurance in the Odyssey. But it is
observable that, amidst the long list of epithets bestowed upon him, none have reference to personal
beauty, except when, in Scheriè, Athenè had endowed
him with it in a manner, which seems to have gone
much beyond mere restoration from his weather-beaten
aspect [7]. He seems to speak of himself, even among
the Phaiakes, as not possessed of this special gift equally
with them [8]. On the other hand, we ought perhaps to
set the attachment of Calypso as tending in the opposite
direction; and when he returns to Ithaca, Athenè dis-
guises him by wrinkling his fair flesh, and by spoiling his
hair, now auburn but elsewhere hyacinthine [9]. His age,

[1] Od. ix. 224.   [2] Od. ix. 492-502.   [3] Il. iii. 210.
[4] Od. ix. 515.   [5] Il. iii. 211.   [6] Il. xxiv. 709 seqq.
[7] Od. vi. 227-235.   [8] Od. viii. 166-175.
[9] Od. vi. 231; xiii. 399.

too, is of course to be taken into account. Perhaps it is on this ground that Homer may have meant to ascribe to him majesty, rather than simple beauty, of countenance.

Although a prudence ever wakeful, and sometimes leaning towards craft, is the most commonly noticed characteristic of Odysseus, and became in after ages the key-note of the character, it is in Homer only one of several features highly distinctive, by means of which the Poet has raised this extraordinary conception to something very near a parity of rank with his Achilles. Though he does not compete with the son of Peleus in his grand prerogatives, in each one of them he is left second to no other hero. He wrestles with Ajax in the Twenty-third Iliad, and beats him in the contest for the Arms of Achilles, thereby establishing for himself the second place among the Greek chieftains. The depth of his passion, and the power of his eloquence, as they are exhibited in the encounter with Eurualos, if they are still behind Achilles in each point, are before those of every other Greek. But by way of compensation for their being only second, Homer has awarded to him a many-sidedness, such as is possessed by no other hero. He is a master not only in war, but in government, and in every industrial pursuit; and the sole approach that we find in the Poems to anything like Fine Art from the hand of a Greek, is in the bed[1] which he had wrought. There is yet another capacity in which Homer has assigned him a clear pre-eminence; the capacity of father and husband, of a model of the domestic affections. After an absence of near twenty years, he is still yearning for the day of escape from the arms of

[1] Od. xxlii. 195–201.

a goddess, that he may return to his wife and child;
and the very smoke of Ithaca would be dear to his
eyes [1]. Of the Odyssey this is the theme. But the
Iliad, too, sustains by its slighter indications the sister
poem; for he alone among the Greek chieftains desires to be known as the father of his son; and touch-
ingly sets forth his sense of the hardship of being
detained, even but a single month, away from a wife [2].

The faculty of tears is generally ascribed to the
Greek chiefs and soldiery; and the Poet did not think
their susceptibility derogated from their manhood. But
even here Odysseus has a specialty. This man of iron
nerve and soul, who within the Horse's ribs saved the
lives of his comrades by sternly compelling silence; who
in the cave of Poluphemos executed his vengeance, and
then clung beneath the great ram as the blinded monster
felt its back; and who again gave place to a profound
and inexorable wrath not only against the Suitors, but
even against their helpless and miserable minions; even
this same man it is, who weeps at the recognition given
of his return by the dog Argos in his twentieth year [3].

3. AGAMEMNON.

The Agamemnon of Homer is described as a good
king and a stout warrior. He shows a natural affection
to his brother, and is not deficient in the courtesy
which, then as now, marked his race; but he is not in
other respects an amiable, nor a decidedly estimable
man: and Homer seems to take care that we shall not
love him. His besetting sin is personal; it is an avarice,
which seems to make him both cruel in war, with

[1] Od. L 58.   [2] Il. ii. 360, 292.   [3] Od. xvii. 304.

a view to spoil, and niggardly in general conduct. His
marked virtue is official; he has a profound sense of
responsibility to the army. To this responsibility he
greatly defers; and though avarice, appetite, and pride,
were alike gratified in the acquisition of Chryseis, he
yields her up [1]. And a circumstance, disclosed later in
the Poem, shows us that, doubtless from motives of
policy, he did not assume an absolute possession of the
woman he had taken from Achilles. Yet he has neither
the fire of genius, nor any gift of profound political
sagacity. On the contrary, while, like so many poli-
ticians, he is a practitioner in finesse, he contrives by
it to outwit himself. This seems to be, in part at least,
the explanation of the unhappy device in the Second
Iliad, where he seeks to provoke the people to an attack
on Troy, by counselling them to go home forthwith [2];
which they would have done, to his utter confusion,
unless the error had been retrieved by Odysseus.

It is a remarkable illustration of the power of the
Hellenic anthropomorphism, that the characters of the
Olympian and the Pelopid chief have some close resemblances. Zeus, wielding the highest power, is
strong in the sense of responsibility, while inferior in
intellect to some members of the group around him;
and he partially redeems the meaner elements of his
character by a strong touch of natural affection for
his son Sarpedon, just as that of Agamemnon is in
a degree ennobled by his fraternal love for Menelaos [3].
He may be in part the reflection of a human prototype.
Whether he be or not, it is in great part true that
Zeus is the Agamemnon of Olympos, and Agamemnon
the Zeus of Greece.

[1] Il. L. 117.   [2] Il. ii. 139-143.   [3] Il. iv. 148; vii. 107.

4. DIOMED and AJAX.

In the same manner the characters of Ajax and
Diomed, allied by resemblances in action, are profoundly and broadly distinguished. Each is superlative
in its degree; but while Diomed is gallant, Ajax is
sturdy. Diomed is impassioned, Ajax is calm; Diomed
is rapid, Ajax is slow. Diomed can brag; Ajax moves
in a simple unquestioning self-reliance. Diomed is not
above taking a circuitous advantage, as we find when, in
the act of fulfilling the duties of guestship, he makes an
extraordinarily profitable exchange with Glaucos: Ajax
ever goes direct to his point. With a fine discernment,
the Poet selects Ajax and Odysseus as the envoys to
Achilles, in the Ninth Book, to attempt a conciliation.
The favourable prepossessions of the great warrior are
commanded by his sympathy with the powerful intellect
of the one, and the straightforward simplicity of the
other. A certain vein of craft and of talk in Diomed
carried him away from the type of the first without
giving him the weighty attractions of the second.
And it may also be observed that, although Achilles
is in truth incomparable, yet the combination of intellect and spirit with activity and rapid force in
Diomed make him the one chieftain of the Iliad, who, if
any, would be placed in a direct competition with the
hero of heroes. Hence probably there was a latent
estrangement. And hence, probably, Achilles selects
Diomed for the chief subject of the matchless passage
in which, gloating over the miscarriages of the Greeks,
he combines bitter taunt with fiery exultation [1].

[1] Il. xvi. 74-78.

Diomed, indeed, possesses every quality necessary to make up a complete Achaian hero. Acute, prompt, intelligent, decided in mind, daring, constant and resolved in spirit, active, strong, and seemingly resistless in strength of body, he is more than able to cope with the brute strength of the god Arès. Of any other poem he might have been the model man. But even the extraordinary composition of his gifts is artfully employed by Homer with a view to the greater glory of that one character, which, in all qualities and all proportions of intellect and soul and body, without deviating from true humanity, is nevertheless colossal.

5. HELEN.

The Helen of the Homeric Poems has been conceived by the Poet, himself of peculiar delicacy, with great truth of nature, and evidently with no intention to deprive her of a share in the sympathy of his hearers. He has made her a woman, not cast in the mould of martyrs or of saints, nor elevated in her moral ideas to a capacity of comprehension, and of endurance, beyond her age; but yet endowed with much tenderness of feeling, with the highest grace and refinement, and with a deep and peculiar sense of shame for the offence into which she has been forced or tempted, and from the consequences of which she is unable to escape.

In order justly to appreciate the character of the Homeric Helen, we must begin by casting aside, if we can, all which later times have added, and which poets more widely familiar than Homer have conveyed into the modern mind. That she was a willing partner in the crime of Paris at its inception, we are not informed by

the Poems; in which, on the contrary, Paris describes
himself as having carried her off by violence[1]. We
only know that she acquiesced in the consequences of it,
by which she became his mate through a series of years,
and by which also, on his death, like other widows, she
was apparently transferred to another husband, his
brother Deiphobos[2]. In this no general baseness or
depravity of character is implied, but only the absence
of a power of resistance, which would have exceeded that
of Penelopè, and would have been almost preterhuman
at a period, when the condition of a woman withdrawn
from the regular family order was one of great, nay
total, helplessness.

After the fall of Troy, Helen resumes her place in
the palace of Menelaos, as his Queen. The subdued
tone of her character, and the absence of self-assertion
in her, are still observable; but by her husband, and by
all around them, she is treated with the same sentiments, as if nothing had happened to break the original
tenor of her married life. Indeed we find in the
Odyssey a passage, which seems to indicate a remarkable tenderness on the part of Menelaos, in connection
with the most questionable act recorded of the conduct
of Helen during the war. When the Greeks were
inclosed within the frame of the Horse, the Trojans,
suspecting the ambush, brought her down to the spot,
and she imitated the voices of the wives of the chieftains, in the hope that they, if there, would reply. This
act, done against the Greeks, savours of that slightness of character, which seems to be represented as
the source of her great error. But Menelaos, when
he mentions the subject, shifts the blame from her.

[1] Il. III. 400-402.   [2] Od. iv. 276.

'Thither,' he says, ' thou camest; but no doubt it was some deity, favourable to Troy, that prompted thee [1].'

Helen was the object of much reproach in Troy; not, however, from the mild Priam [2], nor from the virtuous Hector [3], but from Hecuba, or from the princes and princesses. This is amply to be accounted for, from their natural sense of the suffering which by her means had been brought upon their family and country, without presuming unfavourably of her beyond what has been already stated. But it could hardly have been the general rule; for when her sister-in-law Laodikè summons her to the Wall in the Third Iliad, she addresses her by the title of ' dear bride [4].'

Among the Greeks of the War, she is never made the subject of reproach. In one verse of the Iliad, Achilles speaks of her as that dreadful Helen. But this is in the agony of his mind: and in his conference with the Envoys, where it would greatly have enhanced the force of his argument if he could have represented her as worthless, he does nothing of the kind [5]. Penelopè says of her, that the deity impelled her to do an evil deed [6]. But in the context of this very passage, she speaks of Helen simply as deluded, without any malice prepense, and uses the deplorable result to justify her own extraordinary circumspection in the matter of the recognition of Odysseus. Compare this with the words in which the Poet describes the sin of Clytemnestra, ' To his home Aigisthos led her, as willing as himself [7].'

In truth, Homer awards to Helen, when in his own person he speaks of her, an honourable, not a dishonour-

---

[1] Od. iv. 276.　　[2] Il. xxiv. 770.　　[3] Il. xxiv. 771.
[4] Il. iii. 130.　　[5] Il. ix. 337.　　[6] Od. xxiii. 223.
[7] Od. iii. 272.

able treatment. The epithets attached to her name are chiefly descriptive of beauty and birth; but they are never coloured with any tint of blame. And when in the Odyssey he compares her to his Artemis[1], we see on the positive side that favourable bias of his mind, of which we may recognise the negative side in the fact that he never once compares her to Aphroditè. In truth, the only censures of her that we read in the Poems, are those pronounced by herself.

The scene between her and Aphroditè in the Third Iliad exhibits the highest aspect of her character. The goddess endeavours to excite her passions, by a glowing description of Paris in his beauty and his splendid garments, and desires her to repair to him. Struck at first with fear when she perceives who it is that is addressing her, she then kindles into indignation, and makes a bitter and stinging reply; reproaches Aphroditè for interfering to prevent Menelaos from taking her home, and bids her assume to herself the odious character she was seeking to force on another, who had too long borne it. It is only under violent threats, that she at length and with shame complies; and, on arriving in the presence of Paris, she addresses him in terms of scorn and aversion[2].

Upon the whole, I think that no one, forming his estimate of Helen from Homer only, could fall into the gross error of looking upon her as a type of depraved character. From the odious Helen[3] of the Second Æneid she is immeasurably apart. Her beauty, grace, refinement, are not contaminated by vicious appetites; they are only not sustained by an heroic, almost a superhuman, firmness.

[1] Od. iv. 122.   [2] Il. iii. 390–436.
[3] Æn. ii. 567–587.

Her fall once incurred, she finds herself bound by the iron chain of circumstance, from which she can obtain no extrication. But to the world, beneath whose standard of morality she has sunk, she makes at least this reparation, that the sharp condemnation of herself is ever in her mouth, and that she does not seek to throw off the burden of her shame on her more guilty partner. Nay, more than this; her self-abasing and self-renouncing humility come nearer, perhaps, than any other heathen example, to the type of Christian penitence.

6. HECTOR.

The character of the Homeric Hector has been so exaggerated, and so defaced, by the later tradition, that it has lost every distinctive feature of the original, and has come to stand as a symbol of the highest bravery and chivalry. But neither bravery nor chivalry are, in a proper sense, distinctive features of the Homeric Hector.

In the original portraiture itself, which is perfectly simple and intelligible, there is nothing to account for this change. Hector, in the Iliad, is a person of warm domestic affections, of upright purpose, of feeble will, of considerable, but not first-rate, fighting force; with all the convictions of a good citizen, though without the light of imagination or the fire of enthusiasm. He seems to be born in a family of lower tone, and weaker fibre, than his own; hence upon him is laid the whole burden of war and government in a terrible crisis, and his responsibilities are beyond his powers. Hence, probably, come the discords of his character; between boastfulness, feebleness, and even shabbiness on one

side, and fundamental rectitude, worth, and attachment
to virtue on another. The contrast seems to result
from an overstrain. And hence it may be that, though
much looked up to in the Poems by his own family, he
does not seem to enjoy the confidence or respect either
of the self-centred Æneas, or of the circumspect Poludamas [1], or even of the gallant and good Sarpedon [2].

It may be truly said, that Hector is the most inconsistent character in the Iliad. No man is braver, than
he is at times: on the other hand, no man shows more
palpable signs of cowardice. No man is more rash;
yet none has a deeper presentiment of the future. No
man is so improvident, it might almost be said so
insolent, in repelling wise counsel tendered to him;
and yet none shows more unequivocal signs of personal
humility. But the faults in his character, though
numerous and glaring, do not form its main tissue.
They are flaws in a delineation essentially good, and
occasionally noble. No act of cruelty or bad faith
or violence, of greed or lust or selfishness, associates
itself with his character; the stream of his thought is
pure; the love he has for his country, his parents, his
wife, his child, overflows even in a protective care for
Helen [3]. In the measure open to his day and people,
he is one who fears God, and regards man; and perhaps
the total absence of vice, as it is contradistinguished
from infirmity, in his character, co-operated with other
causes in bringing about his adoption in the Christian
literature of the middle ages, as the model, for the
olden time, of the heroic man.

But the very inconsistency of Hector affords a marked

---

[1] Il. xii. 211; xiii. 726.   [2] Il. v. 472 seqq.
[3] Il. xxiv. 767-772.

testimony to the skill of the Poet. Had he been consistently great, he would have been a real rival to those prime Achaian chieftains, to whom Homer sought to secure an undisputed supremacy of admiration. Had he been consistently mean and small, he would have been a foe so unworthy, that no honour could redound to them from overcoming him. One of these dangers he has avoided by the flaws in the character of Hector; the other by his virtues and his merits. It is not easy to see by what other means he could effectually have attained the ends of his art. And he has further contrived, that the virtues of Hector shall be mainly of a stamp, in which the Achaian chieftains shall not be tempted to compete with him; the affectionate sorrow of his anticipations of the future, the stern rebuke of an unworthy brother, the dignified endurance of misfortune, and that form of resigned heroism, which can only be exhibited in the extremity of disaster.

7. PARIS.

The character of Paris is as worthy, as any other in the Poems, of the powerful hand and just judgment of Homer. It is neither on the one hand too slightly, nor on the other too elaborately, drawn; the touches are just such and so many, as his poetic purpose seemed on the one hand to demand, and on the other to admit. Paris is not indeed the gentleman, but he is the fine gentleman, and the pattern voluptuary, of the heroic ages; and all his successors in these capacities may well be wished joy of their illustrious prototype. The redeeming, or at least relieving, point in his character, is one which

would condemn any personage of higher intellectual or
moral pretensions; it is a total want of earnestness,
the unbroken sway of levity and of indifference to all
serious and manly considerations. He completely fulfils
the idea of the *poco-curante*, except as to the display of
his personal beauty, the enjoyment of luxury, and the
resort to sensuality as the best refuge from pain and
care. He is not a monster, for he is neither savage
nor revengeful; but still further is he from being one
of Homer's heroes, for he has neither honour, courage,
eloquence, thought, nor prudence. That he bears the
reproaches of Hector without irritation, is due to that
same moral apathy, and that narrowness of intelligence,
which makes him insensible to those he receives from
Helen. No man can seriously resent what he does not
really feel. He is wholly destitute even of the delicacy
and refinement, which soften many of the features of
vice; and the sensuality he shows in the Third Book[1]
partakes largely of that brutal character which marks
the lusts of Jupiter. No wise, no generous word ever
passes from his lips. On one subject only he is determined enough; it is, that he will not give up the
woman whom he well knows to be without attachment
to him[2], and whom he keeps not as the object of his
affections, but merely as the instrument of his pleasures. One solicitude only he cherishes : it is to de-
corate his person, to exhibit his beauty, to brighten
with care the arms that he would fain parade, but
has not the courage to employ against the warriors of
Greece.

Paris, though effeminate and apathetic, is not gentle,
either to his wife or his enemies; and, when he has

[1] II. iii. 437-448. [2] II. iii. 428.

wounded Diomed, he wishes the shot had been a fatal
one. The reply of Diomed cuts deeper than any arrow
when he addresses him as

> ' Bowman ! ribald ! well-frizzled girl-hunter !''

Again, the Poet tells us, as if by accident, that when,
after the battle with Menelaos, he could not be found,
it was not because the Trojans were unwilling to give
him up, for they hated him with the hatred which men
feel to dark Death[2]. And again we learn, how he uses
bribery to keep his ground in the Assembly; how he
refuses to recognise even his own military inferiority,
but lamely accounts for the success of Menelaos by
saying that all men have their turn[3]; and how he
causes shame to his own countrymen, and exultation
to the Greeks, when they contrast the pretensions of
his splendid appearance with his miserable performances in the field[4].

The immediate transition, in the Third Book, from
the field of battle, where he was disgraced, to the bed
of luxury, is admirably suited to impress upon the
mind, by the strong contrast, the real character of
Paris. Nor let it be thought, that Homer has gratuit-
ously forced upon us the scene between him and his
reluctant partner. It was just that he should mark as a
bad man him who had sinned grossly, selfishly, and
fatally, alike against Greece and his own family and
country. This impression would not have been consistent and thorough in all its parts, if we had been
even allowed to suppose that, as a refined, affectionate,
and tender companion, he made such amends to Helen,

---

[1] Il. xi. 385.   [2] Il. iii. 454.   [3] Il. vi. 339.
[4] Il. lii. 43, 51.

as the case permitted, for the wrong done her in his hot and heady youth. Such a supposition might excusably have been entertained, and it would have been supported by the very feebleness of the character of Paris, and by his part in the war, had Homer been silent upon the subject. He, therefore, though with cautious hand, lifts the veil so far as to show us that, in our variously compounded nature, animal desire can use up and absorb the strength which ought to nerve our higher faculties, and that, as none are more cruel than the timid, so none are more coarse than the effeminate.

SECTION III.   *The Similes of the Poems.*

The detailed similes of the Iliad are about 194 in number; besides near sixty comparisons without any detail or varied ornament.

They are very unequally distributed. The First Book has none; the Sixth only one. In both these the action is of highly sustained and varied interest. On the other hand, the Books occupied exclusively with battle are largely embellished with them. The Fifteenth has sixteen similes, the Sixteenth has eighteen, and the Seventeenth has nineteen. In the Second there are thirteen, all of them intended to set off the gatherings and array of the Army.

In the Odyssey, the greater or detailed similes become very much fewer. They are only forty-one; and this not only before the arrival in Ithaca, where the action is highly varied, and the movement quick; but also in the latter half of the Poem, after the arrival of

L l

Odysseus in Ithaca, when it is more relaxed: since the lower tone of the diction and of the subject does not call for, or perhaps even admit, this kind of gorgeous ornament; perhaps also, according to a very natural and reasonable supposition, because these books were composed in the declining years of Homer, as they certainly indicate, with some noble and brilliant exceptions, a lower standard of power.

The character, too, of the greater similes in the Odyssey entirely changes. The lion appears but four times[1], the vulture once[2], war never, storm never. Industry, domestic life, the phenomena of outward nature when she is tranquil, now supply the materials to the hand of the Poet

The similes of the Odyssey, then, have the same harmonious relation to the Poem they embellish, as we find in the Iliad. And we should bear in mind, that in nothing has Homer more emphatically established a type of his own, than in the matter of similes. This being so, a treatment so remarkable and characteristic, found in each of the two Poems, furnishes of itself one among the very large number of particulars, which go to make up an inductive argument for the unity of their authorship.

The similes of Homer may in one sense be considered as a miniature of the Poems themselves. Accompanying the movement of the action, they sweep the entire round of human life. There is in them the same elasticity and variety, as in the thought and the style: these they follow over hill and dale, as the faithful dog follows the step of his master. Their tone

---

[1] Od. iv. 335, 791; vi. 130; xxii. 402.   [2] Od. xxii. 303.

changes in precise proportion to that of the subject, and of the effect that the Poet seeks to produce.

The similes afford, as I conceive, one among the incidental proofs that, if Homer was indeed blind, he was blind not from his birth, but from subsequent failure of the organ, or calamity. The experience of hunting in the woods and among the mountains, for example, is detailed with a vivid exactness which implies a knowledge founded on experience, just as experience in this case seems probably to imply vigorous limbs, hardy habits, and the perfection of the organs of sense.

CHAPTER XV.

SECTION I. *The Idea of Beauty in Homer.*

THE conception of beauty in the Poems of Homer is alike intense and chaste. He never associates Beauty with evil in such a manner, as to attract our sympathies towards a bad or contemptible person. This is markedly shown by his treatment of Aphroditè, of Nireus, and of Paris, on whose personal beauty he never dwells as he does on that of Nausicaa[1] or of Euphorbos[2]. Only on the one occasion when he has shown some sense of shame and duty, and is going forth full-armed to battle, is this prince allowed to appear for a moment otherwise than despicable[3]. It is not by a didactic morality, but by a genuine impulse and habit of nature, that Homer thus joins and severs, as far as in him lies, what ought to be joined and severed respectively. The legend of Ganymede[4], which was afterwards perverted to the purposes of depravity, is

---

[1] Od. vi. 149-169.
[3] Il. vi. 332-305.

[2] Il. xvii. 50-60.
[4] Il. xx. 233-235.

in Homer perfectly pure, and indeed seems to recall, though it is in a lower form, the tradition of Enoch, who ' was not, for God took him[1].'

We may, however, mark the downward course of these traditions, following the lapse of time. Two generations after Ganymede, Tithonos, of the same family, is appropriated by the goddess Eôs as a husband[2]. One generation more gives us the lawless love of Aphroditè and Anchises[3]; and the same goddess, in the next generation, promises to Paris a beautiful wife, whom he was to obtain by treachery and violence as well as adultery. Priam seems wholly without rule on this subject; he charges the fall of Helen[4] on the gods, and, even when reviling Paris inclusively with his surviving sons, makes no reference to his peculiar crimes[5].

It would appear that in ascribing so much beauty to the royal family of Troy, Homer may have been following tradition. When treating of the Greeks, he appears to award it in pretty close proportion to general excellence. Achilles, the greatest hero of the Greeks, is the most beautiful[6]; and Thersites, their basest wretch, is loaded with ugliness and deformity[7]. Odysseus, the counterpart without being the rival, of Achilles, has undoubted beauty of a different kind, although without lofty stature[8]; and Ajax, the second of the army in strength, is in the Odyssey called second in beauty also[9].

We may trace the value set by Homer on personal

---

[1] Gen. v. 24. [2] Il. xl. i. Od. v. i. [3] Il. ii. 821.
[4] Il. iii. 164. [5] Il. xxiv. 260.
[6] Il. ii. 674; xxiv. 629. Od. xi. 470. [7] Il. ii. 216-219.
[8] Il. iii. 169. [9] Od. xi. 470.

beauty not only in the loving spirit of passages such as those that relate to Euphorbos and Nausicaa, and in his assignment of the gift to his two protagonists, but also in some notes appertaining to the two nations respectively. No Trojan is allowed the glory of that auburn hair which is ascribed to Achilles[1], in one place to Odysseus[2], and habitually to Menelaos. Nor are they ever adorned collectively with epithets of personal attractiveness such as those given to the Greeks of the flashing eye (ἐλίκωπες)[3], of the flowing hair (καρηκομόωντες)[4], and of the admirable beauty (εἶδος ἀγητοί)[5]. And while, in the case of Nireus, Homer has carefully discriminated between mind and body, he has so marked his perfection of form that no reader of the Iliad, however careless, can fail to be impressed by the record. Manifestly, too, he delivers his own sentiments from the mouth of Odysseus at the Court of Alkinoos, where he speaks of beauty, the power of thought, and the power of speech, as the three great gifts of the gods to the individual man[6].

Stature, as well as form, entered very much into the conception of beauty among the ancients; and this for women as well as men. Yet he was sensible, at least with respect to women, that tallness might pass into excess. Accordingly, among the Laistrugones, when two comrades of Odysseus meet the queen, 'they found her big as a mountain's top, and loathed her[7].'

Homer had a profound perception of the beauty of animals, at least in the case of the horse, as to colour, form, and especially movement. We trace in him a

---

[1] Il. i. 197.   [2] Od. xiii. 397.   [3] Il. i. 389, *et alibi.*
[4] Il. ii. 11, *et passim.*   [5] Il. v. 787; viii. 228.
[6] Od. viii. 167-177.   [7] Od. x. 112.

commencement of the pedigrees of this animal[1]. It is
with an intense sympathy that the Poet describes the
lordly creature and his motions, which he has idealised
up to the highest point by the tears of horses, their
speech, and their scouring the expanse of sea and the
tips of standing corn[2]. The whole series of passages
relating to the horse in the Iliad is noble and emphatic
throughout; and in no parts of the Poems can we more
distinctly trace, by the slower or quicker movement of
his verse, his adaptation of sound to sense. Space
does not permit me here to exhibit in detail the proofs
of Homer's admiration for the beauty of the horse[3].

The appreciation of landscape was a faculty less
highly developed in Homer; yet it surely existed.
The mountainous country of Lacedæmon, which he
calls hollow, he also calls lovely[4]; the epithet employed
(e rate in os) being the same which he uses to describe
Hermionè, the daughter of Helen, a person endowed
with the beauty of golden Aphroditè[5]. Corfù, to which
he applies the same descriptive word[6], is in our day of
the highest fame for the beauty of its scenery.

Again, Telemachos apprises Menelaos that Ithaca is
a goat-feeding island, without meadows, and more
epēratos than a horse-feeding country[7]. The epithet is
equivalent to the one last before mentioned; and as the
meaning is that a hill-country is more beautiful to the
eye than champaign, we seem here to have a distinct
appreciation of the beauty of scenery. The famous
simile of the watch-fires and the sky by night appears to

---

[1] Il. v. 265–273; xx. 221.   [2] Il. xx. 225.
[3] See Studies on Homer, lil. 410–416.
[4] Il. ii. 581; iii. 239. Od. iv. 1.   [5] Od. iv. 13.
[6] Od. vii. 79.   [7] Od. iv. 606.

carry something of a like interpretation[1]. And as regards the more limited combinations of what may be termed home-views, we have at the least two great instances in the Odyssey: one of them the garden of Alkinoos[2]; the other the grotto of Calypso, of which he closes his description by saying that 'even an Immortal, on beholding it, would be seized with wonder and delight[3].'

At the same time, I do not doubt that life, and not repose, is the grand and vital element of beauty in the conceptions of Homer, whether they are applied to nature, or to the animated world.

SECTION II.   *The Idea of Art in Homer.*

The Homeric Poems give us a view substantially clear of the state of art in the time of the Poet. They also contain conceptions of the principle of art, so vivid as perhaps never to have been surpassed. And, unless I am mistaken, they indicate to us the source from which the specific excellence of Greek Art, in its highest form, proceeded. By the term Art, I understand the production of beauty in material forms palpable to the eye; whether associated with industrial purposes or not.

First, then, there are many works of art mentioned in Homer: but, in the whole of them, it is associated with some purpose of utility. The greatest of them all is the Shield of Achilles. Next to which, perhaps,

[1] Il. viii. 557.   [2] Od. vii. 112-132.   [3] Od. v. 63-75.

comes the armour of Agamemnon[1]; various bowls,
mentioned in different places[2]; the baldric of
Heracles[3]; and the golden clasp of the mantle of
Odysseus[4]. In all of them, living form is represented.
There are other objects of a less defined class, but
belonging rather to mere decoration. Such are the
necklace of gold and amber, carried by the Phoinikes
to Suriè[5]; the couch or chair of Penelope, with a stool
to match[6]; and the burnished sheets of copper in the
palaces of Alkinoos and Menelaos[7]. There are also
works of simple mechanical skill, such as the airy net
of metal worked by Hephaistos[8]. We find in the Poems
no production of what is termed pure art: everything,
to which art is applied, has an object beyond itself:
utility aspires to be decked with beauty; and beauty is
never dissociated from utility.

Next, as to the material of art. We have in Homer
no sign of the use of any material, except metal, for the
production of beautiful forms; and, specifically, the
metals of gold, silver, tin, and copper. It seems
probable that there were, at least in Troy, statues of
the gods. But probably also these were rude images
of wood, such as Pausanias describes under the name
of x o a n a, in which Homer would find nothing
answering to his conception of beauty.

As to the range of art in point of subjects, we must
consider it, in all likelihood, as almost entirely confined
to the exhibition of form, and of form too, in the solid.
Of painting proper, and therefore of colours as connected

---

[1] Il. xi. 15-46.
[2] Il. xxiii. 740-750. Od. iv. 613-619.
[3] Od. xi. 609-614.
[4] Od. xiii. 226-231.
[5] Od. xv. 459.
[6] Od. xix. 55-58.
[7] Od. iv. 72; vii. 86.
[8] Od. viii. 277.

with painting, we have no sign; though we have one case of the use of a single colour, in the staining of ivory [1]. But the use of the sheets of copper, already mentioned, is a step in that direction; and the intermixture of varieties of metal, especially on the Shield of Achilles, and in the armour of Agamemnon, show what was perhaps the fullest resort to the principle of colour that the limited command of material permitted.

As to the seat of art, we cannot affirm that it had as yet for any purpose been practically established in Greece. No single operation is recorded in the Poems which gives an indication of high metallic skill as having been attained anywhere in that country. By far the most considerable is the bedstead of Odysseus, which is adorned with gold, silver, and copper: but then Odysseus is a master in every art, almost a magician: and we are not told that even his art included the representation of living form [2]. The colouring process, to which reference has been made, is supposed to be carried on, not by a Greek, but by a Meonian or a Carian woman. And in most of the cases where a true work of art is mentioned, it is referred directly to Sidon or the Phœnician; in one or two instances to Thrace, on the shore of which the Phœnicians seem to have had settlements. In other cases it is referred, like the Shield, to Hephaistos, a god of Phœnician associations. In the case of the bowl, presented by the king of the Sidonians to Menelaos [3], we are told expressly that it was the work of Hephaistos. The gold-beater and the χαλκεὺς, or smith, are known to Homer; but only, as far as appears, for the simplest operations; the former simply attaches a

[1] Il. iv. 141.   [2] Od. xxiii. 195-201.   [3] Od. iv. 615-619.

plate or band of gold to the horns of the sacrificial ox,
and it appears from the passage that he did not ply a
separate trade, but was merely the copper-smith engaged in beating gold[1], inasmuch as he is called
chalkeus, as well as chrusochoos. All that related
to the execution of works of art, so far as we can
judge from the Poems, the Achaian Greeks had yet to
learn.

But as in other points, so in this, the Poet opened
the way for his countrymen, and taught them how they
should walk along it in the after-time. As his perception of beauty in living form was most keen, so
his idea of art in forms inanimate, copied from nature,
was alike powerful and simple: it was that which
brought them up to life. In the nature of things, we
perhaps may say, it cannot be carried farther. The
chairs of Hephaistos moved spontaneously[2]. The
porter-dogs of Alkinoos, wrought in gold and silver[3],
were of an immortal youth. The metallic handmaids
of the god himself were endowed with thought as well
as motion[4]. In the ploughing scene upon the Shield,
as the furrow is turned, the earth darkens, though it is
of gold[5]. And in the battle compartment, the sculp-
tured warriors fight, and the dead are dragged off the
field, with actual movement as in a scene of war[6].
Such is the bold delineation by which the oldest poet
of Art has given the challenge to his successors, and
bids them excel him if they can.

But all these representations, however raised into sub-
limity by genius, must have had a basis in fact; and it
seems difficult to resist the conclusion that Homer,

[1] Od. lil. 432-438.   [3] Il. xviii. 375.   [5] Od. vii. 91.
[4] Il. xviii. 417.   [6] Il. xviii. 549.   [2] Il. xviii. 533-540.

and the Greeks of his time, must have seen, though they had not yet learned to make, art-works of a high order, imported, without doubt, in general from Phœnicia, and produced either there or further eastwards.

The Sidonian works themselves, if executed, as Homer commonly represents, in gold and silver, were doomed without doubt to perish, so soon as the time should arrive when men might come to prize the workmanship less, than the application of the mere material to other uses. But if we may judge from the testimony of such remains as are now accessible, there were two great schools, with which Phœnician artists must have been in relation, alike from their political and their geographical connections: the Egyptian and the Assyrian. It is not, I suppose, too much to say, that we perceive, in a portion at least of the actual remains of these schools, the attainment of high excellence in intention and design, with no inconsiderable progress in execution. They seem, however, to me to represent different principles: the Assyrian appears to embody the principle of life and motion; the Egyptian, the principle of repose. If this be true, there can be little doubt, I presume, that the ideas of Homer had their base and fountain-head much more in the former than in the latter. But in any case, it would really seem probable, from the vivid and stirring descriptions of Homer, that these Phœnician importations supplied patterns, and suggested ideas, which might well, in process of time, become the nucleus of the first great efforts of Greek art.

When that nucleus was once supplied, and when the new life began to grow, then the Olympian system of religion provided it, through the union of the divine nature to the human form, with that lofty aim, which braced it to a perpetual effort upwards, and so conveyed to it the pledge and the talisman of all transcendent excellence. Every idea, appertaining to deity, was held capable of representation in matter; but it could only be matter moulded according to the shape of man. Thus Greek art was a perpetual untiring pursuit of the highest standard of the ideal, while it seems to have had for its starting-point foreign models which, though not similarly inspired, were of such high merit as to suggest to Homer that imitation might run no unsuccessful race with nature. This happy union of the most fundamental conditions of design and execution was seconded by the lights of a fine climate, by the possession of the purest marbles, and by the corporal perfection of a race abounding in the noblest models. We cannot wonder that, with these advantages, Greece, within her limits of knowledge and experience, should have held down to our own day the throne of Art.

Section III. *Physics of Homer.*

Homer's ideas of physics were extremely simple, as well as apparently few. He perceived that rivers were fed by rain and snow; and therefore he calls them Διιπετέες, Zeus-fallen, which we should probably understand to mean ‘coming from the realm of Zeus.’ Fire is the single element which he seems in any direct mode to identify with an Olympian Deity, and this only in one undoubted instance, where he calls it Hephaistos. He considered the human body to be

composed of the elements which make up earth and
water, for he treats it as resolvable by Death into
these substances[1]. It is not easy to arrive at a positive
conclusion about his conception of the figure of the
Earth, beyond the fact that he considered it to be oblong,
which may be probably shown from a comparison of
many passages in the Poems. The land, as known to
his experience, was limited. A circle, of from 350 to
400 miles in diameter, would have comprised more
than all the places, that were within the limits of
ordinary Greek knowledge and experience. All his
ideas of vastness were connected with the sea. From
his placing the River Ocean at all points of the compass, and his making it flow round the Earth, together
with the general disposition of objects on the Shield of
Achilles, he may be imagined to have conceived of our
planet as a flat surface. On the other hand, he seems
to connect the extreme East with the farthest West,
Sunset with Sunrise, as if he thought it were a surface
wrapped (so to speak) round a cylinder. For, placing
in the far east the Island of Thrinakiè and the Oxen
of the Sun, he makes that deity declare that with these
animals he amused himself not only when he rose, but
when he returned from heaven to earth; that is to
say, at the time of his setting. To this idea there is
a partial approximation in the formation of a shield,
such as it appears either uniformly or commonly to
have been in the time of Homer, namely an oval, or
oblong. The Homeric shield is called ἀμφιβρότη as
covering the human figure. But it is also called εὔκυκλος.
Does this refer to a rounding at the top and bottom?
or does it more probably mean that an horizontal sec-

[1] Il. vil. 99.

tion of the shield represented a segment of a well-drawn circle? If the latter be the meaning, the two epithets are placed in thorough harmony. For, the more the shield is rounded horizontally, the more does it shelter the warrior who uses it. And this form might agree with the passage in Od. xii. 380[1], where the 'return' of the Sun may mean his passing from the point at which men lose him in the West, to his bed or place of rising (ἀντολαί) in the East[2].

The amusing threat of the Sun, that he will go down to Hades and shine there, is not so strange or far-fetched, relatively to Homeric ideas, as might at first sight appear. For, while he set and rose in the περικαλλὴς λίμνη[3], the exceeding beautiful expanse of Okeanos, as he had to make his way from the Okeanos of the West to the Okeanos of the East, he might easily be thought, in doing this, to pass through, or near, that underground region, in which dwelt the Gods-Avengers, and which was the realm of Aïdes and Persephonè. Aïdes, says Poseidon, obtained by lot the ζόφος ἠερόεις[4]. Now zophos in Homer is used to signify the West: and yet Odysseus enters the realm of Aïdoneus in the East, near the Sunrise. With all that dark subterranean space between, the Olympian Immortals had no concern: for them, as for us, the light of the Sun both came and went; 'He rose on gods and men, over the teeming earth[5].' The change threatened to be made

---

[1] We might be tempted to treat as Phœnician this piece of cosmology. But we should then perhaps be pushing to an extreme the doctrine of a Phœnician origin for the Theotechny of the middle Odyssey, which would hardly reach so far into details.

[2] Od. xiii. 4.   [3] Od. iii. 1.   [4] Il. xv. 191.
                    [5] Od. iii. 3.

may have been only this, that the Sun, instead of passing through or round the dwelling of Aïdes, would
remain there. Zeus therefore takes his menace as
perfectly serious, and replies in effect, ' Do as hereto-
fore, and all shall be right [1].'

SECTION IV. *Metals in Homer.*

Archæological inquiry is now teaching us to investigate and to mark off the periods of human progress,
among other methods, by the materials employed from
age to age for making utensils and implements. And ·
the Poems of Homer have this among their many
peculiarities; they exhibit to us, with as much clearness perhaps as any archæological investigation, one
of the metallic ages. It is moreover the first and oldest
of the metallic ages, the age of copper, which precedes
the general knowledge of the art of fusing metals;
which (as far as general rules can be laid down) immediately follows the age of stone, and which in its
turn is probably often followed by the age of bronze,
when the combination of copper with tin has come
within the resources of human art.

The grand metallic operation of the Poems is that
of Hephaistos in the production of the Shield. The
metals used [2] were gold, silver, tin, and chalcos, which
has been by mere licence of translators interpreted as
brass, for there was no brass till long ages after Homer
had rolled away: which has been more plausibly taken
to mean bronze : but which, after a good deal of
inquiry, I am satisfied can only mean copper, either

[1] Od. xii. 384-388.   [2] Il. xviii. 474.

universally and absolutely, or as a general rule, with very insignificant exceptions.

The discussion would be too long for this place. But the passage immediately before us of itself affords almost sufficient instruction.

In the formation of the Shield, there is no mixture or fusion of metals. The same, and all the same, which are put into the roaring fire, reappear, each by its original name, in various portions of the Shield There is indeed one passage, where a trench is represented, and this is called kuaneè, a word meaning either made of kuanos, or like kuanos in colour. There are two reasons for giving the latter signification to the word. One, that it commonly bears that sense in Homer; the other, that though kuanos may have been a mixed metal, yet there is no sign of founding or casting in this great masterpiece of Hephaistos.

He could only mix by melting; and had he melted metals, we must have heard of moulds to receive them. Instead of this, the only instruments which he makes ready for the work[1] are

 1. The anvil.

 2. The hammer in his (right) hand.

 3. The pincers in his left.

It is plain, then, that he was supposed not to melt, but only to soften the metals by heating, and then to beat them into the forms he wished to produce.

Had Homer been conversant with the fusing or casting of metals, this is the very place where we must have become aware of it; especially as his works of skilled art are all of Phœnician origin or kin, and his Hephaistos is a god of Phœnician associations.

---

[1] Il. xviii. 476, 477.

If chalcos be not copper, then copper is never mentioned in Homer. But, in an early stage of society, copper was commonly by far the cheapest and most accessible of metals; and it is quite impossible to suppose, that we never once hear of copper from an author, who incessantly makes mention (so it is argued) of another metal, whereof it is by far the largest component part.

One of Homer's epithets for chalcos is eruthros, red; and this it is impossible under any conditions to apply to bronze.

There is abundant evidence of a correspondence between the seven metals of Homer, and the seven metals of the ancient planetary worship of the East: but one of these is copper, and from it Cyprus was named; and Homer introduces Mentes sailing to a port of Cyprus (Temesè) for chalcos [1].

We find chalcos in Homer a very cheap and common metal; tin a very scarce and rare metal, only used in very small quantities, and even approaching in some degree to the character of what we now term a precious metal. It is very improbable that the defensive armour, and all the meaner utensils, in Homer could have contained an eighth part, or thereabouts, of tin.

So Hesiod, in his age of chalcos, represents not only the arms and implements, but the dwellings as made of that material [2]. This could not have been bronze.

And I have high metallurgical authority for stating, that the sheathing of chalcos on walls as already mentioned must, for mechanical reasons, have been some material other than bronze.

It is said that chalcos cannot be hardened so as to

[1] Od. L 184.   [2] Opp. 143-155.

make a cutting tool; whereas this material is named in Homer as used for peeling bark, and cutting twigs and young branches, as well as for making weapons of war [1]. We have, however, in at least one place its imperfection by reason of softness noticed [2]. But, as portions of tin are found in some copper ores, may it not be that there were also small portions of it in virgin copper used for these purposes? I find, moreover, that ancient nails have been discovered, containing 97¾ per cwt. of copper, and only 2¼ of tin: and surgical instruments made of copper alone have been discovered recently in a tomb at Athens [3].

But although it seems clear that chalcos in general means copper, this may not compel us absolutely to exclude from its signification all compositions of the nature of bronze. In later times the word appears to have included both senses. The Latin æs without an epithet described a compound metal; with the epithet cyprium it meant copper. Some bronzes with a polish are not wholly unlike copper, though they want its redness. Possibly some sharp instruments of this composition might be imported into Greece, without at once leading to a distinction of name, especially if there were native copper, or kinds of copper, in use, which had some slight natural admixture of tin. But these cases must have been exceptional, so far as the use of the word in the Poems is concerned.

Kuanos is generally the type of a very dark colour in Homer, and the word may possibly mean bronze. The Greeks had it in small quantities: it was more

---

[1] Il. i. 236; xxi. 37.   [2] Il. xi. 237.

[3] Göbel, Einfluss der Chimie auf die Ermittelung der Völker der Vorzeit, pp. 25, 35.

valuable than copper, but apparently less prized than tin. In the planetary worship of the East, six deities were connected with six pure metals, and one with kuanos. In Homer we find the six metals, and the kuanos. Now as the septiform system was apparently represented in the seven gates of Thebes, and as the Greeks evidently depended on the Phœnicians for imported metals, I conclude that kuanos is the seventh metal, a mixed one; and I know no conclusive reason why it should not be bronze. It was used only for ornamentation, and in small quantities: if we except the cornice of kuanos in the quasi-Phœnician palace of Alkinoos[1]. Metals in those days seem to have been the great basis of commerce, when there was no apparatus available for storing, sheltering, or distributing with rapidity, perishable materials.

The metals of Homer, then, are—

1. Gold.   5. Iron.
2. Silver.   6. Chalcos or Copper.
3. Tin.   7. Lead.
4. Kuanos.

Silver appears to have been rarer than gold: as might be expected, considering that it is chiefly obtained by scientific means. It came but from one place[2], Alubè in Asia Minor. We do not hear of it as used in exchange, nor, I think, in stored wealth; but, in plating only, and in works of art.

The respective order of value for the metals is, I believe, that in which I have just placed them. Not so their quantities. Of lead we hear very little indeed. Iron was greatly more esteemed than copper, and was very rare, though seemingly more abundant

[1] Od. vii. 86.   [2] Il. ii. 857.

than tin or kuanos. We hear of it, together with
gold and copper, as an article of stored wealth[1]. It
was only used for cutting instruments; and chiefly, as
far as appears, for woodmen's axes. The quantities of
all the metals would seem to have been very limited,
except of chalcos only.

Gold was employed in plating, for works of art; it
appears also as stored wealth, and moreover, as in the
Suit on the Shield, with a slight approach to the character of a measure of value[2].

Tin was used in small quantities for ornament, and
was plated on copper[3]. The only articles entirely
made of it were the greaves of Achilles; and these
proceeded from a divine, not a human, workman[4].

SECTION V.   *The Measure of Value in Homer.*

Although the Greek of the heroic age was eminently
temperate, and abhorrent of excess, the spirit of acquisition was already strong within him. Not only were
the crude elements of wealth carefully stored, but works
of art had begun to be prized; and beautiful armour,
garments, and even personal ornaments, were in use
among the great. We have, however, no distinct case
recorded of inland commerce as among the Greeks;
and the business of exchange had not passed beyond
the form of barter.

Yet it appears that gold had begun to be used as a
convenient material for the requital of service, and
probably also for the liquidation of penalty. On the

[1] Il. vi. 48, *et alibi.*   [2] Il. xviii. 507.
[3] Il. xxlll. 561; xx. 271.   [4] Il. xxi. 582, 590–594.

Shield, the most approved Judge was to receive two
talents of that metal [1] for his sentence. And as we
hear of the payment of fines on various occasions [2]
(distinguished, in the terms of the Pact, from the
restitution of the stolen property), it is probable that
there is a reference to a precious metal. The epithets
τιμήεις and ἐρίτιμος or 'priceful [3],' applied to gold, and
to that only, may have a relation to this custom. In
the Twenty-second Odyssey, we have a τιμή or fine of
gold and copper [4].

But a measure of service is one thing, and a measure
of value for exchange is another; and we have no sign
that gold or silver was used as a common standard, to
place commodities in any definite relation of value to
one another; although the hoarding, of gold in particular, was a step towards this further development. Another initial sign was the division of the metal into
fixed and equal quantities, which is recorded on the
Shield.

The only commodity which approximates, in the
actual usage exhibited by the Poems, to a measure of
value, is the ox; for in this alone other commodities
are priced. The arms of Diomed are worth nine oxen;
those of Glaucos are worth a hundred [5]. The tripod,
which was the first prize for wrestlers in the Twenty-
third Iliad, was valued at twelve oxen; the woman
captive, skilled in works of industry, at four [6]. This
case does not probably exhibit the normal relations; for
in the camp women-captives would be cheap, and oxen

---

[1] Il. xviii. 507.
[2] Il. ix. 632-634; xiii. 699.   Od. ii. 192.
[3] Il. xviii. 475; cf. ix. 261.   [4] Od. xxii. 57-59.
[5] Il. vi. 236.   [6] Il. xxiii. 702-705.

dear. Accordingly we find that, when Eurucleia was
brought to Ithaca, she was purchased by Laertes for
twenty oxen, or for the value of them [1].

When Euneos sent ships laden with wine to trade
with the Greek army, his men took in return—(1) copper, (2) iron, (3) hides, (4) slaves, (5) oxen. Probably the
demand for wine was universal: each paid for it with
what he had to spare, in the different kinds of booty
acquired. It is not likely that oxen would be sent
away from the camp; but it may be intended that the
men of Euneos took them from those who had them
beyond their wants, as a commodity which they could
easily dispose of to others of the chiefs or soldiery less
amply supplied [2].

And we have seen from Æschylus, in the Agamemnon, that the figure of the ox was the sign first im-
printed upon a coin; doubtless one intended to represent the equivalent in the metal of the animal [3].

SECTION VI. *The Use of Number in Homer.*

The idea of number is one which, up to a certain
point, is readily grasped by an average adult of the
present day. Persons with a special gift apprehend
the idea, with the same clearness, on a larger scale.
Children fall short of those who are grown up, and in
early youth have no distinct conception beyond a very
few units. It seems that, in the childhood of the world,
men even of the capacity and grasp of Homer had no

[1] Od. l. 431.   [2] Il. vii. 472-475.   [3] Agam. 37.

definite idea of numbers beyond a very narrow range.
By a definite idea of numbers I mean that, which grasps
the whole without losing the separate conception of
the parts.

We find in Homer as round numbers the sums of
ten thousand, and nine thousand. An accomplished
person knows ten thousand things [1]. The shout of
'Arès was like that of nine thousand or ten thousand
men [2]. These expressions are evidently altogether
vague.

Erichthonios had three thousand horses [3]. Euneos,
who came to trade with the Achaian army, presented
the two Atridai with a thousand metres of wine [4].
At the Trojan bivouac, a thousand watchfires were
kindled on the plain [5]. Iphidamas, having given a
hundred oxen to gain a wife, promises a thousand
goats and sheep [6]. Some of these instances are obviously figurative: and it is even possible that all are so;
for we find the rough and indefinite use of the numeral
descending as low as to the single hundred. It is
plain, from many passages in the Poems, that the
hecatomb does not mean a hundred oxen, but only
a batch of oxen, sufficient for one of the more solemn
sacrifices. Crete has in one passage a hundred cities,
in another ninety [7]. Lucaon says, that Achilles sold
him in Lemnos for the value of a hundred oxen [8]. But
though a prince by birth, he could only be worth a very
small fraction of that number of oxen, when sold as a
slave from the Greek camp. Every gold drop or tassel

---

[1] Od. ii. 16.   [2] Il. v. 860.   [3] Il. xxi. 251.
[4] Il. vii. 571.   [5] Il. viii. 562.
[6] Il. xi. 244.   [7] Il. ii. 649. Od. xix. 174.   [8] Il. xxi. 79.

of the Aigis of Athenè was worth a hundred oxen [1].
This, if taken literally, would assign to the Aigis itself
a weight of perhaps not less than a ton and a half,
which is inadmissible, since she carries it in the field
among the Greeks, and must be in a certain relation
of stature to them [2].

The negative evidence of the Poems is in consonance
with these instances of the positive class. The Poet
nowhere states the numbers of the Greek Army; not
even of any of the separate contingents. And when
he gives the number of ships for each contingent, it
is in every instance, except a very few, of which the
highest is twenty-two, a round number. In two cases
he states the crews; they are 120 and 50 respectively.
These numbers have been taken as a key to an exact
computation. But it is impossible that all the chief contingents should have been in round numbers; and we
are told that Agamemnon's division was by far the
first in number of men [3], whereas in number of ships
it was but very little beyond some others.

Homer has clearly shown us how weak he felt himself in the use of numbers, by the curious passage in
which he compares the relative numbers of Greeks and
Trojans proper. Were they to be counted, says Agamemnon, the Greeks in tens, and the Trojans appointed
singly to serve them with wine, many a party of ten
would be without a cup-bearer [4]. Had he been in any
manner familiar with the use of numbers on a large
scale, he could not, on a point of such interest, have
been contented with so slight and vague an approxi-

---

[1] Il. ii. 448.   [3] Studies on Homer, vol. iii. p. 430.
[2] Il. ii. 580.   [4] Il. ii. 123-128.

mation. We may therefore be sure that when he
speaks of the thousand watchfires of the Trojan
bivouac, and adds that by each fire there sat fifty
warriors [1], he had never performed the mental process, to us so simple, of reckoning the force in arms
at fifty thousand.

The largest number which I find in the Poems with
any sign of definite use, is that of the fat hogs under
the care of Eumaios. They are 360 [2]; and, as one is
daily sent down to the banquet of the Suitors, they
correspond with the days of the year; of which it is
probable that, with the help of the months as an intermediate step, a real computation had been made [3].

Except where aided by the revolutions of the seasons,
or by some fixed usage, Homer is extremely vague in
the specification of periods of time. Odysseus describes
as 'yesterday and the day before,' which we may take
as the equivalent of our 'a day or two ago,' what had
happened at a distance of time between a fortnight and
three weeks back. The periods of years which go beyond a generation are never mentioned; but time is
always computed, and with a remarkable accuracy, by
the genealogies of notable persons. The generation,
or γενεή, appears to have been conceived by the Poet
as equal to thirty years; and yet here we ought probably to say, to thirty years more or less. The age of
Nestor was evidently about or over seventy; he was
bearing the kingly office in his third γενεή or generation [4]. And it seems as if the ten years of the war,
with ten of preparation preceding them, and ten of

[1] Il. viii. 563.   [2] Od. xiv. 20.
[3] Od. xiv. 93.   [4] Il. i. 252.

wanderings which follow, were intended poetically to make up this whole, so that an entire generation should be spent upon it. Yet the first of the three terms would appear incapable of a literal interpretation. We may be sceptical as to the other two; but it seems clear, that the Poet could hardly have intended us to believe that ten years were expended in gathering the force.

Only in one place does Homer refer to any actual process of reckoning. He describes Proteus counting his seals by the word pempassetai[1]. I understand this to mean no more than that he reckoned them on his five fingers. It is however somewhat remarkable, that this only reference to any part or element of the decimal scale, which we are still supposed to derive from the East, should be found upon an Eastern scene, and in connection with a personage of purely Phœnician associations.

Section VII. *The Sense of Colour in Homer.*

In the 'Studies on Homer,' I have considered at some length the manner in which Homer handles the subject of colour. I can in this place only lay down certain propositions without attempting the proof of them in detail.

To us of the present day, colour, and its broader distinctions, are familiar from childhood upwards. But, in the first place, it is to be borne in mind, that the acquired knowledge of one generation becomes in time the inherited aptitude of another. In the second place, much of our varied experience in colour is due to

[1] Od. iv. 412, 451.

chemistry, and to commerce, which brings to us the productions of all the regions of the world. Mere Nature, at any one spot, does not present to us a full and well-marked series of the principal colours such as to be habitually before the mind's eye. Thirdly, the curious investigations [1] of late years have shown us that, even now and in our own country, no inconsiderable proportion of persons are without the faculty of perceiving some of the primary distinctions of colour.

With respect to Homer, my main conclusions are

1. That his perceptions of colour, considered as light decomposed, though highly poetical, are also very indeterminate.

2. But that his perceptions of light not decomposed, as varying between light and dark, white and black, were most vivid and effective.

3. That accordingly his descriptions of colour generally tend a good deal to range themselves in a scale (so to speak) of degrees, rather than of kinds, of light.

The primitive experience of the prismatic colours must have been principally drawn from the rainbow. But Homer only once mentions the rainbow [2], and here he compares it with the snakes of dark metal on the breastplate of Agamemnon; of which comparison I can discern no other ground than that they would flash a varying light as the chieftain moved.

His goddess Iris is in evident relation to the rainbow. Yet he never gives her an epithet of colour [3]; though he calls her golden-winged. I think these facts go some way towards proving my main theses.

---

[1] See Wilson on Colour Blindness.

[2] Il. viii. 398.

[3] Il. xi. 27.

There are no words in Homer which can with any certainty be held to mean any one of these three colours : orange, green, and blue. His word kuaneos, which is more like indigo, does not seem to have been clearly separated in his mind from black[1]; while he also applies it to wet sand[2]. His word porphureos for violet, runs into his word eruthros for red. His word xanthos for yellow is applied to auburn or red hair, to the ears of corn, to a chestnut horse, to a river (apt to be swollen I suppose, and darkened by mud). In truth, there is not one single epithet of colour which we can affirm to be thoroughly defined. The word phoinix, which seems to intermix with xanthos, is also used as the equivalents of the words which would be rendered purple and red. Only a minute examination could collect the whole evidence in the case; but I will close with observing that oil is once called rosy[3], iron and wool violet, and oxen wine-coloured. But in the use of the words white and black, light and dark, which is abundant, Homer's eye seems rarely or never to go astray.

[1] See Il. xxiv. 94.   [2] Od. xii. 243.   [3] Il. xxiii. 186.

INDEX.

A.

ACHAIANS, who, 65; epithets applied to, 60; local force of the Achaian name in the historic ages, 64; distinction between them and the other inhabitants of Greece, 65; Achaian race in Crete, 66; closely related to the Pelopids, 159; the Achaian 'succumbs to the half-savage Heraclid,' 172.

Achaiic Argos, 47.

Achaïs, force of the word, 45 et seq.

Achilles, lands occupied by his contingent, 109; his powerful denunciation of falsehood, 386; and elevation of character, 386; his singular courtesy, 392, 421; general survey of his character in Homer, 495-497.

Actoridai, house of the, 136.

Adultery, crime of, held in abhorrence, 395; fine imposed upon the adulterer, 411.

Advent of our Lord, previous history a preparation for that event, 374.

Æneas and the title 'Anax Andrōn,' 160; case of his birth, 170.

Agamemnon as Anax Andrōn, 151; account of his sceptre, 154; and of his extraction, 155; unjust and rapacious, 389; his threat in regard to Briseis, 407; his suzerainty over other princes, 416; his succession hereditary, 423. See Polity, Kings, &c. Description of Agamemnon in Homer, 501.

Aïdoneus, 252; obscurity of his figure, 252; particulars concerning, 252, 253; Homeric adjustment regarding the anterior and the present Olympian dynasty, 255.

Aiguptioi, the, visited by Menelaos, 125. See also Egypt.

Aiguptos, an Ithacan noble, 125.

Aiolids, the question of their Phœnician origin discussed, 135.

Aiolus, a Phœnician, 138; force and derivation of the name, 140.

Ajax, 503.

Anax Andrōn, 149; to whom applied, with facts relating to the phrase, 151; the term disappears from use after Homer, 151; title applied to Agamemnon, 153; to Anchises and Æneas, 160; title a sign of affinity between the Greeks and the Trojans, 164; ap-

N n

www.ingramcontent.com/pod-product-compliance
Lightning Source LLC
Chambersburg PA
CBHW021936110726
47901CB00003B/863